CAIO

Book 1
The Limerent Series

LS Delorme

Dedication

This story is for those who see time not as the ticking of a
clock but as a mosaic that we dance on
and for those unafraid to connect the dots.

Authors Note/ Trigger Warning

This novel includes some very intense scenes including, but not limited to, graphic depictions of violence, including physical assault, abuse, and psychological trauma. *Caio* explores the fluidity of time and how it reshapes human relationships and power structures. So the characters are placed in brutally challenging situations that test their limits.. These elements are integral to portraying the stark realities the characters face, which are essential to understanding their development.

This is not for the faint of heart so reader discretion is advised.

Chapter One

The Boy in a Hole

April 28, 1905

The boy was stuck at the bottom of a hole. It was raining, and his body had sunk so deep into the mud that it was lodged there. It would have been hard for him to move even if he had the energy to do so—which he didn't. He didn't have the energy to do much of anything besides breathe, hurt, and think.

He had been thrown down here after his foreman had tried to rape him, and he had made the unfortunate decision to fight back. Fighting back had done him no good. It had only resulted in him being beaten to the point of death, and *then* raped. Still, unlike other slaves brought into the Amazon to harvest latex, he refused to accept his situation and work himself to death, if only because that's what his captors wanted. Of course, if he was honest, it was more than stubbornness that kept him alive. His almost paralyzing fear of death probably played a part as well.

Fate must have a dark sense of humor because now, as he lay in the hole, he didn't seem to be *able* to die. At first, he had been afraid of death and then, as the cold, pain and gnawing hunger set in, he finally became resigned to it. As the days went on, as the pain grew, he began to wish for death and eventually to pray for it. And now he was beginning to believe the only hope of ending his suffering was for the daily rain to become a downpour so that there would be enough water in bottom of the hole for him to drown himself. If he could make himself do that—because despite the pain, cold, hunger, and his desire for this torture to end, he was still afraid of death. Even as he prayed for it, as worms were going in and out of his body, even when he could see large white ones exploring his exposed abdomen and burrowing into his flesh, even now he was still afraid of death. Maybe this was why he couldn't die.

1

Sometimes his brain would give him relief, and he would drift out of consciousness. In these moments, images of people he didn't know flickered like old movies onto the backs of his eyelids. The image he saw most often was the face of a laughing woman. She was no one he had ever seen. She was pale as the moon, with dots on her face. When she laughed, she opened her mouth wide enough to see her back teeth, and they were beautiful, clean and straight. He would try to speak to her, but he couldn't. Then he would wake up, still in his hole, with the mud and the water and the white worms and the pain.

Eventually his vision began to dim around the edges. Shortly after that, he heard voices above him. By then he couldn't see anything through the haze of his vision, so he wondered if this was a hallucination or the final pathway to death. Some of his fear finally began to abate.

Then, suddenly, he felt a jolt as the earth around him was shifted.

Miracle of miracles, he felt the agony of someone's strong arms pulling his body from the mud.

Chapter Two

Sarah's Birthday Blues

Friday May 2, 2025

So far, Sarah Baker's day had been just glorious. She had awakened with both a nasty head cold and a potential stomach bug. Her water heater had apparently died in its sleep, so she had only been able to take a cold shower. Then, first thing on entering the offices, she had been asked to document a deposition. This meant that she had experienced the joy of spending two hours sniffling and grinding her teeth through intestinal cramps until the blessed relief of bathroom breaks. When these breaks had come, she had bolted to the ladies' room to relieve herself and blow her nose, usually simultaneously. In the afternoon Michael Angel, the partner she worked for, got called to court for a case that would take the better part of the day. Most of the time this would have been a break for her, but today she had been given the task of collecting, reviewing, and updating everyone's billable hours. So she spent her afternoon having her calls ignored by partners and being snarled at by junior attorneys.

On top of all that, just as the day was ending, her boyfriend Karl had called to break up with her, because it was her birthday.

"So was that the annual breakup call?" Angela asked, turning to her with a smile that would have been more fitting on a hyena than a human.

Angela was one of the other paralegals in the office. She had mouse-blonde hair, a large beak nose, and a groveling, subservient manner anytime an attorney or partner was around. Around other administrative staff, she was all smiles and sweetness, until you found the knife in your back. Then she would look at you with a condescending smirk that said *You mean you weren't smart enough to see that coming?* Angela may have looked like a mouse, but she was actually more like a trapdoor spider. She was an ambush predator. Sarah had had the good fortune of sitting in the cubicle just next to hers for the past five years.

At the moment, Angela was faking sympathy during what was actually a probe for weaknesses.

She needs to probe? asked the voice of Sarah's mother in her head. Sarah winced internally, as she always did when her mother's voice spoke. Her mother's was one of the nastiest voices that inhabited her head.

"Do you think he does that just so he won't have to buy you a birthday gift?" Angela asked, cocking her head and putting on a look of sisterly concern.

"No. He's not stingy like that," Sarah responded as she flipped through a pile of receipts and files that one of the attorneys had thrown on her desk while she had been on the phone.

She forced herself to laugh. "He's not perfect, but he's not stingy."

No, he's good with his money, that one. You should respect that more, piled on the self-righteous voice of her father.

"Still, he breaks up with you every other year or so on your birthday. There has to be a reason, right?" Angela asked, placing her chin on laced fingers in a move that had probably been coquettish when she was young, but now just drew attention to the fat residing under her chin. The fat placement was odd given that the rest of her was bone thin.

"Oh, I don't know. Maybe it's just coincidence," Sarah replied, trying to come off as rational and cool but succeeding only in sounding defensive. She had done her best not to cry during her conversation with Karl, but tears were threatening now.

"Well, I guess I should scan these into the system. I suppose that's what Jonathan meant when he threw these on my desk," Sarah said, picking up the files and heading toward the copier room.

The files didn't need to be scanned at that exact minute, both she and Angela knew that, but being alone in the copy room gave Sarah a chance to process the conversation she had just had with Karl.

"I just don't know how compatible we are," Karl had said. "You are a nice woman, but you just aren't all that sexually compelling. I mean, you know that, right? I'm not telling you anything you don't already know. It's not your fault. It's just what happens as women get older and dried-up."

Sarah felt her eyes well up. One single tear teetered on her bottom lashes before making the final plunge down her face ... then the tears were gone. It took less than ten seconds for them to get sucked back into her apparently now dried-up body. The tears were a reaction to the words, and not to the speaker of the words. The truth was that she didn't really like Karl very much, despite the fact he had been the only man she had dated since the death of her husband six years earlier.

"Sarah?" Angela's voice interrupted her train of thought. She quickly swiped at her face, but not fast enough. Angela had stuck her head in the room and was now looking at her with shiny, serpentine eyes.

"Oh, sorry honey. But there's a client for Michael on line one. I told him Michael was in court this afternoon, but he insisted on speaking with him today. Can you grab it?"

Sarah nodded and left the room, walking quickly to her desk.

"Who is it?" she asked Angela.

"He said his name was Andrew Davies," Angela replied, sitting down and looking back to her computer screen.

Sarah picked up the phone. "Culp, Moore and Rosen, can I help you?"

"You made me wait. I hate waiting," said a snippy and distinctively clipped voice on the other end of the phone. It sounded almost British, but not quite. It actually sounded like an actor's bad attempt at British.

But of course you hate waiting, you entitled dick. That's why you chose this firm to begin with, said a voice in her head. This was a new voice. It came into her head unbidden and she was shocked at herself.

"I'm so sorry sir, what can we help you with?" Sarah asked sweetly, shaking her head a little to dislodge the voice.

"As I told the other woman I spoke with, I need to speak with Michael today. And before you tell me he's in court, I already know that. I want to set sometime early this evening."

"Let me take a look at his calendar. What did you say your name was again?"

The man sighed audibly.

"Andrew Davies. I already said that."

Sarah quickly typed the man's name into Michael's color-coded client list. Green people she could put off for a week. Yellow people she should schedule in the next couple of days. Orange people should be scheduled that day if possible. Red people were to be scheduled immediately, even if it meant bumping someone else. Bright red and underlined meant to schedule them immediately, even before calling him. Sure enough, Andrew Davies came up in bright red and underlined. She had to schedule him no matter what. Sarah did a quick check on Michael's personal contact list; Andrew Davies was listed there.

This was one of Michael's asshole friends, but, surprisingly, not one she had spoken with before.

"What time would you like to see him? He won't get out of court until five, so he won't make it back to the office until six. Maybe—"

"I can do the math of how long it takes to get to the office from the court-house," Andrew interrupted.

"Of course," Sarah said, forcing herself to smile into the phone. "Should I book you in for an early dinner?"

"Fine. Just book him with me for 6:30. I'll text him the restaurant. I don't trust you to make restaurant reservations."

"Certainly, I will—" she began, before realizing that he had hung up on her.

"What a douchebag, right?" Angela said, eyes not leaving her computer screen.

"Hmmmm," Sarah replied. She had learned the hard way to be noncommittal with Angela. "Do you know anything about him?"

"Not much. I know he was one of our divorce clients a few years ago. The ex-wife is a nutcase. That's about all I know," Angela replied and then put on her headphones, signaling that she was bored with the conversation.

Sarah sighed. She quickly closed down her computer and put on her tennis shoes. It would be best to get out of the office before she could allow herself the one birthday present she gave herself every year.

Every year, on her birthday, she allowed herself a serious cry.

Chapter Three

What is Basketball without the Balls?

Friday May 2

When Sarah stepped outside, it was raining. Rain had not been forecast, but there it was. She had walked to work that morning because she didn't want to fight with finding a parking space. She should have known better, given the state of her intestines, the start of her day, and the fact that it was her birthday. So now she had to walk home in the rain carrying her crap from work, with her intestines continuing to grumble ominously.

The rain was very light, and it was warm, so there was that. She could also hear music in the white noise that it made, and that always gave her a sense of contentment. She made it to the one major intersection that she had to cross on her way home. If she went left, then she would pass by the park and the basketball court, and straight home. On her right was the parking lot for the local co-op food market.

"Damn it, if I am going to be miserable tonight, then I might as well enjoy it," she muttered to herself, as she made her way into the grocery store. She wasn't going to bother with dinner tonight. She would just buy two tubs of ice cream, consume both of them, and then wait for the eventual sugar crash before bed. If she was going to have a good cry, she might as well do it right.

Despite her vow to only buy the ice cream, she found herself picking up some meat, vegetables, and fruit for the weekend as well. On the positive side, she wouldn't have to cook for Karl tonight. As she checked out in the self-service lane, she wondered for the millionth time why she bothered dating Karl anyway. She didn't like him very much. He obviously didn't like her very much. And yet they had been together for six long years.

You're lucky to have him, you know. He's been a good provider for you, snapped her mother.

Although most of the things her mother's voice said in her head were nasty, most were also true. Sarah usually justified her relationship with Karl by the fact that he had helped her get her life back together after her husband's sudden death. Paul had surprisingly few assets at his death for someone who was a partner at a top law firm. That was even more surprising as Paul had inherited money from his wealthy mother, who had inherited it from her wealthy mother and so on. He must have lost the money somewhere along the way because, after his death, Sarah had found herself with a mortgage she couldn't afford and bills she couldn't pay. Karl had taken care of all that. Later, he had found her a job as a paralegal at another law firm. He had paid for everything in her life for the first few years, as she was getting back on her feet. In fact, he continued to pay her mortgage now, even though she was capable of doing it herself. So even if he wasn't a nice man, he had been good to her in tangible ways.

For his part, she had no idea why he dated her. It might have had something to do with a loyalty that Karl had to her late husband. Paul had hired Karl and had mentored him throughout his career. So maybe he felt some obligation. He certainly treated their relationship as more of a duty than a pleasure. Then there was the fact that he was sleeping with Meghan, one of the junior attorneys at his firm. Sarah knew this and had known it for years. She had no idea why he didn't just dump her for Meghan.

Oh, maybe he just had.

That thought brought both sadness and relief.

By the time Sarah stepped out of the co-op, the sky had cleared. She walked quickly across the co-op parking lot, juggling her work bag and groceries. She crossed the intersection at an angle, so that she could walk next to the park. The trees were past the flowering stage but the green smell coming off them was elixir after the reconditioned air of the office. There was a huge playground in the center of the park, and she could hear the voices of children, even though there was no one there. The sound caused her heart to both twinge and beat a bit faster. She picked up her pace.

When she turned the corner, she saw the basketball court. Despite the earlier rain, there was a handful of teenage boys playing there. Teenage boys made her very nervous. She sped up to get past the court as quickly as possible. She hadn't liked teenage boys when she was a teenager, so not having to interact with them was one of the benefits of adulthood. At her age, teenagers mostly ignored her but on those rare occasions that she was noticed, it was usually acknowledged by whispers and snickering. However, from the look of it, the ones currently on the court were the boys who played there routinely, and they completely ignored her.

Sarah turned one corner of the court, adjusting the bags on her arms. They were cutting into her forearms because she had overloaded them again. She wasn't very good at gauging the weight of things. Her relationship with the physical world had always been one of a tolerated acquaintance only. Her late husband had teased her about that a lot. His teasing had not meant to be mean-spirited, but it had been demeaning nonetheless. Just as his insistence that she was "not cut out for law" had not been designed to destroy her life but had resulted in a situation where she was now doing a lawyer's work for paralegal pay.

Having her late husband intrude into her brain while she was watching young men play basketball felt incongruous. Paul had been the least physical person she had ever known. He had also been thirty years her senior when they got married. She had wondered many times since his death whether she had married him *because* of his age rather than in spite of it. He had married her after her first year of working in a firm in which he was a partner, and he had insisted that she leave work immediately. She often suspected that marrying her alleviated him from the unpleasant task of having to fire her. She was very smart, but she hadn't been a very good attorney. She was too timid, too conciliatory, for the cutthroat culture of Patterson & Van Allen.

Sarah was lost in these thoughts when she felt eyes on her. She looked up to find that one of the boys on the basketball court had stopped playing and was looking at her, dribbling the ball. Her mind placed him as one of the younger-looking ones she saw on the court. He was thin and either deeply tanned, or of a race with a darker complexion. His shoulder-length brown hair was a tangled mess. He was sweaty, dirty and wearing a weather-inappropriate red sweatshirt that must have been sweltering, given the heat. Said sweatshirt had definitely seen better days and his sweatpants had holes in them. His sneakers were disgustingly dirty, and he was standing closer to her than she had realized.

She looked away quickly and kept walking until she had passed him. She heard the noise behind her stop. Curious in spite of herself, she turned back to see what was happening. The other boys had stopped playing and were staring at the boy. He was standing with the ball under his arm still looking at her, without a trace of self-consciousness. For a moment he met and held her gaze. He didn't smile; he just looked at her like he was studying her face. Sarah found herself frozen in that gaze. Then someone called out, he turned back to his game, and she was released.

Sarah walked away from the basketball court as quickly as she could without looking like she was running. She hoped she wouldn't hear laughing or derogatory comments, but she heard nothing, just the boys calling to each other and the sound of the basketball striking the asphalt.

Before she reached the corner, she turned around. She could see the court and the boys jumping beneath the basketball hoop at the far end. The boy in the red sweatshirt was crouched in the middle of the court when he suddenly stood up, turned around, and looked straight in her direction again.

Sarah ran past the last three houses before running up her front walk. When she got to her front door, she found that her hands were trembling.

"Stop it. What is wrong with you?" she muttered to herself as she dropped her keys before finally letting herself in.

#

Her front door opened directly into her kitchen. She dropped her groceries and purse on the kitchen table and sat down for a minute. Her heart was hammering, like a rabbit.

Rabbit.

That was Karl's pet name for her. She suspected that it wasn't because she was little and cute. No, he tended to use it when he was making fun of her for being timid or meek.

Well, that's what he'll see if that's what you are, her mother pointed out.

Be something else, whispered that new voice, the one that had just appeared that morning.

Sarah shook her head. Her little attack of nerves was ridiculous. There was no reason whatsoever to freak out because some teenage boy looked at her.

Or was there?

She closed her eyes and replayed the scene detail by detail in her head. No, his expression hadn't been hostile or aggressive. It hadn't been particularly friendly either. It had looked more like someone studying her ... or assessing her.

"Oh god, I'm being assessed by a teenager," she muttered to herself with a little laugh. She was surprised to hear the laugh come out of her mouth. She hadn't even considered that laughter might be on the agenda for this evening.

She stood up and put the ice cream in the freezer. She didn't think she would be eating it immediately. Her urge to cry had suddenly dried-up.

"Dried-up, just like me," Sarah muttered, but now felt the sudden urge to giggle at Karl's comment rather than cry.

Her phone suddenly pinged. And then again. And then a third time.

She got up and checked her texts. All three were from Michael.

Schedule office time with Andrew Davies for Monday am. Bump things if you have to, was the first text.

The second text read, *Monday, review the original Davies child support and custody order. Prepare response to petition for custody/visitation modification.*

The third text contained an attachment with the Petition for Custody Modification that had been filed by the other side.

Sarah opened the file to find an attached petition. The petitioner was listed as Melissa Taylor. It listed a previous case number, and the names of the three children: Alexander, sixteen, Andrew Jr., nine, and Christopher, seven. There was only one sentence on the reason for custody modification, which stated, "Alex wishes to attend a private boarding school."

As Sarah had nothing else to go on but the motion, she decided to let it rest until Monday morning. For now, she would celebrate her birthday the way she always did, with tears.

After putting on her PJs, she sat down with a tub of chocolate mint chip ice cream. She then turned on the TV, in search of something to prime the pump.

But she couldn't cry.

Sarah flipped through the movie channels, but nothing worked. The movie about the gorgeous handicapped boy who dies after finding true love with his gorgeous eccentric nurse left her dry-eyed. It was a full two hours of wrenching heartbreak acted by painfully sincere actors to an overwrought soundtrack—but nothing, not one tear. Maybe it was because, as she was watching, her mind kept returning to the boy she had seen earlier. Something about him had been strange. People didn't look at her like that. The look on his face had been odd.

After the movie was over, she found that she had finished the entire tub of ice cream but not one tear had been shed. So, for ten minutes, she flipped through channels stopping at every sad-looking story, but her eyes remained stubbornly dry.

Finally, she got up in disgust and went to the bathroom to wash her face and get ready for bed. She was annoyed with herself.

Why are you annoyed with yourself? Because you can't wallow in how miserable you are in your completely normal life? You should be annoyed about that? This wasn't her mother's voice, it was the voice of her ex-husband, Paul. Seemingly concerned but patronizing.

She turned the lights off, crawled into bed and switched off the bedside lamp. She closed her eyes and relaxed her eyelids, but she wasn't drowsy. Her mind kept bringing up the face of the boy on the basketball court. She found herself scanning his face and expression with her inner eye.

With a shock she realized that, despite his dirty clothes and unkempt appearance—and let's not forget his age—she had found the way he looked at her attractive.

Oh stop it. It is mortifying for a middle-aged woman to find a teenage boy attractive, her mother's voice chided. *Get your head out of the clouds and go to sleep.*

Without realizing it, Sarah nodded and rolled over obediently.

#

When sleep came, it brought a recurring nightmare. She was standing in the rain, ankle-deep in mud. She was in a doorway looking out into a clearing in a dark, wet jungle, standing in front of a freshly dug hole. The sound of the rain almost blocked out the sounds of moaning coming from the hole—almost. As she moved forward, she saw a tan-skinned teenager at the bottom of the well. He was lying on his side in the mud, curled up into a fetal position. Even in the dim light, she could see that his body was covered with sores and wounds, and the smell of vomit, piss, shit, and infection was enough to make her gag. Around him water was beginning to pool, and in that water were various worms. As she watched in horror, a very large white worm slithered across the boy's body and began burrowing into the skin of his stomach. Sarah cried out and reached for him.

Suddenly, Sarah was no longer seeing the boy; instead, she was inside his head. His body had sunk so deep into the mud that it was lodged there, not that he would have had the energy to move it even if he could. He didn't have the energy to do much of anything besides breathe, hurt, and think.

As he closed his eyes, trying to will death, she saw the image of a woman flickering on the insides of his eyelids. It took Sarah a few moments to recognize that she was looking at herself. He tried to speak to her, but he couldn't. His vocal cords no longer worked. As the vision began to dim around the edges, Sarah was jolted awake.

She woke up crying. She instinctively switched on the lamp on her bedside table, but it popped and blew out the minute she touched it. So she lay back down and took deep breaths. She used to have this nightmare regularly as a child, but not since then.

So why do you think it's coming back now? asked the new voice. *Must have taken something important to trigger it.*

"I need to sleep," she muttered in response as she rolled over and shoved a pillow between her legs.

But sleep was a long time coming.

Chapter Four

Playing Paparazzi

Monday May 5

On Monday morning, after a totally Karl-free weekend, Sarah woke up strangely refreshed. She had spent her weekend planning what herbs she would plant this year and sketching out designs for the little garden that she kept in front of her house. It had rained heavily on both Saturday and Sunday, so she couldn't really start anything, but she enjoyed researching plants. She enjoyed researching almost anything, to be honest. So her weekend had been relaxed and stress-free.

She arrived at work by 7 a.m. on Monday feeling almost perky, and ready to dig into her casework. She immediately began to collect what files they had on the Andrew Davies case and was surprised to find that there was nothing in the computer. As a matter of course, all filings, depositions, and motions were scanned and/or uploaded as soon as they were completed or received. But there was nothing in the files except for the current motion.

"I can't seem to find any files on Andrew Davies," Sarah said as soon as Angela came in.

"Yeah?" Angela replied with marked disinterest.

"Do you—" she began, but Angela cut her off.

"Nope. I know nothing about any of it. And I have a stupid deposition to retype." She turned her back on Sarah and flipped on her computer. She wasn't even faking friendliness, as none of the partners were yet in.

At around 8:30, Michael came in with not much more than a quick nod before closing himself in his office.

At 10 a.m., Andrew Davies swaggered into the office. She knew it was him on sight. He was short, with graying hair, a pointy nose, and ratty face. He was handsome but in a snooty upper-class British sort of way. He stopped at Sarah's

13

cubicle and leaned on the reception desk.

"You must be Sarah, right?"

What gave that away, the nameplate that says "Sarah Baker?" snipped the new voice.

"Yes, that's me," she said with a placid smile. "You're Andrew Davies, right? Let me call Michael for you."

"Oh, let's not be so formal. I know I started things off on a bad foot," Andrew said, winking at her.

"Oh, it's no problem," Sarah said, as she picked up the phone. "Michael, Andrew Davies is here to see you."

"Sarah," Andrew said, walking around the desk to put his hand on her shoulder. His touch made her skin crawl, but she plastered on a smile.

"Thank you so much for working me in last Friday. I know I might have been a little short with you. It had been a stressful day. My ex-wife is having one of her episodes again."

"I'm sorry to hear that. Is she unwell?" Sarah asked all wide-eyed, knowing full well what he meant.

You need to stop being sassy. Michael wouldn't appreciate it. This is your workplace, snapped her father.

"No, not physically," Andrew responded with an exaggerated rolling of his eyes. "She's just a bit mentally unstable. Sometimes she's a lot mentally unstable. She has these moments where she imagines me as some sort of monster. Usually, she just calls me and accuses me of a whole host of imaginary horrible things. But occasionally, like this week, she decides to pursue frivolous lawsuits."

"That a serious charge, a frivolous lawsuit," Sarah said before she could stop herself. Andrew raised his eyebrows and his eyes glinted. The glint was not a friendly one. But he quickly composed his face and laughed.

"You're right, but believe me, it's not nearly as serious as some of the things she has accused me of."

At that moment, Michael Angel appeared at the doorway to his office.

"Ah Michael, there you are, you fat bastard," Andrew said with a laugh.

Michael laughed and shook his hand. Sarah had never heard anyone refer to Michael Angel as anything derogatory before, at least not without paying a hefty price for it. But he seemed completely unfazed about being referred to as fat, which was all the more perplexing because he actually was fat.

"More problems from the ex?"

"Sadly, yes," Andrew said, shaking his head. "I need to tell you about what she came up with over the weekend."

With this the two of them went into his office and closed the door.

Sarah shivered. Something about that man did not sit well with her. She wasn't sure what it was, but intuition was her strong suit. It had helped her in her job more than any training she had received, including law school.

At that moment, the phone rang and Sarah's day began in earnest.

It turned out to be one of those unfortunate "response days." The days where all she had time to do was answer the phone, rearrange the court calendars, and return emails. She had wanted to get a little more information on the Davies divorce, just in case Michael asked about it, but she couldn't find time. Angela was being no help in that department. In fact, she seemed to stymie her efforts whenever she got up to try to go to the file room. To be fair, Jason, the partner who was her boss, was in the office today and he was known to be high-maintenance when he was present.

Despite the mindless conversations, painful emails, and routine scheduling duties, Sarah found herself thinking again and again about the boy from the basketball court. The one with the grungy clothes and intense stare.

"What are you daydreaming about?" Angela asked her suddenly, sometime around lunch. Sarah realized that while she had been eating at her desk she had been staring off into space.

"Oh, I'm not daydreaming. I'm falling asleep. I slept crappy last night," she lied.

"Of course. Of course. Did you hear anything else from Karl over the weekend?"

Karl? Karl who?

"No. I didn't expect to," Sarah replied quickly. She should appear to be gutted about this. It wouldn't do for Angela to guess she was thinking of someone else.

There is no someone else here. There's only some kid I saw for thirty seconds. It's not like I'm cheating on Karl or anything.

"Listen, I bet he calls back today, or tomorrow at the latest," Angela said, with aspartame sweetness. "There must be something about you because he can't seem to stay away too long."

Sarah gave Angela what she hoped looked like a thankful smile.

"Maybe you are a hidden firecracker in bed," Angela winked at her. Sarah cringed and turned back to her computer.

"Don't worry. I'm sure he'll call soon," Angela said as she turned back to her own computer.

It actually took him until Thursday afternoon to call.

15

Thursday May 8

"Culp, Moore and Rosen," Sarah answered the phone on Thursday afternoon.

It had been a long and trying week. She had accomplished nothing, at least nothing that she enjoyed. The most interesting thing she had done all week was some legal research on change of tax status and the possible impact of change of circumstance on the alimony of an older client.

"Hi Sarah," said Karl's voice on the phone. She felt herself cringe.

"Hi Karl," she said, with no inflection. She didn't have to fake that. The lack of inflection reflected a very real lack of feeling.

"Listen, Sarah. I was a bit hasty when I called you last week. I was just going through a lot of stress at that particular moment, you know."

"Really, what sort of stress?" she asked. Even in her own ears, her voice sounded sharper than usual. This seemed to catch Karl off guard.

"Oh. Well, you know Michael and I are friends. So, he's being thrown into this Davies custody dispute ... and the opposing attorney is Phillip Seider." Sarah couldn't help but smile a bit at this.

Phillip Seider was the founder and lead attorney of the Seider Firm, the top family law firm in the area. He was mean, smart, and a bit more ethical than was the norm for family law attorneys. Plus, there was a history of competition between their firms on family law matters. So, if Seider took this on, it was likely to get ugly.

"Sarah, are you there?"

"Yes. And yes, Michael sent me the motion about the case."

"Well, what you don't know is that there's a history there."

"There's always a history," she said dryly.

Wow, she was being much more distant with Karl than she usually was on his make-up calls. She was usually all smiles and agreement because she was relieved to still be able to say she had a boyfriend.

"Right. Of course," Karl said quickly. His tone had changed from one of supreme confidence to something more conciliatory. "But the history is more personal. Maybe we can talk about it over dinner tomorrow night."

Sarah was quiet for a moment.

Do you really want to do this? Do you really want to get back with this guy who's mean to you and has another woman on the side? Do you want to have sex that is boring at best and gross at worst? Is having the appearance of a boyfriend important enough to have this guy in your life? asked the new voice. She was going to have to give this one a name

16

if it kept talking.

"Sarah, are you there?" Karl asked.

"Yes."

"I know you're angry at me. And it was insensitive of me to break up with you on your birthday. So I have a present for you."

Well, that's a first.

"Can I give it to you tomorrow night?"

Sarah sighed. "Okay."

"Great, then I will see you tomorrow night."

"Okay," Sarah said, but Karl had hung up, once again safe on his superior ground.

Why am I getting back into this?

The truth was that she didn't know how people would react if she was the person to dump Karl, as opposed to the other way around. She was working for his friends. She was taking his money.

So, he's your pimp then? asked the new voice.

Of course not. He's your boyfriend, and you should be thankful to have one, said her mother.

Just at that moment, Sarah noticed that Angela was looking at her with entirely too much interest.

"So you and Karl back together now?" she asked with a smug look. Sarah wasn't sure what Angela had to be smug about, but it made her uncomfortable.

"I guess so. He's coming for dinner tomorrow night," Sarah responded as she got her things together.

Angela shrugged and turned back to her computer, satisfied that nothing interesting was happening.

"Well, he told me that he got me a birthday present," she said, before she could stop herself. Her voice sounded defensive and pathetic even in her own ears.

Angela had turned and was about to respond when Michael came out of his office and handed Sarah a single file folder.

"This is the Davies file. Can you take a look at the divorce decree, equitable distribution and custody papers? Also, I want you to do a little Internet digging on the wife. Her name and info should be in the documents," he said, as he pulled out his phone and began texting someone.

"Do you have any previous depositions that I should go through?" Sarah asked.

"Huh? No, I didn't dig that up yet. Just work with what I gave you for now. And I am really interested in what the ex-wife is up to these days. Oops, I have to go. I'm late for dinner with the new girlfriend, and she's pissed off."

With this Michael bolted out of the door.

As soon as Michael had left, Sarah put on the sneakers that she kept under her desk, gathered her stuff and left the building with a cursory goodbye to Angela.

On her walk home, she decided to stop by the grocery store again. She felt edgy somehow. Michael was an asshole, but he was a thorough asshole. It was unlike him to give her an incomplete file when he was asking her to research. She knew for a fact that they kept copies of all previous motions, court appearances, and depositions. The fact that the file was so light was suspicious.

At the grocery store, as she picked out some grapefruit for breakfast and salmon for dinner tonight, she thought about how funny it was that Paul had always thought of her as too thin-skinned to work in a law office. She wasn't. Sure, she was timid at times and unassertive at others, but she would never have survived growing up in her family if she had been thin-skinned. Her parents and praise were not well acquainted. As a result, Sarah had a fairly comprehensive list of all the things that were wrong with her.

How can you be as smart as you are and have no backbone, girl? or *You're not pretty enough to be able to expect a man to take care of you, so you better find an administrative job so you can support yourself,* or *Self-consciousness is just another form of vanity. It's just you thinking about yourself too much.*

That simply scratched the surface of what she heard on a daily basis growing up. On the positive side, she could take criticism with the best of them. She had also learned to channel her sensitivity into an awareness of people's motivations that coworkers called "uncanny." On the negative side, when her parents died, she had absorbed their voices into those that already spoke inside her head, and now they were the loudest ones.

It was her heightened awareness that told her that something was not quite right with the Davies case. She wasn't sure what, and she would need to be careful about how she researched, but it tickled her curiosity.

Sarah was lost in these thoughts as she left the grocery store and made her way home, past the park and toward the basketball courts. When she realized where she was, her heart started to race a little bit at the thought of seeing the boy she had seen last week.

There were some boys playing on the court. She scanned them for someone in grungy clothes, but from a distance, they all looked like they were wearing appropriate attire.

Sarah's heart sank a little.

Don't be ridiculous, she told herself. Although she wasn't exactly sure what she was chiding herself about, it was nice when the voice doing the talking was her own.

As she got closer, she saw the tall, red-haired boy miss a shot and retake the ball. He was one of the regulars. When the red-haired boy landed, he jostled one of the other boys near him. That boy staggered, regained his footing, and in the process deftly stole the ball. When she saw his face, Sarah actually heard herself gasp. The boy who had been pushed, the one who now had the basketball, was the boy she had seen before. She hadn't noticed him because his appearance was quite different. His shoulder-length dark hair had been cut. He had on a red-and-black striped shirt that didn't look expensive, but did look brand new, as did the matching shorts. His sneakers were black with pristine white soles. And right at the moment, he was dribbling the ball down the court—straight at her.

Sarah froze. She was standing on the sidewalk behind the basket on the other side of the chain-link fence. She felt like her feet had grown roots as she watched him set up, jump, and make the basket. He came down right in front of her. As he landed, before turning to run back down the court, he stopped and caught her eye. His eyes widened ever so slightly, and he smiled. For a moment, he looked directly in her eyes and she felt a strange dizzy feeling in seeing him and being seen by him. No one in her life ever seemed to actually see her. No one ever had.

That pleasure was quickly replaced by anxiety. She looked down and began to adjust her bags. Without looking up, she forced her feet to move and began walking around the corner. Her feet did not want to move. It felt like she was pushing against a current. She desperately wanted to look at him again, just one more time. She turned quickly and saw that he was standing mid-court, watching the other boys under the hoop at the far end. He must have felt her gaze because he turned around quickly and gave her another smile, but this one looked more self-conscious.

You need to get a photo of him, whispered the new voice.

Why? That's creepy, she responded in her head.

He isn't what he seems, Sarah! Do it now, while you can. Then look at it later, the new voice snapped in her head.

Before she could talk herself out of it, Sarah pulled her phone out of her purse and took a snapshot of him. He had just been thrown the basketball and was holding it, not looking at her, thank god. When she took the photo, her phone clicked at a volume that sounded like a sonic boom in her ears.

Frazzled, she promptly dropped her bag of groceries. The two grapefruit rolled out in opposite directions. She dropped to her knees and began grabbing for them. She heard the boys on the court laugh. She wondered if they were laughing at her, as she hurriedly shoved her items back into the bag. She felt stupid, embarrassed, and completely foolish. She got up, berating herself for being ridiculous, and quickly walked away.

When she let herself into her house, she immediately went upstairs and put the phone in the charger on her bedside table, disgusted with herself. She then went to her kitchen and started cleaning, from the top down. She scrubbed the sink, the counter, and the tiles. But as she did this, her mind kept turning to the photo she had just taken. She decided that now was the time to clean her oven as well. So she got out the oven cleaner and spent a good thirty minutes border-line asphyxiating herself with oven cleaner vapors. But still, through all this, the thought of the picture weighed on her.

She then made herself some grilled salmon and ate it with a grapefruit, some rice, and a salad. But she didn't taste a bit of it. She went to her living room, turned on the TV and flipped through the channels but nothing could keep her interest.

Why was she making such a big deal out of this? It was probably just a nothing photo. Surely, it would be too blurry to even see much of anything. And he had been looking down anyway.

Finally, Sarah could stand it no more. She was fixating on this. She got up and went upstairs to her bathroom where she brushed her teeth, washed her face, and put on her PJs. Still her mind kept returning to her phone on her bedside table.

"Okay, enough is enough," she muttered to herself. "Why am I torturing myself about this? I'll just look at the photo, delete it, and go to bed. It's no big deal."

In her bedroom, she pulled her phone from the charger. She quickly opened up the camera and tapped the last photo. Almost immediately, her hands began to tremble.

The boy had not been looking down in the photo. His head was down but his eyes were looking up from beneath his dark hair directly into the camera. And the expression on his face ... well, it was an expression that had no place being on the face of a teenager. He was smiling, but it wasn't an innocent smile. It was crooked, suggestive, and knowing.

Sarah quickly closed the camera and dropped the phone on her bed, as if he could see her from the device. She felt jittery, and her hands were shaking.

He knows, she thought to herself, shame welling up inside her. *He knows that I took his picture.*

She sat down quickly on the bed to keep from falling.

Oh god. He was probably mortified, or horrified, or both.

But that had not been his expression. He looked amused. Oh god. Suppose he had told his friends. Suppose they had talked about her.

Okay. That was enough. She was going to stop this right now. She put the phone back in the charger, turned off the light, and got into bed. In time, fatigue finally coaxed her into sleep.

She hadn't deleted the picture.

Chapter Five

Return of the Grind

Friday May 9

Sarah overslept on Friday morning and so, for the first time in years, she had to rush to get to work. By the time she got to the office, everyone was in panic mode. The equitable distribution hearing for one of Jason's major clients had been moved forward from Monday to today, so Angela was speeding around the office like she was on meth. Jason, for his part, was in his office making angry calls. His door was closed, but he was loud enough that everyone in the office heard him anyway.

This meant that all of the phone and email responses went to Sarah. She didn't mind, it kept her brain busy and away from dwelling on yesterday's possible humiliation by a teenage boy.

Karl called her at five o'clock on Friday evening to tell her that he would be running late for their date and probably wouldn't be there until seven. He also told her that he would pick up some Chinese food on his way to her place so that she wouldn't have to cook. That was rare. He never brought food. He expected her to cook. Sarah closed out her workday and was home by six, bringing work home with her.

Karl didn't make it to her house until nine that night. By that time, Sarah was hungry *and* tired. She hadn't bothered preparing food because he said he would bring it, and by 7:30 pm she had regretted this decision. When he finally showed up, he came with the promised Chinese and nothing more. Apparently, he had forgotten the birthday gift.

"I got the Chinese food," he said as he entered. He had let himself into her house with his set of keys. He never bothered knocking. She wondered if this was because he paid the mortgage and therefore, in his mind, he owned the place.

"I thought you would be here by seven," Sarah said, surprising herself because her words sounded like an accusation.

"Yeah, well I got roped into some last-minute client phone calls. Plus, there was a line of idiots at the Chinese joint and it took them for-fucking-ever just to put together a simple takeout. I ordered some cashew chicken and Mongolian beef. It's not like it's exotic. Fucking idiots."

As Sarah listened to this, she noted his appearance. His tie was badly knotted. His hair was pressed flat against his head. And, despite his words, his body posture was unusually relaxed. He also reeked of sex, which told her that he had been visiting Meghan earlier that evening.

On the positive side, it meant she wouldn't be subjected to make-up sex, as Karl was a once-a-night man. On the negative side, it meant that she would, for all intents and purposes, be smelling Meghan's crotch for the rest of the evening. Sarah didn't hate Meghan because she was fucking Karl. She didn't need to, there were so many other reasons to hate her. She was young. She was beautiful. She was vain and arrogant about being young and beautiful. She thought she was brilliant, when she was only passably smart. And she was always stevia-sweet and condescending to Sarah whenever their paths crossed.

Karl dropped the brown paper bags containing the Chinese food on her kitchen table and sat down on one of the chairs. They almost never ate at the table. Usually, Karl opted to eat in front of the TV, so eating at the table was probably some diluted act of contrition on his part.

"Did you get a chance to look at the Davies case file?" he asked her, putting his feet up on one of her other chairs.

Sarah got a couple of plates and laid out the food on the table with some silverware.

"Yes. I looked at what Michael gave me, but it wasn't that much."

"Well, the ex-wife is a psychotic bitch. She had a mental breakdown and was under a psychiatrist's care for a couple years before the actual divorce. Andrew Davies is a good guy. He has sole custody of the kids, but he's still paying his ex monthly alimony."

"He's paying her $150 a month," Sarah interjected before she could help herself.

"Yeah, but he didn't have to pay her anything. The court didn't order it. He's just doing it because he's a good guy and she's the mother of his kids."

Never mind that she probably worked to put him through law school. That's the usual scenario, Sarah thought to herself.

23

"You know a lot about this," she said out loud.

"Yeah, the original case was a bitch."

"Why?"

"It was long and ugly. And there's a history between Phillip and Michael that I mentioned to you. That made it harder for him. I wanted to tell you about it, so you'll understand if Michael is testy during this case."

Sarah put a plate with some of the Mongolian beef with rice in front of Karl. Then she sat down and began serving herself.

"What's the history?" she asked. She was trying to ignore the fact that Karl's perfectly manicured and buffed fingernails were filthy.

"Phillip is now married to Michael's ex-fiancée. She left Michael during that trial."

"Oh. Right. So they don't like each other," Sarah's voice sounded flat and bored to her own ears, but Karl didn't notice.

"They won't even golf together," Karl responded, jabbing viciously at a piece of beef.

Not golfing together? No, say it's not true.

"I think Michael's better off now, because she was super high-maintenance, but I think he's still in love with her. That's why he hasn't had a serious relationship since."

Poor Michael. High-powered attorney boy can't get over being dumped.

Sarah tried not to smile. She shouldn't be so sarcastic. Michael wasn't all that bad—well, most of the time, and comparatively. Karl was giving her an odd look, so she quickly returned her thoughts to the case.

"What's weird about the filing is that the ex-wife is filing for change of circumstances, and she wants the kids. *But* the rationale she states is that her oldest wants to go to a private boarding school. That doesn't stand up."

"Of course it does!" Karl interjected. "If the kid's living with her then she will try to arrange for the funds to go through her. And she can then get child support."

"But no court would fall for that. He wouldn't be living with her; he'd be at the boarding school. That's not a real change of circumstances, and, despite whatever else you may think of him, Phillip isn't an idiot."

"No, I think that was just to get the ball rolling and to see if we will play along. She doesn't want to mention the real change of circumstances before we have responded because she knows that we won't react well to it."

What's with the "we"? This isn't your case.

"What's the real change of circumstances then?" Sarah asked.

"Andrew just got remarried and the ex is furious about it."

"Ah. Does she know the new wife? Was she part of the original case in any way?"

"No," Karl said, looking away. "But they've been together for a while. I think they got together a year or so after his divorce."

You really know an awful lot about this case. So much for confidentiality.

"What has Michael asked you to do so far?" Karl asked.

"Not much. Draft a reply requesting it be dismissed."

They were quiet for a moment as they ate. Sarah was wondering why Karl implied that Phillip thought Michael might just roll over on this case.

"What about the kids?" she asked. "I saw there were three, right? Do you know anything about them?"

"The oldest, Alex, the wannabe boarding school kid, is a brat," Karl said, before adding hastily, "Andrew never actually said that. It's my interpretation of what I have heard about him. What Andrew did say was that the kid is still furious about the divorce and resents the new wife."

"That's not abnormal or surprising," Sarah replied with a shrug.

Karl snorted and leaned back in his chair.

"Has Michael asked you to do anything else?" he asked.

"Look at the divorce decree, equitable distribution, and custody documents. That's all he gave me," she said. "But he asked me to do a little research on the wife, Melissa Taylor, this weekend."

"That's a good idea. No one researches like you, rabbit." He reached over and patted her hand with his dirty fingers.

Sarah tried to smile but she was having a hard time doing it. As she looked at Karl's face, and his guarded expression, she thought of the open look on the face of the boy in the photo. Karl's eyes always looked dry and flat, like a snake's. The boy's eyes had been bright in that photo.

They were really that shiny, right? You need to check that again, honey, to make sure you aren't just imagining it, whispered the new voice.

"You're somewhere else tonight," Karl said, narrowing his eyes. "Are you mad that I was late? I did call to tell you."

"No, I'm not mad," she said. This was true. Now that she was fed, she didn't care much.

Do I always feel this much nothing when I am around him?

Karl's eyes were scanning her face, so she adopted a totally neutral look.

"Oh. You think I forgot your birthday present. That's it," he said suddenly with a slight smirk. "But I didn't. I was planning to give it to you tomorrow night. See, I cleared my Saturday evening schedule so that we can have another date night tomorrow."

25

He said this with a wide grin. Normally they had one date a week on Friday evenings.

So that's his great surprise, said the new voice.

Smile quickly. Smile quickly. Smile quickly.

"That's great. I can cook dinner tomorrow," she offered quickly, before he had time to notice anything amiss in her face.

"Good. I love the stew you make. That would be great," Karl said.

Smile. Smile. Smile.

"Hey, I have to go now. More work to do. I really shouldn't have left the office at all tonight. I wouldn't have if I hadn't promised to have dinner with you," Karl lied. His gaze felt like ants crawling on her face. His brows were still knit.

"Oh," Sarah said, making her voice sound small and weak.

Karl's face relaxed. "Don't worry, rabbit. I will make it up to you tomorrow night," he said, standing up and walking toward the door. "Plus, this will give you some time to look up Melissa Taylor."

With that he walked out of the door without a backward glance.

#

After Karl had left, Sarah let out a sigh of relief and got up to clear the food off the table. Without Karl there to actively distract her, she started thinking about the photo on her phone again. She had not allowed herself to look at it while she was at work. Angela was too eagle-eyed to make that safe. She had not allowed herself to do so while waiting for Karl because it wouldn't do for him to catch her staring at a photo of a teenage boy.

No, that would not do at all.

She should have deleted the photo, but she didn't do it this morning because she was late. She had also been afraid that the shame she had felt the night before might still be clinging to her. But now, after a full day and dinner with Karl, she was sure that she had been overreacting.

Sarah sighed. Clearly, she wasn't going to be doing any research tonight. She had left her phone upstairs on the charger, so she went to retrieve it. The light in her bedroom was off but the light from the hall was bright enough to gently illuminate the room. Sarah sat down on her bed and pulled her phone out of the charger. She took a deep breath and opened the camera function, clicking on the last photo taken.

When the photo of the boy appeared, she saw the same knowing expression she had seen before and her heart began hammering in her chest, just as it had the night before. This time she closed her eyes and forced herself to calm down.

Sarah, that boy looks like he knows that you were taking a photo of him. That's just humiliating, he's a teenager! said her mother's voice.

Wrong, said the new voice

That's neither here nor there at the moment, said a different voice, cutting off the new voice. This particular voice had appeared about a year ago and was the one she now thought of as her attorney voice.

Just look at the photo. Think of it as part of your job. Be a researcher. What do you see? She looked at the photo. Yes, the boy had seen her taking a picture of him, for sure. His eyes were looking straight into the camera. His smile was harder to translate.

Don't try to translate that until you have analyzed the rest of the photo. What can you learn about him from the photo? the attorney voice asked.

Well, he wasn't from one of the wealthy local families. She knew that from her previous encounter with him. Even if he was wearing nicer clothes this time, they were not any of the high-end sports brands. On closer inspection, his skin wasn't tanned per se. He looked like he had Hispanic or Latino ancestry. His arms and legs were muscled but very thin. His hands on the ball were delicate-looking with long fingers.

Okay, so he could be Mexican or South American. He could also be from Europe but that would be less likely, unless he was second generation. Now that her brain was clearer and more focused, she returned her gaze to his face.

On closer examination, his eyes weren't nearly as big as she had thought they were. In fact, they might have been slightly on the small side. It was the intensity of them that made them look big. He also had dark circles under his eyes. This could mean lack of sleep, lack of nutrition, allergies, or any combination of the above. From the lack of inflammation, she suspected sleep problems.

Sarah turned her attention back to his smile, the one that had freaked her out. There was no denying that it looked a like a smirk, but it wasn't like the smirks she saw with Karl. It didn't seem particularly malicious. She tried to scan her brain for where she had seen that sort of smile before. It took a couple of seconds for her to pinpoint it. She had seen it on the faces of male celebrities. It was almost a self-satisfied look.

Great. He feels full of himself because I am taking his picture. Fantastic. So he's an egotistical asshole.

Disgusted, she was about to throw the phone down again when the new voice stopped her.

No, don't stop. Read his eyes, said her attorney voice.

Sarah looked at the picture again and zoomed in on his face. She felt a little kick in her gut. The photo was grainy at this level of magnification, but one

27

thing was clear. His eyes didn't match his grin. If the grin was lazy and self-confident, the eyes were not. They were open and very intense. And his eyes were glued to the camera as if searching for something. There was a desperate quality to his gaze.

"Eyes and mouth don't match. If eyes and mouth don't match, believe the eyes," she muttered to herself. She then lay back down on her bed, eyes scanning his face. After a while she got sleepy, but found it was hard to look away from the photo. Something strange was going on here.

When sleep finally took her, the phone was still in her hand.

Chapter Six

By Any Other Name

Saturday May 10

Sarah woke up Saturday morning with drying spit in her hair and her phone on the mattress next to her. She had fallen asleep in her clothes. The last time she had done that was … never.

You're having some sort of midlife crisis.

"Shut up, Mom," Sarah muttered to herself. She looked at her phone. It had run out of battery charge. This meant she couldn't stare at the picture anymore, at least until the phone charged. As it was the weekend, she would have to find some way to distract herself from it.

Okay, first, shower. The phone will be charged by then and I can erase the photo. It's not like it's doing me any good. It's just embarrassing, Sarah thought as she got out of bed and stretched.

It also reminds you of other things, doesn't it? The things you don't have, said the new voice. Sarah suspected she might come to hate this one as much, if not more, than the others.

"Oh, shut up," she muttered to herself, as she got up and walked to her master bathroom. There wasn't much that was "master" about it, except that it was connected directly to her bedroom. She brushed her teeth, showered, dried off, and grabbed the first things she found in the closet, which were a white shirt and a pair of jeans. She didn't bother looking at herself in the mirror through any of this. She had been okay-looking in her youth, but age had made her skin pale and washed-out. Her freckles had also become more accentuated as she got older. So, in short, she didn't like her looks and only looked at herself when required.

She went downstairs, grabbed a can of Coke out of the refrigerator and a banana off the counter. While she was eating, she opened up her laptop. As she powered it up, she turned her thoughts to the Davies case. She concentrated particularly on Melissa Taylor's situation. In these claims, people were always presented in the best and worst possible lights. While Karl had called Melissa the "psychotic ex-wife," Sarah knew that truth was always hidden in the gray area between the conflicting points of view. Of course, the attorneys in the office didn't care about the truth, they only cared about winning the case for the client. But it was important to Sarah to know the truth, if only for herself.

This desire to find out the truth had hindered Sarah at law school. Law was not about truth; it was about the ability to argue either side. It took Sarah almost two years to figure that out in school and her grades had suffered because of it. Still, she had learned this lesson by the time she took the Bar and had passed the first time. She had carried this lesson with her once she began to work, and again when she rejoined the workforce after her husband's death. So she knew what Michael wanted her to find. What he wanted was what every lawyer wanted in a custody battle, the smoking gun that proved the other side to be an unfit parent. Drug or alcohol problems, abuse, and mental illness were the gold standard proof of bad parenting. Unemployment and/or abject poverty could work too, but courts sometimes felt sorry for the parent in question in these cases, especially if the child wanted to stay with the parent in poverty. Poor judgment in romantic relationships could also work if you could prove that the unsavory significant other would have direct contact with the children.

She had very little to go on about Melissa, except her full name and the fact that she was the ex-wife of Andrew Davies. The file Michael had given her included a photo of Melissa from their wedding. The woman in the photo was a tall, pretty brunette who was beaming at the camera from behind a three-tiered wedding cake. Andrew Davies had a smile that was showing lots of teeth, but no crinkling of the eyes. In short, she looked truly happy and he looked like he was pretending to be happy. It was an old, dingy photo but at least it was a visual of the woman. The names of Melissa's three children were also in one of the filings.

These things together were enough to start the ball rolling. Sarah started with the low-hanging fruit: social media. Social media was great because people tended not to think about the long-term implications of their picture posting and political comments. These could be gold mines of bad judgment, which could be dragged out in a court case. Unfortunately, Melissa didn't seem to be on Twitter, Instagram, Snapchat, or Pinterest. She didn't even seem to have a Facebook or LinkedIn account.

Sarah rechecked and cross-checked with the names of her children. Her oldest, Alex, only had an Instagram account but his page was private, so she couldn't see much, just his profile picture and that he followed five people and was followed by five. Her nine-year-old, Andrew Jr., had an Instagram account and was surprisingly active, with lots of photos of friends and family. While Chris, the seven-year-old, had no accounts on his own, he was featured heavily on Andrew's page. On Andrew's page there were lots of photos of their stepmother, but their birth mother was nowhere to be seen. Sarah checked the woman's age again. She was in her forties, so she was surely aware of the social media sites, as well as their importance in the lives of teenagers. Sarah had noticed that most mothers, at least the ones that she had run into, were obsessive about keeping up with social media, often to keep track of their kids. But Melissa was nonexistent on all social media. This meant that it was likely to be an active choice on her part, but it didn't explain her absence from her kids' sites.

Next Sarah checked photos, just to see if there were images of Melissa anywhere on social media. She looked at the Facebook pages of the boys' friends and their friends' mothers. She was hoping to see that Melissa had mom friends within their circle of friends, but there was no joy there either. So social media was out.

Sarah then began the more detailed, more physical searches. She searched public records for birth records, current address, and phone number. There wasn't too much interesting here, except for the current address. A quick search on Google Maps confirmed what she already knew. Melissa lived in an apartment in a so-so section of town. There was a pawn shop a few blocks from her and a check-cashing store on the next street over. She owned the apartment she lived in, based on the property records, and it looked like she had bought it just after the divorce settlement. There was no one else listed on the deed with her and no one listed as ever having lived with her in the online 411 data.

She got lucky on Ancestry.com. Apparently, Melissa's mother had tagged her in a family tree. This told Sarah that Melissa had one sister named Maria. She felt an immediate dislike of Melissa's parents for subjecting their children to a cutesy naming scheme. She also found out that Melissa had been born in San Jose, California. She was a California girl who had moved from the west coast to the east coast, which probably had something to do with Andrew.

She was about to start her research on Andrew Davies himself, when she looked up at the clock. To her shock, she realized that it was already 3:30. She had worked all day and hadn't had lunch.

She grabbed herself a sandwich and was sitting back down to her computer when it suddenly hit her.

"Shit. Karl is coming over tonight," she gasped aloud. "And I said I would cook that beef stew, which needs at least three hours to simmer. Shit. Shit. Shit."

She had forgotten because Saturday was never a date night for them. It was always Friday night and then Saturday was her time. She realized that she was feeling no small amount of resentment.

This is not a healthy relationship, the new voice said, which Sarah was trying to ignore.

She ran upstairs to grab her purse and dashed out the door. She grabbed her phone on the way and realized with a shock that she had managed not to think about the photograph all day.

But she also hadn't deleted it.

I'll do it when I get back from the store, she promised herself.

#

Sarah left her house at a trot. She was already short on time, but now she would need to go to a different butcher. The co-op never seemed to have stew beef. Luckily, there was a specialty butcher down the street, on the other side of the basketball court. She hoped she could find what she needed there.

It only took her ten minutes to get to the grocery store with the butcher. It was a bit expensive, but the higher price tag on the goods wasn't due to over-head, it was due to the unique range of meats they offered. Once there, Sarah picked up the various vegetables she needed on her way to the meat depart-ment—onions, garlic, carrots, celery, potatoes. As she approached the meat department, she smiled politely at the tan-skinned grocer she didn't know, as she compared the various weights and ratios of the different parcels of stew beef. The man watched her with a strange expression on his face. Sarah won-dered if he was worried she would steal something, but she was fairly sure that she didn't look gutsy enough to be a thief. When she looked up at him and smiled again, he quickly looked away.

Ah, maybe he was thinking I would take something and is embarrassed that I caught him in that thought. Sarah smiled a bit. Thinking that someone might think she was dangerous enough to be a thief brightened her mood substantially.

Just as she had decided on the largest parcel of beef, as Karl liked his meat plentiful, she heard a chorus of voices coming from the front of the store. She threw the stew beef in her basket, sighed and began walking toward the registers. It was against her nature to walk toward commotion, but she needed to get home quickly to have time to get everything in the pot and simmering. She had made it halfway up one of the aisles when a few teenage boys walked past the top of her row.

Sarah froze. She recognized them as the basketball boys. She hadn't seen *him*, but he might be with them. Her heart began to hammer in her chest again. She could feel her face heating up as she began backing down the aisle. When she saw them walk by again, she whirled to head in the opposite direction and ran right into someone. Her grocery basket with the meat fell to the floor and she landed unceremoniously on her butt.

She looked up to see a face smiling down at her. At first, she didn't recognize him because he was so close, but this lack of recognition lasted for only a second. When she met his widened eyes, she realized that this was none other the boy whose photograph she had been staring at obsessively for the past twenty-four hours.

"Here, let me help you up," he said, offering a hand and a smile. She shook her head and struggled to her feet. Her face was burning and must be the shade of rhubarb.

"Are you okay?" he asked.

"Oh, I'm fine. Nothing hurt but my pride," she said, trying to laugh, not looking at him. She managed to get to her feet and was turning to flee when she heard, "Ms. Baker."

She turned back, shocked. The boy knew her name.

"Yes?"

"You forgot your groceries," he said, picking up her grocery basket … but *not* holding it out to her. This forced her to move closer to take it from him. She extended her hand, but he still didn't hold out the basket. His gaze was open and direct.

"You don't remember me, do you?" he asked her.

"No. I'm sorry. Do I know you?"

I've only been stalking you and falling asleep with your photo.

"My foster family lives a few blocks from your office. I moved in last year. My name is Caio."

He pronounced this name with a hard C, like a K, a long I, and a long O. He also had a slight accent that she couldn't discern.

"I'm sorry. I didn't remember. Very nice to meet you properly, Caio," Sarah replied, holding out her hand. She wasn't sure if this was coming across polite and proper, or just stuffy. But he only smiled and took her outstretched hand. His hand was more calloused than she would have expected for such a young man. He didn't shake her hand. He just held it warmly for a moment before letting go. His hand was extremely hot.

"My foster father is the butcher here," he said, nodding to the back. "If you

33

want, I can get you a better cut of meat. This doesn't look very good." He nodded at what was in her basket.

She only managed to nod in response. What the hell was she supposed to say? She was too busy staring at the curve of his nose, how it looked just the same as it did in her photo.

He walked to the back and rang the bell. The butcher came out and greeted him with a marked lack of warmth. Still, some exchange happened, and he came back with a different parcel.

"This is better," he said. "I am originally from Brazil, so I can recognize good meat." He smiled at her as he handed back her grocery basket with the new parcel inside. He regarded her with a little smile that she could not read.

Did that statement make any sense? Would I be able to tell if it did? Jesus, Sarah, get yourself together.

"Thank you," she said quickly, taking back her basket. She knew that she should leave, but she didn't want to. She wanted to keep talking to this boy. This was stupid and ridiculous, and she was making a fool of herself, but she just couldn't leave, her feet wouldn't let her.

"You play basketball very well," was all she was able to get out.

"Nah. I'm too short."

"You're not short," she said, before she could stop herself. She was 5'4" and he was taller than her, and that made him tall in her estimation.

"I'm 5'10". I'm the shortest on the team. But I'm fast. So I can keep up, but that's about all," he said, looking directly into her eyes.

Most teenagers don't make direct eye contact like this, do they? Is this weird? Oh shit, I'm staring.

She started to feel faint. She was afraid she might fall down.

"Thank you very much for the meat," she said, looking down before flushing at how bad that sounded. Then feeling worse because normally she would have thought nothing of uttering that sentence.

"I need to go. I am fixing Karl a stew," she blurted out. Caio's face darkened, and his brows came together to form a deep crease between his eyes. Once again, the depth of the crease was something she wouldn't have expected on such a young face.

"Karl Renfield?" he asked.

"Yes, do you know him?" she asked.

"Um hmmm," he said. Now he was looking down. Sarah felt confused and she was becoming aware that people were looking at them.

"Well, thanks again, Caio," she said turning to go. She had walked about five steps when he called her.

34

"Ms. Baker."

"Yes," she replied, turning.

"Can I ask your first name?"

"What?" The world seemed to be getting slippery beneath her feet.

"Your first name? What's your first name?" he asked, regarding her with those strange wide-open eyes.

"Sarah," she said, and he smiled. She then turned and walked as quickly as she could to the register. She didn't remember paying, walking home, or even beginning the stew. It was only as she began browning the meat that her brain re-engaged.

"Caio," she thought. "His name is Caio. And why did he want to know my first name?"

And at that thought, a little sun was born into the grayness of her heart.

Chapter Seven

Reunited and It Feels so "Ick"

Saturday May 10

Why did he ask my first name? For that matter, how did he know my last name?

These thoughts came into her mind continually as she cut up the vegetables for the stew. Once she had added them to the meat, she sat down and allowed herself to look at his photo again.

Caio. It was a photo of Caio.

She couldn't delete it now. They had been introduced and he was someone she knew. Even more, he was someone who knew her, and who had wanted to know her name. She couldn't remember the last time anyone had been interested in knowing her name.

Sarah found herself holding her phone next to her chest and hugging herself.

Would you stop acting so ridiculous! You are going to make a total fool of yourself, said her mother's voice.

Maybe it's okay to make a fool out of yourself sometimes, if it makes you happy, said the new voice.

You are playing a dangerous game, little girl, her dad's voice chimed in.

Sarah shook her head to dislodge the conversation happening there. She wasn't going to ruin this moment. Certainly, it would be taken away from her soon enough. Happiness always was.

Caio. What a beautiful name.

When she thought of him asking her first name, she felt a light go on inside her. It was silly. It was stupid. It was borderline creepy, but it was what she felt. Her small, bounded world felt bigger and more open at the thought of him. The sky she could see from her window seemed to stretch further. The music she heard on the street seemed more exciting than jarring. People up and down the

36

sidewalk seemed less frightening, some even friendly.

She had a bit more information on him as well. She knew his first name. She knew that he was Brazilian. She knew that he was a foster child and that his foster father was the butcher in the alternative grocery store. She searched her brain for when she might have met him with his foster family. Neither Caio nor his foster dad had looked familiar to her when she first saw them. It must have a quick meeting, or at a place where she had not been formally introduced.

My foster family lives a few blocks from your office.

Wait, he knew where she worked. Maybe she had met him at work. That was possible, but what was making her blood rush was the fact that this person bothered to remember her AND remember where she worked.

Sarah hugged herself again.

When the stew was almost ready, she brought the docking station down from her bedroom, put her phone in it and played music. For the first time in forever, she danced as she mashed potatoes and drained peas.

"What are you smiling about?" asked a sharp voice. Sarah jumped and spilled some hot water from the peas onto her foot. The pain caused her to gasp and hop on one foot. She quickly grabbed a towel from the door of the stove and began to wipe it off.

Karl was standing in her kitchen, glowering at her. He had let himself in with the key without her hearing him. Apparently, he hadn't had the best day.

Sarah's foot was turning an angry red. She moved past Karl and grabbed some ice from the refrigerator and began to rub it on her foot.

"Perhaps you didn't hear me, but I asked you a question," Karl said quietly but with punctuated words.

"Perhaps you didn't notice that I just spilled boiling water on my foot," Sarah snapped back.

For a moment Karl looked as stunned as Sarah felt. She had never smarted back to him before. He made it very clear, on a very regular basis, that he was doing her a great favor by dating her. The fact that he had also paid her mortgage since her husband died made the inequality of their relationship even more pointed.

The shock on Karl's face morphed into a smile that was much worse than his glower. Sarah had a bad feeling that she had just made her evening much worse than it might have been.

"Well, then you should bandage that little foot right up. I wouldn't want you to be uncomfortable or anything. I mean, I'm sure it's a life-threatening wound and all."

He walked past her quickly, grabbing a beer from her fridge and moving into the living room without giving her another glance.

She put some butter on her foot, and then put food on plates for both of them and brought them to the living room. Normally, Karl was fastidious about manners, neatness, and decorum, but at her place he had no problem eating on the couch and dropping things on the floor. Eating at the table last night had been a conciliatory gesture on his part, and he apparently thought there was no more need for such niceties.

He ate quickly, not looking at her. He didn't like it if she spoke to him while he was eating. When he was done, he handed her the plate. She obediently took it, and hers, into the kitchen.

"How was your day?" she asked as she came back into the room. This question was expected.

"I had to deal with a bunch of goddamned idiots as usual. But I had a deposition, so that made the day a bit more exciting."

He then went into a detailed description of said deposition. Karl liked depositions, because he liked having the chance to "push someone over" as he called it. He was ugly that way.

In truth, Karl was ugly in quite a few ways, including sexually. While he wasn't someone who openly participated in BDSM, or other such sexual behaviors, he indulged in little abuses on a regular basis. He held her head tightly when she gave him a blowjob, occasionally resisting when she tried to pull back. He preferred sex "doggie style," where he would knead her ass hard as he penetrated her. He also liked to squeeze her breasts and pinch her nipples. None of these things were extreme enough for her to complain about. In fact, the one time she complained about him pinching her nipples, he smirked and said that he knew she liked it. This was how he reacted to any even slight insinuation on her part that she didn't like his sexual behavior. In a lot of ways, a true BDSM relationship would have been better for her. At least she would have had a safe word.

Tonight, when he stood up, signaling it was time to go to the bedroom, she feared he would be worse than usual for her sassing him, and he was. His hands were rough on her body. He squeezed her breasts so hard she got tears in her eyes. So she forced herself to do what she always did when he did this—drift away.

When he was finished, Karl got up and went to the bathroom. Sarah rolled over on her back and looked up at the ceiling. She found herself wondering what her life would be like without Karl. She had a decent job now, unlike when her husband had first died, so she could pay her own mortgage. But it was hard to imagine telling Karl that she was breaking up with him. Even the thought of that was scary.

Karl came out of the bathroom and began pulling his clothes on. He then exited the bedroom.

"Hey, get me a beer," he called back to her. Sarah dutifully got up and pulled a robe on.

Sarah grabbed a beer from the fridge and brought it to Karl as he sat on her sofa with his feet propped up on one of her chairs. He was watching a reality TV cop show.

She sat down next to him, but not too close. Karl was not affectionate. In fact, he had told her that it was the natural tendency for men to want to pull away from women after sex. Once, when he was drunk, he said it was because men felt "disgusting" after sex. This had been the same occasion that he been drunk enough to tell her that her only problem was that she "wasn't a man."

As Karl sipped his beer, she pretended to watch the program, but her mind was racing. In her mind, Sarah thought of Karl as the "gray man." His hair was ash brown. His skin was neither pale nor dark, and he had an unhealthy sort of gray pallor. He wore glasses all the time, but they were light silver wire rims and therefore virtually transparent. His skin, his hair, and his glasses tended to blend to make his whole head look like a large gray blob. If it weren't for his very large nose, fleshy lips, and orthodontically straight but grayish teeth, his face would have been completely nondescript. Sarah found that she was beginning to feel nauseated even glancing at him. She thought about Caio. How different he looked from the man sitting next to her. His skin was deeply tanned, and his hair was a beautiful rich dark brown. But it wasn't the way he looked that had struck her, it was his behavior. When he had smiled at her, it had looked real, not forced like all of Karl's smiles. His eyes had also been open and direct, not sneaky and darting. She wondered if his behavior was a Brazilian thing or if it was just him.

Stop it. Stop comparing a boy to a man. It's not like you can have a relationship with this boy, snapped the voice of her mother.

"What are you thinking about?" Karl asked her suddenly.

"What?" Sarah responded, startled out of her thoughts.

"This is the second time today that I have caught you staring off into the distance and smiling. Is there something I should know about?" he asked, turning his gaze to scrutinize her face. She knew he was watching her face for "tells."

"Well. Actually, I was thinking about South America," she said. A half-truth was always better.

"Why the hell would you want to think about a godforsaken place like that?" he asked, rolling his eyes. "This is not going to be another one of your 'ideas' to go traveling again, is it?"

"Well, it would be nice to travel a bit. I always wanted to go—"

"Want. Want. Never get," he said, interrupting her. It was a favorite phrase of his mother's that he threw at her often. He then turned back to his TV program.

Sarah pretended to watch with him. This was their pattern. He would watch TV until around 11:30, then he would go home. He wouldn't kiss her when he left. He never kissed her, not even when they had sex. He would just get up and leave, expecting her to follow him to the door and let him out. Over the next week, he would send her texts asking her to do whatever little tasks he needed done during the week. She was basically his at-home admin during the week.

Don't you mean slave? asked the new voice. Sarah almost told it to shut up but somehow, she couldn't. There was too much truth in the statement to squash it.

At promptly 11:30, after all his shows were off, Karl got up and walked toward the door. No mention had been made of the "great present" that he had supposedly bought for her.

Oh right, the date was supposed to be the great present.

Just as Karl reached the door, he turned to look at her hard.

"You know, if I found out you were doing something behind my back, I would be very unhappy," he said.

"What do you mean?" she asked, as this would be the correct response.

"I mean, if you ever make me look stupid, I will make sure it goes badly for you," he said. Then he turned and walked out without another word.

Sarah closed the door behind him and heaved a sigh of relief. He was gone. She could breathe again. And that little sun inside her was still shining.

Chapter Eight

Falling Down the Mountain

Friday May 16

Sarah spent the next work week in a strange, cushioned bubble. By midmorning on Monday, Angela had sensed there was something different about Sarah, so she had done her very best to insult her, first subtly and then not so subtly. Somehow none of it seemed to matter. Every moment her brain was not actively engaged in something else, Sarah was thinking about Caio.

The one thing that had managed to distract her a tiny bit from her obsession was the Davies case. She had spent her quiet times at work reviewing the case files. They seemed to be completely run-of-the-mill divorce and custody papers. Still, all she had seen were the motions, counter motions, and final decrees. She hadn't seen any of the depositions, which is where a lot of the meat of a case history is found. She had gently asked Michael for these more than once, but as of yet, he had not seen fit to find them for her. What she *had* managed to dig up on Melissa Taylor over the weekend was equally uninspiring.

Sometime around midweek, Michael left her a copy of a new motion from Phillip Seider stating a change of circumstances. The change was more than simply the boarding school issue. It was a motion for modification of both custody and child support. Melissa was claiming that her son had become withdrawn and depressed since Andrew's new wife had moved in, and that this woman had been a bad influence on him. She was seeking a change of custody and modification of child support because Alex had been accepted to a prestigious boarding school, but that the school was in another state and it would be better for Alex if she was nearby. So she was offering to move to be closer to him. She also stated that she wanted custody of Andrew Jr. and Chris as well, as it was in the best interest of the boys not to be separated for too long. If they were with her, then Alex could see them on weekends. She also stated that there had been a change of income. Like so many women, she had given up her career for her husband's, and Andrew's income had been supplemented in a meaningful way by his new wife's business. Toward the end of the week, the firm received a notification that the court would hear the petition. The whole office knew when this happened because they could hear Michael swearing from one side of the building to the other. Michael was usually a cool customer but when he did lose his temper, he did so in spectacular fashion.

So it wasn't surprising that midday on Friday, Andrew Davies marched into the office with a woman and three children in tow. The woman was dressed like an archetypal teacher from a Broadway musical set in an idyllic Midwestern town. She sported wavy brown sun-kissed hair that was pulled back in a navy-blue fabric headband, and a glowing tan. Her dress was of a blue gingham print, cinched at the waist and falling demurely down to just below her knee. Her flats could have been cheap but were not. These were Repettos or Sarah was no researcher. In short, the woman looked perfect, but Sarah wasn't quite sure what kind of perfect. All three boys, on the other hand, were easy to pin down. Each of them looked like a model for an upscale skiing brochure. They were fair-haired, blue-eyed and attractive. As they entered the reception area, the two younger boys were bickering with each other. Alex was lagging behind the others, face buried in his phone.

"Good afternoon, Sarah," Andrew said, as he came over and leaned on the counter above her desk.

"Good afternoon, Mr. Davies," she smiled. Even Andrew Davies was not dimming her sun this week. "Let me buzz Michael and let him know that you are here."

"Excellent. And I am happy to see that you seem to have forgiven me for last week." He reached out and touched her shoulder. His wife narrowed her eyes and was about to say something when the youngest boy grabbed her arm.

"Anne Marie, can I have your phone?" asked the youngest boy, Chris. His name was appropriate, as he looked like a miniature Captain America. The Captain America backpack only added to the effect.

At that moment, Michael came out of his office. "Andrew," he said, grabbing his hand. "And Anne Marie, you look as beautiful as ever."

Well, I guess, if you go for that Marian the Librarian look, said the new snarky voice.

"Alex, can you watch your brothers while we have a quick chat with Michael?" Anne Marie asked.

The question seemed harmless enough, but the older boy, who had taken a spot at the far end of the waiting room, jerked as if he had been slapped. Then he caught Sarah looking at him, noticeably composed his face and went back to looking at his phone.

"Don't worry, I can keep an eye on them as well," said Sarah.

"Thank you, Sarah," Michael responded. "We shouldn't be too long."

As the adults entered Michael's office, the two younger children took seats at different points in the waiting room. Andrew Jr. plopped down in the middle of the seating area and pulled out what looked like a vampire comic book. Chris, the youngest, sat close to Sarah.

The boys were quiet, so Sarah continued going through the emails she had received since lunch. But she was watching them out of the corner of her eye. They didn't interact with each other at all. Usually, siblings in the same room would sit in the same vicinity, but these kids didn't. Still, they were quiet so that was something to be thankful for.

After about ten minutes, Chris came up to her desk.

"Hi," he said.

"Hi yourself," she said, turning to smile at him. The boy was looking at her intently. She realized his eyes were on her blouse. It was a simple orange silk blouse, but the boy seemed riveted by it.

"I like orange," he said. "It's my favorite color. It makes you look pretty."

"You shouldn't say that to strangers," Andrew Jr. said from across the room.

"Why not?" Chris asked.

"Because it's inappropriate to talk to women like that if you don't know them," Alex said from further across the room, eyes still on his phone.

For a moment Chris looked perplexed, but then a little impish smile appeared on his lips. He stepped closer to Sarah.

"Alex is talking about S-E-X. Alex is a teenager, so that means all he cares about is S-E-X," Chris said in a singsong voice.

"Chris, you need to shut up," Alex said from across the room. His pale skin was turning red.

"I don't have to shut up if I don't want to," Chris replied.

"Alex'll tell Anne Marie," Andrew Jr. said, looking up from his comic book.

"So what, she's the one that told me that," Chris said. "Alex needs lots of S-E-X."

Alex jumped up and was next to his brother before Sarah could get out from behind her desk. He had grabbed his brother's arm painfully. Chris was struggling to pull away and beginning to cry.

"That is just about enough of that," Sarah said, moving around her desk and grabbing Alex's arm. Alex immediately dropped his brother's arm and flinched

43

backward, as if he had been struck.

Something's wrong here. Something's really wrong here.

Alex stalked back across the room, and Sarah bent down in front of Chris to examine his arm. He was still sniffling.

"I bet I know your favorite superhero," Sarah whispered to him.

"Who?" the boy asked.

"Captain America," she said. Chris looked up at her, a small smile coming to his face.

"You just guessed that because you saw my backpack."

"No, I guessed it because you look just like him," Sarah said with a wink.

"I do?" Chris responded with a big grin.

"Absolutely," Sarah said.

At that moment, the door of Michael's office opened.

"I see we have made a friend here," said Andrew, looking at Sarah sitting with his youngest child.

"She said I look like Captain America," Chris proclaimed loudly, tears forgotten.

"Well, she certainly knows the right thing to say, doesn't she?" replied Anne Marie, cornflower-blue eyes narrowing for a split second.

Just at that moment, the phone rang. It was a woman in tears asking for an appointment because she had just found out her husband was cheating on her. It took Sarah ten minutes to calm her down enough to get her contact information and schedule an appointment. By the time she was done, the Davies family had left the building.

The rest of her day was equally hectic, but the conversation between Alex and Chris kept interjecting itself in her brain.

There's something off in that family. Something more than a narcissistic stepmother and a dickhead father. The fact that the youngest said the stepmother had implied that Alex needed lots of sex was awkward at a minimum, but the extreme reaction of Alex to this comment and the way he flinched when I touched him … yeah, there was something really not right here.

At the end of the day, Sarah was asked to review a response that they were sending to Phillip Seider on the Davies case. It had been drafted by one of the younger paralegals and it was fairly typical. She pulled up the recent emails between Michael and Phillip just to make sure that they weren't forgetting anything. There were several from today. As Sarah had access to Michael's email, she was able to access this part of his communication.

In skimming the emails, it seemed the usual fare. But in an email from just before he left, Sarah found a reference to mental health problems of the mother and something about her being institutionalized.

Interesting. Why wasn't that brought up in the filings?

Sarah didn't leave work until well after dark, and just as she got home Karl called her and said that he had too much work and couldn't make it for dinner. Sarah could hear a woman's voice in the background. It was Meghan's voice. Sarah told him that it was okay. And in truth, this was a relief. She didn't really want to see Karl. She just wanted to think about Caio.

That night, as she lay on her bed in her PJs, she looked at his photo on her phone, wishing she had more than this one. She knew that she was acting like a schoolgirl with a crush, but she felt good. The photo no longer scared her. He was now someone she knew. He had acknowledged her, and had wanted to know more about her. But as she was looking at the photo, it struck her that the expression in his eyes looked not just intense, but sad and wary. The expression was not unlike the expression she had seen on the face of Alex Davies today.

Sarah shook her head. That was a thought she didn't want to have, and an association that she didn't want to make. Instead, she focused on memorizing the lines of his face.

In this manner, she fell asleep.

Saturday May 17

The next morning, Sarah got up earlier than usual to get ready for her regular trip to the co-op. If she went early enough then the boys might be on the basketball court by the time she came back with her things. She got up, showered, and took the time to blow-dry her hair. She had brownish, auburn hair. Normally, she hated this because, together with her freckles, she thought that she looked a lot like Raggedy Anne. But today, when she looked at herself in the mirror, she thought she looked okay. At 9:30, she put on a simple yellow swing dress and some sandals. She didn't want to look like she was trying too hard, but she wanted to look nice.

Why are you doing this? What are you hoping to achieve? her mother's voice said, but Sarah swatted it down.

Of course, this was going nowhere, but it made her happy for now, and it had been such a long time since she had felt happy. Leaving her house, she noticed the smell of mint in her herb garden. The freshness of it made her happier still.

She knew that the boys played basketball off and on most of the day, so she decided to do half her shopping this morning and then go back for the rest in the afternoon. She told herself that this made sense anyway because she had a lot to buy, and it was always very heavy carrying it all at once, but she knew that this was an excuse. As she approached the basketball court, she saw three of the boys she often saw. One was the tall African American boy with braided hair. Another was the red-haired, super-skinny boy with the slumped shoulders and the gawky walk. The third was the boy with long-ashen hair that he pulled into a ponytail. All of them were shooting hoops as she walked past them completely unnoticed. Caio was not there.

At the grocery store, she began to feel jittery and nervous. She told herself that she was simply getting her groceries, but she couldn't shake her nerves. As she was wandering down the bread aisle, she noticed that her dress was beginning to stick to the skin on her stomach and under her arms. She quickly picked up her bread and walked over to the refrigerator section to cool herself down. She picked up a small chicken and a couple of pork chops, then put back the chicken. She wanted to have a good reason to come back later in the day. Next, she went to the butcher.

Mitch was behind the counter. He was small with slight bones and a delicate face, completely at odds with every butcher stereotype Sarah had ever known.

"Hi Mitch," she said, walking up to the counter.

"Hi Sarah," he replied. "What can I do you for?"

"Well. I was wondering if you knew what sort of meats were used in Brazilian cooking," she asked. Mitch's face became a bit cloudy.

"I didn't know Karl was into that sort of food," he replied.

"Oh, he isn't. But I like to try new things for myself from time to time," Sarah lied. She never tried anything new. But Mitch didn't seem to notice the lie and his face brightened again.

"Well, I can't say that I know but I'll look it up and have the answer for you the next time you come back," he said. Sarah smiled at him and got a bigger return smile than usual. She felt the little sun inside her chest expand a bit more.

She waved at Mitch and went up and down the remaining aisles, killing time but reminding herself that she didn't need to buy too much just now. At about 10:25 she got into the checkout line. As she was paying for her food, she started to get butterflies in her stomach again. She smiled at the cashier, who was a lady she didn't know, but who returned her smile warmly.

Leaving the store, with her two small bags, Sarah tried not to rush. She wanted to look calm and casual, never mind the fact that she never ever looked calm and casual. Still, it would be good if she looked a little less flustered than usual. She slowed her walk down as she neared the intersection that led to the street where the basketball court was located. She took a deep breath before she turned the corner.

As she turned, she saw boys already in the midst of a game. Her eyes searched their faces and forms, but she didn't see him. She felt her heart sink. She had been looking forward to seeing him all week, but he didn't seem to be there. Of course, he might be there later today, but she had hoped to see him twice today. That had been her goal anyway.

As he was obviously not there, she felt it was okay to walk slowly and watch the other boys playing basketball a bit. She didn't usually do this, but these kids didn't notice her anyway, so there was no harm done.

There were six or seven on the court now. Caio had been right, all of them were very tall. They heckled and pushed at each other as they played. Although it was only 10:30 in the morning, they were already sweaty. Then, as she turned the corner of the court she saw him, sitting on the ground tying his shoelaces. She felt herself flushing red. As she got closer, he turned his head. For just a moment, he met her eyes.

"Hi," she said quietly, and smiled. He smiled back, but briefly and tightly, before getting up and running over to where the other boys were playing.

Running.

Running away from you, said her mother's voice.

Sarah felt like she had been stabbed in the chest. And the little sun that had been inside her for the past twenty-four hours was suddenly blotted out by black clouds. She turned away quickly and walked toward home. She had made him uncomfortable.

Of course you make him uncomfortable. He knows you are a forty-seven-year-old woman, with obviously questionable mental health, obsessed with him. I'm sure that makes him uncomfortable. Even if you were really beautiful, it would be creepy. But you aren't, are you? said her mother.

Each word felt like a knife. She quickened her step but told herself not to run. She made it home quickly, unlocked her door, let herself in, and then closed and locked the door behind her.

"What was I thinking?" she said to herself, ignoring her mother's voice as much as she could.

Well, that's enough of that. I won't walk that way anymore. I don't need to humiliate myself any further on this one. It was fine when he didn't know me, but if he recognizes me then that's too humiliating. I just won't see him anymore. It's that simple.

She picked up a head of lettuce and turned on the water in her sink. She was okay. This was fine. She couldn't have kept up with this little obsession forever. It was better that it was over now. She didn't need to get unrealistic expectations. Of course, she would have to avoid the basketball court from now on, but that wasn't too much of an inconvenience.

47

Thinking all this, she hit the lettuce forcefully on the table and pulled out the core. As she held the lettuce under the running water, she barely noticed that she was crying. Her tears mixed with the water from the tap, and both swirled down the drain.

Gone and forgotten.

Chapter Nine

Proverbs and Romans

Thursday May 22

For Sarah, the next week was the same as it had been every week for the last five years. She did nothing particularly different nor did she go out of her way to do so. She just stuck to her routines.

And she felt dead inside.

On Monday morning she was given new documents to review regarding the Davies divorce case, which was both helpful and distracting. She went through these things, mechanically documenting everything they had received. She didn't dig into these in any detail initially, as she was overwhelmed with the emails and phone calls that always flooded in on Monday mornings. All she had time to do was to collect and collate what she had. To add fuel to the fire, the emails between Michael and Phillip were becoming heated.

On Thursday morning Sarah woke up sobbing. She had dreamed of the boy in the hole again, but this time he saw her. His anguished eyes had met hers, as she had desperately reached out for him. After calming herself, she decided to go to work early, to escape what was happening in her own head. She was ready and in the office by 6:30 a.m. As she was the first one there, she walked into a dark, silent space. She reached for the light switch—but stopped. There was something calm and reassuring about the darkness. Her childhood had taught her that it was safer to stay in the shadows of life. She seemed to have forgotten that in recent days.

God knows she should have learned the value of being unseen in her youth. When she was only five years old, her parents took her to a doctor because she would speak to herself using different voices. When the doctor had asked her who she was talking to, she had answered in all innocence that she was talking to the friends in her head. Her mother had gone ballistic. She would have no daughter of hers embarrassing her by having mental problems. Sarah had seen several psychologists and had been assessed for everything from schizophrenia to dissociative identity disorder. In the end, the consensus was that she was simply a very creative child. This had gone down a little better with her mother, but only a little.

That's because most "creative" people are just slackers and can't take care of themselves, said her mother's voice, still so clear and vivid inside her.

Sarah shook her head, there was work to be done. When she flipped on the lights, her eyes were accosted by the glare of the fluorescent bulbs. She made her way to her desk and unlocked the cabinet where she stored the box with the copies of documents and the memorabilia related to the Davies case. Taking the box to the conference room, she spread everything out on the large table and organized it, based on type of evidence. Looking at these, she noticed for the first time that there were three different scrapbooks that the client had dropped off.

Sarah sat down at the table and scanned the objects in front of her. She reviewed the motions, counter motions and whatever other legal documents she could find. She was still missing the transcripts of the depositions for the original custody case. She picked up the bank statements. There were none from their client, only from the ex-wife. These didn't show much except that Melissa made previous payments to a psychological center. This was not good for them as Melissa was clearly not loose with her money or resources, and she didn't seem to have much. The one useful piece of information was the fact that Melissa was receiving regular checks from a local bookstore, so Sarah suspected that this was where she was employed.

Putting away the financials, Sarah reached for the scrapbooks. Scrapbooks could be an incredibly useful thing in painting clients as loving and dutiful parents. She picked up one and flipped through it. It was filled with photos of picnics, parks, and days at the beach. Honestly, the photos could have been laminates for scrapbooking, they looked that staged. Underneath each photo was either a cutesy saying like "fun in the sun" or a verse of scripture. It was enough to make bile rise in Sarah's throat. But, upon further inspection, Sarah noticed that in all the photos, the older boy Alex looked away from the camera. In most, either his stepmother or father had an arm around him. The two younger boys looked like typical boys: mugging for shots, fighting and laughing. Their body language was loose and relaxed. In comparison, the older boy looked stiff and uncomfortable. Sarah would have written this off as normal sullen teenage behavior if she had not seen the interaction between the boys in her office.

Sarah began reading the captions under all the photos, looking for something that might be telling. But page after page, it was the same treacle, until she noticed something. One of the photos was a picture of the whole family sitting on a couch dressed in ski pants and turtleneck sweaters. Alex was sitting between his dad and stepmom again. Beneath the photo read "Annual Family Ski Trip to Aspen" with little smileys and hearts. Underneath it said Proverbs 7:10. Sarah was fairly sure that the Bible didn't mention ski trips to Aspen, so she pulled out her phone and typed in the scripture verse.

"And behold, there met him a woman with the attire of a harlot, and subtle of heart." Sarah sat back in her chair.

What the hell? Is this woman using random scripture numbers to make it look like she's religious?

She scanned through the album for more verses. On a picture of the family at Christmas, after the cutesy message, was written Romans 7. When she searched for this scripture, she found, "So then if while her husband lives, she be married to another man, she shall be called an adulteress." And next to a photo of a picnic at the park was Proverbs 7:26. This one was even sweeter, as it read, "Many are the victims she has brought down; her slain are a mighty throng. Her house is a highway to the grave, leading down to the chambers of death."

Sarah went through the rest of the scrapbook, writing down all the scriptures referenced. When she looked them up, she found every one of them related to adultery or the sinfulness of second marriages or fornication.

What the fuck is going on here? asked the new voice in her head. *This is clearly the second marriage for him. But what about her?*

Sarah went back to the notes from the case, shuffling through for any information about the new wife. There was very little there. Her name was Anne Marie Davies. According to the paperwork, she was a stay-at-home wife and stepmother. She and Andrew had had no children of their own. She was just pulling out her phone to start a bit of research on Anne Marie Davies, when she heard someone come into the office. For reasons she didn't quite understand, she tore off the pages where she had scribbled the scriptures, folded them and put them in her pocket.

At that moment, Angela stuck her head in the door of the conference room. She was eyeballing Sarah suspiciously.

"You're here awful early," she said, eyeing the papers in front of Sarah.

"Yes. I wasn't sleeping very well. So I thought I might as well work on the Davies case," Sarah replied, putting the papers into a stack.

"Something bothering you then?" Angela asked, stepping into the room. Although it was just Angela, and although it was a normal move, Sarah stiffened and felt her heart begin to race.

Don't be ridiculous, little girl. It's just Angela, said the voice of her father.

Sarah was about to utter some oatmeal sort of response but when she opened her mouth to speak, something else came out.

"Actually, Karl skipped a date last week," she said. It was her voice and her mouth, but the words were coming from somewhere else.

Angela's eyes widened. Normally, Sarah would never have said anything this personal to Angela, but another part of her was leading the conversation.

"I was wondering," Sarah asked, putting a slight tremble in her voice. "If you knew if Meghan had changed her schedule?"

"Oh no!" Angela whispered, coming to sit beside her. "You know about that then?" Angela asked, putting her hand on Sarah's arm. It took everything in her not to yank her arm away.

Sarah nodded, looking down.

"Listen honey. Karl doesn't care about Meghan. I know that. It's just this physical thing they have," she said, patting Sarah's arm. "He would never leave you for her. They don't have a relationship."

"Seems like Karl doesn't have much of a relationship with me either," Sarah whispered, pretending to look down but really watching Angela carefully out of the corner of her eye. The look on Angela's face was the strangest thing. She looked anxious, almost panicked.

"Listen Sarah, I've been here for years and I know everything that goes on in this office. And because we're so tight with the crew at Patterson and Van Allen, I know everything that goes on there too. So I know that Karl values his relationship with you. I absolutely know that. This thing with Meghan is a nothing little thing. Do you want me to say something to Karl about it?"

"No, no. It's fine," Sarah said, strategically wiping at her eyes.

Just then the main door opened, and Sarah heard Jason's voice swearing in the hall.

"Shit, he's here early," Angela said, jumping up from her seat, but before fleeing the room she turned and touched Sarah's arm again. "Don't do anything drastic because of something this meaningless, okay?"

Sarah nodded, continuing to look down until Angela was gone from the room. Then she quickly gathered up her papers and put them back in the small brown box.

Why did I talk to Angela about Karl? she asked herself.

You were distracting her. There's something weird with the Davies case, and Angela knows something, said her attorney voice. *As she said, she knows everything there is to know at these two law firms, but she's completely amnesiac when it comes to details of this case. Michael won't give you the past depositions. Add that to the fact that Phillip Seider seemed to think that there was a chance that their firm would just roll over and give the other side what they wanted on child support, and then these scrapbooks. This is not looking like a normal case.*

Sarah decided that she would need to find some time to do a bit more research into Anne Marie Davies, as well as Melissa Taylor, as soon as possible. Sadly, she spent the rest of the week working on sudden emergency hearings for one of their clients who beat his girlfriend until she had to be hospitalized. Working on ways to exonerate abusers and assholes was the hardest part of her job. At least it was consuming, from both the time perspective and the mental perspective.

All of this distracted her from her emotional life, for a bit.

Chapter Ten

End up Kissing Dirt

Saturday May 24

On Friday night, Karl had called her to say that he had to work late for the second week in a row, so he wouldn't be stopping by. That meant it was pretty certain that Meghan's schedule had changed and that she was demanding that he spend time with her on Fridays. For the hundred-millionth time, she wondered why Karl didn't simply dump her for real and date Meghan. But now she was asking the question with more intensity and less resignation than she had before. They were both single, so there was no real reason not to dump Sarah and get together with Meghan. He certainly didn't love her. On top of this, she was beginning to feel an intuition that there was some strange link between her personal life and the Davies case, but that was absurd.

Of course, it's absurd, little girl. You need to get your head out of the clouds and back into your work before you get yourself fired, said her father's voice.

Still, Sarah stayed at the office until well past eight on Friday, reviewing the scrapbooks and files yet again. She didn't find anything beyond more of what she had seen before. All three scrapbooks were filled with religious allusions to the sins of adultery and fornication. When Sarah finally got home, she was exhausted and fell into her bed without much more thought.

Early on Saturday morning, Sarah had the dream about the boy in the hole again. She woke up calling out, with her heart pounding. The alarm next to the bed told her it was 6:30 a.m. but she couldn't go back to sleep. Instead, she went downstairs, made herself a cup of coffee, and sat at her kitchen table to drink it. She stared at the scratches in its white top and wondered where and when they had come to be there. She couldn't remember. She had no need to notice or mark moments like that in her life. It was not like she had children, someone to whom she could say "Remember when you used the knife to carve a picture in the table when you were five?" In her world, stains, marks, and scratches were never more than just stains, marks, and scratches. They never gained weight with nostalgia.

These were her thoughts as she drank her coffee and stared at her walls. She felt like she was searching for some form of life within the walls. But the only living thing here was her, and even that was in question. To break up these thoughts, images of that dream she had last night would occasionally insert themselves into her head. She found her eyes welling up at those moments. She could no longer deny that the boy in this dream looked like Caio.

After what seemed like no time and yet forever, she looked up at the clock and realized that it was 10 a.m. She had done nothing all morning.

"I need to get up, get dressed and go outside," she muttered to herself. She needed to move, or she was afraid she might never be able to move again. She had no idea what had gotten into her. Usually, she could just shake things off, and get on with life. Yesterday, and throughout the week, she had been mostly okay but today—well, today she felt like she was walking through molasses.

Sarah got up, went to her bathroom, and splashed cold water on her face. The shock and slight pain of this made her feel more alive. She then decided to get dressed and go out to the gardening shop. She threw on a sundress and a cardigan and left her house. She studiously avoided going the route that took her by the basketball court, even though that was the quickest. Instead, she walked the back roads.

Once at the gardening store, the smell of the dirt and plants lightened her spirit. Maybe it was the oxygen they produced, but she always felt that there was something inherently good about plants. She wandered the small aisles of the store, gently touching the leaves of some plants and breathing on others. She had stopped at the seedlings of oregano when she felt someone come up behind her. She turned to find Jerry, one of their local police officers, smiling at her.

"Hi there Sarah," he said. "You find anything interesting?"

Jerry was a "plant person" and another one of the regulars here at the nursery. At least a couple of times every month, she saw him here. He was always kind and they usually engaged in a bit of light conversation.

"I'm just thinking about planting some oregano or basil. They usually do pretty well in my garden," Sarah replied.

"Well, there's never a good reason to say no to Italian herbs, after all," Jerry replied, smiling. Jerry was a proud Italian-American and to him all herbs were Italian in origin.

Sarah laughed a bit. It felt good to talk to a non-work person, even just for a little while.

"Where have you been keeping yourself?" he asked as they walked through the aisles.

"Oh, I've been around. Doing the same old things. Working. Reading. Puttering around the house. Date nights with Karl. Working in my garden."

"Uh huh. Didn't you tell me once that you were going to try to travel a bit this summer?"

"Oh. I wanted to, but Karl didn't like the idea at all. He thinks it's a waste of money," she said. "Maybe he's right."

She suddenly felt sadness come raining back down on her.

"Well, let me get back to it," she said with forced cheer. "Nice seeing you, Jerry."

"Sarah," he called as she started to walk away.

"Yes?"

He looked at her for a moment before sighing.

"Have a great weekend," he said after a moment.

"Thanks Jerry," she replied.

He feels sorry for you. Everyone feels sorry for you. Everyone knows that Karl is a shit, and you are too much of a rabbit to do anything about it, said the new voice. It was critical but honest.

On her walk home, Sarah began to assess again why she stayed with Karl. She didn't really need the money anymore. She could pay for things herself, if she just tightened the belt a bit. But the thought of saying that she was "single" at age forty-seven made her feel something close to panic. Sure, Karl wasn't the best but at least she wasn't completely alone. She knew if there was a real emergency, she could call on him.

Could you? Is that what you really believe? the new voice asked again.

"Of course. He's my boyfriend," she replied.

It's more like he's your nasty employer or your pimp, the voice said. *Maybe the truth is that you are afraid of what he would do to you if you decided to break up with him. Could it be that?*

Sarah shook her head and shut this voice down.

It was then that she noticed where she was. She had taken the path by the basketball court without meaning to do so.

Did you not?

Shut up.

And Caio was there, playing ball with the other boys.

She walked slowly on the path next to the court. She kept her head focused forward but watched him out of the side of her eye.

He was right, he was quite a bit shorter than the others, but he moved better than they did. He was faster and more agile. As she watched, he made a move under the basket, swiveled on his heel, jumped and dropped the ball through the hoop. There were whoops and jeers, and he smiled and laughed.

Then he saw her. Without realizing it, she had stopped and had been staring at him.

When he saw her, he stopped laughing. Instead, he gave her that quick, tight smile before looking away.

Now she was sure. She made him uncomfortable. She felt her eyes well with tears while her face burned. She picked up her pace as she walked away, but not too much. She didn't want to seem obvious. Her eyes were leaking onto her cheeks. She wiped at them quickly, hoping she didn't meet anyone she knew between here and her house.

That dimmed sun, the one in her chest, now imploded. Chunks of it dug holes in her heart, her confidence, and her sense of belonging. She felt a blackness creep inside her. She made it back to her house after what seemed like a lifetime and stepped quickly into the building.

She dropped her purse, along with the oregano and basil plants, on her kitchen table and walked into the downstairs bathroom. She pulled on the light and stared at herself in the mirror. The woman who looked back at her was pale and gaunt, with dark circles under her eyes. Despite the perky nose and freckles spread across her nose, she looked like a specter.

She averted her eyes from herself and began to cry. What man would find that attractive? What grown man or even old man would find that attractive? None. And the thought that a boy in the flower of his youth would even look twice at her was laughable. And that's what she had been thinking, wasn't it? Somewhere deep inside, after he had asked her first name, she had secretly hoped it was because he liked something about her. She looked back up at herself and the woman looking back at her had red eyes and a dripping nose. She hadn't been beautiful even in her youth, but now she was just embarrassingly plain. So, it wasn't surprising that the only relationship option was with a man who was with her only as some sort of favor to a deceased colleague.

Sarah turned away from the mirror again. She stared instead at a cup sitting on her sink. In this cup were the things that Karl needed when he was there. He kept a toothbrush, comb, and razor there. This was for the rare occasions that they went out at night after work. His razor was one of the more traditional ones, with an inserted blade. Sarah took it out and looked at it. She fiddled with

57

it a bit until she figured out how to open it. When she took out the razor blade, it looked clean, bright, and surprisingly beautiful.

Taking the blade gingerly between her fingers, Sarah pushed one corner of it against the skin of her forearm. At first, she felt nothing but a slight resistance. She pushed a little bit harder, and was rewarded with the feeling of a prick followed by a bit of red that appeared under the brightness of the blade. Red surrounded the blade, staining it, making it less beautiful and more sinister. Suddenly there was more red, a LOT more red.

Sarah threw the blade into the sink and ran from the bathroom back into the kitchen. Once there, she grabbed a kitchen towel and pressed it tightly against her arm. When she removed it, there was a larger bloodstain than she expected. She pressed it back again and held it more firmly.

What is wrong with you? You are crazy, aren't you? came her mother's shrill voice.

Sarah's head began to spin, and she quickly sat down at her table. After a time, when she withdrew the towel, there was a smaller bloodstain. She waited five or ten minutes after that before going back to the bathroom and getting a bandage. She loaded it with antiseptic and salve before placing it on her arm. When she put the bandage on her arm, the blood was already clotting fairly well.

Okay. Enough now.

She then replaced the razor in Karl's cup. She returned to the kitchen, picking up her plants and gardening gear, and heading out to her herbs. She would not think anymore. She would push all of this from her mind.

She spent the rest of the morning and all afternoon planting her new oregano and basil plants. The earth felt good and solid in her hands. The smell of it was calming. After she finished with the plants, she plotted, designed, and then cut out a new garden area next to the old one. She removed the grass that was there before adding soil that she happened to have from last year.

By the time she had finished, she was sweaty, and the sun was hanging low on the horizon. She was also covered with dirt. She could almost forget that this morning she had cut her own wrist with a razor blade.

When she stood, Sarah noticed for the first time that she was still wearing a sundress. The hem and skirt were now plastered with wet dirt. She must have looked a sight, out there gardening in a dress. She walked to her porch and dusted some of the loose dirt off her before stepping through the door. Once inside, she went straight for the shower. She pulled her dress off and dropped it on the floor. She found that even her underwear was covered in mud and bits of grass. Looking at this made her feel better. The earth didn't judge.

She got into the shower and felt the water run over her. She turned it as hot as she could bear it. Her skin began to turn pink then red under its caress. But it felt so good to be able to concentrate on nothing but this. Afterward, she pulled on a robe and went to her kitchen where she began to wash a few pans that had been in her sink from the night before.

Staring out the window at the setting sun, Sarah felt something stir inside her. Something different from the flat dull resignation that she knew was a part of her everyday life. This was a sharp twisty snake uncoiling in her belly. It took her a minute to recognize that it was anger. Sarah suppressed anger, but now it reared its head in her belly, baring its fangs at the world.

Okay. I'm obsessed with a teenage boy. Who cares? I'm not doing anything wrong. It's not like I'm ever going to do anything about this. It's not like I could ever do anything about it. For a teenage boy, a forty-seven-year-old woman is pretty much invisible. If watching this boy makes me feel happy, then why shouldn't I do it? It's not like I'm hurting him.

She said this to herself and to the voices in her head waiting to judge her. She knew the comments they would make. She was ridiculous. She was a coward. She was a pathetic loser. But as she had already acknowledged what she knew they would say, this seemed to take the power back from them, and they were unusually silent.

The problem was that she did want to avoid the obvious humiliation of having him know that she was stalking him. She couldn't take any more of that particular torment. So she would have to be careful. Sure, she could watch him out of the corner of her eye as she walked by the basketball court. She didn't want to catch his eye anymore, as she had obviously made him uncomfortable in their previous meetings. Maybe she had acted too happy when he wanted to know her first name. Clearly, she had read too much into that but that didn't change the fact that he had stirred something in her—something she didn't want to die. She would need to feed this obsession tenderly and secretly. The boy himself didn't really need to have any input into it.

She finished washing her pans. It was now 6:30 p.m. and the sun was heading down the sky toward the horizon. If she was going to stalk this boy in any serious way, she would need to be careful about it. If anyone found out, they wouldn't understand her motives. They wouldn't be able to see that she didn't want anything from him besides simply being able to watch him. She would never be able to express that watching him made her happier than she had been in years. And surely that was not a bad thing? As long as he never saw her, because she made him uncomfortable. But in some small way, maybe even that was kind of cool. Someone was having an actual, real reaction to her. Most people treated her like she was the wallpaper.

With these thoughts, she got up and went into her living room. *A Princess Bride* was on TV. She loved and hated this movie in equal parts. She loved the romance of it and hated herself for loving something so unreal. Tonight, she watched it anyway, self-loathing and all.

After crawling into her overly soft bed that night, she replayed the movie again in her mind until she finally fell asleep.

Chapter Eleven

The Secrets of Beauty

Sunday May 25

Sarah spent Sunday working on the Davies case and trying NOT to think of Caio. She didn't have the Davies family scrapbooks with her, so she could do no more work on that angle, fascinating as it was. Instead, she decided to research the client, Andrew Davies, and his wife Anne Marie. No one had asked her to do this. They had specifically told her to concentrate on finding out about the ex-wife, Melissa Taylor. But there was something about that directive that seemed weird, particularly in light of the behavior of the oldest son, Alex, and the things she had seen in the journal. She didn't want to jump to conclusions, but conclusions were already inserting themselves in her head.

A basic image search of Anne Marie Davies retrieved pages of pictures, mostly with her husband at social events. Sandwiched between these were family photos of the sort that Sarah had already seen in the scrapbooks. Next, Sarah searched what corporate holdings the couple might have. This angle proved fruitful. Andrew Davies was on the board of a whole host of small local companies including, to her surprise, many of the clients of both Culp, Moore & Rosen and Patterson & Van Allen. It seemed that he was a partial owner of much, if not all, of their community. This made something in Sarah's belly twist.

Anne Marie Davies, on the other hand, only had one listing for company directors, and it was originally under her maiden name, Anne Marie Laure. It seemed she was the owner of a business called Laure & Co. that made leather goods for horse riding. When Sarah went to the company website, she discovered a slick page which boasted pictures of green pastures and beautiful women on horses. On closer inspection of the opening page, Sarah noticed that many of the photos were of Anne Marie herself. Every photo seemed to be staged to highlight her assets: her bronze-streaked hair, her perky breasts, her well-toned, voluptuous butt. If Sarah hadn't already disliked this woman, knowing that she had picked these photos of herself to feature on her company website would have sealed the deal.

When she clicked on a link for Services, there were photos of gleaming bridles, clamps, sewing machines, and knives. On the Store page there were links for Saddlery, Leather Goods, and Contact Info. The link for Our Story contained a paragraph that made the back of Sarah's neck tingle.

Anne Marie grew up with a love for horses and riding, working odd jobs until she had enough saved to buy her first horse. Her company now produces a unique collection of leather goods based on timeless design and craftsmanship. This range includes belts, whips, briefcases, bags, phone and computer cases, and knife pouches.

She wasn't sure what it was about this paragraph that made her feel so uncomfortable, but something about it did. It might have been that it was almost impossible for her to imagine "Ms. Repetto" mucking out a stable, cutting leather, or doing any actual physical work. She looked more like a sorority girl than a craftswoman.

When her stomach started growling, Sarah got up and made herself a peanut butter and jelly sandwich, which she ate in front of her computer. She went back to her computer and created a list of all the companies Andrew Davies had a vested interest in. Looking at it she felt queasy.

She peppers her scrapbook with biblical quotes about the wickedness of second wives, when she's a second wife, Sarah thought to herself, as she scanned the company names and business activities. *Her oldest stepchild is clearly uncomfortable in her presence. Her younger child says inappropriate sexual things. These are flashing red signs of sexual abuse. That's a no-brainer. The fact that the firm doesn't want me to see the previous depositions could be because this was one of the accusations during the original child custody hearings. But why exactly would they do that? It certainly wouldn't be the first time that the firm had knowledge that one of their clients was an abuser. There were no mandatory reporting requirements in New York. Why is this time different?*

That's a good question, said the new voice in her head. *Wasn't there a new DA elected recently? Maybe he isn't in their pocket.*

Let's not get paranoid— Paul began.

Sarah slammed an internal door on this conversation. It was time to change gears and do the work that she was actually being paid to do. She opened the list of Melissa Taylor's expenditures that had been forwarded to her by Michael. She referenced and cross-referenced each expense to try to get a picture of how this woman lived and what she did with her time. From all she could see, Melissa spent her time and resources on her kids when they were with her. Most of her expenditures were related to kids' clothes, kids' after-school classes, food, and the occasional purchase of a book. She seemed to spend very little on herself.

The picture of Melissa Taylor that was coming into focus wasn't looking like the psycho demon ex-wife that Andrew Davies had painted. She looked up the bookstore chain that was paying Melissa. There was an outlet not more than two or three blocks from where the woman lived, so it was likely that this was the branch where she worked. Sarah toyed with the idea of dropping by the shop, just to get a look at her. It was unusual for mothers to lose primary custody, even in this day and age. Sarah couldn't even imagine how hard it must be for her to have lost her children.

Her phone pinged and buzzed on the table. It was a message from Michael.

Can you do a little research on the Cheshire Academy in Connecticut? This is where oldest kid got accepted. Good? Difficult to get into? - M

Sarah sighed, shook her head, and got up for a second. This was a good change of pace. She needed to pull herself out of being ridiculously emotional. That part of her had gotten out of control recently. So, despite the emotional pull of Melissa Taylor, Sarah dutifully spent the rest of the evening researching Michael and the firm's interests.

Monday May 26

Sarah got into the office at 8:44 a.m. on Monday morning. The phone rang at exactly 8:45 a.m.

"Culp, Moore and Rosen," she answered.

"Hi. Listen, I know that I stood you up on our last two date nights. So I want to go out to dinner on Friday night," Karl said. He didn't bother identifying himself and he had recognized her voice. Maybe that should be something that she considered a compliment.

"Are you there?" he asked. She hadn't responded quickly enough.

"Yes. I'm here. Someone had just messaged me," Sarah lied. "Dinner sounds nice. Is there somewhere you want to go in particular?"

"Let's go to the Italian place on Third Avenue. Can you make a reservation for around seven?" he asked.

Sure. Why not? I'm your admin anyway, right?

No, he's your boyfriend who just apologized, so stop being such a baby, said her mother's voice

"Okay—" she began but he cut her off.

"Hey. I gotta go. I'll text you later in the week." And then he hung up.

Just then Michael came out of his office.

"Sarah, can I have a word with you?" he asked, motioning her into his office. Sarah nodded.

"Angela, can you watch my calls for a few minutes?" she asked as she got up.

"Of course," Angela replied briskly. It was amazing how she was immediately infused with energy anytime there was a partner around.

Sarah went into Michael's office. He closed the door behind them and motioned for her to sit down.

"The judge has agreed to a hearing on change of circumstances in the Davies case. We were hoping that the wife would just let this go. She's done that before," Michael began.

"Why would she let it go?" Sarah asked, before she could stop herself. She was still in research mode and not admin mode. But Michael simply nodded.

"She likes to stir things up. Most of the time, she runs out of energy or money to pay her attorney bills before it goes too far. But things are a bit different this time," he sighed.

"Because Phillip Seider took the case?" Sarah asked.

"Yes. And I suspect that Phillip doesn't really care much about whether she pays him. He might even be doing this pro bono. I'm sure that Karl has told you that he and I don't have a great history together."

Sarah nodded.

"I am guessing that he will be unwilling to drop the case or settle. So we need to prepare for a court battle. What did you find out about Cheshire Academy?"

"It's one of the top boarding schools in the US. Very prestigious, with big money investors. If her son got accepted there, it is a big deal. They have a reputation of giving a lot of one-to-one attention to kids, particularly special needs kids."

"I'll need to talk to Andrew about this. He's coming in this afternoon," Michael muttered to himself.

"Does he have any emotional-" Sarah began gently but Michael cut her off.

"Issues? With the mother he has, it wouldn't be surprising," Michael said quickly, but for a moment he narrowed his eyes, assessing her a bit too much for her comfort. It was never good to have an attorney like Michael Angel assess you. She had seen him emotionally shred men, women, children, and grandmothers. No one was safe if he was acting in the "service" of one of his clients.

There has been abuse and he knows it. Don't let him know that you know, whispered the new voice.

"I also did a bit more research on Melissa Taylor. It seems that she's holding down a job at Reddux Books," she said quickly.

"Is she a responsible employee there?"

"Not sure, but I was planning on stopping by the bookstore, just to check it out," said Sarah.

"Excellent. But do it before the deposition. Anything else about her?"

"No. But that was strange in and of itself. She has no presence on social media."

"Well, a lot of paranoid people try to avoid being online," Michael said, shuffling through papers. "And with her history of mental illness, it's not surprising for her to be paranoid."

Is this the second or third time that he has mentioned her mental instability? And it's been, what, five minutes?

"Speaking of that, I didn't see any doctors' notes or depositions from doctors—" she began, and Michael slapped his head in an overly dramatic fashion.

"The depositions, right. I'll get the copies to you this week. By Friday at the latest," Michael said, standing up to indicate that he had finished the discussion.

Of course you will, Sarah thought as she went back to her desk.

#

The rest of the week came and went in a whirl, but when Friday close of business came around, Sarah was still deposition-less. On top of that, she was supposed to be meeting Karl for dinner and she didn't much feel up to it. While she knew she had no chance of having any sort of relationship with Caio, he had still brought Karl's behavior toward her into sharp contrast.

Sarah sighed.

"What's wrong with you?" Angela asked from her cubicle. Sarah had been under the impression that Angela was still under her headphones, but she had apparently been wrong.

"Nothing. I just haven't gotten those depositions from Michael yet," Sarah replied. "And I don't feel like I can do a good job of research without them."

"Oh Jesus. Wait here," Angela said, getting up from her desk and stomping off. She returned a couple of minutes later with a large manila envelope, which she threw on Sarah's desk.

"Now, will you stop whining about those?" Angela snapped.

"Are these the depositions for the Davies case?"

"Yeah. You can stop obsessing now. Just don't tell anyone where you got them from," Angela said, as she threw work from her desk into her cabinet. She then switched off her computer and stomped out the door without another word or glance in Sarah's direction.

She's giving you something you aren't supposed to have. Why would she do this? the new voice asked.

Maybe she's just trying to help you. Stop being so paranoid, said her mother's voice.

Of course, she's the milk of human kindness, that one, replied the new voice. She really needed to give this voice a name. It was inserting itself more and more often these days.

Sarah quickly shoved the papers into her bag and put her shoes on.

Somehow, she felt like it would be better to read these at home.

Chapter Twelve

Mousetraps

Friday May 30

On her walk home, Sarah took an alternative route. She had been tempted to look for Caio, but she was afraid what her reaction would be if she saw him, and she had a date with Karl. It was never good to show vulnerability around Karl, as it tended to make him meaner. Once in her house, she dropped the envelope with the deposition papers on the kitchen table. These papers had meaning. She could feel it radiating through her fingers when she touched the parcel.

Yes, it's a place where you might be able to make a difference … if you are brave enough, whispered the new voice.

Sarah shook her head.

First things first, her dinner date with Karl.

Sarah went upstairs, washed her face, put on a bit of makeup and changed into a simple-cream silk shirt and some dark pants. Karl told her that she looked much better in pants because her legs weren't good enough for dresses. Of course, the truth was that she could wear whatever she wanted to because he usually didn't really look at her much anyway.

A picture of Caio appeared in her head unbidden. It was not the picture from their last few meetings when his face had been closed and uncomfortable. It was the picture her mind had captured in the moment when he was trying to help her up at the grocery store. He had looked genuinely glad to see her, almost desperately glad.

"No. No. No." Sarah shook her head as she went downstairs. She needed to get out of this mindset. She needed to distract herself. She picked up the manila envelope from the table and pulled out one of the documents.

The first document she extracted from the envelope was an old deposition of Melissa Taylor. There was a yellow sticky note on it that read "SB to research per client." The words kicked her in the gut. It made sense that SB would be her, but Andrew Davies had asked for her by name? She didn't know him, and he hadn't seemed to know her when she first spoke to him. Something about this was making her heart beat faster, so she turned her attention to the deposition itself. It began like most other depositions, with questions about Melissa's full name, etc. A bit further down was slightly more useful information about her work.

Q: Did you attend university?
A: Yes.
Q: Which one?
A: UCLA.
Q: Did you graduate?
A: Yes, I graduated from their nursing program.
Q: And did you practice nursing?
A: Yes, I was an ER nurse while I lived in California.
Q: And when did you move here?
A: I moved here when I got married. We wanted children, so I didn't get a full-time job. So I trained to be an electrocardiographer as something I could do part-time.

The page continued with more detailed questions about Melissa's work. This was designed to get evidence that she was capable of working so that they wouldn't have to pay alimony for as long. It wasn't until the third page that the attorney got into the reasons for the divorce.

Q: Did you love your husband when you married him?
A: Of course, otherwise I wouldn't have married him.
Q: And you loved him through the birth of all three of your sons?
A: Yes.
Q: Why are you filing for divorce?
A: Because I discovered that he was abusing my oldest son, Alex.
Q: Abusing?
A: Sexually abusing.
Q: And how did you discover this?
A: I walked in on it.
Q: Where did this occur?
A: It was in my husband's office.

Q: Your husband was sexually abusing your son in his office?

A: Yes, I had left Alex to stay with his dad while I went to a dentist appointment. When I came back, the receptionist at the front desk was gone, so I just walked into the office.

Q: And what did you see?

A: I ... I ... I'm sorry ...

Q: Take your time.

A: I saw my husband sitting behind his desk. He was leaning back, and his eyes were closed. He looked ... he looked like he was about to have an orgasm.

Q: How did you know that?

A: He was my husband; I was his wife. I know what that looks like.

Q: Okay, please continue.

A: Okay. He, well, I coughed, and he opened his eyes quick. Then my son crawled out from under his desk. He ... he ...

Q: You hadn't seen him under the desk?

DEPONENT'S ATTORNEY: Can we take a recess?

(Returning)

Q: We are back. Are you okay to continue with this?

A: Yes.

Q: You believe your son was sexually abused by his father?

A: Yes, I saw it.

Q: Did you talk to your son about the incident?

A: Yes, but he said it was nothing. He didn't want to talk about it.

Q: If your son was being abused, as you say, why didn't he want to tell you about it? Why does he deny it when he's asked directly and under oath?

A: Because he's afraid.

Q: And who would he be afraid of?

A: His father, among other people.

Q: I see. Mr. Fritz will be testifying at the hearing as well, am I correct?

A: Yes.

Q: And he's your current psychologist?

A: Yes.

Q: And are you taking any medication right now?

A: Yes.

Q: Which medications are you taking?

A: Klonopin.

Q: And you are taking this for anxiety?

A: Yes.

Q: And it was prescribed by Dr. Fritz?

A: Yes.

Q: Have you taken any other psychiatric medications?

A: Yes, clozapine.

Q: I am not familiar with that one, what is it used for?

A: It is an antipsychotic, but I am not taking it anymore.

Q: And was this prescribed by Dr. Fritz?

A: No.

Q: Who was it prescribed by?

A: Dr. Iselle Summers.

Q: Is this a psychiatrist?

A: Yes.

Q: Are you still under her care?

A: No.

Q: Is this the doctor who was seeing you when you were committed to the psychiatric facility?

A: Yes, when I asked to be committed to a psychiatric facility.

Q: Why did you ask to be committed?

A: Because my husband and Dr. Summers were messing with my mind.

DEPONENT ATTORNEY: Can we go off record for a moment?

(Returning)

Q: We are back on record now. You said that your son was afraid of his father, among other people. Who are the other people?

A: His father's friends.

Q: And has he told you that he's afraid of them?

A: No, but he doesn't have to, they are scary people.

Q: In what way are they scary?

A: Umm. Well. They have a lot of power.

DEPONENT ATTORNEY: I don't think we need to cover all this. You can ask the boy.

Q: Well, we already have asked the boy, and his response is very different from his mother's. I am just trying to understand why she believes her son to be afraid of his father. It doesn't seem—

A: Alex is afraid of him because he's a monster. I know that you are trying to make it look like I am crazy and making this up, but my son is in danger if he stays with his father. He puts him in contact with people who are Illuminati or something—some other group like that—but whatever they call themselves, they are evil. And one day … one day … something is going to happen to my baby. And then you will all be back in this room trying to figure out what went wrong. And everyone will be wringing their hands, but my son will be hurt or gone. And if you let this happen, I will never forgive you—any of you.

DEPONENT ATTORNEY: Can we take a moment?

Suddenly Sarah heard footsteps on her porch. She looked up at the clock. It was 7:00. She had lost track of time.

Shit. Karl is here.

She was standing across the room reading the papers when Karl walked through the door.

"Hi. You are a bit earlier than usual," she said, quickly dropping the papers behind her on the counter.

"I thought that would make you happy," Karl said, looking at her and then at the counter behind her.

"What were you reading?" he asked.

Don't lie. He's going to look at these at some point and it will look suspicious if you move them, said her attorney voice.

"Some of the depositions for the Davies case," she said as the turned to go wash her hands. She didn't need to but didn't want him to be able to read her face.

"The old ones?" he asked.

"Yes, a few. Michael kept promising to get them to me, but I didn't see them until today. I wanted to review them this weekend before the initial hearing next week," she said.

She could feel Karl's eyes on her back.

He knows something too. Shit, there really is something going on here.

"Hmmm. Okay. Well, we need to go if we are going to make it to dinner on time." He walked to the door. He waited and held the door for her, which he never did, but his eyes had taken on that flat, snake-like look again.

On the drive to the restaurant, Sarah kept up a stream of chatter, asking him about his day and his workload. He answered her questions, but without the usual annoyance or arrogance that he usually displayed. When they arrived at the restaurant and sat down, his subdued mood and demeanor did not change. But his eyes kept drifting to his phone, which he had left on the table.

You're in trouble. Just get out of here. Go home. Or to a motel, whispered the new voice.

Don't be ridiculous. You are just having dinner with Karl. You are just being hypersensitive again, said her father's voice.

Karl's phone pinged, and he picked it up.

71

"Who gave you the depositions?" Karl asked sharply, looking up from his phone.

"What?" she asked, taken aback.

"Michael just texted me. He said that he hadn't given you the depositions."

"You texted Michael about that?" she asked.

"Yes. I wanted to see if there was something in particular that he wanted you to look for. But he said he didn't give them to you. So who did?"

"One of the admins. Michael had said that he would give them to me by today, but I thought he just got too busy and so I asked another admin," she said.

"You know you shouldn't push things so much, Sarah. If Michael hadn't given them to you yet, there must be a reason," Karl said softly, looking down at his phone. "Did you read all of them?"

"Not yet. I read part of the first one. I didn't have time," Sarah lied, looking directly into his eyes.

"Sarah, you aren't an attorney," Karl said, rearranging his cutlery on the table.

Actually, I am.

"You shouldn't overstep your—"

"Hi Ms. Baker." A voice cut Karl short. Sarah looked up to see the smiling and earnest face of the red-haired boy that she always saw on the basketball court with Caio.

"Hi," she replied.

"You don't recognize me? I'm Mouse. I play basketball on Saturdays, and I always see you coming back with your groceries," he said, pulling out a pad of paper from his apron.

"How do you know her name?" Karl asked coldly.

"I make a point of knowing the names of all the pretty ladies in the neighborhood," Mouse said, giving her an exaggerated stare from underneath his eyebrows. Sarah smiled despite her earlier misgivings about the evening. But when she saw the dark expression on Karl's face, she stopped.

"Pretty ladies, I understand, but old women?" Karl asked. Mouse's jaw dropped open for a moment. Then he composed himself.

"I'm your waiter—" he began.

"Obviously," said Karl. Sarah winced. Karl was looking at his menu. Mouse looked at her with eyes that were hard to read. They were both hard and soft.

"What would you like?" he asked her.

"She will have the grilled chicken salad, because she could do to lose a few pounds," Karl said, causing Mouse's eyebrows to shoot up again.

Clearly this boy had not learned facial control. Neither was he hiding his clenched jaw and narrowed eyes.

"And I will have the filet, medium rare, with a loaded baked potato," Karl continued. "And a bottle of sparkling water for the table."

Mouse nodded and walked away silently. For a tall boy, he was surprisingly successful at it. Maybe that was why they called him Mouse.

"You really shouldn't make of fool of yourself flirting with teenage boys," Karl snapped.

"I wasn't flirting. I didn't even say anything."

"Oh yeah." Then Karl faked a giggle and pantomimed flipping long hair. She didn't do that. She had never done that. She didn't even have long hair. But it would be pointless to argue.

Mouse brought out their food quickly. As Karl ate, he stared around the room as people came and went. He was always looking for potential clients. And, as was their habit, they did not speak while they were eating. It was hard for Sarah to watch Karl eat. It was harder for her to eat because a feeling of dread was filling up her stomach.

It's called fight or flight. So that's what you should do—fight or flee. The chemical is not released so that you can sit there and stare at the cat as it chews your head off, said the new voice.

At this moment, she didn't resent this voice. She found it somewhat comforting to think that she had choices. She pondered whether she should just get up to go to the bathroom and leave. But she knew Karl would simply show up at her house.

You could stab him in the hand with the steak knife, said the new voice.

Sarah. Don't you get like that, said her mother's voice. But the thought made Sarah smile to herself.

As they were finishing their meal, Mouse returned to the table.

"Hi. I just wanted to let you know that my shift is over. Myra will be taking over your order from here. She's great, so you will be well taken care of."

Karl flipped his hand dismissively.

"Thanks Mouse. I hope you have a lovely evening," Sarah said. Karl glared at her.

"Not so lovely. I have to study for a social studies test tomorrow. It's about world cultures. I'm terrible at this stuff."

"Oh. But that sounds so interesting. I would love to be able to travel, and studying other countries is the next best thing, right?"

"Sarah, you sound so naive when you say stuff like that," Karl said, then turned to Mouse. "She hasn't traveled enough to know how incredibly annoying and boring it is. She thinks it's all like some glamorous Condé Nast advertisement."

Sarah felt herself color again. Karl's behavior was normal for him but apparently not for Mouse, who looked really uncomfortable.

"Uh yeah. Well, have a great night," he said, turning and leaving quickly.

"He was a little asshole, wasn't he?" Karl said as Mouse walked off.

"I thought he was nice," Sarah said.

Karl looked up at her and narrowed his eyes. "Really? I guess you didn't see how disrespectful it is for him to be flirting with you in front of me."

"He wasn't—" Sarah started, but Karl put up his hands.

"I don't want to talk about it."

They finished their meal in silence. Karl paid the bill without so much as a glance in her direction. The ride home was also silent.

Sarah knew trouble was coming. She knew it even more when Karl opened the door of her house and let her enter first. For a brief second, she considered slamming the door in his face, but she wasn't fast enough. She did quickly move to the far side of the kitchen to where she kept her utensils.

Karl closed the door behind him, locked it, and strode over to her. Without a word he backhanded her across the face. It was a hard blow and it knocked her off balance. She fell to the floor.

Cry! Start to cry! Let him think he has won this battle! Do it now! yelled the new voice.

Sarah began to cry. Karl crouched over her body and grabbed her by the hair.

"Don't you ever disrespect me like that again. After everything I have done for you. I pay your mortgage. I take care of you. I even got you a fucking job. And you repay me by becoming sassy at work and flirting with teenage boys like a slut."

He let go of her and her head banged against the floor, making her see stars. She was beginning to tremble all over.

Karl was now standing at her counter, looking at the transcripts she had left there. When he turned to her, he met her eyes for just a moment.

"I don't want to hear about this evening again, do you understand? If you mention it to anyone you will be very sorry you did," he snarled. With this he walked out the door, depositions in hand, and closed it softly behind him.

He closed it softly.

Even though she was trembling, she noticed that. Karl didn't slam the door. This was not about the restaurant or her behavior there. This was about the depositions that she had seen. She had known there was a problem from the

74

moment he had seen them. His expression had told her that. And his expression just now, the moment after he had struck her, was just as telling. His expression had not been one of anger.

His expression had been one of fear.

Chapter Thirteen

Insubstantial Cavalries

Friday May 30

Sarah lay shaking on the floor for a long time after Karl left. She had stopped crying, but she couldn't stop her body from shaking. Her face and head both throbbed. This was the only thing that kept her connected to the real world. In her head, she felt like she was drifting. Images flashed through her mind. The face of her mother looking down on her, her eyes aflame. The sound of her own voice, but much higher.

I'm sorry, Mommy. I won't do it again.

How could she forget that? Her mother had hit her. When she was little, she had hit her. She had forgotten it. She forgot the fear, the pain, the guilt. It was over by the time she was a teen, so she just forgot.

She hit me.

He hit you, said the new voice, breaking into her thoughts. *That asshole actually hit you.*

Well, you should have known better than to flirt with someone in front of Karl. You know he can be jealous, said Paul's voice.

What the fuck is that about? Karl has never been jealous of you a day in his fucking life. He doesn't care enough about you for that. This was about those deposition papers, said the new voice.

You don't know that. You are just guessing again. And you are going to end up without a boyfriend or *a job if you keep this up*, said her father's voice.

Good. Get rid of the asshole for good, said the new voice.

And what would you do then, with no boyfriend and no job? You think someone else is going to take care of you? said her father's voice.

But Sarah, why were they both so panicked about you seeing that deposition? Karl texted

Michael about it the minute that he knew about it, asked her attorney voice.

Because that boy was being abused and is still being abused, replied the new voice.

Yes. But there's more. Abuse is terrible, but it wouldn't be the first time that your firm represented an accused abuser, would it? Something is different here, besides run-of-the-mill abuse, said the attorney voice.

Sarah squeezed her eyes shut and a picture formed on the red-black screen of her eyelids. She could see herself sitting at a large round table. It was covered in a lace tablecloth with an ornate and gaudy candelabra in the middle of it. Around the table were five people. Three were the owners of the voices she had been hearing in her head for years—her mother, her father, and her ex-husband. Her mother looked younger and thinner than she had been when Sarah was growing up. Perhaps this was how she had looked in her youth. Her father looked about the same age as he had been when she was a child. But sadly, her ex-husband looked pretty much the same as he had a couple of weeks before he died of cancer.

It was the other two people at the table that caused Sarah to gasp internally. One was her torts professor from law school, Larry Boger. The other was Valerie "Val" Rigby, her best friend during law school.

When Valerie spoke, Sarah realized that this was the new voice she had been hearing in her head.

Listen, sweetie, Val said. *Your asshole parents are trying to keep you in the same emotional place where they kept you when you were a kid. The place that you broke out of for a while when we were in law school. Then you went and married him, a guy who was just as nasty as your parents but just put a better face on it.*

"Why are you in my head now?" Sarah asked.

The same reason I am, said Larry Boger, in the fast, clipped, analytical voice he had always used in class. Sarah now recognized this as what she had thought of as the "attorney voice" that had appeared in her head a few months ago.

We're here because we want to help you, Val said, reaching out across the table to touch her hand. Sarah could almost feel it, although this was happening in her head.

And because we recently died, continued Larry. *All of us here in your head are ghosts.*

"What?" Sarah said.

We're ghosts, said Val. *Me, Larry, your parents—*

That's quite enough of that, said her mother, tapping her hand on the table.

"Shut up!" Sarah snarled.

Don't you talk to me— her mother began, but Val stood up.

She told you to shut up, you old bag! growled Val. Sarah almost smiled. Valerie had been loud, crass, and irreverent when she met her at law school. She had been no different when they graduated. The years she spent as Val's best friend were the best of her life. Sadly, they had grown apart after her marriage to Paul.

Sarah, sweetheart, that asshat you are dating just slapped the shit out of you because you are getting too close to something. It has nothing to do with your relationship with him. It is a much bigger thing.

That girl is just trouble-making, like she always does, snapped her father, never a big fan of Val's.

She is not. Valerie is simply trying to warn Sarah, Larry said. *You are at a juncture point in your life. We are here to help you with it.*

You know you have to leave Karl, right? Val asked her.

She has to do no such thing, said Paul.

You can shut the fuck up too, Val snarled at him.

"I'm afraid to leave him," Sarah whispered. "But after, this I am afraid to stay with him too."

He stepped over a line. If he does that and you forgive him, he'll do it again. You lived with your parents and you work in a family law office, you know how this works, said Val.

But she has to be careful in how she leaves him, said Larry. *It's not just him you will be leaving. You will be leaving your—*

You aren't allowed to say anything else, Paul interrupted sharply. *We aren't allowed to reveal the future.*

Because we can't, asshole. We don't know what will happen. We only know what is happening now, Val said.

"And what is that?" Sarah asked.

That's the problem actually. Ethically, we can't tell you all we know. We can't tell you anything more than what you know, Larry said.

"Well, that's convenient, because as voices in my head, that's all you would know," Sarah sighed.

Look us up. Research our deaths, Larry said. *Find out if what we have told you is true.*

And let us help you plan your way out, Val said. Sarah's mother started to speak but Val turned on her and actually bared her teeth.

But first, let us help you sleep, Larry said. *When you get up, go straight to bed. Sleep will help you recover, and we will help you sleep.*

With that, the table and the visions in her head disappeared and Sarah found herself still lying on the floor of her kitchen. She got up gently, her head pounding. She wondered momentarily if she should avoid sleeping, just in case she had a concussion, but she couldn't be bothered. She made her way up to her bedroom and lay down on her bed. She felt her eyes becoming heavy. She felt almost as if she had been drugged. While she was still barely conscious, she reached for her phone. She typed in the name Valerie Rigby.

The first thing to come up was an obituary, stating that Valerie Rigby had died four months ago.

Monday June 2

Sarah slept through the entire rest of the weekend, only getting up to pee and drink water. She dreamed a lot, and most of those dreams were pleasant, including a few law school dreams that featured Valerie. Still, even in her sleep fog, she was starting to get worried that she might have a concussion, but she woke up when her alarm went off on Monday morning famished and alert.

She stumbled downstairs with her phone in hand, scrambled herself an egg and had it on a piece of toast. Her headache was gone but her face was still throbbing. She was halfway through her egg when she heard her phone beep. It was a text from Michael.

I need to talk to you when you get in today, was all it said.

With that, the events of Friday came back into full focus, along with the vision she had. She quickly typed up the names of Valerie Rigby and Larry Boger. Valerie had died four months ago of ovarian cancer. Larry had died a little over a year ago from a heart attack.

She sat back in her chair. This is what the voices had told her. Had she known this before and just buried the knowledge? Had the stress of Karl hitting her opened some weird psychic connection to them?

Sarah found that her heart was racing. This was way outside of the norm for her life. It was probably related to having a concussion or something, but what if it wasn't? What if she was actually hearing ghosts in her head? What if these voices were more than simply her own voice tearing herself apart? What if they had just wanted her to think that?

Suddenly the room felt like it was glowing. The sun outside looked brighter than it should be at this time of day.

Sarah looked at the clock. It was already 8:30 a.m.

"Damn it. I'm late," she said as she ran upstairs to throw on clothes and head out the door.

Chapter Fourteen

Dorian Gray Throws Angela under the Bus

Monday June 2

As it turned out, it took Michael until almost noon on Monday morning to call her into his office. This provided enough time for most of the office to see her face, and for the gossip mill to be in full production. Angela was surprisingly absent from her desk all morning. She showed up at 11:35, just before Michael rang Sarah and asked that she come to see him. He did not ask for her to bring any files or documents. She knew what this was about.

"Please sit down, Sarah," Michael said as she entered his office.

She sat down on the small chair facing his desk. Most of the chairs in his office were noticeably shorter than his. She didn't know if he had intentionally done this to make the client feel small, or if it came from his natural Machiavellian instincts.

"You know how happy I am with your work overall," he began, lacing his fingers on the desk in front of him. "We have always been very impressed with your organizational skills, your researching prowess, and your attitude."

Sarah found herself staring at his upper lip, which had a slight sheen of perspiration. He was also blinking a lot more than he usually did. And while Michael didn't usually make that much direct eye contact, he always made some. But right now, he was staring hard at her earlobe.

"So I don't want you to take what I am going to say to badly," he said.

"Are you firing me?" Sarah asked suddenly, surprising herself and him.

"No, no. Of course not. I wouldn't dream of it. You are too much of an asset to this firm. However, I am a bit concerned about you overstepping your authority with the Davies case. I had specifically asked you to research Melissa

Taylor. That was your directive. It was not your directive to go digging for depositions until I gave them to you."

"I didn't go digging for them, they were given to me," she replied.

Michael's bushy eyebrows crawled up his face like caterpillars.

"Really, by whom?"

Sarah hesitated for only the briefest second. Then she remembered Angela's expression just now, when she saw Sarah's face. The look had been smug.

"Angela gave them to me," Sarah said flatly. Michael's eyebrows now met each other in his face to form a unibrow.

"Really. Angela did that? Are you sure?"

"Yes, I'm sure. I have no reason to make that up and a lot more reasons not to tell you. I'm sure she won't be happy with me about it. But I assumed that if she had them, then they are available for the admin staff to see. She isn't even your paralegal."

Michael's jaw tightened to the point that she almost expected to hear teeth crack.

"Yes. I can see how you would think that, but Angela should not have had access to those files either. I will have a word with her," Michael said. Then he suddenly gave her his attempt at a sympathetic smile, reached out and patted her hand.

"Don't worry, I'll make sure there are no repercussions for you."

Oh really, how do you think you are going to do that? Do you think you can watch Angela every minute of every day? She will bite me as soon as your back is turned.

Still, Sarah realized that she was much less nervous about retaliation from Angela than she normally would have been. This was because it had suddenly dawned on her that she was more important to the firm than Angela was, or ever would be. Angela was also paid more than Sarah. So, while Sarah was doing an attorney's work for half the pay, Angela was doing a paralegal's work, badly, for probably twice what she was worth. It might have been useful to keep Angela on her good side in order to get information out of her but now she realized that she couldn't trust what information she was given, it was better to openly treat her like the snake that she was.

You don't want to get in fights with your girlfriends in the office. They are the ones who can help you, said her mother.

And it's always better to be polite. That way you don't antagonize people. And you know that you don't do well with confrontation, said Paul.

Well, maybe you better learn how to deal with it. Your supposed boyfriend slapped the shit out of you last Friday for nothing. Are you just going to accept that? And accept everyone else walking all over you? asked Val.

81

Sarah shook her head.

"Sarah, are you all right?" Michael interrupted her thoughts with a tone that was probably intended to sound gentle but sounded more like Kaa from *Jungle Book*.

"Yes, I'm fine," she said.

"Did Karl hit you?" he asked her suddenly, directly.

Sarah thought about the lies she could use. I ran into the door. I fell down the stairs. I was in a kickboxing class. These were the answers that Michael wanted from her. She knew that, like she knew that he had already talked to Karl about this. He was asking her to probe, but she didn't know to what end. She opened her mouth to tell him that she had fallen, but that was not what came out.

"Yes," she said, looking him straight in the eyes. He flinched a bit and looked down. Some other part of her had come forward. Some stronger part. The part that had made it through law school despite all the doubts of her parents. And for a moment she could feel the presence of Val in the room with her.

"I see," Michael said, then he was quiet for a bit. She knew he was hoping the silence would pressure her into speaking to fill it, but she refused. Finally, he looked at her again.

"Karl can have a temper, but I have never heard of him doing anything like this before."

So it must be your fault, is what he's implying.

"Do you want me to talk to him?"

"No," Sarah said. "It's my problem. I'll handle it."

She surprised herself further with these words. Her voice sounded calm and strong.

Michael must have been surprised too, because he raised his eyebrows again, staring at her. Sarah said nothing, she just stared back at him. When she didn't look away, he began moving papers on his desk.

"Well, let me know if you need anything," Michael said. "And don't worry about that other little thing. I know you meant well, but Angela was the one in the wrong here. It will be sorted out."

He stood up and walked her to the door of his office, opened it for her and walked her to her desk.

"Angela, would you care to join me for lunch?" he asked. Angela looked up suddenly and her eyes narrowed.

"Thanks Michael, but I have to finish up all the transcripts for Jason's hearing tomorrow, so I need to just eat at my desk," Angela said with an attempt at a doe-eyed simpering smile.

"That wasn't actually a request," Michael said coldly. Angela shot Sarah a quick but venomous look. Sarah's initial response was to wince but then she felt this warm feeling rush through her. She realized that the thought of Angela catching shit from Michael made her happy.

That's not very Christian, her mother said scornfully.

Neither is the behavior of many so-called Christians, including Angela, she responded in her own head.

"I don't have much time for lunch, so I would like to leave now," Michael said. Angela immediately nodded and scurried to get her stuff together.

Sarah felt a surge of relief as they walked out the door together. She had felt completely under the microscope all day. People in the office had been drifting by, always on the way to somewhere else, but they slowed to look at her. Clearly the news had gone around that someone had hit her. Most people probably guessed it was Karl.

The phone rang.

"Sarah," said Karl's voice. "I just wanted to call you about what—"

"I don't have time to talk right now," Sarah said, hanging up the phone. This was the first time in the six years she had dated him that she had dared to do that. It wasn't the first time she had wanted to, but it was the first time she had actually done it.

You need to be careful here. You need to play this like you are scared, not angry, said Larry.

Why? she responded in her head, but got no reply.

The other voices in her head were strangely silent and they stayed that way for the next hour, as she quietly ate her lunch at her desk.

#

When Michael returned from lunch, Angela was not with him. When Angela had not returned by midafternoon, Sarah assumed that she had been chewed out in a spectacular fashion.

Sarah decided to do no work on the Davies case today, in any way, shape or form. Instead, she worked on paperwork needed for traditional cases that they had coming up: one separation agreement to draft, one protective order and one request for summary judgment. As she worked on these, admins and paralegals continued to trickle by her desk to gawk. Sarah ignored them, but by five o'clock the whispers were beginning to take their toll. This, added to the fact that her face was still throbbing despite taking twice the prescribed dosage of Tylenol, made her decide to pack up and leave just at closing time. As she was putting on her shoes, she saw the delivery boy enter the office at the other side of the building. He was carrying a huge bouquet of roses.

Please don't let it be for me. Please don't let it be for me.

But sadly, the boy turned her way. She got up quickly and moved out of her cubicle, hoping to avoid the encounter but the boy stopped her as she walked by.

"Are you Sarah Baker?" he asked as she tried to slide by.

"Uh huh," Sarah replied.

"So you are the lucky—" he began with a big smile, but stopped when he got a good look at Sarah's face. His smile disappeared and his face tightened.

"Can you just put them on my desk back there?" she asked.

"Sure," he replied quickly.

"Or you can just throw them in the trash," Sarah muttered under her breath.

"Do you want me to?" the delivery boy asked, reaching out and touching her arm. She felt her eyes well with tears. His obvious and sincere concern affected her much more than Michael's prefab speeches.

"No, no. It's okay," she said quickly, wiping her eyes. "Just drop them on the desk."

With that she put on sunglasses to hide her eye and left the building.

Once on the street, she took a deep breath. The air was cooling down with the end of the day, and it was moist. She could taste the evening on her lips. As she began her walk home, she thought about the Karl situation.

He had hit her. He had crossed that line and actually hit her. Before this, he had certainly been emotionally abusive. As Larry had said, this would happen again.

No, he's just not demonstrative, said her mother.

He's an abuser, Sarah replied.

She hadn't wanted to admit that before, but being hit by him put this in stark relief. There was no denying it anymore. As there was no denying it, there was also no way around the fact that she would have to make a choice now. If she stayed with him, not only was she saying that all his other abuse was fine, she was also saying that she was okay with being hit. Even worse, it would be saying that she was okay with the fact that she would most assuredly be hit in the future. And, on some deeper level, she was probably saying that she deserved it.

It's not about what you deserve. It's about what you can get, said her mother.

And it's about not being alone. You know you don't do alone very well Sarah. You need someone there to look out for you, said Paul.

Let's face it, Sarah. If you go back to Karl, then you are exactly the rabbit and weakling that he has always thought you were, said Val. *Then there will be more hitting and more abuse. And that won't make you stronger, it will make you weaker and more afraid.*

She listened to these voices differently now. Before, she had assumed it was all just in her head. But now, with the emergence of Val and Larry's voices and the information concerning their deaths that they had given her, she wasn't so sure. And if ghosts could talk in her head, then there was a whole world out there that she had never been aware of.

No, you just never let yourself be aware of it, said Val.

Sarah had crossed the road and was walking by the park. There was a young boy of about seven standing in the center of a seesaw, balancing it with his weight. A woman, probably his mother, was walking toward him with a face full of concern. Sarah wondered if she would have been a different person if she and Paul had ever had children. Maybe in some other dimension, that was the life she had chosen. The thought that some part of her might be having a better time of it in another life was strangely comforting to her.

"Hey, Ms. Baker," Mouse called to her from the other side of the basketball court.

Sarah started. Mouse was standing with a group of about six boys, including the African American boy, whose name was Dex, and Caio. The sun that had shone in her life for those first few days after her meeting with Caio now seemed like a distant fairy tale.

She waved her hand at Mouse and kept walking quickly but he ran across the court toward her. She pulled her sunglasses up on her nose. The glasses didn't hide the part of the bruise that was on her cheek and the injured cheek was the one facing him. She hoped he wouldn't notice. At least it was sunny outside, which would explain the glasses.

"Ms. Baker,' he said, catching up to her. "I wanted to ask you—"

She turned and smiled at him as convincingly as she could.

Apparently, it was not convincing enough, as his words died on his tongue. He stood just staring at her for a moment. Behind him she saw Caio walking toward her holding the ball under his arm. His eyes were focused intently on her, and as he got closer, his face seemed to harden, and he dropped the basketball. As it hit the ground, it sounded like a gong in her ears.

She suddenly felt such shame well up in her that her eyes swam with tears.

She had become one of *those* women. The ones that other women feel sorry for. The ones that other women secretly feel superior to, clicking their tongues and muttering, "I would never put up with that." She was Dorian Gray, after his sins caught up with him. Her weakness was now physically stamped on her face.

85

She turned quickly and started walking home.

"Ms. Baker, wait. Are you okay?" Mouse called after her.

She started to speak but what came out was a sob. At that point she broke and ran toward her house. She heard voices behind her and thought she heard someone call her first name but that was probably just her imagination.

She ran up her steps and fumbled with her keys, fearing that she heard footsteps behind her. When the key turned, she threw her weight against her door and slammed it behind her. She then let herself slide down it into a crouch.

There she sat, sobbing until she had no more tears, and the sound that came from her sounded less like crying and more like dry heaves. When she was finally calm enough to breathe normally, she went upstairs and crawled into bed.

Humiliated and exhausted, unconsciousness came quickly.

Chapter Fifteen

Pastries and Spies

Tuesday June 3

On Tuesday morning, Sarah woke up feeling like she had been sucking a woolen sock for much of the night. Her mouth was dry, and her eyes were crusted with a lovely mascara/mucus mix. When she sat up, her head throbbed. She felt like she had a hangover but without the fun of the drinking. She looked over at her clock to see that it was already 9:05 a.m. She got up from her bed and stumbled to the bathroom. The mirror revealed that she looked even worse than she felt. Her eye was more swollen and the bruise on her upper cheek was darker and more prominent today.

She quickly got dressed for work, but, as she was standing at her front door, she couldn't bring herself to go out. The expressions on the faces of the boys last night still burned in her memory. Mouse might as well have had a bubble over his head with the words "Ms. Baker is a victim." And Caio? She cringed when she thought of his look. She hadn't been able to read it, or maybe she just didn't want to try. She already made him uncomfortable, and surely seeing her as a woman whose boyfriend beats her up would not do much to put him more at ease.

Sarah went back into her kitchen and sat down at the table. She couldn't bear going into the office and facing those stares and looks of false pity from people who didn't give a shit about her. And god only knew how Angela would react to her after the events of yesterday.

She pulled out her phone. Surprisingly, no one had messaged her yet. She typed a quick message to Michael.

Hi Michael. I am feeling a bit under the weather today, so I am going to stay home. I hope this is not a problem. If you need me to work on something, I am happy to work on it from home.

Michael responded almost immediately. *Of course, Sarah. Just rest. But if you start to feel better then maybe you could go check on Melissa Taylor and see if you can dig up anything. But only if you are up to it.*

Sarah smiled a bit, despite herself. Michael was notoriously nasty about absences, and she had only had one or two absences in her past five years with the firm. However, he was also sensitive enough to public scrutiny to be aware that people who came in would be assessing him through her. That wasn't a problem unless the person knew that she was dating Karl, and that Michael was a friend of Karl's. That could potentially tarnish his image. Sarah guessed this was why he seemed relieved to not have her in the office.

It must be very awkward for him, said Val. *That's a good reason to get your butt back to work tomorrow, just to make him squirm.*

Sarah smiled to herself, and it was good to smile. She decided that she would follow up on Michael's request and go see the bookstore where Melissa Taylor seemed to work. It would be a good way to distract herself from thinking about Karl, Caio, and her life in general. The bookstore was in a strip mall about eight blocks from her house. But it wouldn't open until 10 a.m.

Are you just going to sit around here and mope all day? asked her father.

You should be at work. You don't want to risk losing your job because you are lazy, said her mother.

"Then I'll go out and get some pastries and then walk to Reddux Books, will that shut you up?" Sarah snapped out loud, as she grabbed her purse and stomped out the door. The bookstore was in the opposite direction from her work. She decided to get the pastries at the expensive French patisserie. Normally she didn't see the value in spending a lot of money on food just for her. Also, it was a bit out of the way, but she felt defiant.

The bakery was at the end of the street that was home to one of the local high schools. As she turned down this road, she saw a boy running down the street in her direction. He was wearing shorts, a red-and-black striped T-shirt and black sneakers. He jumped gracefully over a pile of garbage left on the sidewalk. She felt her stomach clench inside her. She knew his movements. It was Caio.

Oh god, why now? Of all the teenage boys in the city, why him and why now? Fate hates me.

He was running with his head down, so he hadn't seen her yet. She looked around frantically for somewhere to hide but saw nothing but parked cars and a scattering of trees.

What if he thinks I came this way on purpose? He must go to school here. Shit, what if he thinks I am stalking him? Oh god, what if he thinks I am someone who would hang out at schools waiting for young boys? Jesus.

This thought made her desperately wish for someone to sideswipe her, but, as there were no cars on the road, she just kept walking, head down. She could hear the sound of his shoes on the pavement now. As her eyes were focused on her feet, she felt him see her before she saw it. Or maybe she heard the approaching steps falter and stop.

She looked up to see him standing a few yards away from her. There was no place to run or hide. His face lit up and he smiled. This smile was like the one he had given her in the grocery store. For a moment the caution that had been there in their last few meetings was gone. Then his smile changed to a more casual one. At least it wasn't that tight uncomfortable one she had seen recently. As they got to the point where they were almost directly in front of each other, he suddenly froze.

"Hi," she said. Her voice sounded shy and frightened to her own ears.

"Hi," he replied, his eyes lingering on her face. She could almost feel them moving across the bruise on her cheek. She looked down and kept walking past him. She wasn't going to read anything into anything, and, god knows, she didn't want to get into a conversation about the state of her face.

She was just past him when he turned. "Sarah?"

She spun around at the use of her first name.

"Are you okay?" he asked.

"Yes. I'm fine," she said.

"Are you sure?" he took a few steps toward her.

"Yes. I'm … I'm just fine. Really. I'm on my way to the bakery and then to work," she lied and started backing away.

"Well. Okay," he said, standing still and staring at her. "Have a good day, yeah?"

She wasn't sure if that was a directive or a question but, in any case, whatever he had been in a rush about seemed to have been forgotten.

"You too," she said and waved a bit.

That was stupid. Why the hell are you waving? You said goodbye already. For god's sake Sarah, you are acting like a skittish schoolgirl, said Paul.

Sarah inwardly cringed as she turned to walk away. She desperately wanted to look back, but she was too nervous to do so. She didn't want to make him uncomfortable again.

He called you Sarah, said Val.

That could mean a lot of different things, said Paul, *but the one thing it does not mean is that this child is harboring some romantic interest in you.*

Don't you go making a fool of yourself again, said her mother. *You are in enough trouble with Karl already after your scandalous flirting with that teenage boy the other night.*

"I didn't flirt," Sarah muttered to herself. "And I'm not going to overthink this thing with Caio. He's just being polite, so I am not going to let myself go down that rabbit hole again."

Because the rabbit hole you are currently in is so much better? responded Val.

It's not ethical for her to be swooning over some teenage boy, her mother snapped.

Oh shut up, you pompous windbag, Valerie snarled. *You know as well as I do that he's no more a teenager than I am.*

VALERIE! Larry snapped. Then the voices in her head became silent. Sarah wanted to bring them back. The ball of jittery energy that had appeared in her stomach when she saw Caio was now spreading outward to her trembling limbs.

She was standing at the door of the bakery. An old man came out with a bag of pastries and her stomach growled. The man laughed and held the door open for her.

The bakery had quaint red-and-white-checked curtains and "La Petite Boulangerie" written in large gold cursive script on the window.

Once inside, the smell of bread and sugar combined with her jittery mood resulting in her buying a ridiculous number of pastries for one person. She left the bakery with two pains au chocolat, two croissants, and two pains aux raisin.

Eating like that will make you fat—well, fatter, sniffed her mother.

"That's enough," Sarah said out loud, proceeding to eat as she walked. She ate as noisily as she could in order to drown out the sound of the voices in her head.

#

"Can I help you with something?"

Sarah jumped. She had been in the small bookstore for a good five minutes and had seen no one present. Now she turned to find herself face-to-face with the person she was here to spy on, but it took her a couple of seconds to recognize Melissa Taylor. The woman was tall, probably close to six feet. She had gorgeous, curly, deep brown hair that cascaded around her face and midway down her back. Her face was pretty but mannish, with a sharp jawline and thick, dark eyebrows.

"No, I am just looking. But thanks," Sarah said. The woman had a name tag that said "Melissa," confirming her guess.

"Fine. But let me know if you need any help," Melissa said. Then, as she looked pointedly Sarah's face, her expression softened noticeably which transformed her face making it truly beautiful. As she turned to go, she lightly touched Sarah's arm. Her hand was warm.

Sarah wandered through the books, keeping Melissa in her line of sight. Now and then she snuck glances at her out of the corner of her eye. Melissa sat on a chair next to the register, reading a book. The woman was definitely beautiful. Even though she was wearing a loose poet's shirt and jeans, this could not hide the fact that she had a figure that other women would die for. She looked like a model. No, she looked like a lingerie model.

"I bet she's had trouble with other women," Sarah thought to herself. If there was any upside to being somewhat forgettable, it was that other women didn't feel threatened by you.

Sarah wandered over to the self-help section. The books there were arranged by problem. The vast majority of them were about relationships: *Getting the Love you Want, He's Just Not That Into You, Co-dependent No More,* and *Women Who Love Too Much.* There was also a whole section on abuse with titles such as *Breaking the Cycle of Abuse, The Verbally Abusive Relationship,* and *Will I Ever Be Good Enough?* Sarah picked one up and began skimming through it. When she glanced over, she found that Melissa had disappeared from view. But then someone touched her arm and she jumped.

"I'm sorry. I didn't mean to startle you," said Melissa. "I just wanted to tell you that I read that book, and it's one of the better ones of that genre."

"Really?" Sarah said, studying the woman's large brown eyes. "Have you read a lot of these?"

"There's probably not a book on abuse that I haven't read," she replied, "and yes, that is because I was in an abusive relationship."

"Oh. I'm sorry," Sarah replied. Melissa didn't say anything, she just nodded and looked at her. Then she smiled.

"If you need any advice on these, don't hesitate to ask," she said, turning to go.

"Do you have a book that talks about what happens when verbal abuse turns physical?" Sarah asked.

"This the first time he hit you then?" Melissa asked. Sarah was a bit shocked by the directness of the question, but the woman looked at her with such real compassion in her eyes that she felt her own welling up again.

"Yes," she replied softly.

"Well, the books will tell you a lot. But I guess you need to ask yourself what you really need to know," she said.

"What do you mean?"

"Well, what you really need to know depends on what you plan to do. If you plan to try to stay with him, then you need a book that talks about his psychology and how to get him to seek help. Honestly—that almost never works. If you plan to leave immediately, you need books about how to separate and protect your assets. Even if you aren't married, you need to know your rights to any joint property and to privacy. You may need to know how to get a protective order. If you plan to leave him, but can't do it right now, then you need to get something that tells you a bit about the cycle of the abuser, so that you can get an idea of how long it will be before he hits you again."

"Isn't it about avoiding things that provoke him?" Sarah said.

"No!" Melissa snapped. "Sorry, I just hate it when people blame themselves. It has nothing to do with anything you do. There's an internal cycle with people who do this. Whoever hit you is probably going to be sweet as pie for the next three months, particularly if this is the first time. It's not because of anything you do, neither the abuse nor the following sweetness. It's a part of their disease, their illness. It's part of their evil."

Evil, that was a strong word.

"Was your ex emotionally or physically abusive?" Sarah asked. "Sorry, I shouldn't ask."

"No, you didn't ask. I offered. And the abuse was both physical and emotional. But the cycle of physical abuse was very long in the beginning, so the relationship lasted a lot longer than it would have if the cycle had been shorter. Still the abuse increased exponentially with each cycle. In the end—well, in the end I spent some time in a mental hospital because of it."

"Why a mental hospital if you were the one being abused?" Sarah asked.

"Because it was like *Gaslight*, the movie. Have you seen it?"

Sarah shook her head no, but of course she had seen it. She, and most of the legal world, were well aware of the term "gaslighting." She wanted to see what Melissa said about it.

"Well, the movie is about a guy who convinces his wife that she's crazy. That's what my ex did to me. He convinced me that everything I saw was in my head. I'm still not completely sure about what was real and not real, and about some pretty important things."

"I'm sorry, that sounds horrible," Sarah said softly.

"It was, it still is," Melissa replied, and her voice broke a bit on her words. "I'm sorry, I shouldn't be bothering you with my problems."

"No, it's helpful to hear that someone else has had the same problem," Sarah said. "Thank you for sharing. I think I will get this book."

She handed the book to Melissa, who smiled and walked to the register.

"Do you live nearby?" Melissa asked as she scanned Sarah's book.

"I live a few blocks away," Sarah responded.

"Well, I work on Tuesday and Thursday mornings and all weekend, if you want to stop by or you need someone to chat with," Melissa said. Sarah felt a pang of guilt. By all appearances, this woman was kind, genuine, and sincere. Sarah, on the other hand, was lying to her by her very presence here.

"Thanks. You've been a big help," Sarah replied as she took her package. She waved a bit and turned to go.

"Do you have children?" Melissa asked suddenly.

"No."

"Well, that's one thing going for you in all this. Stay safe," Melissa said. Sarah smiled and nodded.

You too, she thought.

That night, lying in her bed, images flashed through her head as if in a slideshow. The tears in the eyes of Melissa Taylor when she spoke about her husband's abuse. The ratty face of Andrew Davies when he put his hand on her shoulder. The tension in Karl's body when he saw the deposition papers on her table. The way Caio's face lit up when he saw her today.

Sarah had always prided herself on her ability to research and read people. That was her area of expertise at her job. She had developed this ability during the cacophony of her childhood. Her parents were prone to eruptions, so it was better to be able to see those coming. This ability to predict people's behavior had allowed her to find an island of stability in her head. But now, people were acting in new and unpredictable ways.

The inside of her head felt like a hurricane, and she didn't know in which direction the winds were blowing.

Chapter Sixteen

A Heart and a Spade

Wednesday June 4

As Sarah sat down at her desk on Wednesday morning, she did not make eye contact with Angela. Instead, she busied herself by putting away her bags and starting her computer. Her face was throbbing less today and the bruise was fading from purple to a lovely greenish yellow. She had refused to make any effort to conceal this with makeup. Karl had marked her with this, so let he and Michael deal with what people thought.

"Sarah," Angela said just as Sarah's screen was coming up.

"Yes?"

"I need to talk to you."

Here it comes.

"Okay," Sarah said, not turning around.

"I wanted to apologize to you for what happened," Angela said. Sarah felt reality shift again and swiveled her chair around to face Angela. The downward turn of Angela's mouth and her slightly raised eyebrows were probably an attempt at a doleful expression but her eyes told a different story. Normally, they looked flat and ratty. Today there was actual emotion in them, and it looked like fear.

Just like Karl when he saw the deposition papers.

"I didn't know when I gave you those papers that it would make Karl mad enough to hit you," Angela continued.

"Who told you that he hit me?" she asked.

And who gave you that as a reason why? He told me it was about flirting with Mouse.

"Michael," Angela whispered, her eyes darting around. "Don't get mad at him. He's just worried about you. And I never thought that Karl would be angry about that. I thought just like you did, that Michael had been too busy to get them for you."

Like hell you did, said Val.

"I know you must be really mad at me, and I understand that. I also understand if you don't want to talk to me for a while," Angela said. Sarah finally let herself make eye contact with Angela. The fear was still there.

Just at that moment, her phone rang, and Sarah turned her back on Angela.

"Culp, Moore and Rosen," she answered.

"Is this Sarah?" came the clipped, fake British voice of Andrew Davies.

"Yes, may I ask who is calling?" she replied coldly.

"It's Andrew Davies. How are you doing today?" he asked. There was a knowingness to his tone that irritated Sarah.

"Just fine," she replied. "Do you want me to get Michael for you?"

"Actually, I was wondering if you could squeeze us in this morning. My ex-wife called over the weekend with some new delusional accusations, so I wanted to run through that with Michael before her deposition next week."

Sarah looked at Michael's calendar. It was packed and she hated to move someone for this asshole.

"He only has availability before 10:30 or after 5 p.m. Do either of these times work for you?" Sarah asked as sweetly as possible. Andrew sighed. She could almost hear him grinding his teeth through the phone line.

"How about 9:30? Do you think he can make that?"

"Of course, I'll book that in," Sarah replied. As she got off the phone, she inwardly cringed at the thought of Andrew Davies seeing her face and making assumptions about her life based on it. Never mind that the assumptions would probably be true, she still hated it.

The other line rang, and she got sucked into what she could tell would be a "phone day."

#

The whole Davies clan showed up at the office at 9:20. Andrew came in wearing a suit with an actual vest. Anne Marie was wearing a simple green wrap dress. Her bronze-streaked hair was loose around her shoulders. She looked less uptight than the last time she had come into the office but now Sarah couldn't get the images of her riding horses out of her head. The two younger boys were trailing close behind her. Alex, the oldest, was walking further behind, carrying his phone.

The minute they entered, Michael came out of his office to greet them and

95

usher the adults into his office. No one looked at her. Without further prompting, all three boys assumed the positions in the waiting room that they had taken the last time they were there. Chris was on the sofa closest to her. Andrew was in the middle, with yet another comic book. Alex was on the far side of the room, on his phone. Sarah turned back to her emails and was just answering a query from a new client when someone touched her on the shoulder, and she jumped.

"What happened to your eye?" Chris asked her. She hadn't seen or heard him approaching.

"Oh nothing. I just fell down my front stairs and into my garden. You should see my knees," Sarah said with a forced laugh. Chris laughed too.

"Would you like me to get you something to drink?" she asked him.

"Do you have any Cokes?" he asked her.

"Of course, but does your mother allow you to have it?" Sarah asked, aiming the question across the room at Alex.

"Yeah. Our stepmom lets us drink it," Alex replied from across the room. Rather than looking down at his phone, as he had been doing, he was now staring at her intently.

"Okay then. Let me get you a Coke," she said, getting up. Alex's gaze was unsettling.

"Can I have one too?" Andrew piped up from his comic book.

"Certainly."

"I would like one as well, please," said Alex.

Sarah nodded and headed to the refrigerator in their tiny canteen on this floor. She knew that Alex had clocked her, and knew that her story about falling was a lie. It sounded like the typical battered woman lie that one heard on bad TV dramas. She cringed a bit when she thought of saying it, but it had fooled Chris easily enough.

When she returned, she came with three cans.

"Does anyone want a glass and ice?" she asked but all three shook their heads.

As she handed Alex his Coke, his hand lingered on hers for a moment.

"That bruise looks painful," he said quietly.

"It's not so bad now," she replied. "It was much worse a few days ago. I hope it's gone in a few more."

"It takes a couple of weeks for them to completely heal. Much longer than you think it will," Alex said, making direct eye contact with her.

"You've had a lot of experience with black eyes then?"

"I did at school. It was bad a few years back, but it's better now."

96

"What changed?" she asked, sitting down next to him. He tensed for a moment, but then, looking at her face, he relaxed again.

"I made a few friends. None at the school, but a few friends. They are going to a private school next year."

"Is that the one that your mother wants you to go to?"

"Yes."

"Would that be a problem for you? Being away from home?"

Sarah almost jumped out of her seat when Alex barked out a laugh. The sound was rough and jagged. It was no expression of joy. It came across more like an animal exposing its throat.

"No, I'm fine with living away from home," he said. He pronounced the word *home* with disdain that was apparent.

"Do you dislike your stepmother?" He looked away.

"I have no opinion about her."

"Your father?"

"I don't want to live with him."

"And your real mother?"

"What about her?"

"Do you want to live with her when you are back home from the school?" she asked. Alex looked away again.

"Is this a deposition?" he asked sharply.

"No, no. Of course not. I'm sorry. I shouldn't have bothered you with this," Sarah said, starting to get up but Alex put his hand on her arm. Sarah forced herself not to pull away. He was touching her a lot, but this sort of behavior wasn't uncommon for teens who had been sexually abused. They could become hypersexualized. She suspected he might also be using touch to unnerve her.

"Look. I know where you are going with this. You want me to say that I hate my mother because she had a breakdown. Yes, she had a breakdown. Yes, she beat me once. Yes, I was hospitalized for it. But there was more to it than that."

"What do you mean?" Sarah asked. She had not been aware of the fact that he had been beaten or hospitalized.

"I mean things aren't always as obvious as they seem. I would think you would know that," he said, touching her face suddenly.

"Meaning?"

"Meaning you got that shiner from, what, falling down some stairs? That's what you said, right?" he said softly, leaning forward, "Because you couldn't bear telling people the truth."

"So, what would be the truth?"

"That you are either too insecure to leave him, or you like it." His words, the jaded words of a survivor coming out of the mouth of this child, cut her.

"What was the truth in your case?" she asked.

"The truth is that my mother was right," he whispered.

"She was right to beat you?" Sarah asked with horror.

"Yes. She was trying to—" he began, but then he stopped. His eyes met hers and visibly hardened. "Look, sometimes people can really fuck things up when they are trying to help. And sometimes people are trying to help when it looks like they are fucking up. But it takes an insider to know the difference."

Sarah was shocked by his casual use of the word *fuck* but more shocked by the content of what he was saying.

"So your mother was trying to help you by beating you? How does that work?" she asked softly. But Alex just shook his head, his eyes hard. Then he suddenly took out his phone.

"Sorry, but my friend keeps texting me. I need to respond to him. I don't mean to be rude," he said, as he got up and walked toward the window. She stood up as well and moved back toward her desk. Sarah had heard no pings, but knew a way out when she heard one.

It was hard for her to imagine the woman that she had met at the bookstore striking her child. It was almost impossible to imagine her injuring him to the point that he needed to be hospitalized.

She vowed to see Melissa Taylor again soon. Not for work. Not for her job. But because her gut told her that Melissa would be the only source of truth she would get about this case and the boy who might be a victim here.

Chapter Seventeen

A Connection is Made

Friday June 6

For Sarah, Thursday went by in a blur. It was the day of the deposition with Melissa Taylor. The deposition was being held in their offices, but Sarah spent most of her day on a different floor, as Michael didn't want Melissa to see her and know that she worked for the firm. This might interfere with Sarah's ability to get information from her later. So her day had been filled with ongoing administrative tasks, everything from booking spaces and ordering lunch, to making sure that the technology teams were on standby in case something went wrong. The level of attention to detail on this case was up to a standard that Sarah had never seen before. It seemed like the entire firm, the entire building, in fact, was aware of it and riveted by it. As a result, Sarah didn't get much done during the day, or at least nothing of substance. The fact that she was sitting next to Kathy Denning, one of the chattiest paralegals in the firm, didn't help.

The deposition didn't start until late in the afternoon, and it wasn't over until after seven. As Sarah needed to be on standby, she was stuck at the office until the last minute. Unfortunately, Kathy felt the need to stay and keep her company. Sarah didn't know Kathy very well, but she noticed Kathy staring at her face repeatedly and she guessed that she was trying to get Sarah to open up. Everyone had dinner at the office, so Sarah was stuck listening to Kathy babble about her recent vacation to Bermuda and the fact that her five-year-old son was already reading "big-boy books." By the time she got home from work, she didn't bother with much besides crawling into bed and going to sleep. Given her past week, this was an emotional relief.

By the time she was back in the office on Friday morning, things had calmed down. All she really had to do was answer the phone, respond to emails, and wait for the transcript of the Taylor deposition. But this morning, she was very light on emails and the phone just wasn't ringing. On top of that, Angela was AWOL. As this left her brain unfettered by immediate tasks, it began to drift toward Karl, Alex, and Caio. She purposely turned her attention to Alex Davies.

The conversation she'd had with Alex on Wednesday had been weighing on her mind. The detached manner in which he spoke about himself, the directness of his statements, and his clinical assessment of his mother's behavior was not something usually seen in a person his age. At this point, he should just be making the transition from being a video game junkie to being awkward and girl-crazy. He should not be ruminating on the existential nature of "good" actions. That was too adult, and it was this that hit her the hardest. She knew that sexually abused children often acted much older than their years. She also knew that, contradictorily, they were also often very skittish around adults.

When she thought about these things, it was impossible for her not to make some of the same connections with Caio. His initial interaction with her in the grocery store had felt very adult. In fact, he had treated her in a manner more befitting a man than most men she knew. And yet ever since then, he had been very uncomfortable with her. She wondered if he had ever had trouble in this area. He was a kid in foster care, and it was well known that the system could be a cesspool of sexual abuse. She had seen more than a few sexually abused kids in her years working in a legal environment. What was striking was that some of these kids had a very sexual presence and vibe. Alex had that vibe about him. So did Caio. She herself was attracted to Caio in a very sexual way. There was no denying this. She reacted to him as if he were a man and not a teenager. With no small amount of horror, she realized that she might be attracted to someone who has had many adults be attracted to him before. Maybe that was why he closed down with her, when he realized that her attraction to him had taken a sexual turn.

The thought that she might be causing pain or discomfort to someone from the foster care world, who had probably known enough pain and discomfort for an entire lifetime, brought a burning ache to her chest.

What are you going to do about it? asked Val.

I don't know if I can do anything about Caio. Except to avoid making him uncomfortable, Sarah replied in her head.

But what about the other one? What about Alex? asked Larry. *You may be able to help him.*

She would lose her job! snarled her mother.

Yes, she would, replied Larry. *And we can't underestimate what Karl will do.*

He will try to hurt you, said Val.

100

So you need to have an escape plan, said Larry.

You shouldn't be thinking about all this. None of this is your problem, said her mother. *You should be happy that Michael considers you such an asset to the firm.*

And Karl— her father's voice began, but her inner conversation was cut short by the devil entering the front door. Michael was just stepping out of his office when he caught sight of Karl and moved over with outstretched hand.

"How did it go yesterday?" asked Karl. Sarah felt her heart begin to hammer at the sight of him.

"Very well," Michael replied, motioning Karl inside his office.

Sarah's hands were beginning to tremble. She wanted to get away. She didn't want to have to talk to him. She didn't want to have to see him. She was just standing up to head for the door when Karl came back out of Michael's office and walked straight toward her.

"Hi Sarah," he said, approaching her, putting his hands on her shoulders and giving her a quick kiss on the cheek, the cheek with the bruise on it.

She pulled away and he smiled a bit.

"I was hoping that maybe I could take you to lunch today," he said, looking at her with his head cocked.

He's trying to look like he's being sympathetic, said Val.

"I don't want to leave the office. I have a lot of research to do," she said, not looking at his eyes.

"Then can I speak to you for a few minutes?" Karl asked.

"You can use our conference room," said Michael, coming up behind Karl.

Sarah nodded. Karl gently took her elbow and ushered her toward the conference room. Once inside, he started to close the door behind him.

"Leave it open," Sarah said, surprised at the force in her own voice. Karl's eyes widened, but he nodded. He sat down at the conference table. She sat down catty-corner to him, so that she didn't have to be too close.

"Listen Sarah, I wanted to talk to you about the other night," he began.

Sarah said nothing. She just stared at him. His face was placid, but his eyes had the same panicked look that she had seen the other night.

"I'm so sorry that I did that to you. It's not an excuse, but I have been under a lot of stress at work. And, whether you know it or not, I can get a bit jealous too. I was very hurt by the fact that you were flirting with that boy at the restaurant. I try to do everything I can to please you, so it felt really disrespectful."

See how he tries to blame you for this. It's classic abuser shit, said Val.

But don't let him see that you know this. Let him believe that you are softening. You need to buy time to plan your exit, said Larry.

Sarah sighed and looked down.

"Listen Sarah. I'm not trying to excuse what I did. I'm just trying to explain it. I know that you'll be suspicious of me for a while. I know you are going to think that this is the beginning of a trend, but it isn't. I never did that before and I will never do it again. All I am asking is for you to give me the chance to prove it to you," Karl said.

As he was speaking, he was leaning forward and looking at her with what must have been an attempt at intensity. It ended up looking like someone with gas.

"Are you willing to do that? Are you willing to give me a chance to prove that I'm not that bad?"

You see, he's a good guy. He cares about you, said her mother.

He cares about something here, but it's not you. You need to buy the time to find out what it is, said Val.

Sarah looked down. Karl waited, scanning her face.

"I promise that I won't touch you again in any way until you say it is okay," Karl said. At these words, Sarah felt a weight lifted from her.

"Okay," she said, still looking down.

She knew this promise wouldn't last but it bought her time. For what, she wasn't exactly sure, but she felt she would need it.

"Well, I guess I should get back to work now," Sarah said, standing.

"Of course," Karl replied. "But can you let me take you out to dinner sometime next week. It doesn't have to be Friday. We can change our date nights if that is easier for you."

Wow, even now you are trying to reorganize around Meghan's calendar. It would be smooth if it wasn't so obvious.

"Okay," was all she said. Karl nodded.

"I'll call you later in the week and we can plan something for the next week. Okay?"

Sarah nodded and Karl walked out the door, without a backward glance. Yeah, he was going to make big changes for her.

When Sarah got back to her desk, Angela smiled at her from her call and gave her a thumbs-up. Sarah had to avoid openly shuddering.

As she sat down at her computer, she toyed with the idea of working on the Davies case. But she realized that what work she wanted to do would not be for her partner or her law firm. If she wanted to keep her discoveries secret, she would need to research at home, or when no one else was around. Of course, she would still be working on it here, but not from the angle she wanted.

Sarah felt frustrated by this, but fortunately it didn't last. Her day heated up after lunch and she was kept busy on the phone until almost the end of the day.

As she was putting her shoes on to go home, Michael came up to her desk.

"Hey Sarah," he said. "I just sent you a copy of the deposition with Melissa Taylor. It went well, but I wanted you to review it for any holes in her testimony. Also, look at what you might be able to probe on if you see her in person, particularly from the mental health perspective."

"Okay. I can look at it this weekend," she said.

"That's fine but don't overstress yourself about it," he replied. This was completely out of character for Michael. Usually, he *wanted* people to stress themselves. "Take some time for your personal life too."

With this, he smiled at her, turned, and walked out the door.

Oh, this was about Karl. Somehow everyone was pushing her back toward Karl. What was up with that? Why did they really care who she was dating?

Why indeed? asked Val.

With this running through her head, she collected her laptop and began her walk home.

#

Sarah decided to walk by the basketball court. She had a new take on Caio now, and she was concerned for him. She wouldn't look at him directly, but she wanted to check out his friends and try to get a visceral sense of his well-being. She told herself that she would not think about him in romantic terms anymore. In fact, she would think about him as a project, which meant she wouldn't have to think of him all the time.

These thoughts were running through her head as she crossed the street toward the basketball court. From a glance, it looked like all the regulars were there. She could see Dex towering over everyone else. Mouse was jostling for the ball with the boy sporting the ash ponytail. The boy with the spiky blonde hair was standing just behind Dex. And Caio was standing bent over at center court. To avoid humiliation and notice, Sarah crossed to the other side of the street, opposite the court, before she got too close.

As she walked by, she refused to look. Instead, she kept her head down. She wanted to go at least a few days without any humiliating encounter, so that she could get her bearings on what she was feeling. She had developed so many different theories and just as many feelings about this boy in the past few weeks that she wanted to clear her head. She knew that looking at him would do nothing to clear anything.

"Ms. Baker," she heard someone call out. She looked over to see Mouse walking across the court toward her. She waved and kept walking.

"Hey, Ms. Baker. Can I ask you a question?" he called.

103

Great.

Sarah stopped. If she kept walking, or worse, if she ran, it would look weird. No, it would look neurotic. She took a deep breath and turned toward Mouse. He was standing at the chain-link fence that separated the court from the street. He motioned for her to come over. Sarah took another deep breath and crossed the street.

Please don't make fun of me. Please don't ask me about my face. Please let Caio not give me one of those awful tight looks. Please let me get through whatever exchange this is without it resulting in a suicide attempt.

As she approached, Mouse smiled at her. The other boys were walking over toward her as well, Caio was among them.

"Hey. You know me and Dex and Caio, right?" he asked. Sarah nodded. "Well, these other two are Ash and Mickey." He indicated the boy with the ashen ponytail and the one with the short platinum hair.

"Hi," she said. They all smiled and nodded.

What the hell is this about?

"I wanted to ask you a question the other day when ... well ... whatever," Mouse started, stumbling over his words. "Well, you know Caio, right? Caio, come over here."

Please don't be weird. Please don't be weird. Please don't be weird.

She wasn't sure if she was focusing this thought on him or herself.

Caio walked over, running his hand through his hair. He looked up at her from beneath his bangs, which were now growing out.

"So, Caio's failing geography and civics. You work in a law office, right?" Mouse asked.

"Yes, I do. I do paralegal work there, but I am actually a licensed attorney. I'm just not practicing right now," she said, standing up a little straighter.

At least I'm smart. I may not be pretty or strong or charismatic, but I am smart.

"Caio was asking us if you tutored people. I told him that you were a lawyer, you would have to know civics. So, do you tutor kids?" Mouse continued with an odd little smile playing at the corner of his lips.

"I haven't before ... but I probably could," she said slowly, gauging the expressions of the boys around her. They were all looking at her intently. She felt like she was waiting for the other shoe to drop. For someone to jump out and yell, "Surprise!" Or more likely, for someone to start laughing.

"What grade are you in?" Sarah asked.

"I'm just finishing tenth grade," he said. His dark eyes were completely unreadable.

Tenth grade ... that would make him ...

"I could come on Saturday evenings," Caio said abruptly, interrupting her thoughts. "After I get off work." He spoke with that accent again, the one that she couldn't place.

"I'll pay you. Of course, I'll pay you," he continued quickly, beginning to stumble over his words. "But, if you have other things you do on Saturday night, then, you know, it could be another time."

Sarah forced a casual shrug. "Saturday's fine."

He smiled at her. It was that tight shy smile and then he looked down. Sarah cringed a bit inside.

"I live just around the—" she began.

"I know where you live," he said, making pointed eye contact with her. She must have looked shocked because he looked away quickly.

"Why don't you come by around seven tomorrow? If you want to start that soon," she said as coolly as she could. Her heart felt like it was beating a thousand beats a minute and she could hear her own blood in her head.

"That's perfect. That's great," he said, smiling briefly at her before turning and dribbling the basketball down the court. At least it had been a real smile this time.

"He's shy," Mouse said. "He was too shy to ask himself. So thanks for helping. He doesn't need another reason for his asshole foster family to get on his case."

Mouse raised his eyebrows then turned and walked off before she had a chance to ask him more about it.

And a new sun was born in her chest.

Chapter Eighteen

Elastic Brains

Saturday June 7

Sarah woke up very early Saturday morning, excited about seeing Caio that afternoon. As much as she might try to deny it, the fact was, she liked this boy—a lot. She liked his calm demeanor and intense eyes. She liked the ease with which he had addressed her in the grocery store, the intelligence that she saw on his face and the thoughtfulness with which he spoke. She liked the fact that he had seemed concerned about her when he saw her on the street the other day. These simple things were completely missing from her life, and she felt a deep sense of longing when she thought about what life would be like with someone like him as part of it.

Still, even if that was not an option for her, she could take a small piece of happiness by being able to help him. Maybe they could even form some sort of friendship. That was probably another pipe dream, because why would a teenager want to be friends with a grown woman? Still, it was a nice dream to have.

Listen, you can't afford to get yourself all worked up like you did last time. This was her own voice, not one of the cast of characters that inhabited her head, be they separate personalities or ghosts.

She threw on a white shirt and some jeans. No dresses today. She was NOT going to dress up and look ridiculous. Picking up the papers that Michael had given her yesterday, she went outside. Stepping out onto her front porch felt like stepping into someone else's skin. She felt calm, confident and in control. She had been put in a position where she could actually help several people—if she could keep her wits about her. She wasn't sure if she believed in fate, and if she did, it had certainly not been kind to her. But she somehow felt that something else was leading her along her current path. She wasn't sure if it was wise to trust whatever this was, but she was tired of running all the time. So for once, she would just follow her feelings and see where things took her.

The air outside was surprisingly fresh, and the sky was clear. She sat down in the chair on her front porch and began to read the papers she had been given. As expected, this was the recent deposition of Melissa Taylor that he wanted her to review. He wanted her to look at it for irregularities and any conflicts with facts already at their disposal. Sarah didn't want to do this. She already knew that she liked Melissa Taylor, and depositions were a place to intimidate and dig for weakness.

As she read, Sarah found herself grinding her teeth. The deposition had taken four hours and in most of it, Michael had grilled Melissa over every little expenditure she had made. If there was anything that was not strictly for survival or for the good of her children, he played it off as trivial and selfish. A cup of coffee at the coffeehouse was an outlandish expenditure. She should be saving for her child's education. And on and on. Michael did a superb job. She had to admit that he was excellent when it came to breaking people down. By the end of the deposition, the more junior attorney working for Phillip Seider had lost it and went after Michael. He called him some choice names and the deposition was ended. It made the other attorney look like an amateur and it made Michael look polished and professional. In what other profession would the obvious asshole be the obvious winner?

It took Sarah most of the morning to read it and take notes. She then took a break for lunch so that she could refocus her mind to go through it again looking only for inconsistencies. She hated reading these things at the best of times, and hated even more helping a client who she thoroughly despised. Still, it was her job and she needed to continue doing her actual job while she looked for additional angles to this case. After lunch she settled herself on her kitchen table to cross-check the expenditures that the wife claimed she had with the ones that they had on file. Everything checked out, but that is not what Michael would want her to find. He would want a discrepancy, something he could use to discredit Melissa.

If you found one, would you give it to him at this point? asked Val. Sarah pushed the question from her mind for the moment.

She re-read the transcript looking for something she might have missed. She found herself focusing on a small series of questions that didn't seem to have to do with anything, yet it called to her.

Q: If you are requesting a change in child support, there must have been some substantive change to warrant it?

A: Yes, there was. My son wants to attend a private school.

107

Q: But you had already covered that in your divorce agreement. You had agreed that he would attend public school.

A: He's not doing well there.

Q: Maybe you aren't helping him enough at home.

A: I help all the time. But he isn't with me very much, is he? His father has primary custody. And he needs some extra help.

Q: Well, then you will need to cover half of the difference, that is what is in your divorce decree, isn't it?

A: Yes, but I don't have enough money to cover even half of the private tuition.

Q: Well, did you think about these things before you signed the agreement?

A: No. I didn't think about much before I signed the agreement, to be honest. And I certainly didn't understand the implications of it.

Q: Are you saying that you signed a legal agreement without understanding it? You thought that was a good idea? You thought that was sound judgment?

A: I signed it because I was told that it was fair. I signed it at a time when people had made me feel like I was being paranoid and delusional in my assessment of my ex. Everyone around me, my friends, my work associates, my psychiatrist, told me that I was being overly harsh. They told me that no matter what horrible things my ex might have done to me, he would never make his children suffer.

Q: Even so, signing a legal document without understanding it is far from good judgment, under any circumstances. And if you have such questionable judgment, do you think it warrants you regaining custody? You were checked into a psychiatric hospital at some point, were you not?

A: Yes, I checked myself in a few months before I filed for divorce. Going through counseling gave me the courage to finally file.

Q: Is that so? Or was your filing for divorce just another symptom of your own ongoing mental problems?

A: Oh, that's what my ex-husband would say, most certainly. But he is very good at manipulating people's images, particularly his own. Monsters are often good at that.

Q: Well, if he's a monster, then you certainly felt okay staying with that monster for over ten years. Oh, and having three children with him. If he was good enough for you then, it seems odd that suddenly he turns into a monster after all that time.

A: Sometimes we don't see things we don't want to see. Sometimes we forget even more. The brain is an elastic thing.

Sarah stared at that sentence for a long time. There was something there, something that made her uncomfortable. She wasn't quite sure what it was. Maybe it was the fact that Melissa was referring to the disturbingly extreme allegations in the depositions from the first case. Or maybe it was because, as she read the words, she heard them in the jaded voice of Alex Davies.

Chapter Nineteen

Civics and Chicken Hearts

Saturday June 7

Sarah was startled from her paper when she heard a knock at the door. She was even more startled to look up and realize that it was 7:00 p.m. already. She cringed. She hadn't applied even a bit of makeup.

Stop it. He doesn't care what you look like. He's here for your brain not your body. You are an old woman to him, said Paul.

She squared her shoulders, got up and opened the door.

Caio stood there and gave her one of his tight smiles, then looked down. He was carrying a book bag, and a couple of plastic bags containing what could only be groceries.

He saw her looking at the bags and shrugged a bit.

"I realized that I don't have any cash right now, so I hoped that I could pay you by making you dinner. Mitch said that you were interested in Brazilian food. So I thought I could make a sampler of things. Is that okay?"

He looked up from the bags and caught her eye. He looked both guarded and hopeful in equal measure.

"Uh. Sure, that's great. But you, you really don't have to pay me—"

"Yes, really I do," he interrupted, his lips suddenly tight and his jaw set.

"Okay. Come on in then," she said, stepping back and letting him in.

She was struck again by his height. He was taller than her but not by so much as to feel threatening or overbearing. He smiled that slightly tight smile and dropped the grocery bags on her counter. He was obviously uncomfortable again.

"You know, you really don't have to do this, if you don't want to," she said quickly.

He turned. "Why do you think I don't want to?"

"Well, you kind of look really uncomfortable," she blurted.

He winced. "Sorry. No, really, I'm sorry. I want to do this," he said, turning back to the groceries. "But I think we should eat first. I, uh, didn't eat before I left so I'm really hungry."

"Oh, I have some snacks," she blurted again. He turned and smiled openly for the first time.

"No, I don't want to snack. I want to eat decent food." He then began to pull out a variety of meats from the bag.

"I know you liked meats from what Mitch said, so I got a few options. Some you may not like but I thought I would make them for you to try. I got some steak, some calf's liver, and some chicken hearts. You want to try all of them, or should I not bother making one? The chicken hearts might be too much but—"

"No, I would be happy to try anything you want to make. I've never had Brazilian food. I didn't know you were Brazilian," Sarah lied, then realized that he had told her that himself and inwardly cringed, but he didn't seem to notice.

"Yeah. Originally. But I haven't been back in a long time," he said.

A long time ... how long could it be?

"Where are your pans?" he interrupted her train of thought. "Or are you okay if I just make myself at home?"

"They are there, but yes, make yourself at home."

He dug around her kitchen, looking for different things. He obviously didn't feel the need to make ambient small talk. This gave her a chance to really look at him, maybe for the first time.

He was wearing jeans and a simple black shirt with some logo on it that she didn't recognize. His black sneakers looked fairly new, and he had a single woven bracelet on his wrist. He had long legs for his frame, and he was thin. He also had small, delicate bones. Maybe his bone structure was normal for someone his age, but she didn't know. She wondered if he was thin because he didn't eat enough. From the back, she could see the tiny hairs on the back of his neck. His skin color had looked Italian to her, but she had never met someone from Brazil before.

"Mouse said that you were failing geography?" she asked.

"Yeah, but I'm worse at civics. We have a geography test in two weeks and a civics test in three weeks, and I can't really afford to fail them."

"Are your grades bad?"

"No, not usually, but my foster parents don't like to be bothered by the school. If I get a bad grade, then they involve my foster parents."

111

"Oh. Ummm. They aren't—"

"No. No. Don't worry. It's not like they are abusive or anything. It's fine, besides I won't have to stay with them long. The age of emancipation in New York is sixteen, so I just need to do the paperwork," he said quickly. But he was twisting his foot back and forth as he spoke.

"So you're sixteen?" Sarah asked.

"To be honest, I have no idea how old I am," Caio replied, turning to face her. "I was born in a small village in northern Brazil. We didn't measure time in the same way that you do here. So they just kind of assigned me an age here. Here they say I'm sixteen. Time is a weird concept in my world."

"But how—" Sarah began, but he cut her off.

"Hey, could you do me a favor? My hands are messy, could you get my wallet out of my bag?" he asked.

She nodded and opened his book bag. Inside were several notebooks and textbooks. Everything was very neat and orderly.

"The wallet is in the front pocket," he said. She reached in and pulled out a very old, very soft leather wallet.

"Inside it, in the note pocket, there's a little piece of paper. It's got a recipe for chicken hearts on it. It's been a long time since I made it, so I wanted to make sure I don't forget something."

"Do you cook a lot?" she asked, opening the wallet.

"Whenever I get a chance."

As she reached into the wallet, she saw three things that made her freeze for a moment, and made her heart race. The first was roughly $150 in cash. The second was not one but two driver's licenses. The third was a condom.

She stared for just a second before quickly locating the piece of paper, closing the wallet and putting it back in his bag. She then handed him the piece of paper.

Caio turned to look at her directly in the eyes as she gave him the paper, his hand touching hers for just a moment, and he smiled. His hand was very hot.

"So you are okay for the chicken hearts? You are courageous about food, then?" he asked, turning back to the meat.

Sarah laughed.

"No, I'm not courageous about much really."

"That's a bit rude to say about yourself. Besides, it's not true," Caio replied.

"How do you know?" she asked.

He turned and looked at her.

"You just let a sixteen-year-old boy that you barely know into your house. A frightened person wouldn't have done that," he said with a strange expression.

"Maybe I'm just foolish," she said. "Or naive. But I think someone making me dinner is probably pretty innocent."

Caio laughed lightly.

"Do you think most men who are making dinner for women have innocent intentions?"

She felt herself flushing. And for a split second she wondered if she had made a mistake letting him in. Then she felt a twinge of excitement that he might feel that way about her. This was immediately followed by a wave of self-loathing. Surely, he had no such thoughts.

How many girls who get raped start out thinking the man is attracted to them? It's not about attraction, it's about power, said Paul.

Shut up, she told his voice in her head.

"But you don't have anything to worry about with me," Caio said quickly, before turning to drop several different meats into the pan.

She thought she heard him say something else at the end of that sentence, but it got lost in the sizzling of the meat.

"Just sit down and relax. I am guessing you don't get people cooking for you too often," he said over his shoulder.

And why would he think that? You are too old? Too plain? You don't have a real boyfriend? You are a loser? said someone's voice. She wasn't quite sure whose. It might have just been her own.

She watched him as he cooked. It was wonderful just to have the freedom to watch him without feeling embarrassed. She was a bit shocked when in less time than she would have expected, he pulled the plates from her cupboard, loaded them with food and brought everything to the table.

It was the first time in years and years that she ate dinner with someone she actually liked. He served meat, rice, and some salad, which he said was not Brazilian, but he thought she might like it. All the food was delicious. She had been a bit put off by the look of the chicken hearts, as they looked exactly like what they were. But she was amazed at the richness and complexity of the tastes in the dish. Even if the food hadn't been wonderful, the fact that someone else had prepared it for her made it one of the best meals of her life.

Not someone else, this person you are obsessed with.

"How did you meet Karl?" Caio asked suddenly, shoving a forkful of rice into his mouth, none too daintily and chewing even less daintily.

"What?"

"Karl … that guy … your boyfriend," he asked. His face was expressionless, but he was twirling his fork in circles in the air.

113

"Well, Karl was a partner in the law offices where my husband was a senior partner, before he died," she said.

"I'm sorry," Caio responded.

"It's okay. It was six years ago, so it's been a long time and—" she stopped talking.

She looked up and saw his face, eyes glued to her, but there was no judgment in them.

"And?" he asked.

"And I guess if I am completely honest, it wasn't much of a marriage to begin with."

She laughed a little as she said this but then stopped in horror, realizing what had just come out of her mouth.

"That sounded terrible. I'm sorry, I shouldn't say that sort of thing to you," she stammered.

"That's okay. You don't have to be sorry. I'm a foster kid, remember? I've seen the inside of a lot of marriages. There are some really good ones, but there are more than a few really screwed up ones too."

"Oh, ours wasn't really screwed up. It's just that he thought of me more as his daughter than his wife," she said, beginning to feel unreal. "That might be why he never wanted to have children."

Are you really actually having this conversation with a sixteen-year-old? asked Paul's voice with no small amount of bitterness.

"And you wanted children?" he asked.

"Yes. I did. A lot," she said, almost more to herself.

"Hmmmm. Do you still want them?" he asked.

"With Karl? No. No. And he would never want to have kids. He made that clear when we first started dating. Besides, he had a vasectomy a long time ago."

Stop talking. This is so inappropriate, snapped her mother.

"Karl isn't the only man on the planet," Caio said.

He was still looking directly at her with that open yet unreadable expression. She just laughed and shrugged, hoping for casual but fearing she was failing.

"Well, he may be the only man on the planet who notices me," she said.

Caio's eyes suddenly flashed, and his eyebrows knit together, causing that deep crease to form between his eyes. "Don't say shit like that."

"Excuse me?" she replied, startled that a boy of his age would swear in front of her and defensive in spite of herself.

"Sorry," he said, looking down. "I shouldn't swear, and I know it's none of my business, but I don't like it when people self-denigrate."

Denigrate? Really? What teenager uses that word? Or adult for that matter?

114

"I wasn't—" she started, then realized that she had indeed been doing that. Caio was saying nothing, just looking at her.

"I guess we should set up studying before it gets too late," she said, quickly getting up.

"Yeah. Right. Okay," he said, getting up with her and beginning to clear the table. He was actually cleaning the table. That, as much as anything else, made her feel completely unreal.

She removed the glasses and quickly wiped the table with a sponge.

"You want to get your stuff?" she asked, and he grabbed his bag from the counter where she had placed it after she had retrieved his wallet. This reminded her of what was in his wallet, and she felt lightheaded again.

He pulled books out of the bag with one eye on her, and a slight smile on his face.

"Do you want to start with geography?"

"Hmmmm, yeah. That's the next test I have so I guess that makes the most sense."

"Maybe we should start with going over what exactly you are studying in geography right now," she said, sitting down across from him at the table.

"The distribution, processes and effects of the movement of the human population across our planet," he said, pulling books out of his bag.

Oh shit. I will have to read about this, she thought to herself.

"That's ambitious for tenth grade, isn't it?" she said out loud.

"Yeah, it's the advanced class," he said with a smile.

He's in advanced classes. Why the hell does he need my help?

"Do you have your textbook?"

He nodded and handed it to her.

"We are being tested on chapters twenty-five to thirty-five."

"That's a lot of material," Sarah said, skimming through the book. The material was dense and covered a multitude of causal factors for geographical changes. It was good to have something to focus on as it cleared her brain and distracted her from making ridiculous conclusions about what the hell was going on tonight. This was like reading a brief or a deposition, so it brought a different part of her brain to the surface.

"How do you want me to help you?" she asked, a bit bluntly after reading through the chapters.

"Any way you can," was his answer. She looked up to see that he was staring at her intently again. Flustered, she looked back down at the book.

"Well, to be honest, I'm not sure if I'm much of an expert on any of this stuff. I'm not sure how much help I would be," her analytical brain answered, and her heart heard this with horror.

She looked and saw that Caio's eyes were wide.

"Well, actually, there is a section about the effect of legal enactments on global movement patterns and the consequent changes in environment," he said quickly.

"Wow. Really? That's a cool thing to study," she said. She never remembered studying anything that cool in her high-school classes.

"So, I thought you might be able to help me with that bit. I'm not very good at regulations and legislation and stuff. It all sort of gets blurred inside my head. It changes so much over time," he said, looking up at her from underneath his bangs.

"Yeah. I can definitely help with that. But I will need to read this and then come up with a game plan. How long until your next test?"

"Two weeks," he said.

"Oh. That's not much time and this is a complex subject."

"I can come earlier or something, if that helps."

Sarah's heart bloomed.

"Okay. So, by next week, can you make sure you have finished reading all of this?"

"Yep. I already did actually."

"And will your test be multiple choice or essay?" she asked.

"Both."

"Well, then I can give you a practice test next time you come. Do you need your book this week, or can I borrow it to come up with questions?"

"No, you can have it. I know the material," he replied.

"Also, can you leave me your last few tests, if you have them? It would be good to look over what you have done," Sarah asked.

Caio cringed openly.

"Uh, I have the last one but not the ones before."

"That's fine. I can look at that one."

As she watched, he opened a folder and pulled out a test with a lot of red marks and handed it to her. He quickly closed the folder but not so fast that she didn't see that the paper beneath this one had a large "A" on it.

Why would he—

"Okay. I guess I should go," he said.

"Of course," Sarah said looking up at the clock, it was 9:00. He had been here for two hours, and she had barely noticed the time going by. They had also done no actual studying. She should suggest that he not cook dinner. That would be the adult responsible thing to do. After all, she was supposed to be helping him.

"We didn't get too much studying done, so—" she began.

"It's okay. I'll come earlier next time," he said, and he slung his backpack over his shoulder and backed toward the door.

"Uh, okay. Thanks for dinner, you don't have to—" she began.

"I know, but I want to," he said, his hand on the doorknob. He paused for a second, rocking back and forth between his feet.

"Right. Okay. I'll see you later," he said finally and walked out the door.

Sarah stood in the middle of her kitchen feeling a bit like she had been hit by a truck. She walked to her sink and began to load dishes mechanically into her dishwasher.

Wow, what just happened? Val asked in her head. Sarah could almost see her smirking.

I set up studying sessions, that's all, she responded.

Really, you think that's what this is about? You saw his last grade. It was an A. He's an Advanced Placement student. This kid doesn't need your help, Val said.

Why is he here then? she asked.

Why indeed? said Val.

Don't you start getting yourself worked up or getting ideas in your head. It's not healthy and ideas like this are not ethical. You don't need to be thinking too much about anyone's motivation, said Paul, in a more accusatory tone than usual.

No, of course not. I am sure there's some rational explanation, she told him and herself.

She kept telling herself that at regular intervals as she cleaned up and got ready for bed. But scenes from the evening kept inserting themselves into her head and she found herself just standing and staring at things. The comment he made about men not having innocent motives when they cook for women. The fact that his grades were obviously fine. These things were distracting enough but the physicality of his presence here stopped her in her tracks. She found one of his hairs on the table. He had left the grocery bag in the trash. And when she found that he had surreptitiously boxed the remains of the food and put it in her fridge (when did he do that?), it froze her in front of her fridge until it started beeping.

That night, as she lay in her bed, she felt a deep ache in her gut. It felt like period cramps, but it wasn't that time of the month for her. She finally allowed herself to think about not only about the three things that she had seen in Caio's wallet, but about the implications of them.

The condom was the easiest one to explain. He was either sexually active or hoped to be soon. That wasn't too surprising. He was gorgeous. She was pretty sure he would be sexually active. That thought made the ache in her gut worse.

Then there was the money. If he had 150 dollars, he could easily have paid her, yet he chose to cook for her instead. Maybe he's just saving money? No, sirloin does not come cheap. It would have been cheaper to just pay her $20 or something. She didn't want to read things into this, but she found it hard not to. He had wanted to cook for her. For some reason, he had wanted to do this rather than pay her.

So, was this a date? Val asked.

No. That is a ridiculous thought, said her mother. *Why would a boy who looks like that, and who could get any young girl he wanted, be interested in you? That's just delusional.*

Is it? Did it really play out much like a tutoring session, honey? Even you can't be that blind? Val laughed.

Sarah shook her head. The final thing she saw in his wallet was the most confusing. He had multiple licenses in there. There had been at least two and maybe more. Maybe they were just fake IDs but something about them made her intuition tingle.

As she began to nod off to sleep, she thought about the dream she had about the boy in the hole, and how he had looked like Caio.

Chapter Twenty

Beyond Coincidence

Sunday June 8

Sunday morning Sarah woke up with her heart racing. She sat up in her bed, trying to figure out what was scaring her.

Karl? No, not a current threat. *Work?* No, also not a current threat. So what was she trembling about? Suddenly it hit her. She wasn't scared, she was excited. She was actually feeling excited about her life. She was feeling excited about the world.

Why wouldn't you be? Val asked in her head. *You've had a lot of changes in a short period of time.*

"What changes? Nothing's really changed?" Sarah replied.

Well, to start with, you didn't know that we were here before, said Larry.

"I still don't know you are there. Or that you are real anyway," Sarah said, getting up out of bed and stretching.

Do you really think you can make up the sort of things I would say? asked Val.

"Yes, actually I do," Sarah replied out loud with a laugh.

She had loved Val deeply during their time in school and it had scarred her so much when they fell out after law school, but Val had hated Paul. She hadn't just disliked him, she had passionately hated him. One night they had had a terrible fight over the phone about Val's attendance at her wedding. Sarah had told her that if she didn't come, she wouldn't be able to forgive her. Val hadn't come and they had never spoken again. It still hurt to think about it.

I was wrong, Val said. *I should have come. I should have called you. I should have just told you that I was jealous.*

"Jealous?" Sarah said, stopping mid-route to the bathroom. "What do you mean, jealous?"

Oh, not in a sexual or romantic sense. Well, maybe a bit in the romantic sense. I was jealous that I would be losing the intimacy. You wouldn't be calling me every day or sharing your problems with me or falling asleep on my couch with your head in my lap after watching late-night TV. I was grieving losing those things, and I couldn't just tell you that because I thought you were all head over heels in love with a guy who was an asshole.

"I wasn't," Sarah said softly but out loud.

I know that now. I know it from being in your head. But I can tell you that you were one of the greatest loves of my life and one of the last people I thought about before I died.

"I missed you," Sarah said, tears forming in her eyes. "I still do."

You don't have to anymore. I'm here, laughed Val.

"But how can I know you are real? I've always heard voices in my head."

I know, Val replied. *Odd, isn't it?*

Sarah could feel the knowing grin behind the words.

"How do I know you are anything more than the voices I have always heard? How do I know you are who you say you are? I want to believe that but—"

But you need proof, Larry said. *That's understandable. Ghosts get this all the time.*

How about we tell you a bit about that boy you were "tutoring" last night? Val interjected.

Oh, no, said Paul suddenly, as if he were just waking up. *You don't tell other people's stories. That isn't allowed.*

Hmmm. It is a conundrum. How can we give you proof? muttered Larry. *Paul is right. We can't—well, we shouldn't tell other people's stories. At the very minimum, that's very rude.*

The voices in her head went silent for a moment. Sarah used the moment to go and brush her teeth. She had just finished and was looking at herself in the mirror when she was suddenly taken aback.

She didn't look bad to herself. She didn't look plain or old or ridiculous. In fact, with her tousled hair and freckles, she looked almost cute. She smiled and saw, maybe for the first time, that she had a very sweet smile.

I know, said Larry suddenly in her head. *I can tell you about myself. That's my story. It's not infringing on anyone else's, so it's not breaking any ethical rules or universal codes. I can tell you some things about my life that you wouldn't have known, something that couldn't be coincidence. But you would also need to be able to look it up.*

I don't think Sarah needs any more distractions from work or her real life. She has had enough problems with that in her life, she— began her mother but her voice was suddenly cut off.

Don't worry about her. I got her covered … literally, said Val.

Sarah smiled as she headed downstairs. When she opened her fridge, she saw again the food that Caio had boxed the night before and, for a moment, felt so dizzy that she had to sit down on the floor. After her head cleared, she took the box out gingerly and opened it. He had arranged the leftover meat on top of the rice.

It's easy to microwave that way, she thought to herself, with a flush of heat in her chest. She then took the box and put it in the microwave. Normally, she would have added some water to the rice, but she didn't want to make changes to anything he had done.

Her phone pinged as she was eating. It was a text from Michael.

We need to change court dates for the Henderson case. Know it's short notice. Can you do first thing Monday morning?

Of course. Will go direct to courthouse Monday, Sarah replied. Monday was usually a mess at the courthouse, so it was always better to get there early.

The food Caio had made was even better today. As she sat down at her kitchen table and ate, she thought again about the night before. He had been uncomfortable in the beginning but once she had mentioned this, he had seemed to relax. In fact, by the end, he hadn't seemed any more eager to go than she had been to have him leave.

During the course of the day, Sarah thought several times about going to the grocery store with the hope of seeing him playing basketball, but she didn't. She didn't want to leave her house right now. It still smelled of the food that he prepared, and she still found little things to remind her that he had been there. A rearrangement of things in her fridge, a grain of rice on the floor and even a footprint on her Welcome mat. She wanted to stay in here with these things. Also, she was afraid that he would be cold and distant with her if he saw her while he was with his friends. She didn't want to deal with that just now.

Plus, I'll see him next Saturday. He will come here again. And he said he wanted to come earlier.

Instead of going outside, Sarah pulled out the textbook he had left with her. The material was dense and complex. It was clearly an advanced course, and it was challenging even for that. Sarah spent the next few hours reading through the text and coming up with questions related to the material. She wanted to make it challenging for him, but she also wanted to be realistic. It was hard to know what he would know and what he wouldn't know, but she decided to target it as a high-school senior question. Somehow, that felt right to her.

After a few hours had gone by, a voice interrupted her study.

Okay. Hmmm, I think I have one for you. Have you read, heard, or deduced anything about my family of origin? Larry asked her suddenly.

"No."

Did I tell you much about it when you were my student? I did speak to you more out of class than most of my other students.

"No."

Good. Well, then let me tell you that I was a twin, but my sibling died when I was born. That isn't information that most people would be able to track down or that most people would know, Larry said. *So go and see if this is true. Her name was Linda.*

Sarah nodded to herself and went to her computer. For some, this search might have taken a long time but not for Sarah. A few clicks on Ancestry.com followed by a couple of public records searching came up with "Linda Boger", who was the stillborn sister of Larry Boger.

Sarah sat back in her chair, staring at the screen. There was no way she could have known this. This information was in no way a part of the personal knowledge database in her head. This information came from somewhere else. Either she had developed some sort of psychic ability, or it was as she was being told—there were ghosts in her head.

Right now, said ghosts were very quiet. Sarah got up and walked outside to stand on her front porch. The sun was now low on the horizon, the day almost gone. Time in the outside world had raced forward while she was in the bubble of her house.

Yet, despite the bubble, she could feel her world was expanding around her. She wondered where it would stop.

Chapter Twenty-One

Dating With the Damned

Monday June 9

Sarah got up early Monday morning and was at the courthouse when it opened. She had received another text from Michael last night telling her that, in addition to changing the Henderson court date to a later time, she should also try to get a temporary restraining order started for Mrs. Stetz. Mrs. Stetz was a new client with an abusive and volatile ex-husband, who had apparently broken into her car over the weekend. Her car was an expensive but older model with a CD player and the ex had inserted CD of a woman screaming into it, so it was the first thing she heard when she turned her car on that morning. As a result, Mrs. Stetz was more than a little freaked out. Michael forwarded her the paperwork for the restraining order on her phone. He suggested that she could print it out at the courthouse.

When Sarah got to the courthouse, she immediately went to the see Laura in the clerk's office to borrow her printer. Laura was short, curvy, with curly salt-and-pepper hair and strong opinions. She was also smarter than most of the attorneys that she worked with and the unofficial matron of the courthouse. Most of the attorneys referred to her as "the pistol." If she didn't like you, she could make things very difficult. But you had to be a serious asshole to make Laura dislike you.

Laura was already logged in and looking at her computer when Sarah got there. She was an early riser.

"Good morning, Laura," Sarah said, coming up to the reception desk.

"Hey there lady, I haven't seen you in a while," Laura said, beaming, but when Laura saw Sarah's face her smile faded. She raised her eyebrows. Sarah knew that Laura had seen lots of this before, so she didn't need to be told what had happened. Laura was an unusual combination: an outspoken woman who could also keep her thoughts to herself.

"What do you need today, beauty?" she asked.

"I was just wondering if you could print some documents from my phone. I have a temporary restraining order to file."

"Of course, of course," Laura said, taking Sarah's phone. For a moment, Sarah felt panic. She still had the picture of Caio on her phone. But then she relaxed. Even if she saw it, it would mean nothing to Laura.

"What have you been up to these days?" she asked, eyes on her computer as she uploaded the paperwork.

"Same old, same old," Sarah lied. "I have to reschedule the Henderson hearing. And then the protective order."

"Isn't your firm working on the Davies case? I heard that the ex-wife is filing for change of circumstances."

"Yes, we are. But how did you hear about that?"

"Everyone has heard about it. It was a really nasty divorce the first time out. Have they got you researching it?"

Sarah nodded. Laura gave a low whistle.

"Get ready to lose your faith in humanity," she said softly. "Have you spoken with Scott Thomas yet?"

"No, who is he?"

"You don't know him? You've probably run into him around here. He runs a spy shop downtown. But he's a huge ancestry buff, and he occasionally does part-time research work for people looking for their roots. He comes in here to look for court records."

"But who is he to this case?" Sarah asked.

"He's Anne Marie Davies's ex-husband, that's who. I guess they haven't wanted to fill you in on him yet. But if this is going to trial, and rumor is that it will, you better know about him because the other side will reference him at a minimum."

"Do you know where his shop is?"

"It's called Spy Gifts and it's on Union Street," Laura said, as she pulled the petition for temporary restraining order off the printer and handed it to Sarah.

"You should go, girl," she said, meeting Sarah's eyes and holding them. "Even if your attorneys don't tell you to, you should see what you can see there."

Sarah noted the name and address of Spy Gifts as she was filing the petition. As she had come to the courthouse very early, she had the petition filed and the court date changed by a little after 10 a.m. Michael wouldn't expect her in until after lunch. Without much more thought on the matter, Sarah typed the address of Spy Gifts into the GPS in her car and started driving in that direction.

Spy Gifts was not an opulent shop by any stretch of the imagination, nor was it particularly large. It was a tiny store with a black front and a black awning with a red and white sign that proclaimed nothing but its name. It was sandwiched between a paint store and a pizzeria.

Once inside, it was not as dark as she had been expecting from the somber exterior. The lighting was good and there were lots of display cases around with bluish-white lights highlighting them. A man was standing behind a display case at the back of the store. He looked up, a bit startled, as she walked in.

"Can I help you?" he asked.

Sarah realized that she hadn't concocted a story, so she made one up fast.

"No. Well, actually yes, I was wondering if you had anything that takes pictures? You know, that someone wouldn't know was a camera," she asked.

"Sure, we have lots of hidden cameras," the man said, stepping out from behind the counter. "What sort of resolution do you need?"

Think quick. What would you be taking photos of? Legal documents.

"I just want to be able to take some photos of some documents that's all," she said.

"Nothing illegal though," she added quickly.

"Divorce?" he asked, staring at her face.

"Yes" she said. "I think he has assets that he's hiding."

"If you think he does, then it's likely that he does. Did he do that to you?" he asked bluntly, looking at her face. This fading bruise was turning out to be a door opener for her in some perverse way.

"Yes."

"Fucker," he muttered under his breath. "Sorry."

"No, you are completely right. He's an asshole," Sarah said.

"I'm Scott, by the way. I own this place," he said, extending his hand to her. She took it. It was dry and cool.

"I'm Lila," Sarah lied.

"So, Lila. What situation will you be in when you want to take the pictures? Will the asshole be near you?"

"Yes. And I won't have much time to do it or a lot of chances. I need to make sure that the photo works the first time. I have been postponing a meeting with him just so I can have something."

"Then glasses are best," Scott said, handing her a pair of innocuous-looking black-framed glasses. They looked a bit like Sarah's reading glasses. These were not cheap plastic things; they were fashionable high-end frames.

"They have a camera in the bridge of the nose. They also have lenses that will darken in the sun, so you can wear them like sunglasses," said Scott.

"I bet those are really expensive."

"Yes. They are kind of expensive. Before you waste money, I should ask if this document isn't something that you or your attorney can just request through discovery. That would be much easier," Scott asked.

"No. It's something he claims not to have. But if you know the word 'discovery' then it sounds like you went through a divorce as well," she said with a smile.

"Oh yeah. I did. It was really nasty."

"Well, at least she probably didn't divorce you because she thought you were 'old and dried-up,'" Sarah said, a tremble coming into her voice. The tremble was real. She could still find the pain in that statement.

"Son of bitch didn't actually say that, did he?" Scott asked.

Sarah nodded.

"Listen. You are neither. And don't you go thinking all men are bad because of this. We aren't. My ex was a monster, and she was a woman, but I refused to let that make me think all women are bad. I have a girlfriend now who would be very unhappy if I thought that," he said with a smile.

"Is that why you got into this business, because of your divorce?" she asked. Scott shrugged.

"Indirectly yes. I wanted to be a historian growing up. I wanted to go to NYU and get a PhD in history, but I didn't have that kind of money, so I went to a junior college. I met my future ex-wife there. But it's a pretty gruesome story," he said.

"I'm okay with gruesome. She can't be any worse than my ex," Sarah said. Scott laughed.

"Oh, for your sake, I hope that's not true," he said. Sarah raised her eyebrows at him.

"You want to hear? You sure?" he said. Sarah nodded.

"Okay. Well, I should start by saying that I actually met Anne Marie at a Nyotaimori restaurant that one of my friends dragged me to. Do you know what that is?"

Sarah shook her head.

"It's the Japanese restaurants where they serve sushi from a naked woman's body. Yeah, I know," he said, stopping. Sarah must have looked shocked, and she was. She wasn't shocked by the practice. She'd heard of it. She was shocked that super-clean gingham woman had done that.

"You still want me to go on?" he asked.

Sarah nodded.

"Okay. Well Anne Marie was a model there. I thought she was so beautiful, but I forgot about her a couple of days after we left. Then, later, I saw her at school. She had an economics class with me, and she recognized me. She caught me after class and asked me not to say anything. She told me at the time that she was just doing that to save enough money to start her own business. She loved horses and wanted to start a company that made saddles. I thought it was charming. I thought she was charming," he said, shrugging a bit.

"After that we started dating. I was crazy about her. I barely flinched when I found out that she was doing fetish modeling as well. She swore that she didn't engage in any sex in these things, and I believed her. Crazy what you will believe when you are in love, right?" he said.

Sarah nodded.

"We got married just after we graduated. Well, around that time, my father died. About six months later, I lost my mother as well. Even though my parents weren't super-wealthy, they left me a pretty sizable chunk of money, what with their life insurance and savings. I could have used that to go to NYU, but Anne Marie convinced me to use it to start the leather business. She said once the business was up and running, we would have loads of cash, so I could pursue my PhD or anything else I wanted to do. So I agreed. I was crazy about her, and she was crazy about the business."

Sarah said nothing. Scott wasn't looking at her. His eyes were unfocused, staring into the distance.

"And she was great at it, the business I mean," he continued. "She made all the contacts. She found the vendors. She sorted out a website. Basically, I did the money and accounting, and she did the rest. I didn't think about her contacts. I didn't even pay much attention to what we were selling. Everything was great."

He sighed and shrugged.

"Until I got a call from one of our employees saying that she was quitting because she was being sexually harassed. The girl was eighteen years old and barely coherent over the phone. So, I met her for coffee, and what she told me … well, at first I couldn't believe it. She said most of the buyers of our leather goods were not equestrians but owners of sex shops and fetish enthusiasts. She said that Anne Marie had encouraged some of the women who worked there to go to certain parties at certain clubs wearing their leather gear. Like I said, I didn't believe it at first. Of course I didn't. Anne Marie was my wife."

"But later that week, I went to our factory after closing hours, and I caught Anne Marie having sex with one of the managers there. I say 'having sex' very loosely. He was doing things to her. It was—well, it was disgusting. But it got a lot more disgusting after that. First, I moved out and filed for divorce. Initially I put up a fight. I was hurt and I wanted her to hurt as well. Then as our court date got closer, I started noticing weird things. When I got home from work, things in my apartment would not be in the same places that I left them. Once the table had been moved to the other side of the room. Another time the fridge door was open, and everything inside completely warm and had to be thrown out. Finally, I found a dead dog in my bathtub. I don't know whose dog it was, but it wasn't one of those little ones. It was a golden retriever. No more than a few minutes after I found the dog, I got a phone call from Anne Marie's lawyer. He said that they would like to settle the estate without having it contested. Somehow, I knew that they were watching me and had been watching me all this time. I was freaked out, but I met with them. Her attorneys really did look like something out of a mafia movie, and they offered me a deal I couldn't re-fuse. Anne Marie would get the business. In exchange I would get a huge wad of cash and a promise that she would never contact me again. Of course, that was meant to convey the message that none of her 'friends' would 'contact me' either. I got the hint and took the money. It was better anyway. I had no desire to have anything to do with what that business had become."

There were no tears in Scott's eyes, but his face looked blank and haunted. These stories put paid to statements like "It is better to have loved and lost than never to have loved at all." Clearly it was not true in a case like Scott's.

"I'm so sorry," Sarah whispered. Scott shook his head and gave her a small smile.

"I told you it was bad. But the good thing is that I got paid a lot more than I got from my parents' estate. It was easily five or ten times as much. I'm pretty sure that I was paid much more than the value of the business. I guess that's because she had influential clients. In fact, she's now married to some big-shot business guy."

Sarah wanted to ask more questions about that, but she didn't want to appear suspicious. As she glanced at her watch, she realized that it was already 11:30.

"Have I freaked you out with my awful story?" Scott asked.

"Oh, no. Not at all. I just need to get back to work by noon. I've been here longer than I realized."

"Time flies when you are listening to a train wreck," Scott said smiling.

Sarah laughed a bit.

"Listen, I really appreciate you telling me about it. It makes me feel less alone in this. But I should get going or my boss will yell," she said.

"Here," Scott said, handing her the glasses she had been looking at. "You go ahead and take these."

"Thanks, they are great, but I am sure I can't afford them," she said, smiling.

"That's not a problem because I'm giving them to you," he said. "I don't mean to be rude but the bruise on your cheek says you may need as much help as you can get. I'm not short of money here, so it makes me happy to think that I could help someone, particularly if that someone is a pretty lady."

He said this last bit with a wink. His heart appeared to not be really in it, but he was trying.

"Thank you. I don't know what to say."

"You don't have to say anything. Hey, it's a floor model, so it's already set up to work. It also has a memory card in it. Here's the manual," he said, dropping a small booklet into a store bag and handing it to her.

"Just promise me that you will be careful. There are some scary people out there in the world. I wish I had known that before I got married. I might have seen what was coming if I had."

Sarah nodded and smiled.

When she got outside, she put the glasses on. Scott had been right. They did work as sunglasses, turning the sunshine of the day into shadows.

Chapter Twenty-Two

Accidental Bullets

Monday June 9

From the moment Sarah stepped into the offices of Culp, Moore & Rosen on Monday afternoon, she knew that something inside her had changed. She couldn't continue to close her eyes to the little evils that were around her every day. The place was a cesspool and if she continued to contribute to it then she was contributing to that evil. She could no more do that than she could continue to accept Karl's nastiness. Something in her had flipped. She wasn't sure when exactly it had happened. Was it her conversation with Scott Thomas, which confirmed what she already felt about the Davies clan? Was it the dinner she had had with Caio, which gave her a peek into what life would be like with a kind person? Was it when she was given some evidence that the voices in her head were not simply a sign of her mental instability or weakness? Or was it simply when Karl hit her? In the end, maybe it didn't matter. Her world was changing, and she felt that she could either embrace these changes or be consumed by them.

The work that she did from this point onward would be at odds with the firm because now she would do whatever she had to in order to save Alex Davies. While she didn't actually know that Andrew Davies was into the BDSM scene, she did know that his wife was, so it seemed very likely that he would be as well. And while Sarah had no qualms with kink between consenting adults, as long as there was consent, she knew from personal experience that consent was a malleable thing. Was it consent if she agreed to something only because she was afraid of repercussions? If the repercussions were physical, then of course. But what if the repercussions were emotional, or the withholding of approval? Would that be real consent? On the child question, it was not a question: a child could not consent to this sort of behavior.

And could a child consent to a romantic relationship with a grown woman? Paul asked, but she brushed his voice aside.

"This is not about Caio," she said.

Is it not? Are you sure you aren't trying to save Alex as a way to relieve the guilt you feel about desiring that other teenage boy? Paul asked.

Val, are you there? she asked inside her head.

Of course, honey. I am always here, Val replied.

Then can you shut those two up while I work? she asked.

My pleasure, said Val. And Sarah's head suddenly became strangely serene.

Sarah sat down at her desk, started her computer and faked scanning emails as her brain raced. If she broke this down, the facts painted a picture that was hard to misconstrue. Melissa Taylor had testified to seeing Andrew Davies sexually molesting their son in the initial divorce. According to Melissa, Andrew and a psychiatrist had done their best to try to convince Melissa that she was crazy. Alex would not admit to the abuse, but much of his behavior was consistent with a boy who had been abused. There were the weird things written in Anne Marie's scrapbook about the evils of second marriages, even though both she and Andrew were in second marriages, not to mention all the scripture verses about fornication. And now, she had verbal confirmation that Anne Marie had a business that serviced the BDSM community and that she had forced employees to engage in that world without their consent.

There was no question in her mind now that Alex Davies was being abused. The problem was that all the evidence she had was either hearsay or circumstantial. She had no smoking gun. If she was going to give information to the district attorney or leak it to Phillip Seider, then she would need the smoking gun. She needed Alex to be willing to make a statement under oath that he had been abused. Or she needed someone else who had witnessed it to come forward, someone besides Melissa, who they had painted as crazy. Or she needed photos. She had none of these things.

Sarah was sitting at her desk, pondering this as she replied to emails, when Michael came out of his office.

"Sarah, I need you to dig a little more on Melissa Taylor this week. Seider moved to change the judge because the judge we had was a friend of mine from law school. It's ridiculous, because there are so many of us who know each other from law school."

"Are you arguing it?" Sarah asked. Michael cut his eyes downward and looked away.

131

"No. We have to pick our battles on this one. The new judge he's suggesting is fair enough, and she's a woman, which means that we will be less likely to be accused of any sort of bias related to gender."

Sarah nodded.

"But that means that the new judge won't have seen Melissa Taylor's craziness first-hand. So we will need to prove that again. Can you look at that this week?"

Sarah nodded. As he walked back into his office, the phone rang.

"Culp, Moore and Rosen."

"Hi Sarah. It's Karl," the sound of his voice made her skin crawl.

"Hi Karl," she said.

"How has your day been so far?"

Karl had never once asked her that. Ever. At any point.

"Fine," she replied.

"I was wondering if I could take you to dinner on Thursday night. We could go to the new sushi bar that opened. What do you think of that?"

Is there a way you can get out of this without it looking suspicious? No. But you can get out of part of the date with illness, but she couldn't do that until the last minute and it wasn't assured.

"Sarah, are you there?" he asked.

"Yes. It's just that I have a lot of work for the Davies case. Michael just asked me to get some more information on Melissa."

"That's fine. It doesn't have to be a long date. I understand if you are suspicious. We can just get a quick bite. Oh, and I have a few mortgage papers for you to sign, but that's no big deal," he said.

Papers to sign? How interesting.

"Okay," Sarah replied.

"Good. Maybe I can pick you up from the office on Thursday at around six? Is that too early?"

"No, that's fine."

"Great. I'll see you on Thursday, honey," he said before hanging up. Sarah held back the urge to gag.

Honey? Really? Gross.

He's making an effort, Sarah, said her mother.

"Val?"

Sorry, that slipped through. I'm on it. It's not easy though, said Val. As if to prove the point, Sarah heard the voice of her dead husband next.

You are being hypersensitive about this firm, this case, AND Karl. You know, I always told you that you were too sensitive for the practice of law.

Shutting him down, said Val. And then there was quiet in her head.

It didn't really matter. Sarah knew that her reactions had nothing to do with the practice of law, per se. She had no problem with the concept that everyone deserved representation. She had no problem with the idea that everyone is innocent until proven guilty. It was how these concepts played out when put into practice that distinguished between ethical and unethical. A prime example was right in front of her. Lawyers hold the notion of attorney/client privilege and confidentiality as sacred, even though there were definite requirements to report child sexual abuse. Attorneys had developed ways of "not knowing" certain facts about their clients and clients had learned not to admit to anything. So, what about kids like Alex Davies? After her conversation with Scott Thomas, she knew that her firm knew Anne Marie's history.

The brain is an elastic thing.

Sarah got a flash of intuition. She typed those words into a search engine. Nothing came up initially. But when she narrowed the search to only blogs, she found that this phrase was used in the signature block of someone called Gaslight44. Bingo. This was Melissa for sure. She did a quick search under this name and her screen was filled with hits. Some were from abuse forums, others were from boards that looked like they were all about conspiracy theories, with titles like "AliensAmongUs" or "Y files" or "Illuminati are here." Sarah had just opened one when she felt a presence at her shoulder.

"What's that?" asked Angela, who had returned to her desk.

"Nothing. I was just looking at some of the forums that Melissa Taylor visits," Sarah replied, regretting the words the minute they were out of her mouth.

"Aliens Among Us?" Angela said loudly. "Yeah, she's a fruitcake."

As black serendipity would have it, Michael was coming out of his office at that moment.

"Who's a fruitcake?" he asked.

"Sarah just found a whole list of forums that Melissa Taylor is on. You should see this. It's great."

Michael immediately came over and leaned over her shoulder.

"This *is* great. This looks like the profile of a complete paranoid. But how do you know it's her?"

Come up with something quick. No. Wait. It's okay. Tell the truth. They already know.

"When I saw her at the bookstore, she said that her relationship with her ex was like *Gaslight*, the movie. Her handle is the movie and the date of the movie. Plus, she has the statement 'the brain is an elastic thing' in her signature. And she said those exact words in the deposition. I googled them and found this."

Michael patted her on the shoulder. "You really are amazing, do you know that? I've never worked with someone as good at research as you. This is fantastic. And it's out there for the public to see. Well done, Sarah. Remarkably well done."

Sarah tried to smile but she felt like she had a knife in her stomach. They were going to use this to paint Melissa as a crazy again. She felt like she had just betrayed a friend.

"You know, you should just take the rest of the day off, Sarah. You have more than earned your pay today."

Angela laughed out loud.

"Michael, it's already 5:30," she said. She stopped laughing when Michael cut her a venomous look. That was the sort of slip-up Angela didn't usually make. One did not correct Michael Angel—ever.

"Of course, of course," he said sweetly, but with an edge. "Well, maybe Angela can take your calls and emails for the rest of the week. That way you can focus more on this Davies case. You wouldn't mind that, would you, Angela?"

"Of course not," Angela replied, smiling but with her teeth alone.

Michael then strode out of the office.

"Asshole," Angela muttered under her breath.

"Listen. You don't have to do that," Sarah said. "I can catch my own calls. But we'll tell him you did."

Angela whirled on her.

"I don't need your pity," she snapped.

"I'm not giving you any. I just don't think that was fair," Sarah snapped back. Angela's eyes widened but then a different look came into them.

It was that same look of fear she had seen before. The same one she had seen in Karl's eyes. As she packed her things to go, she racked her brain for reasons that they might be afraid of her.

But she could find none.

Thursday June 12

The idea of wearing the surveillance glasses on her date with Karl did not come to her until she was already at work on Wednesday. She had been carefully filtering the work that she did on the Davies case during her working hours. She didn't want to have a repeat of Monday, when she unintentionally handed Michael a weapon against Melissa. Instead, she was answering calls and emails. When Michael gave her a warning look as she was talking on the phone, she pointed to her screen, which had a picture of Melissa from one of the forums, and he smiled and gave her a thumbs-up. The picture was nothing, but it gave the appearance that she was working on this. What she was really working on was reading through what Melissa had discussed in the forums to find clues regarding Anne Marie and Andrew Davies's potential BDSM activities. As they already knew about Melissa's moniker and presence on the forums, it didn't hurt for her to scan them. The fact that Melissa said nothing particular incendiary or crazy on those forums made her feel a bit better. Most of Melissa's comments were conciliatory responses to people who were going through a rough time.

It was while she was reading one of these that the idea came to her. Someone had written that he was sure that he had been followed for years by beings that were too fast to be seen and that he was scared. Melissa wrote a conciliatory note saying that she was sure that even if he was being followed, surely nothing meant to hurt him if it had been happening for years. This was a nice, bland response. It was the next statement that piqued Sarah's interest.

"Dude, you should wear some of those glasses that record video. Get a recording of everything around you and then play it back slow-mo. You should be able to see the things if they are there."

Hmmm, well, maybe your glasses are fit for documents after all, said Larry's smiling voice in her head.

Documents … Karl said that he wanted her to sign documents tonight. It was about time she started really reading these things, but Karl never let her do this. If she asked now, he would be suspicious, but if she could wear the glasses and get a photo of it, then she could at least get an idea of what she was dealing with.

The problem was that the glasses were at home. And it was 4:30, so she wouldn't really have a good excuse to go home and get them. She would need to call Karl and get him to come to the house, as much as she didn't want to do that.

She picked up the phone and dialed Karl's cell phone. Usually, he didn't pick up when she called him but today he picked up on the second ring.

"Sarah, how nice to hear from you. Is everything okay?" he asked.

"Oh, I'm fine. I was just wondering if you could pick me up at the house. I spilled something on my skirt and I want to change before we go out," she lied.

"You don't have to do that for me, I am happy with you the way you are," Karl lied back.

"Well, I would rather not look horrible tonight. If that's okay with you of course," she said in a simpering tone.

"Whatever you want is fine with me. Should I pick you up at your place at six?"

"That's great," she said and then hung up. She looked up at the clock and it was almost five. She would need to get home and figure out how to use those glasses before Karl got there.

She buzzed Michael in his office. "Yep," he answered.

"Hey Michael. I'm getting the beginnings of a migraine. I think it's from all the caffeine this week. Is it okay if I kick off a bit early? Also, I have a date with Karl."

"A date with Karl. Oh, that's good news. Of course, go on and leave. Like I said on Monday, you earned your keep for the week by Monday afternoon."

Sarah virtually ran home from the office. None of the boys were on the court today, which was both a relief and a disappointment. She would have loved to see Caio, but she wouldn't have had the time to talk.

When she got home, she got the glasses out. True to what Scott at Spy Gifts had said, they were quite easy to operate. There was a button on the bridge of the nose you pushed to take photos and videos. These were transferred to a TF card. She took a couple of pictures quickly and transferred the data to her computer. Sure enough, she was able to see the photos she took.

She had just put them on when Karl knocked at her door.

Wow, he knocked.

"Hi," she said as she opened the door. She was praying that he wouldn't notice that she was wearing her "reading glasses" to dinner. Turns out she had no worries on that account.

"Hi Sarah. You look lovely tonight," Karl replied. "Are you ready to go?"

Sarah nodded and walked with him to the car.

Rather than the usual tense silence that she was required to fill, Karl started telling her about an article he had read in *The Economist* that predicted that research skills would become even more valued in the job market.

"Maybe you should ask for a raise at work, rabbit," he said, reaching over and patting her hand. She had to bite the inside of her cheek to keep from jerking it back.

"Should I talk to Michael about that?" he asked.

Fuck him, you can deal with your own career, Val growled in her head.

"If you don't mind, that would be great," was what she said out loud. And she said it in her best sweet, simpering voice.

"I'll do it first thing tomorrow," Karl said.

When they got to the new sushi bar, they discovered it was one that had a conveyor belt to deliver the food. Normally, Karl would have had a fit about this. He would have considered it too much like "mall sushi," but today all he said was "looks like fun."

They hadn't been seated for five minutes before Karl pulled a pack of papers out of his briefcase.

"Here, before we start eating, can you just sign this mortgage stuff so I can take care of it for you," Karl said, turning the document to the last page to sign. As he was handing it to her, she noticed the bowl of soy sauce and saw her chance. She reached out to take it and knocked the bowl over on to the document.

"Oh Karl, I'm so sorry," she said, grabbing the documents and a napkin to blot the soy sauce from the signing page. She then closed the document pretending to wipe the sides. As she pushed her glasses back up on her nose, she pressed the photo button as many times as she dared. Karl had frozen for only a few moments before reaching out to take the documents back from her.

"Don't panic Sarah, it's just a little bit of soy sauce," he said, with a smile that looked predatory. "It won't invalidate the document or anything. Look, the signing page only has a tiny stain. You can just sign here."

He handed it back toward her with a pen. But this time, he didn't take his eyes off it as she signed it. Afterward, he smiled and put the papers back in his briefcase. He was happy and chirpy for the rest of the meal. Sarah smiled and played along, hoping and praying that she'd got a good photo of the documents. She hadn't been able to see much in those few seconds, but what she thought she saw was causing her stomach to twist with anger. She ate very little but smiled a lot and laughed at his horrible attempt at jokes. Karl's jokes were always of the mean variety, and that didn't change even when he was trying this hard to be nice.

Although they were only in the restaurant for about an hour, it felt like an eternity to Sarah. She was holding everything she felt inside, concentrating on watching Karl chew his food and talk. She was struck by how different she had felt eating with Caio. Karl had impeccable restaurant manners. He never spilled his food. He never ate with his mouth open. He never used the wrong utensil. He was completely at ease and dexterous with chopsticks. And yet he always looked like he got exactly zero enjoyment out of it. When she had been eating with Caio the other night, his manners had not been even close to that level of impeccable. He wasn't rude but he talked and ate at the same time. He laughed and ate at the same time. He used his utensils to illustrate points. But he had obviously enjoyed not only the eating process but eating with her. He hadn't been focused on propriety. He had been focused on enjoyment.

Imagine having sex with someone like that, said Val, but Sarah promptly shut her down. She couldn't afford this sort of thought, particularly now.

When it was time to go, Karl took her home and didn't make any attempt to come inside. He simply kissed her on the cheek at the front door.

Sarah watched the clock. She wanted to wait at least thirty minutes before putting the TF card in the computer. When she finally did, the images that came up were too blurry to read in any detail. She had been taking them too quickly for the camera to focus well. Either that or she had moved. Despite that, one thing that was clear. The document she had signed was a trust report, and it had her name on it.

So, her dead husband *had* left her a trust, and no one had told her about it.

Chapter Twenty-Three

Time and Trusts

Friday June 13

It was well after midnight when Sarah went upstairs and lay down on her bed. Her brain was reeling about the document she had seen. She was sure that it was a trust set up for her by Paul. But in all the years since his death, she had never received notice of such a trust.

Have you not? asked Val. *What about all those papers that Karl got you to sign after Paul's death? The ones that he told you were simply about him taking over the payment of your bills and mortgage. What about those?*

Sarah thought back but she could remember almost nothing about that time. She had been terrified when Paul died. She had become dependent on him during the course of their marriage. After he died, she had had no idea of what to do. She didn't have a job. She didn't even know where her insurance papers were. In their life together, Paul had taken care of all of that. At his death, she had mentally shut down. Karl had stepped in and had taken care of everything. He had come to her house and gone through all her paperwork. The large house she had lived in with Paul had been sold to cover the cost of the funeral and to pay for the debts that Paul had incurred with the firm. At least, that's what Karl had told her at the time. He had also found this small house for her and had secured the mortgage.

Sarah, you and Paul were living in a four-million-dollar house. He was the partner at a large law firm. He wasn't a spendthrift. What sort of debts could he have had? Val asked in her head.

"I don't know," Sarah said.

You could start by asking, Val said.

"What?"

Well, if he is taking up space in your brain, the least he could do is provide a bit of information, Val said dryly.

Of course, why hadn't she thought of that?

So, Paul. You are strangely silent, Sarah said tentatively into her head.

There was silence.

Paul, I need you to tell me if you left a trust for me, she said louder, her voice echoing inside her own skull.

She closed her eyes and saw herself standing in a dark room. Val was standing beside her. Larry Boger appeared at a desk near her.

Paul, Larry said. *Sarah's talking to you. If you are staying here, then there is a requirement that you come when called.*

I can't answer her question, he said, appearing next to Larry's desk. *It's against the rules.*

A book suddenly appeared in front of Larry. It was deep blue but covered with silver writing that Sarah couldn't discern.

It doesn't say anything here about you not being able to answer a question that is related to her life.

But it's my story, Paul said, crossing his hands over his chest.

No, it's your shared story, said Larry. *And you aren't prevented from telling your story anyway.*

You fucking bastard, Val snarled, getting right up in his face. *What are you afraid of?*

Paul backed up, looking at Sarah with large, scared eyes.

She walked toward him. *Paul, did you leave me a trust?*

He nodded, his eyes to the ground.

And Paul, did you assign Karl to be the trustee? she asked.

He nodded.

Why didn't you just leave me the money?

I didn't think you could handle it, Sarah. It's a lot of money, he said.

"I can handle money, Paul. Or I could have figured it out," she said softly.

No, Sarah. You don't know what kind of money I am talking about. It's an amount of money that could put you in danger. It could make you a target. It could draw unscrupulous people to you, Paul said, with a voice that sounded close to panic.

You mean more unscrupulous than Karl!? Val yelled. *What the fuck were you thinking?*

Sarah held her hand up to Val. She then moved even closer to Paul. She felt like he had stabbed her in the heart.

Did you hate me, Paul? she whispered. *I mean, we may not have had the most romantic relationship, but I never would have thought that you hated me. You put my life in this guy's hands. He doesn't care about me. He certainly doesn't love me. And he hurts me. Why would you do that to me? Why, unless you hated me?*

Paul's eyes filled with tears.

I didn't know that he was like that. I mentored him. I got him his first jobs. I coached him through his whole career. I thought he would feel a sense of duty to me and therefore a sense of duty to you. And I knew he was a really good attorney, Paul whispered.

Paul, were you that stupid? Sarah asked. *Did you think being a good attorney meant that he would be a good person? Or that he would do the right thing? After everything you told me about lawyers and working in a law firm? You really didn't see what he was like after knowing him for almost ten years?*

Paul's jaw clenched.

Well, you didn't read him much better, he muttered.

Sarah laughed. *Actually, I've known that Karl is a shit for years now. I just haven't had the guts to do anything about it, but that changes now. And if any of you can't deal with that, then I suggest you find someone else's brain to inhabit.*

She turned to face all of them. Val was beaming and clapping slowly. Larry nodded as her mother and father scowled at the ground. When she turned back to Paul, he kept his eyes on the floor.

"Okay, so for now, I'm going to bed and—" Sarah began.

We'll help you sleep, Larry said softly. *There are some things that can be accomplished more easily because you have ghosts in your head. One of them is sleeping.*

With that Sarah opened her eyes just long enough to pull off her clothes and crawl into bed.

She had one final thought as she felt her consciousness slip away.

If Paul left me that much money, what have they done with it?

#

By the time Sarah got to the office the next morning it was already 8:15. This was much later than she usually arrived and most of the other admin staff and paralegals were already in the office. She had planned to call Laura at the court to see if she could surreptitiously get some information about the trust that Paul set up, but she didn't really know how to start. She didn't have long to contemplate this because her phone started ringing off the hook the moment she got in the door.

It was about 10 a.m. when she got a different sort of call.

"Culp, Moore and Rosen," she answered.

"May I speak with Michael Angel please?" asked a male voice. The voice was soft, but Sarah knew the sound of menace when she heard it.

"Michael's in court today, may I take a message?" she replied.

"This is Phillip Seider, Melissa Taylor's attorney. With whom am I speaking?"

"This is Sarah Baker. I am Michael's paralegal."

"Ah, yes. Sarah. I've heard nothing but good things about you. So please don't take what will be my aggressive tone personally," he said.

"I don't take anything personally at work," Sarah lied.

"Good for you. Well, then would you please tell Michael to call me back the moment he calls in. And if his client threatens Melissa's son one more time, we will press for an emergency change of custody. And I won't give a rat's ass how many hours I have to put in, or how long it takes, I will make that happen. Do you have that?"

"Of course, I will tell him. But just for clarity, do you want me to specify which child," she asked. She was digging a bit.

"He knows the child, and his asshole client knows the child. Excuse my language," Phillip said, but his voice was calm. Sarah understood why he was so respected. He had not raised his voice once in this conversation, but his level of menace was pointed and intense.

"I will relay your message immediately," Sarah said.

"Thank you, Sarah. And once again, please do not take this personally. I hope you have a wonderful rest of your day."

Sarah put the phone down gently. Normally, that sort of message would be something left on voicemail or sent in email. It was unorthodox to relay through a paralegal. It wasn't strictly unethical, but it was unorthodox. And during the conversation, she got the distinct impression that he wanted her to know something, but she didn't know what. There was no way he could know or guess what was happening in her world and how she was turning against the people in this office. Unless he had already seen someone go through that.

Phillip's wife was Michael's ex-fiancée, and she left him during the first court battles on this same case. Certainly, she knows the Anne Marie story. Phillip was not the opposing attorney in the first case, but he was now, and it seemed like he wanted Sarah to know that he wasn't going to back down. What else did he know?

Sarah shook her head. One thing at a time. First, get through her day. Second, find a way to call Laura to get her hands on … wait.

Sarah turned around quickly to see that Angela was not at her desk. To her relief, Angela had stepped away. Quickly, she dialed back the last number that had called her.

"Phillip Seider," he said, answering his phone.

"Hi, this is Sarah from Culp, Moore and Rosen. I thought I would just go to your machine. But I wanted to double-check that you actually wanted a call back from Michael on this number."

She was expecting to be snapped at. That would have been the normal response.

"Thank you, Sarah. That is very thorough of you. This number is fine," he said. Sarah was breathing hard.

"Is there something else I can do for you?" he asked quietly.

"Um. Well, you do trusts and estates, right?" she asked, and she heard the tiniest intake of breath on the line.

"Yes, we do."

"Well, I have a friend who wants to find out if a trust has been left in her name," she started and then stopped. She hadn't thought this through well enough. He would surely tell her to come see him. Or ask questions she couldn't answer. But he didn't.

"Hmmm. Yes. I see," Phillip said. "Well, I would suggest that you go see Laura at the clerk's office. She should know all about it. You should go in person. Laura is on vacation this week but do go see her when she's back."

Sarah felt like her head was expanding. She could see Angela walking back to her desk.

"Thank you. And I will pass that along to Michael," she said.

"Of course. And Sarah, after you see Laura, come and see me if you want to," Phillip said. "Have a lovely day."

And then he hung up.

"Who was that?" Angela asked.

"Phillip Seider. He's really angry, and I need to text Michael about it," Sarah said. She then sent a text to Michael, relaying to him what Phillip had said. Michael texted her back saying to make an appointment for Andrew at 3 p.m. As Angela stayed put at her desk from that point onward, Sarah buried her thoughts about the trusts and the conversation she had with Phillip Seider.

When 3 p.m. rolled around, Andrew Davies charged into the office. His ratty face was a storm, and he came into the office with Alex only. Today Alex was not walking behind his father, but in front of him, as if he were being forced at gunpoint.

"Hello Sarah," said Andrew. "I believe we have a meeting set up with Michael now."

"Yes, you do. Let me buzz him," she said. Andrew nodded. Alex was standing in front of her desk with his head down. He wasn't on his phone, he just kept his eyes downcast.

"Hi Alex. Would you like a drink while you wait?" she asked.

"Oh, *Alex* will be in the meeting with us. It seems that my son has been saying untruths to his mother recently so he can get what he wants. And now the adults must find a way to undo the mess that he made," Andrew said from between clenched teeth.

"Andrew. Good to see you," Michael said as he came out of the office. Andrew put his arm on Alex's shoulder and Alex openly cringed. Sarah instinctively started to stand up, but Alex caught her eye and shook his head. And with that, both men and the boy entered the office.

She had never seen such desperation in the eyes of another human being before. And a phrase from the deposition she read came back to her: *And my son crawled out from under the desk.*

You have to do something about this, said Larry.

Sarah nodded to no one there.

#

On her way home, Sarah's brain was bouncing around so much, she felt like it might just explode out of her skull. When she thought about Alex, she wondered how she might be able to help him, or how she might be able to help Phillip Seider to help him. She had the story of Anne Marie's kinky past from Scott Thomas, but surely they already knew that story. And her being into kink didn't prove anything per se. They also already had Melissa, who had actually seen her son's abuse. What could Sarah add to this situation? What could she provide that Phillip didn't already know? Thinking of Phillip turned her mind to her conversation with him. Could he want her help with this case? Is that why he was so cordial about the trust question?

This made her think about the matter of her trust. If she did have money that she was unaware of, could she find a way to get a hold of it? And if so, what would she do at that point? The minute that she tried to have Karl removed as a trustee, she would be fired from her job. She knew that without a doubt, but she didn't quite know why. But first things first, Sarah needed to visit Laura and see what she could find out.

Her brain had been so engaged that she had been on autopilot on her walk home. But something made her look up when she was by the basketball court. She saw Caio standing mid-court, and her heart stopped. Everything else she had been thinking, all her other concerns, problems, and pains, left her head.

You are just obsessed with a good-looking boy. That's not becoming for a woman of your age, said her father.

Was that true? Was he just beautiful and that was it?

144

Sarah entertained the thought for a moment but then dismissed it. No, it wasn't that. The very first thing she had ever noticed about him was not what he looked like. It was the way he had looked at her. And later, it was the way he spoke to her. It was different from the way any man in her life had ever looked at her or spoken to her.

She was so caught up in these thoughts that she didn't even notice that Dex was standing right next to the fence.

"Hey, Ms. Baker," he said, and she jumped. Dex was well over six-feet tall and an imposing presence, but he had a voice like velvet.

"Hi," she replied.

"Hey, Caio behaving himself with you?" he asked with a small smile. Mouse was standing next to the fence and started to laugh when he heard this. Caio had noticed her and was walking toward them.

"What?" she blurted.

"I mean, he's not hitting on you or anything, right?" Dex asked.

Sarah felt her face begin to heat up. Caio was now standing next to Dex and giving him a look that would freeze lava.

"Oh. Of course not. I mean. He's ... well, I'm his tutor—" she started but Mouse cut her off.

"Oh, come on, Ms. Baker. You gotta know that Caio has a huge crush on you," Mouse said, laughing and poking Caio, who openly winced. "Yeah, I wouldn't be half surprised if he failed his test just so he could have a reason to ask you to tutor him."

Sarah's face now felt like an actual furnace. She knew she must be seven colors of red and that humiliated her even more.

Stop it. Stop it right now. These are teenage boys, and they are just messing with you to see how you react, snapped her father.

"You gotta watch out for that South American type. They are known seducers," Mouse said, hitting Caio on the head. "Lucky for you, Caio is a chicken shit."

Caio looked up at her and his eyes registered something that looked like real pain, mixed with panic. She unconsciously took a step forward. But then he just shrugged and looked down. Suddenly, some of the other boys arrived on the other side of the court and both Mouse and Dex turned to greet them.

Caio then moved closer to the fence that separated them.

"So is it still okay if I come by a little earlier tomorrow night?" he asked suddenly.

"Sure. What time?" she replied, trying for cool but failing as her voice squeaked like a mouse. She had also taken a step closer.

145

"Maybe five thirty or six? Is that okay?" he asked, putting his hands on the fence. It wasn't until that moment that Sarah realized that she was holding onto the fence with one hand. He put his hand through the links right next to hers. He wasn't touching her, but it was very close. His skin was close enough to hers to feel the heat of it.

He glanced around quickly, almost nervously, scanning the boys on the other side of the basketball court.

"Sure. Do your foster family want you home earlier or something?" she asked.

"No. I told them but they don't really care. I just wanted to have more time to talk to you," he said, and then backed away, turned, and began quickly dribbling the ball back down the basketball court.

Sarah made it home and had to sit down at her kitchen table before she fell down. She hadn't realized until that moment how hard her heart was pounding, or how ridiculously physically impacted she was just by that little encounter.

No lady would be reacting like that to a man. And no decent human being would be reacting like that to a little boy, snapped her mother.

He's not a little boy. He's a teenager, Sarah snapped back.

Sarah, you are arguing semantics. You know that he's underage and it's disturbing for you to be thinking of him this way, particularly to be reacting to him this way physically. You have specifically said you wouldn't do that, her dead husband sniffed.

"I'm TRYING not to think of him that way. But I can't exactly control how my body responds to another person, can I? As a man, I would think you would understand that," Sarah snapped before she realized she was speaking aloud.

She was starting to get angry with herself or, well, with the people in her head.

Then she shook her head. The answer was simple, she would make something good of all this. She would help this boy. She felt something for him, and if what she felt was inappropriate, then she would find some way to make it appropriate. Helping him in school seemed like a good start. And he would never know about any of the ridiculous things going on in her head.

Chapter Twenty-Four

Big

Saturday June 14

Sarah had spent most of the day on Saturday trying *not* to think about the fact that Caio would be coming over this evening. She cleaned. She rearranged her wardrobe. She tried to work but couldn't even focus on that. At 4:30 she just gave up and decided to get a shower. She had just finished and thrown on some jeans and a loose-fitting T-shirt when someone knocked at the door. She looked at the clock. It was 5:15. She had a moment of panic, wondering if Karl had decided to stop by to check on her. But as she walked to her door, she knew that the shadow on the other side of the smoked glass window was not Karl. Karl was taller and wider.

As she opened the door, Caio smiled at her. He had his backpack, and he was carrying groceries, just as he had on the previous Saturday. She smiled back.

"I know I'm a bit earlier than I said. I hope that's okay. Your boyfriend isn't here or anything, is he?" Caio said with a little grin as he stepped inside. He dropped his book bag by the door and immediately took the groceries to the counter.

"Did you eat the leftovers from last week?" he asked, pulling things out of the grocery bag.

"I ate them for breakfast the next morning," she replied. He turned and grimaced.

"Chicken hearts for breakfast. You ARE a brave woman. Well, I brought something easier today. I wanted to make something that wouldn't take as much time because I brought a movie."

He brought a what? Val said in her head. *Jesus. This is a date.*

Sarah would have told her to shut up, but was afraid she might say it out loud.

"Really? Do you think we'll have time to do that? I mean we have to study, right?" she asked him.

"Oh yeah. Of course. But I thought you could give me the practice test while we eat. It shouldn't take me more than an hour, right? Then you can grade it and give it back to me this week when you see me on the court. Then I will know what I need to focus on. That would work, right?" he said, as he pulled what looked like a fish from the bags.

"Ummm. Yeah. Okay. That's good I guess."

"I thought I would make fish and chips. Does that work for you?" he said, holding up a white fish for her inspection.

"Sure. I'm happy with anything someone else is cooking for me," she laughed, but a bit nervously.

Caio cocked his head slightly and looked at her intently.

"Hey. I just wanted to clear something up. You know, so you won't be uncomfortable with me," he began.

"Okay," she said.

"So, you heard what Mouse said yesterday, about me having a crush on you?" he began, leaning back against the counter, eyes directly on her face. Sarah felt herself color. He would want her to know that it wasn't true. Of course, he would be embarrassed by that.

"Oh, I didn't take it seriously. I know he was just joking and picking on you—" she began but he cut her off.

"Actually, it's true. I do have a pretty big crush on you. But I want you to know that I won't be disrespectful in any way, and I don't expect anything from you. I'm happy just to spend time with you," he said. His eyes were still on her face. He didn't look away or even down.

Sarah's head began to spin. Thank god she was sitting down. She put her hand to her head to try to slow the world down, but everything seemed to be whirling.

"Hey. Are you okay? Did I upset you?" Caio asked, crossing the kitchen and crouching in front of her.

"No. No. Upset is not what I feel," she muttered and then realized how that must have sounded and felt her face begin to burn. Caio just smiled.

"Okay. Good then. We can eat. Then I can take the test. Then we can watch the movie. Okay?"

"Okay," Sarah said in a small voice.

Caio stood up quickly, went back to the cabinet, and began pulling things out.

"Do you have any corn flour or cornstarch?" he asked.

"On the top shelf on the left," she replied. She normally had to get a stool to reach that shelf, but he was able to access it just by going on his toes. Sarah was having trouble focusing or even breathing.

Did that just happen? He just said that, right? I wasn't making that up, right?

Damn straight he said that, Val said.

I'm sure he didn't mean it. Suppose he's just making fun of you, said her mother.

Oh, shut the fuck up, you old bat, Val replied. *You know as well as I do that that's not what's going on here.*

"This won't take very long. Maybe fifteen minutes tops," Caio said as he began to batter the fish. "I have to watch it a bit, but after I make a salad, I should be able to start taking the test."

"I can make the salad," Sarah replied. Caio's eyebrows came together.

"Look. You are doing all the cooking. I can do that one little thing. It would make me feel less guilty," she said, coming to stand next to him and pulling the lettuce, cucumbers and tomatoes from the bag. For a moment her arm brushed his and she had to focus very hard on the lettuce not to get dizzy.

"Listen. Before you start that, can you get the practice test for me?" Caio said, putting his hand on her arm.

She was only able to nod.

Little girl, you are going crazy. This is not right and not normal, said her dad.

She pulled the practice test that she had put together in the week from the drawer in her living room. When she came back into the room, Caio was standing with his back against the counter, just watching her.

She handed him the test and a pen, which he eyeballed for a minute.

"Erasable pen? Think I'm going to fuck up a lot?" he asked, raising his eyebrows. She couldn't help but smile, despite the language.

"Not necessarily," she said, sitting back down at the table. "I just believe in managing the risks."

Caio was leaning on the counter, beginning to write on the paper she had just given him.

"Do you now? How's that 'managing risk' thing working out for you in your life?"

An image of Karl came to her mind as his words sunk in. She lowered her eyes. When she raised them Caio was crouching in front of her.

"I didn't mean it that way, Sarah. I wasn't thinking of your asshole boyfriend. It was more of a clumsy attempt at flirting. I'm sorry. It's been a really long time so I'm out of practice with this," he said, looking at her face and brushing her hair back from her eyes.

Who are you? What sixteen-year-old boy acts like this?

"It's okay. I just … well, can we not talk about Karl tonight?" she asked, and he nodded.

"I'm completely happy to never talk about Karl again, if that's what you want," he said, walking back over to the counter. "Hey, food's almost done. Do you have any vinegar?"

"No, why?"

"Because that's what you put on fish and chips."

"Not ketchup?"

"God no, we're not heathens. Fish and chips are British, and the British way is with vinegar."

"How do you know?" she asked.

"I lived there for a while," he replied with a shrug.

When? When did you have time to do that? Born in Brazil. Lived in the UK. But you are a foster kid. What happened?

"Really? When did you live there?" she asked out loud.

"It was a while back. Oh, fish is done" he said, changing the subject.

Caio quickly set the table as she managed to get herself moving and finish the salad. He then served their plates with fish, fries, and peas. Sarah put the salad in two bowls and brought them to the table.

"Do you mind if I just do this while we eat? I don't want to be rude, but I want to have time to watch the movie with you," he said, digging into his food as he scribbled on the paper.

"No. Go ahead. It might take you some time though. I designed it to take about an hour," Sarah looked at the clock; it was 6:15. He had already been there an hour. It felt like he just walked in.

And yet, despite her expectations, he was done by 6:45. He looked up and handed her the stack of papers with the pen balancing on top of it.

"You're finished?" she asked, shocked.

"Yep," he said.

"Did you just write a bunch of crap?" she asked glancing at the pages. He laughed out loud.

"Well, that's for you to decide when you grade it," he said. "Okay. Movie now."

He got up and helped her clear the table. There were no leftovers to speak of, and she was a bit disappointed about that. She liked the idea of being able to eat something tomorrow morning that he made with his hands. After the table was cleared, he grabbed his book bag and pulled out a big bag of popcorn with a smile.

"You brought popcorn?" she said, smiling back.

"Yep. Salty and sweet mixed because I didn't know what you liked," he said. "What do you like?"

"I like it mixed," she said, and he did a little fist pump. She laughed out loud. He then took a big bowl, poured the popcorn into it and took it into the living room, where he went to her DVD player and put a disk in.

"I noticed that you had a DVD player last time I was here, so I thought I would bring this. You've probably already seen it, but I think it's kind of interesting," he said.

He handed her the case. It was *Big*. She hadn't seen that film in years.

They sat next to each other on the sofa with the popcorn between them. As they watched the film, Caio was quiet, but she could feel his eyes on her from time to time. She tried not to turn and look at him, but it was impossible not to at times. When he laughed, she glanced at him out of the corner of her eye to watch his face light up. Occasionally their hands would touch when reaching for popcorn. When this happened, she felt her skin tingle at the place he touched.

The movie itself made her feel more than a little uncomfortable. She hadn't really remembered how much of the movie centered around the relationship between the little boy in the man's body and the adult woman. She felt positively squirmy at times. Everything was hitting too close to home.

"Well, I hadn't really remembered the ending was that creepy," said Caio, turning to her as the movie ended.

"Why? You didn't like it?" Sarah asked, trying not to sound like she was freaking out. She felt painfully vulnerable, as if someone had stripped her of her skin.

"Mmmmm, at the end, when she sees he's a twelve-year-old boy, she just kind of looks sad. She was probably sleeping with a twelve-year-old. She was definitely lusting over a twelve-year-old. But what's creepy is that everyone seems okay with it," Caio said.

Sarah felt like someone punched her in the gut.

Like how creepy it is that you are lusting after him, said her father.

"Everyone is okay with sleeping with an emotional twelve-year-old as long as he's in an adult body. I wonder how they would feel if it were the other way around?" Caio continued.

"Meaning?" she asked noncommittally, trying to breathe normally.

Control your face. Control your face. Control your face.

151

"Meaning how would it have gone over if he had been a fifty-five-year-old in the *body* of a twelve-year-old? Would everyone have been okay if he had then slept with a thirty-five-year-old while he was in a twelve-year-old body? What about sleeping with another twelve-year-old while in a twelve-year-old body, but with the mind of a thirty-five-year-old? It kind of seems like people are more concerned with the age of the body than the age of the mind. Or the soul," Caio said.

He said these words very slowly, very deliberately.

Sarah sat staring at him. This had gone in a direction that she hadn't anticipated.

"What do you think?" he asked her, looking straight into her eyes. She felt that rush of panic.

"About?" she asked, stalling for time.

"About the difference between physical and emotional age. What do you think is more important?"

"I think it's complicated no matter which way it is. But—"

She took a breath. She wasn't sure if this was a safe thing to say. In fact, she was fairly sure there wasn't any safe thing to say in this situation. So, she shouldn't say anything at all. Or she should deflect the question.

"I think someone's emotional age is a lot more important than the physical one. I guess ..." was what came unbidden from her mouth.

Caio's face noticeably relaxed, and he smiled.

"But those things are usually linked—the age and emotional maturity," Sarah said quickly.

"Yeah. Usually," he said and looked away.

She wondered, not for the first time, if he had been abused. Abused children often exhibited an unusual adult quality. And she told herself, also not for the first time, that she would not add to that pain.

What exactly are you doing right now, little girl? It was her dad's voice this time, stern and cold.

Caio grabbed a handful of popcorn and stuffed it inelegantly into his mouth. She noted again how long and delicate his fingers were. He had the hands of a pianist.

He turned and caught her staring at him. He smiled slightly.

"I should probably get going," he said, standing up.

You should have been the one to say that. You probably look like some lonely pathetic middle-aged spinster. And he's being nice and humoring you, said her mother.

"Can I come at the same time next Saturday?" Caio asked.

"Sure. But I need to get you your test back before then. When is your test?"

"This Wednesday," he said.

"Oh crap," she said and he laughed. "Okay. I will grade this and get it to you by Monday. I can drop it by the basketball court around five. Will that work? Will you be there?"

"I will be if I know you are coming," he said. "Then next week I can tell you how I did."

"But do you still need to come? I mean, school is almost out for summer—" she started but he interrupted her.

"Yes, I do. I have one more test," he said getting up and grabbing his bag and walking toward the door. Once again, he stopped for a minute at the door, shifting back and forth for just a second before turning, smiling at her and saying, "See you Monday, Sarah."

And then he was gone, and she felt like she had been hit by a truck. She managed to get to a chair before her legs gave out.

"What the fuck just happened?" she muttered to herself.

Jesus, Sarah, said Val's voice. *There is blind and then there is just stupid blanket denial. That was a date. That boy told you he had a crush on you. You may not want to own that, but it took a lot of balls for him to say it, and you shouldn't dismiss it. So yeah, in his mind, that was a date. And you have another one next Saturday.*

You need to stop this right now, said her father. *When you see him on Monday, you need to tell him that he doesn't need to see you anymore.*

Why, exactly, should she do that? She hasn't done anything wrong, snapped Val.

"Can you all shut up for just a minute," Sarah said, holding her head. She went back to the sofa and lay down, with her head where he had been sitting. It was still warm with the heat from his body. She could smell the scent of whatever soap he used.

She didn't know how long she stayed there but she knew that when sleep began to overtake her, she didn't bother to go to her bed.

Chapter Twenty-Five

What the Body Knows

Sunday June 15

Sarah woke up Sunday morning exactly where she had fallen asleep Saturday night, on the couch, in her clothes. As she got up, she was mildly shocked not to see popcorn all over the floor. When she walked into the kitchen, she saw that it was clean as well and the test that Caio had taken while he ate dinner last night was lying on her kitchen counter. She kind of remembered them cleaning up, but she didn't remember that it took long enough to get it into this state of spotlessness. The pans were washed. The counters were crumb-free. There were no ingredients left lying around. Sarah felt a bit sad about this. She would have liked to have some remnants of him left.

Stop it. Just stop it, said her mother. *Get this out of your head.*

"Is it wrong to like someone?"

It's wrong to like someone his age, in that way, snapped her mother.

"That probably won't last," Sarah said out loud. "Attraction doesn't usually last that long. But maybe friendship does or could."

She has a valid point, Larry piped up. *Many marriages, even the best ones, end up as good friendships and that's all. Attraction is a fickle thing.*

Exactly, so why shouldn't she enjoy it while it's here? Val said. *Sarah, when was the last time you actually felt anything? Anything at all?*

"In law school," she said softly.

Exactly, so why shouldn't you go with this. Feeling stuff isn't easy but you are old enough to control it, so use it. Attraction is a powerful thing.

Sarah felt her face turning red as she remembered Mouse's words. *Caio has a huge crush on you*, and then Caio's eyes later, when he said, *Actually, it's true.* She felt her mind begin to tilt and realized that if she started thinking about what happened yesterday, she could end up doing nothing but staring into space all day.

She pulled out her computer with every intention of looking into the law on trusts in New York, but she couldn't make herself focus. All her brain seemed capable of doing was to flash random images of things that had happened the night before: a piece of battered fish on her plate, Tom Hanks crawling into a bunk bed, Caio stuffing popcorn into his mouth. She realized that she would have to get out and go for a walk or something if she wanted to have any hope of regaining concentration.

She was just crossing the room again when her eyes were drawn back to the test that was laying on her counter. *That* was something she could do and it was a way to be with him when he wasn't there. She could read his words and his thoughts. The idea of that sent a flood of warmth through her chest, so she picked up the paper and sat down at the table. Caio had written his full name on the top right of the paper. Caio Silva. Sarah smiled and reached out to touch the paper where he wrote this. Then she shook her head again and dropped the paper to the table, picking up a pen to mark it.

Three paragraphs into his answer to the first question, and Sarah knew something was wildly off here. She had asked a question about the role of regulations, and how that impacted global migration. At best, she had expected him to discuss immigration, or even better, discuss arguments for and against open immigration policies. And he did discuss this in his second paragraph. But then he went on to discuss the notion of "politics of places" and how that contributed to new concepts of responsibility, care, and solidarity in a globalizing world. And it wasn't just this. His writing style, use of vocabulary and sentence structure was something she would have expected from another lawyer, not a teenage boy.

What the fuck?

Sarah put the paper on the table and sat back for a second. Her head was reeling even more than it had been when she woke up.

Look at the facts. Keep it clear.

Okay. What did she know about this boy? His name is Caio Silva. He was a foster child. He was at the end of his tenth-grade year. He knew Karl and didn't like him. He has a crush on her. And he asked her to tutor him in a subject that he clearly had a better grip on than she did. So he was obviously brilliant. Oh, and he played basketball well.

You see, you don't even know much about this boy, said her mother.

Yes, well, sometimes our bodies know things that our minds don't, Larry said. Sarah was shocked. She would have expected that comment from Val, not Larry. Larry was logical to a fault.

But this IS the logical way to think of things, Larry continued. *We don't control much consciously. We don't control our heartbeats. We don't control the regulation of our chemicals. We can't even control the fact that our pupils dilate when we're close to people that we find attractive. Our bodies have knowledge that our conscious minds don't have or can't have. Maybe your body knows something about this boy that your logical mind can't grasp.*

"Like what?" she asked. But everyone was suddenly silent.

Sarah took a deep breath and continued grading his test. What took him less than an hour to complete took her hours to grade. He made statements relating to regulations and history that she had never heard of so had to cross-reference. At noon she stopped for lunch because she was only halfway through. It was almost impossible to believe that he had just thrown these answers together as he was shoving dinner into his mouth. That just couldn't be possible, could it? But despite her incredulity, everything he wrote checked out. All his facts were correct. All his references to regulations were accurate. All his historical references were on point.

This was a boy she met playing basketball! Had teenagers become unusually brilliant in the years since she left law school without her realizing it?

Do you really think that? Val asked.

"No. Of course not. But how do I explain this? What teenager, or even young adult, writes like this or thinks like this?" she muttered aloud.

They don't, Val said.

"And he clearly doesn't need my help."

Well, not with academics, that's clear, said Larry, dryly.

Sarah closed her eyes and put her face in her hands. She felt like she wanted to laugh, and cry, and scream, but she couldn't decide which to do first. She chose to clean instead. She got up and started with her kitchen, working her way through to the living room, and then her bedroom. By the time she finished cleaning her bathroom, it was already dark outside. When she went to bed, the same question kept running in circles through her head, until it finally sang her to sleep.

Who are you? Who are you? Who are you?

Monday June 16

Monday morning at work was tedious, boring, and busy. This was Angela's week of vacation, so Sarah had to cover for both Michael and Jason. Around midmorning, she got a text from Karl saying that he would be out of town for a case and wouldn't be back until next week. Sarah let out a sigh of relief. He had texted her rather than called, which surprised her. Karl usually called; he was old-school that way. Maybe he was traveling with Meghan and didn't want to risk having her speak in the background. Whatever the reason, she was relieved not to have to talk to him, and even more relieved not to have to see him.

There were a few good things about Angela being gone. The first and foremost was that it kept her busy, and therefore distracted. Another was that she didn't feel like someone was looking over her shoulder all the time. The bad thing was that with all the calls, meetings and emails she had to deal with, she didn't have the time to be doing anything that she wouldn't have wanted Angela to see. She did manage one call to the court, where she confirmed that Laura would not be back until next week.

By the end of the day, she was tired and irritable, but there was there was light at the end of it. She was supposed to hand Caio back his paper today, and he said he would wait for her on the basketball court. Michael was in court today, so she could leave at a reasonable hour. As long as she had her phone on and her computer with her, he didn't much care where she was once official office hours were over.

Sarah forced herself to walk at a normal pace on the way to the basketball court. When she turned onto the road, she saw that Caio was sitting on the ground with his back against the fence, looking right toward her. When he saw her, he stood up and walked toward the edge of the court, intercepting her at the far corner.

There was no shyness in him today. His smile was warm, relaxed, and genuine.

"I thought you might have forgotten," he said, as she approached him.

"Of course not. I said I would grade your test, and I did. I actually spent most of yesterday doing it," she said as she pulled his folded paper from her purse.

"How did I do?" he asked with a smile. His dark eyes trained on hers.

"I think you know how you did. And I don't think you need me," she said looking down.

"Yes, I do. I really do," he said. Sarah was shocked by the urgency in his voice and in his eyes when he said this. He was about to say something else when Ash and Mouse walked over toward their corner of the court.

"Caio said you made him take a test last Saturday. That's cold," Mouse said. Sarah laughed, relieved that he obviously hadn't told them about watching a movie.

"Well, he did a practice test, and he did incredibly well. He should do fine on his test Wednesday," she said.

"I get the test back on Friday, so I will bring it to show you on Saturday," Caio said.

"Maybe I should get you to tutor me in history," Mouse said.

"No," Caio said suddenly, "you don't need help."

He then grabbed the ball and started bouncing it back toward the court, but not before catching Sarah's eye.

"Guess he told me," Mouse said, winking at Sarah. Sarah laughed and turned to walk home.

You see, these have been dates, not tutoring sessions. And he's telling you that in no uncertain terms, Val said with a laugh. Sarah could feel heat in her chest. She felt like dancing. She felt like she had been injected with speed or cocaine.

It was Monday. She would see him on Saturday. She only had six days to wait.

Chapter Twenty-Six

Things That Are But Should Never Be

Friday June 20

The rest of the week was just as busy as Monday, with Sarah juggling the schedules of two attorneys. But finally, on Friday, Jason asked her to go to the courthouse to pull a traffic file for one of their clients. The other side had accused one of their clients of jeopardizing the welfare of the children by driving with them while drunk. The opposing attorney claimed that their client had a history of DWI, and their client denied it. As everyone in the office knew that this particular client was a serial liar, Jason sent Sarah to get a certified copy of his driving record. He also asked her to track down any criminal records he might have in his current name or other names. In truth, she could have done most of this from her computer, but she could get more thorough information from the court. At the courthouse, one could also get the gossip that was often infinitely more valuable. But Sarah had other reasons for wanting to go to the courthouse.

When she got there, Sarah immediately went to the clerk's office just in case, by some chance, Laura had come back early from vacation. Sadly, it was Laura's assistant, Vickie, who was at the desk. So Sarah went to get printouts of their client's criminal record, with DWIs. It turned out that the paper it took to print it would have stretched out to be taller than she was. No criminal record, huh? Sarah laughed to herself. On her way out, she walked back by Vickie.

"Hi Vickie," Sarah said, sticking her head in. "Do you know when Laura will be back in?"

"Actually, you are in luck," Vickie said. "She just dropped by a second ago to say hi, so you should be able to catch her on her way to her car if you hurry."

Sarah walked down the hall as briskly as she could without actually running.

She thought she was out of luck but as soon as she walked out of the door, she saw the back of Laura's ponytailed head walking down the stairs.

"Laura," Sarah called, and Laura turned and smiled.

"Hi Sarah. So did Phillip coerce you into buying some Girl Scout Cookies from my grandkids?" she asked with a smile, pulling out a Girl Scout Cookie registration sheet. At first Sarah was confused, but only for a second. Laura had mentioned Phillip's name, so he had spoken with her.

"Yes. He talked me into it when he called the other day," she replied.

"Okay. Here, let's go find something I can write on," said Laura, moving toward a parked car near the road.

"I'll take some Thin Mints," Sarah said. Laura nodded and wrote it down.

"Put your contact details here," Laura said, handing her the sheet.

"You wanted to know about your trust?" Laura asked. "How did you find out?"

"I took a picture of the trust notice that Karl asked me to sign. He said it was about my mortgage."

"How did you get the picture?"

"With camera glasses—"

"That you got from Scott Thomas?" Laura asked with a knowing smile. Sarah nodded.

"Good. You know you have a trust then?"

"Yes" Sarah said. "I could read that much, but the rest was very blurry. I am not sure what else it said in the notice."

"There's probably a lot there you don't want to know," Laura said, touching her arm and laughing. This was all for effect because her eyes were darting around her, surveying everyone within their proximity.

"I thought I could get a copy of Paul's will."

"You don't have one? No, of course Karl wouldn't want you to have that."

"Is there a copy of the trust somewhere?" Sarah asked.

"Somewhere, yes. But not here. Listen. As I am sure you know, if someone sets up a trust, it isn't required to be a public record. But if it was set up in the will, and the will referred to it, then you would have something. But I have to warn you, if I were you, I wouldn't do this alone. I would get an attorney to track this one down. And I would only trust certain attorneys."

"Like Phillip Seider?"

"Phillip is great," Laura replied. "He's more than great. If he wasn't married and I wasn't married, then I am sure he would be the love of my life. But he is not the guy to go to on this. He's too local and too family-oriented. You need an ethical guy who'll know about your situation and who has ties in the city.

Basically, you need someone who can't and won't be intimidated by the fact that he or she will be taking on most of the legal community here if they take this on."

"Most of the community—" Sarah began, but Laura interrupted.

"Yes, dear. Most of the community. It's a bitch of a community and it's railroaded more than a few people. The attorney you need to see is Matt Greenley. He has offices here and in Manhattan. He's not difficult to find. You need to call him and set up an appointment, but you also need to realize, and I'm sure he'll tell you that you shouldn't do this until you've planned a way to cut and run. Karl will be none too happy about this, and he has friends that will be even less so. If you doubt this, get a look at who goes in and out of the Stigmata Club over on Orchard Street. Just park on the street and see what you see.

"I'm gonna go now, because if we chat much longer it will look like it's more than just chitchat. Feel free to mention me to Matt or Phillip, but if you say anything about this conversation to anyone else, I will deny it and hate you forever. Just joking. But not really." Laura said this with a smile and gave her a quick hug, then she turned and started toward the crosswalk. But before crossing the street, she turned.

"I'll let you know when the cookies come in."

Sarah nodded. One sentence stuck in her head.

"It's railroaded more than a few people."

There was one more person she wanted to see today.

#

"Wow, what happened to you?" Melissa Taylor asked as Sarah walked into the bookstore. "Sorry, I should have said 'hi' first."

Sarah laughed. "That's okay. What do you mean what happened to me?"

"You just have a totally different air about you today. You look like, I don't know. You look more solid, or more sparkly or something," Melissa said. "Did you dump the asshole?"

"Not yet," Sarah said. She had come here to tell Melissa that she worked for Culp, Moore & Rosen. She wanted to warn her that Michael knew about her online identities and postings on websites. She wanted to admit that she had provided him with these, but that it had been an accident. But now that she was here, she didn't want to do it. Sarah's intuition told her that Melissa was a good, kind person. Sarah had not had a good female friend since law school and Melissa could have been that person, but telling Melissa that she had betrayed her would certainly destroy any prospect for that in the future.

161

"Well, have you done something you are proud of, or happy about?' Melissa asked. "Because you're glowing."

"I started tutoring a kid in geography," she said, and then was shocked at herself. Still, it felt good to mention him to someone else.

"That's really nice of you. Maybe that's it. Is it helping him?" she asked.

Sarah hesitated for just a moment then blurted out, "Well, that's the thing. I don't really know. You see, he took this practice test that I gave him, and it was really strange."

"In what way?" Melissa asked. She motioned for Sarah to come and sit next to her on the small reading couch in the corner of the store.

Sarah then gave her some of the details of Caio's answers. Melissa leaned forward and rested her chin on her hands. She asked a few questions and nodded a lot. After Sarah finished, she asked. "How old did you say this kid was?"

"Sixteen. Do you think that a sixteen-year-old boy could write something like that?" Sarah asked.

He's not sixteen, Val muttered in her head.

"No. I don't think a teenager would come up with that sort of grasp of subject matter or vocabulary. Are you sure he wrote it?" Melissa asked.

"Yes. I saw him write it. I was tutoring him and gave him a practice test. Then I graded it. It never left my possession," Sarah replied.

"Does he seem extraordinarily gifted?" Melissa asked. Sarah thought for a moment but then shook her head.

"Not exactly. He doesn't seem gifted, he just seems, well ..."

"Older?" Melissa asked.

See, she knows it, Val said.

"Yes. Older," Sarah said. "I know it shouldn't be bothering me, but I'm just perplexed."

"What I am perplexed about is why he would need tutoring if he's that smart," Melissa said and Sarah felt herself freeze. She felt like she had walked into a trap.

"Whoa. Whoa. I'm not accusing you of anything," Melissa said, putting her hand on Sarah's arm. "You're a good person. I know that. I'm a sensitive. I know most people don't believe in that. I didn't believe in it for years, and that's why I married my ex. Logically, he was the perfect guy. He said all the right things, he did all the right things. He was rich. He was funny. He was even good in bed. But deep down I think I always felt like there was something wrong with him. It was in his eyes. It took ten years for him to show that evil side of himself to me, and by that time we had kids together, so I didn't feel like I could escape. But I knew, even in the beginning. I almost called off the wedding the night

162

before, but my girlfriends convinced me that it was just pre-wedding jitters. It's funny how all those girlfriends disappeared when things got ugly."

"Melissa," Sarah started. "I have to tell you something. I actually work for Culp, Moore and Rosen, the firm that represents your ex-husband."

Melissa smiled. She pushed a strand of curly hair away from her face.

"I know that," she said.

"How?"

"When you came in last week, I knew the black eye was real and that you were really in an abusive relationship. I also knew that wasn't the whole story. You were too interested in me and my life. After you left, I called Phillip to tell him about it. He asked me to describe you and he recognized you by my description. He said you were a good person, who worked in a bad place. I believe him."

"I'm so sorry," Sarah said. "I probably shouldn't be here now. But I wanted to tell you that I accidentally let Michael on to your 'Gaslight' online ID."

Melissa's eyes got wide for a moment. "How did you find that? I have kept that very secret."

"Your quote. The brain is an elastic thing. It was in your deposition," Sarah said.

"Damn. You're good," Melissa said with a little laugh that showed signs of discomfort for the first time. Sarah's heart ached for that.

"But I also wanted to tell you that I want to help your son in any way I can."

Melissa smiled a wan smile. "I'm not sure what you can do. But I appreciate any effort on your part. I think Phillip is the best chance I've had in years. Every other lawyer has taken my money and done little to help me. I guess that's what most lawyers do, or lawyers around here. There's a lot of evil here."

"Why don't you leave here then?" Sarah asked.

"Because he has my kids," Melissa said sharply. "They may have maneuvered me into a position where no one will take anything I say seriously, but I can't leave my kids. I have to keep trying. As long as I have breath, I have to keep trying."

Melissa's eyes filled with tears.

"Did Phillip talk to Scott Thomas?" Sarah asked.

"You mean about the stepmonster's BDSM habit? Yes, we know about that. Do you know that they actually tried to pull the discrimination card when we brought it up?"

Sarah must have had some facial response because Melissa nodded.

"Yeah. Amazing, isn't it? But it doesn't surprise me because that's what my ex started doing with me. He would do something, then he would repent and do nothing else for years. And then it would repeat. It was a long, long cycle. It wasn't until he started with my son that I knew we had to get away … but I lost it. I lost my grip on reality and I did stupid things. I even beat my baby, just to put him in the hospital. I guess I hoped the system would investigate the whole family over something like that. But they didn't. They just investigated me. So now, I am just considered abusive and crazy … and I can't help him. I am hoping that Phillip can. If not, I'll have to figure something else out."

"Why are you telling me all this? I could still be spying on you for Michael," Sarah asked.

"Yes, but you're not and I know that. Just like I know that you will eventually leave that asshole you are with. Like I know that there is much more to the story about the boy you are tutoring than you and I could guess. And like I know that there are some fairly spectacular things about you that you are just beginning to discover."

"How do you know all that?" Sarah asked, genuinely taken aback.

"Like I said. I'm a sensitive. And I also know that you need to step very carefully for the next few weeks because your life is going to change a lot."

Melissa reached out and touched her arm again, smiling. "Yes. A lot."

Sarah took a piece of paper from her purse and wrote down her number on it.

"You can call me if you need anything or any information. Don't leave texts, though, because Karl could see them. Only leave voicemails. And don't leave your name. I'll recognize your voice."

"Thank you, Sarah," Melissa said. "If you need to reach me, you can find me here. I have tried to keep a low profile on social media. I know my ex is always keeping his eye on me."

Sarah nodded. She stood up and started to walk out, but Melissa took her arm and pulled her into a hug.

"If you are taking this on, they may fix their eyes on you as well," she whispered in Sarah's ear. "Stay safe."

Sarah nodded and walked out. On the way home, she took a convoluted route for reasons she couldn't exactly explain.

Chapter Twenty-Seven

Summer Solstice

Saturday June 21

Saturday morning, Sarah got up with her heart fluttering. She hadn't seen Caio since their brief exchange on the basketball court on Monday. She had no idea how his test had gone. She was also very aware that public schools went on summer vacation in two weeks. At that point, there would be no legitimate reason for him to be coming over to her house. Of course, he might not want to come over anymore but …

What are you even thinking? Were you present last Saturday? Or this Monday when you dropped the test off? Oh yeah, and the look he gave you when you said that he didn't need you—yeah that was really blasé, wasn't it?

This was Val's voice. Sarah smiled to herself. She was ridiculously excited right now. Melissa had been right. Her life was changing. Maybe it would be something different from the bleak, barren existence she had been living for so many years.

Barren, maybe, but not bleak. Not always, said Paul's voice. *And your life has been safe.*

Safe but with nothing in it. No risk. No excitement. No kids. No passions. Sure, it had been safe with Paul, but without purpose. Since Paul had been gone, she had thought she was safe with Karl, but he had proved her wrong. First thing Monday morning, she would call Matt Greenley and see what he could tell her about getting a copy of her trust. And after that, she would take a little trip one evening to the club that Laura mentioned, the Stigmata Club. But today, she was going to do frivolous things.

Sarah spent the morning working in her little garden. She walked to the grocery store in the afternoon to pick up some food for tomorrow. She didn't pick up anything for this evening because she knew Caio would want to cook. Surprisingly, he wasn't in the store that afternoon, even though she knew that it was his shift. She thought about asking Mitch, but then thought again. That would look odd.

When she went home, she got a long shower, and blow-dried her hair. She then put on a tiny bit of makeup, a simple peasant shirt and some drop earrings. It wasn't fancy, but it made her look nice. At least, she thought she looked nice and that was a change. She did all this early because she thought he might come early. Sure enough, there was a knock on her door at 5:30.

When Sarah opened the door, he was standing there with groceries and his backpack. He smiled at her, and she felt herself beaming back.

"I got my test back," he said, as she stepped back for him to come in.

"And?" she asked.

"And if I tell the other guys my grades, they'll want you to tutor them next year," he said with a laugh.

"That good, huh?" she asked as he put the groceries on the counter and gave her a stern look.

"'Son, this is the best paper I have read in all my years at this school. I don't know what you have done to improve yourself so much, but I applaud you. I applaud you'," he mimicked raising his eyebrows and putting his hand under his chin and stroking it as if it were a beard.

"Oh wow. The pressure will be on for next year then," Sarah said laughing. "I guess you don't have any more tests or anything as next week is the last week of school."

Caio's face fell. "I have one more civics test, but can we not talk about that just now? If that's okay. I'd rather just enjoy the evening."

Sarah felt her heart tug. He didn't want this to end either.

"Are we studying tonight? Or watching a movie?"

"Neither. We're just having dinner. I just want to be able to talk to you. I realized that watching the movie the other night wasted time that I could have had getting to know you better. But I just wanted to know what you thought about it," he said. "So, tonight, just dinner, just us."

Sarah felt her heart skip a beat.

"What are we eating?" she said, coming over to look in his bag. He cringed a bit.

"Well, that's the thing. I also didn't want to spend all my time cooking, so I kind of got lazy on this one. I just got steak for the meat, but I did get everything we need for a Greek salad, which is great in the summer. I know I was lazy last week *and* lazy this week, so next time I promise I will cook something more special. I promise promise promise," he said, crossing his heart.

Next time …

"You are a paralegal now?" he asked as he turned the heat up under a pan and pulled tomatoes and cucumbers out of the grocery bag. "But you said you were a lawyer before. What happened?"

"Oh. I married Paul," Sarah replied. "I told you about Paul. He thought I wasn't cut out for law. So I stopped working. But later, when I had to go back to work, all I could get was paralegal work. I had been out of the profession for too long. And I let my license lapse. That was stupid of me."

"Do *you* think you're cut out for law?" Caio asked her, putting the steak in the pan, where it sizzled and produced a puff of steam.

"You know, I was mad at Paul about saying that for a long time. But I think he just said it wrong. I *could* practice law, but I don't think I'd like it. I like the research. I like to study things. I like to make things grow. I don't like tearing things apart. And that's what lawyers often seem to be doing, tearing things apart."

Caio nodded.

"But I need to ask you about that test. How were you able to do that?" Sarah asked.

"To do what?" he asked, chopping up the tomatoes and cucumbers and putting them into a bowl with black olives.

"To write like that. You write like an attorney or a professor. You don't write like a sixteen-year-old," she said.

He turned and looked at her. She didn't know what she was expecting but she wasn't expecting the blasé shrug.

"No, really. Are you that smart?"

"I guess it depends on how you define smart," he said, as he turned back to his salad. "I have lots of experience with lots of things. That's a type of smart."

She was about to say something, but he cut her off.

"Can you grab a plate and get the steaks? I don't want them to overcook." Sarah nodded, getting the plates out.

They added salad and some grapes to the plates with the meat and sat at the table. Caio sat with one of his legs stuck out of the side of the table at an angle so that it was almost touching hers.

Their conversation was light and easy. They talked about everything and nothing of import, and it felt comfortable and natural. She found herself laughing a lot, for no other reason besides that she was happy.

"Tell me what you were like when you were little," he said suddenly.

167

"What?"

"What were you like as a little girl? Were you shy? Were you the leader? Did you want to be a ballerina when you grew up? Did you dream of being a rock star or having a family?"

"Oh wow. I haven't thought of that in such a long time. When I was little, I wanted to be a police officer," she replied, wincing a little.

"Really? A cop? You wanted to be a cop?" he asked, laughing.

"Yes. I know it's kind of weird but I wanted to make the world a better place."

"Why did you change your mind?"

"I guess I thought it could never happen," she said with a sigh.

"Why?" he asked.

"Well, my parents weren't terribly supportive of lots of things that interested me. They didn't even want me to go to law school. They didn't think I was smart enough. Law school was a bit of a rebellion for me. I thought if I could make it through that then they would know I was smart enough and tough enough and sane enough, but it didn't really work like that. In their eyes, I was exactly the same, just with an added piece of paper."

Caio furrowed his brow again.

"What do you mean, sane enough?" he asked.

Shit did I say that? Damn it, I said that.

"Well, I was a very creative kid, when I was really little. And I used to talk to myself using different voices. It freaked my parents out, particularly my mother. She was afraid that I had dissociative identity disorder. Oh sorry, that's multiple personalities—"

"Yeah, I know," Caio said.

Of course he does.

"So, she wanted me tested for everything. I think she might have been a bit disappointed when the psychiatrists told her I was just creative."

"Did you know the voices you spoke in?" Caio asked.

"What do you mean?"

"Were the voices of people you know or knew?" he asked.

Sarah felt herself freeze. Why was he asking this? He couldn't possibly know that for the longest time it had been the voices of her grandma and grandpa.

"I don't know, I don't remember," she said, but she looked away.

Caio got up and she briefly panicked, but he simply removed her plate from in front of her. She had finished all her food without even realizing she was eating. He had turned on the faucet and was washing the dishes. He was actually washing dishes.

"I can't believe you voluntarily do dishes," she said.

Caio laughed. She noticed for the first time that his canine teeth were disproportionately large compared to his other teeth, and a bit more pointed. They weren't really vampiric, or only a little, mainly they looked more like someone who hadn't really needed braces, so had "natural" teeth.

"Actually, I prefer to dry, if I am completely honest," he said.

"That's good then because I prefer to wash," she said, taking the plate from him. It wasn't until after she said it that she realized it sounded quite odd, as she were pairing them in her mind. She cringed and looked down at the water, concentrating on getting all the salad remains from the bowl.

After a few moments, Caio took the bowl from her and began to dry it, standing right next to her. She felt her skin flush as his touched hers from time to time. Other parts of her body were reacting as well, and she felt both guilty and excited. It was probably the strongest feeling she had ever had for anyone at any time in her life.

You need to get him out of here before you make a fool of yourself, said her mother.

"Wow. It must be getting late," she said, looking at the clock. "Yep, it's almost nine o'clock. Your foster family must be getting worried."

No, please don't let him leave.

He laughed dryly. "My foster family lock me out of the house if I'm not back in by eight."

"What? How could they do that? Where would you stay the night? Wait, you've left here after eight before."

"Yeah, so I usually sleep under the bleachers at the basketball court *when* I stay out late."

"Wouldn't your foster parents be horrified if they knew that?"

"You don't know much about foster families, do you?" he said, turning to catch her eye. "Sure, some people are very nice, but my experience has been that more than a few are only in it for the extra income, or—well, other things. Anyway, if I'm not back for dinner that's less money out of their pocket."

He was smiling a bit, but his eyes looked so sad, and so old. How horrible to be tossed around from family to family, with no one really caring about you. She wanted to take him in her arms, but the feeling was not a maternal one, and this made her cringe internally.

Well, at least she could fix this one little problem.

"Well, you'll just have to stay here tonight then," she said, handing him the last plate and turning to head to her bedroom. In the part of her mind that she would admit to, she was thinking about finding sheets and pillows so he would be comfortable on the couch. But in the deep recesses of her brain, she was

169

imagining sneaking out into the living room in the dead of night, to watch him as he slept.

She flipped the light on in the bedroom. It was that time of summer when there was still light in the sky at nine o'clock, but it was the gentle, fragile remnants of the sun which was passing over the horizon, coloring the sky orange, purple, and gray.

She had found some sheets and had just managed to pull an old pillow from under her bed when she heard him. She stood up quickly, aware that he must have had an all too vivid view of her butt as she had crouched looking for the pillow. When she stood and turned around, he was leaning against the doorframe of her bedroom.

"What are you doing?" he asked.

"Oh, I was just getting some sheets and pillows and stuff so that I could make a comfortable place for you on the couch," she said.

He looked at her with such directness that she had to look down. She wasn't sure exactly what his eyes were saying, but they couldn't be saying the things her traitor mind was interpreting.

"Am I sleeping on the couch then?" he asked softly. And as he said this, he flipped off the light and walked into her room, closing the door behind him.

"Yes of course you are, that's the only proper thing," was what she should have said, but instead, she said nothing. She watched him approach her, probably looking like a bunny being approached by a snake.

"Do you want me to sleep on the couch, Sarah?" he asked as he stood directly in front of her and looked into her eyes. He was taller than her by a good six inches. She suddenly felt small.

This is a dream. None of this matters because I am making this up. I am having a dream and I'll wake up soon.

"No, I don't want you to sleep on the couch," she heard herself say, shocking her to the core.

He leaned forward and put his lips to hers, kissing her softly. At first, she did nothing. She simply lingered in the feeling of his soft lips on hers.

This is a dream.

Well, your curtains are wide open. People can see in.

Why do you think he turned off the light?

He pulled back and looked into her eyes. His were large and liquid brown. His skin seemed darker, more tanned, up close. She could see the little bump on his nose that she had been studying in that stupid picture for weeks. In person and up close, it was even more endearing.

He was breathing faster, and so was she … and her legs were shaking. That

170

had happened to her once before, on a night when sex with her husband had been surprisingly good. It had never happened before sex.

She was terrified—and yet …

When he leaned forward to kiss her again, she let him. She opened her mouth to his and felt the wet heat of his tongue. He put his arms around her and pulled her tighter to him. She went up on her tiptoes, pushing her crotch against his. His kisses were no longer light, they were deep, passionate, and demanding.

He moved her backward until they were next to her bed. His hands were on her back and in her hair. He turned slightly and dropped onto the bed, pulling her with him and then rolling her over onto her back, lying half on top of her. She kissed him with a passion that she hadn't thought she was capable of feeling. He pushed her shirt up and put his hands on her waist, her ribs, and then her breasts. With one hand he reached behind her and undid the clasp on her bra on the first try. She put her hands under his T-shirt to feel his warm chest. He sat up and removed his shirt. She was surprised to see that he was broader across the shoulders than she had been expecting, and he had a few scatterings of hair on his chest. Then he bent to kiss her again.

They wound their limbs around each other. His mouth never left hers. If it had, maybe she could have said something, anything. She should and she knew she should, but he didn't let her.

You are the adult here. This is absolutely not okay. You know this is not okay.

Let go. Just let go. This was her own voice, no one else's. No one else was here now. There was no room for anyone else in this.

Caio moved directly on top of her and moved himself so that his hips were between her legs. Her skirt was now pushed up to her waist. He had managed to remove his jeans so that she could feel the hardness of him at the entrance of her. He pulled back for a moment, looking at her face. His eyes met hers and suddenly she felt beautiful. He leaned down and began to kiss her again, deeply and passionately.

Sarah ached for him in a way she had never experienced. When she kissed him, she didn't hold back, and neither did he. These were not delicate, fluttery kisses, these were kisses designed to consume.

And then he was inside her. She gasped. He was larger and wider than she had expected, and she felt herself being stretched and filled. She clutched him and matched his rhythm. She felt the waves rising again. She covered her mouth with her hand again, but he pulled it off and pinned it to the bed.

"I want to hear you," he whispered in her ear.

When they came, they were both loud.

Chapter Twenty-Eight

Alibis in the Gloaming

Saturday June 21

Afterward, they rolled to their sides. He was still inside her.

She surprised herself by laughing.

"What's so funny?" he asked, furrowing his brow.

"Oh, I am thinking that I'm completely damned now."

"For sleeping with me?"

"Well. Yes."

"It's not your fault. It's not like I gave you much choice," Caio said, stroking her hair.

"Oh, I could have stopped you if I had wanted to."

"Could you? I'm not particularly big, but I'm bigger than you. Do you think you could have stopped me? I mean, assuming you had tried."

"You mean you would have raped me?" Sarah asked.

"No, because it wouldn't have been rape. But yes, this was going to happen tonight. I planned it from the moment I came in the door, but I didn't want you to feel responsible. This was my choice. I've wanted you for a long time now."

"How long?" she asked.

"Since I first moved in. I saw you in your office with my foster parents around a year ago. And then I started seeing you a lot when we were playing basketball. I thought you were so beautiful, but you didn't even look at us. I even tried playing shirtless, but I guess that wasn't impressive enough to get your attention," he said with a shy smile.

"It's not that. You are very impressive," Sarah laughed.

"So what was it that finally made you notice me then?" Caio asked.

"It was the way you looked at me. You stopped playing and everything. You just looked so … so open. I'd never seen anyone look at me in a way that was so open and honest. I guess I felt like you were letting me see inside you."

"Yeah. I was trying to be as obvious as I could. And I saw you notice me for the first time," Caio said softly.

"You saw that?"

"Of course, I'm not stupid. Why do you think I went out and spent money getting a haircut, new clothes, and new shoes? I figured if you were looking at me, I wanted to look good to you."

"You knew all that?"

"Yes."

"Do your friends know?" Sarah asked.

"Hmmm. Well. Yeah. That could be a bit of a problem. They know I have a 'crush' on you. But they think I don't have the proverbial snowball's chance with you."

"Why?"

"Because you are an intelligent grown woman, and you're beautiful. Why would you look at a gawky teenage boy?"

She felt herself glow. Beautiful. There were people out there who thought she was beautiful? *He* thought she was beautiful.

He moved slightly and then he was out of her. She felt a sense of loss at this in a way that she hadn't felt before. It was usually a relief when a man pulled out.

He lay on his back looking at the ceiling. It was the gloaming outside, so there was still enough light to see him, but things were fuzzy. He was so beautiful to her. The bump on his nose, his slightly too large ears that hung a bit too low on his head. But these small imperfections just highlighted his beautiful eyes, perfect skin, and glorious lips. Or that was how she saw him, anyway. She suspected other people might not see what she saw.

"I hate that I look like this," Caio said, suddenly.

"That you look like what?" she asked, turning on her side to admire his nose, his long eyelashes, and his delicate lips in the fading light.

"Like a teenager," he said, cringing as he said this.

It was such an odd thing to say.

"You mean you hate being a teenager?" she asked.

"No, no. I just hate looking like it."

"Why?"

"Because it makes things really difficult."

"What sort of things?" she asked.

173

"This sort of thing," he replied, turning on his side to look at her. She felt herself flush again.

"Well, it's not a problem with girls your own age, is it?" she asked. She was trying to act like his social life was no big deal to her.

He blew his hair out of his eyes.

"No, I guess it wouldn't be a problem with them. But I'm not really interested in them, am I? But looking like this is a big problem with someone I am interested in."

She felt her heart begin to beat harder.

"Well, what you look like doesn't make much difference. You still are actually a teenager."

He sighed and plopped back on the pillow, looking up again.

"Yeah," he said and then sighed again. They were quiet for a moment. It was almost completely dark in the bedroom now, but his breathing seemed a bit irregular.

"Are you okay?" she asked, taking his hand.

"What if I wasn't?" he whispered.

"What's wrong?" Sarah asked, sitting up.

"No, what if I wasn't a teenager? What if I just looked like that, but I was actually much older? Like we talked about in that movie."

"What do you mean?"

"I mean, would you see me differently? Would you take me more seriously? Would you feel more comfortable doing what we have done if you thought I was, I don't know, thirty or thirty-five?"

Sarah was silent for a moment.

"I don't think I would like you any more or less but yes, I guess I would take you more seriously, if I am being honest. I mean, we can't really …"

"But if you thought I was thirty or thirty-five, then you could imagine having a relationship with me?" he interjected.

"Yes."

She couldn't believe that had come out of her mouth. She couldn't believe she had admitted that.

"What if you *knew* I was thirty or thirty-five but I still looked sixteen? What about then?"

"Why do you ask?"

"I'm just curious. Would that change things, if you knew I was older, but I just looked a lot younger?"

174

"I guess so. It would still be weird in public, but if there was actual proof that you were that age, then I wouldn't feel like I was taking advantage of you or something."

He laughed in the fading light, and she could see his slightly protruding canine teeth. "Because you would be so likely to take advantage of someone. I bet you've never done anything completely selfish in your entire life."

"Well, maybe not, until just now," she whispered.

"Good. It's about time then," he replied. Then he rolled over and pulled her on top of him and began to kiss her.

"From now on, we are both thirty-five," he whispered in her ear. "When we are together like this, we are both thirty-five. Okay?"

She pulled back for a moment. "But we can't do this again. It's wrong."

"Not if we are both thirty-five," he said, pulling her back down for another kiss.

#

She only realized that they had fallen asleep when she felt Caio get up.

"Where are you going?" she murmured.

"To sleep on the couch," he said, kissing her forehead.

"Why?" she said, starting to sit up but he kissed her and eased her back down.

"I don't want to, but it's the smart thing to do. I'll explain in the morning. Just go back to sleep," he said kissing her again. He might have said "honey" after that, but she wasn't sure. She was barely able to stay conscious.

Sunday June 22

"Morning," Caio said as she came into the kitchen. He was cooking bacon and the smell of it made her stomach growl.

"Morning," she said. He turned around and when he saw her his eyes widened. She looked down and realized that he was completely dressed, and she was wearing only what clothes had managed to stay on her body the night before.

"Oh, right. Hold on," she said, quickly retreating to the bedroom and pulling on her jeans and a new, clean T-shirt.

When she came out, he had put bacon, eggs, and toast on the table with two plates.

175

She sat down in front of him, nibbling on a piece of bacon. Caio ate with enthusiasm.

"I was famished when I woke up, but I didn't want to wake you with the noise."

"Is that why you left last night?" she asked.

"No, I left because you need plausible deniability."

Plausible Deniability? What the hell?

"If something were to happen. If someone were to ever ask you about this, you need to be able to say that I slept on the couch very convincingly. If I actually spend at least part of the night sleeping on the couch, then you can. You could probably pass a lie detector test, if you had to."

She was dumbfounded for probably the thirtieth time in the past twenty-four hours.

"Aren't you hungry?" he said, indicating her plate with his fork. "If you aren't, then I didn't do my job very well last night."

The corner of his mouth turned up just slightly when he said this.

She felt herself blush, probably violet.

"I want to find a way to see you more often, which means I need a good excuse. The school year will be over in two weeks, so I'll need some other reason to be coming over here. Something that won't get you in trouble if ... well, if someone finds out."

She stared at her food. She felt herself glowing. She should tell him that they needed to stop this now. That would be the adult thing to say, just like it would be prudent not to encourage this. It could go nowhere. And yet she couldn't manage to get the words out of her mouth.

He put his hand over hers and looked at her.

"Do you want that? Do you want to see me?"

"It's not about what I want. It's about what I should do," she whispered.

"But I'm not asking what you think you should do, Sarah. I am asking what you want. Do you want me?"

Yes. In every and all ways.

She could only nod.

"Okay then. I'll figure something out. All right?" he asked. She raised her eyes to meet his.

She was getting in over her head and she knew it.

Suddenly, they heard the mail truck going down the street.

"Right. I need to go home and face the music. And I can't look too guilty leaving, so let me get my books and try to look academic."

He grabbed his books and his bag, and she stood up. He smiled at her and backed up toward the door.

"Hey, I am usually at the basketball court between five and six thirty during the week. And if I know you will be walking by, I will be sure to be there," he said, smiling at her. He had his hand on the door and was turning to leave.

She felt a little twinge in her heart. And the memory of the way he had looked at her before, the way he had ignored her, came rushing back.

"Oh. Well, you didn't always seem comfortable with it when I came by before," she said suddenly. "Maybe you don't like being seen with me or something."

She tried to laugh a bit when she said this, but the hurt in her voice was apparent.

Caio whipped around sharply, dropped his bag, crossed the kitchen to her, took her hand and led her into her living room. The room was still dark as she hadn't opened the curtains yet.

He sat her down on the couch, took her hands and looked at her hard.

"That hurt you. I didn't mean it to hurt you," he said. She felt her eyes well with tears. She felt betrayed by her own body but all she could really do was nod.

He nodded back.

"I thought I had been too forward," he said, taking her face in his hands. "You know, I had asked your first name in a grocery store full of people, when I already knew it. I was trying to get your attention and it wasn't very subtle. You seemed frightened by that, so I didn't want to make it worse."

"I'm sure I didn't look scared the next Saturday," she said softly, looking down.

"No, you didn't. You looked beautiful. You were wearing that yellow dress and you looked like a sunflower. When you looked at me, you looked so hopeful. And that scared *me*."

"You *were* scared. I thought you looked uncomfortable," she said, eyes welling again.

"No, not uncomfortable. I was scared, there's a big difference," he said. "I was scared about what I was feeling and even more scared that you seemed to be feeling something too. Like I said, I have had a thing for you for a long time. The thought that I would ever have a chance with you didn't even enter into my mind until that minute. And when it did, I realized what it would mean for you."

"What do you mean?"

"I mean that I could bring you a lot of trouble. You have a horrible boyfriend, partner, asshole, or whatever you want to call him. I worried about the consequences if something happened between us, and he found out. I worried about what would happen to your life and your reputation. I didn't want to cause you any pain. So, the next few times I saw you, I tried to be friendly, but not too friendly. I could see that this hurt you, but I thought it would be better than the hurt I could cause if I let myself go with this."

"What changed your mind?" she whispered.

"I realized how badly you were already being hurt. And that there wasn't one goddamned person around you who was trying to stop that hurt."

"You felt sorry for me."

"No, not exactly," he said softly, kissing her hand. "It reminded me that we don't get a lot of chances for happiness in life. If we actively push them away because we're afraid something bad will happen, well, something bad will eventually happen anyway. Life is like that. And I haven't felt what I feel for you in a really long time."

"How long can long be with you, you are only—"

"Thirty-five. Remember, we are both thirty-five," he said. She smiled a bit, but his face was deadly serious.

"So I decided to fail my geography test so I would have a legitimate excuse to ask for help."

"Then you don't really need my help as a tutor?"

"We didn't really do much studying, did we? And you saw my grade on this test. No one turns things around that fast."

He smiled, but only briefly. He turned serious again.

"But I want you to know that I would never ever be ashamed to be seen with you. I know that's what you were thinking. For some really ridiculous reason, you don't seem to be aware of how gorgeous you are. If it wasn't … if I wasn't … well, if things were different, I would be so proud to be seen with you. As it is, I have to watch other people stare at you without saying anything about it."

"No one stares at me," she said softly.

He laughed.

"If you don't see them, then you must be blind." Then he leaned forward and kissed her again. It started as a small kiss but quickly derailed into something a lot more. He finally pulled away and blew out a breath.

"Okay. If I don't go now then I won't, and that will start getting harder and harder to explain, if anyone happens to notice."

He kissed her again quickly. "I'll see you next Saturday at the latest. Maybe sooner if I can figure something out."

He then got up quickly, walked to the kitchen and grabbed his bag. But before he went, he leaned back around the corner and blinked hard at her with
both eyes. She didn't quite know what that meant but she blinked back.

Chapter Twenty-Nine

Fear, Felonies and Flexible Time

Sunday June 22

When Caio left, Sarah's heart was still pounding. She could still feel the touch of his lips on hers. When she licked them, she imagined that she could still taste him. She felt a warmth all around her that made her skin tingle.

Unfortunately, the afterglow was short-lived. The voices in her head, which were largely silent while Caio was there, were suddenly wildly vocal.

What the hell have you done? You just slept with an underage boy? shrieked her mother.

"Yes, I slept with him but—"

But nothing. Do you know how much trouble you would be in if someone found out? snarled her father.

Did you think that maybe that is why he did it? continued her mother. *Maybe he did it so he can blackmail you. That wouldn't be all that surprising. Foster kid. No money. And here you are, a woman being taken care of and having her mortgage paid by her boyfriend.*

You know, that's possible, Sarah. Had you thought of that? asked Paul.

Yes, and remember that's the boyfriend that you just cheated on, said her father.

With a minor, Sarah, a minor, said Paul.

"He's not a minor, he's sixteen!" Sarah snapped.

Actually, I wouldn't argue that point, Sarah. Age of consent in New York is seventeen, Paul's replied, dripping in condescension.

"What—?" Sarah began but her mother cut her off.

That doesn't even matter. What matters is that she just took advantage of a young boy.

"I didn't start it. He did. I didn't seduce him. He seduced me. And when the fuck did you start caring about anybody else besides yourself?" snapped Sarah.

Don't you take that tone with your mother, snarled her father.

180

And you were the one who suggested he spend the night, Paul's chimed in.

"I was just trying to help," she said to herself.

You were doing no such thing. You have a thing for this boy, and you were thinking with your privates and not your brain. God knows what sort of harm you might have just done to him, said her mother.

Sarah felt her blood go cold. Could she have hurt him? The idea that she could hurt anyone seemed absurd. But what if she had caused this wonderful person harm? A person who had been nothing but kind to her. A person who had befriended her and treated her with respect. A person who listened to her like her opinion mattered.

Sarah felt her heart begin to pound arrhythmically and it became hard to breathe. She leaned down and put her head between her knees.

Shit. What if Paul's right and he is a minor? *What if this hurts him? What if I hurt him?*

Sarah felt the walls of the room begin to close in on her. The air seemed too heavy and thick to breathe.

Sarah, you need to go upstairs, Val said softly.

What she needs to do is try to find a way to make sure that no one will find out about this and make sure that it never happens again, said Paul.

She also needs to make sure Karl never finds out. He would be furious if he did, said her mother.

Well, I think we can all agree on that at least, said Larry. *She should certainly make sure that Karl doesn't find out. So perhaps she should change her sheets.*

He delivered this sentence slowly and deliberately, as if casting a line.

And they took the bait.

Oh god. Of course. You need to do that right now, Sarah. The smell of that boy is still in your bed, shrieked her mother.

It was this last sentence that sent Sarah up the stairs. Not because she wanted to change the sheets, but because she wanted to lie down in a spot that still smelled of him. Despite all the things that they were saying, and her fears about what she had done and what she might have done to him, she still craved being in his presence. Changing her sheets was an excuse to go to the bedroom where the smell of him would still be the strongest.

But when she got to the room, she was stopped in her tracks by an object lying on her nightstand. She knew what it was the minute she laid eyes on it. She had seen it before. It was Caio's wallet.

She moved toward it almost warily.

Don't you look in that thing. What is in there is none of your business, snapped her mother.

181

Is it not? asked Val. *Do you think he left this here by accident? Has there been anything about this person that would make you think that he's either distracted or forgetful?*

You had sex last night. People tend to forget things in those circumstances, said Paul. He hadn't said much in the past few days, but he seemed to be trying to make up for lost time this morning.

Sarah sat down on the edge of her bed and picked up the wallet. It was made of brown leather and incredibly soft to the touch. When she opened it, she saw that it contained some of the same things she had seen the first time she looked in it. First, there was a lot of money in it. She pulled out the bills and found that he had $520 in cash. She wasn't sure what was normal for teens these days, but this would be a lot of money to have in her wallet, so she assumed it was a lot for him. The condom was also in his wallet, but they hadn't used it last night. She had thought about it a few times since, but she couldn't bring herself to get worried about it. It's not like she was a teenage girl likely to get pregnant and, for better or worse, she had assumed that he was an unlikely candidate to be carrying an STD. These were all after-the-fact excuses, at the time she wouldn't have wanted anything to be between them.

The licenses were also still in his wallet. There were three of them this time, all sitting in different credit card spots. The first one was a current license that listed his birthday as May 4, and it showed that he turned sixteen this year. It was pale blue and had the New York State seal in the background, along with the Statue of Liberty. It looked completely legitimate. The name listed on this was Caio Renato Silva.

The second one was much harder to fathom. It was also a driver's license, but from North Carolina. This one was on whitish pink paper with a photo of Caio on the left-hand side, in front of a red background. It looked much older and when Sarah looked at the date of issue, she had to wipe her eyes and re-look. The date of issue was 04/28/1974. She blinked and rechecked to see if it might be a typo but no, the date of expiry was 04/23/1978. The name on this one was Caio Jose Silva. He looked exactly the same as he did now. The birthday listed was 04/28/1956.

Okay. This looks legit but it has to be a fake, right? But why would someone have a fake ID that made them out to be at an age to get Social Security? Why not just go for twenty-two or twenty-three at the highest?

Sarah put this one down and picked up the last ID.

If the one before was perplexing, this last one was mind-altering. The card was paper, and it looked very old. It was a faded cream color with bright orange lettering and embellishments. On the top was written *NOT A PASS—FOR*

IDENTIFICATION ONLY. Just below that it read *War Department, The Adjutant General's Office, Washington DC.* Underneath these words was what seemed to be a military seal and underneath the seal were the words *Certificate of identity to be issued to Military and Civilian Protected Personnel.*

Underneath all this was his name, Caio L. Silva and his title, Private First Class, with his signature and a countersignature of someone else. To the left of this was a picture of Caio, looking almost identical to how he looked this morning, but with shorter hair. His name was listed on a board he was holding in front of him, along with his military number. But what made Sarah lose her breath and reach out to hold the bed was what was listed beneath his picture. Right below his photograph was a line that read *Date issued.* The date next to it was *29 May 1944.*

Oh my god. What the hell is going on here? This was a military ID from the 1940s. This was not something that you can easily fake, and it would be fairly easy to check.

Easy to check.

Sarah grabbed the IDs and ran downstairs to her computer. She quickly logged in and pulled up Ancestry.com. She put his name in. Nothing came up in the overall search, but when she searched military records, she found a C. L. Silva who died in battle in 1944. It took a bit of cross-referencing, but she finally found of photo of C. L. Silva, and there he was, looking like he did when he left this morning.

Sarah sat back in her chair and put her hands on her head. This was a military record online. It wasn't something that was easy to fake or alter. And it was from World War II. She squeezed her eyes shut because she was afraid her head might explode. Her brain was whirling fast, connecting data, facial expressions, comments and trying to tie them to this new piece of information that she had discovered. She actually was beginning to think she might be having a breakdown when she heard laughing in her head.

She closed her eyes and saw Val in front of her, sitting on the cream couch that had been in the lounge at their law school. There was nothing there, just Val on the couch in a ring of light—and she was laughing.

"What the hell are you laughing about? Did you … can you not … didn't you see what I just saw?" Sarah asked.

Yep, sure did. And you know what I thought?

Sarah just stared at her, as Val put her hand over her mouth, stifling laughter.

I was thinking that it seems like an older man is taking advantage of you, she said, bursting out in peals of laughter and slapping her leg. The tension in Sarah's head was immediately cut by about half and she felt herself starting to giggle.

Jesus, those uptight assholes you call your parents are going to have to eat some serious crow. Seems like you didn't sleep with a minor after all, Val said, wiping the tears from her eyes.

"I don't know. I mean. Could that really be true?"

Oh, come on Sarah, you know it is. It all adds up. The maturity, the weird word choices, the test, the wanting to watch Big *and then grilling you on emotional versus physical age.*

"Still, it seems crazy," she said.

Well, you know the axiom, said Larry, appearing out of the darkness. *If you rule out the impossible, then whatever is left, however improbable, is the truth.*

"Wouldn't not aging be impossible?" Sarah asked.

Larry shrugged. *Not all creatures age, at least not in the way we do. Biological immortality is well documented in bacteria and yeast. Also, a lot of people would think our presence in your head was impossible, but I think we managed to convince you that we are really here.*

"Sort of," Sarah said. She was about to say something else when she felt everyone disappear and she was sitting in her kitchen in the fading light of the day.

Her cell phone was ringing.

#

"Hello?"

"Hi Sarah," said Karl. The sound of his voice felt like roaches crawling across her soul. Just hearing it made her feel unclean.

"Hi Karl," she said.

Why was he calling this early? Was he checking up on her?

"Hey, I just wanted to give you a call and tell you that I will be coming back on Friday, and to ask you if you wanted to go on a date Saturday."

Shit. That's when I usually see Caio. Is there a way that I can get out of this without it looking suspicious? I can't say I have to work, because it's a weekend. I certainly can't say I have other plans. Shit shit shit. I'm taking too long to respond.

"Sarah, are you there?"

"Yes. I'm here."

"Okay. Look. I know there are lots of reasons why you might not be really happy to see me right now," Karl said. There was an abnormal jittery quality to his voice that made it even more grating. "I know there was the unfortunate incident where I lost my temper, but that won't happen again. And I understand it better. I understand why you were flirting so openly with that teenager."

What the fuck are you talking about?

Just stay quiet, said Larry suddenly.

"Angela told me that you know about Meghan."

184

Oh, this is what this is about.

I told you that was a good idea. At least he's on the defensive, said Val.

Hush, said Larry.

"I need to tell you that I took Meghan on this trip with me."

"You did?" Sarah said, putting as much coldness into her voice as could.

"No wait," Karl said quickly. "You need to understand. I took her so I could say goodbye to her. I've called everything off. She's really upset, of course, but everything that has happened recently made me realize what you and I have together. I don't want to lose you, Sarah."

Doesn't he mean "I don't want to lose your money, Sarah"? Val said coldly.

"Sarah, are you still there?"

"Um hmm," she said.

"I understand if you don't believe me, and I want to say how sorry I am that you feel hurt by my actions."

I am noticing how you aren't saying you are sorry for your actions. But you would never guess that I would notice something like that.

And you should be thankful for his ignorance right now, Sarah. But you can't rely on it, said Larry.

"So I just want to be able to talk to you over dinner on Saturday night. You won't have to be competing with Meghan for my time anymore. What do you say?"

"Okay," Sarah said. "We can have dinner Saturday."

Do better than that, Larry said. *He must believe that you still want him.*

"I would like that," she said.

"Excellent," Karl said, and his voice sounded more stable. Now that he felt he was getting some of his control back, Sarah could feel a huge suck of power as if he were pulling energy from her. Had he always done that?

Yep, he sure has.

"Is there anything you want from Chicago?" he asked.

A terrorist on your plane home.

She started to say "no" but stopped herself. That wasn't the right thing to say.

"Anything you want to get me is good," she said instead. She made her voice soft and timid.

"Okay. I will see you Saturday night," he said.

"Okay, Karl," she started to hang up, but his voice stopped her.

"Oh, one more thing Sarah. Do you know Laura at the courthouse very well?"

Danger. Danger. Danger. Speak carefully here. He knows something.

185

"I know her a bit. I go by the court a lot for work," she said, paused and then added, "Why, do you need something from her?"

Don't elaborate too much. That looks suspicious.

"Oh. No. It's just that Ted—you know, the junior associate in our office—he saw you talking to Laura for a long time the other day and asked if you guys were friends."

"No. No."

Think. Think. Think. It has to be near the truth.

"It's just that—look, Karl, don't get mad," she said. "Promise you won't get mad."

"I promise," he said. He said this too quickly and the edge was back in his voice.

"Well, her granddaughter is selling Girl Scout Cookies. She wanted me to buy some. And I did. I bought a couple of boxes."

"And?" Karl asked.

"Well. I know you think I am a bit overweight and that I shouldn't be eating stuff like that. But I only bought two boxes."

Karl laughed out loud.

"Is that what you are worrying about? Listen, Sarah. A couple of cookies won't make much difference one way or another. Don't worry so much about that."

Note he isn't saying you don't need to lose weight, Val said.

"Oh, okay," Sarah said, forcing a brightness in her voice despite the fact that she was stabbing the notebook in front of her with a pen.

"Okay then. See you next Saturday night," Karl said, and then hung up.

What was that about? Val asked.

He thinks that he might lose me, so he's making an effort. Don't worry, it won't last.

Sarah, you can't be cavalier about this, said Larry. It was almost a snap, and he never snapped. *If he is changing his behavior like this, then something or someone put the fear of god into him. This makes him very dangerous right now. He's more dangerous than he was before. He can't guess for one second that you are considering leaving him. If he guesses that, then he might do worse than simply slapping you.*

"What do you mean?"

I mean, he is the trustee of your estate. He has power already. And you don't know what the trust says about what will happen in the event of your death.

"You think he might try to kill me?" she whispered aloud. Suddenly she felt very cold.

Yes. I do, Larry said. *And to the rest of you, I should point out that if Sarah dies, you have nowhere else to go—at least, some of you will have nowhere else to go. Some of us chose*

186

this, so our duty will end at that point. But for those latched on to Sarah's soul because you fractured your own, how do you think it will turn out for you if you have done something that ends up getting her killed?

There was dead silence in her head.

Given that, are we all in agreement that from this point on, we are together in protecting Sarah's well-being? Larry asked. His voice sounded different than she had ever heard it before. It was strong, resonant and commanding.

I bet this is how he would sound in court.

I'm not hearing any answers. Are we together on this? he said, even stronger and a bit menacing this time.

I'm in. But I've always been in, said Val.

Yes. I never wanted to hurt Sarah, I just— Paul started to say but Larry cut him off.

Yes, is all I need to hear. Isabelle?

Yes, said her mother, sounding a bit shocked at the use of her first name.

Derrick?

Yeah. Okay, said her dad.

Good. Sarah, you need to plan to get away as soon as you can. This is not sustainable. If you could arrange to leave by tomorrow, I would suggest doing so, but I know you have some things you want to finish up. Still, you need to start planning your way out now and it needs to be done before things with Karl come to a head, said Larry.

"Yeah, I know. I don't think I can sleep with him again."

Honey, if he tries to do that on Saturday, you will have to do it, Val said softly. *Otherwise, he will be too suspicious. It's been a long time since you two had sex and it's been enough time since he hit you for him to think you should be over it. So, if he wants it, you have to give it.*

"I'm not sure I can," Sarah said, thinking of Caio, his dark eyes, his kind voice and his easy laugh.

You don't have a choice, said Larry. *Your life may depend on it.*

Sarah put her head down on her table and had to fight to keep her nausea at bay. She had six days until Karl came home. She had six days to find her way out of this situation.

Chapter Thirty

Lessons in Snake Charming

Monday June 23

Sarah woke up Monday morning with a raging headache and a cramping bladder. She stumbled to the bathroom to pee and almost fell over. Her head was whirling. She was on emotional overload, and she knew it. Her life, which had been so emotionally dead until thirty days ago was suddenly complicated to the point that she could barely keep up with what emotion she was feeling at any given moment. This morning the overwhelming emotion she felt was the burning desire to talk to Caio, but she was also afraid to see him.

Of course you are. It's very possible that you were just an easy one-night stand for him, said her mother.

Because Sarah is known for being such an easy relationship target. Jesus, are you that blind, woman? snarled Val.

Need I remind you all that we have a pact about keeping Sarah healthy right now, said Larry. *This includes her emotional health. If we mess with her mental stability, then she could make stupid mistakes that endanger her physical health. So right now, we are all going to be nothing but supportive, or we are going to shut up. Understand?*

There was silence. Shut up it was.

Sarah, just think through the things you need to do today, in order, said Larry. *That will clear your brain.*

Sarah looked at herself in the mirror. Her eyes were bloodshot, and her hair was a mess. But strangely, she didn't look half bad. She wondered what that was about.

"First, before I go to work, I should call Matt Greenley about the trust and leave a message. I can ask him if there's a time that I can call him outside of office hours," she muttered to herself.

Good, said Larry. *Then?*

"Work. I need to find some way to help on the Davies case. But I have no idea what I can do," she said as she walked downstairs to the kitchen. She grabbed a bowl and poured some Corn Flakes in it. Thinking about the Davies case helped distract her from the intimate and surreal turn in her relationship with Caio.

We'll get back to Caio, said Larry. *Right now, let's focus on work. Is there any information you can ferret out that will help Melissa or Phillip with this case? And if you do, can you keep yourself from being implicated?*

"If only I had had a video recorder or something with me when Chris had revealed that Anne Marie was the one who said that Alex was all about sex," she muttered.

Yes, that would have been good, but it wouldn't have been enough. If you had known what he was going to say, you might have been able to probe to get more answers.

Probe. Wait—maybe …

An embryonic plan was forming in Sarah's brain. It was something that could work, but it would require a level of subterfuge she wasn't sure if she was capable of pulling off. Michael was a professional at reading people. He was even better at picking up lies and half-truths. And she would have to fool him to a degree that she had never tried before.

I have an idea, she said in her head.

Do you want to share? asked Larry.

You mean you can't just read it from my brain?

No. Not exactly. We can only read concrete thoughts that have gained enough weight, said Larry. *Also, you can shut us out of any thoughts that you want to shut us out of.*

She doesn't need to know this, said Paul.

Yes, in fact she does, said Larry. *All you have to do is put a mental circle around us. In fact, you can do that now. That limits us to only hearing what you directly think to us, but we can still direct questions to you, so it won't stop the barrage of commentary from some of us.*

I don't think that's a good idea, said Paul, but Sarah knew good advice when she heard it. In her mind, she imagined all the voices in her head in a spotlight and she drew a circle around them.

There was silence in her head that felt very much like sulking.

About this idea of yours? asked Larry.

I think it's better if I don't tell you, Sarah thought at them. *I'm not sure how well I can pull it off if I know you are judging me on it. I'll need to act convincing and spontaneous, and I can't do that without it actually being sort of spontaneous. But it might work.*

Sarah was starting to feel more in control, more stable. She had a plan. It might be a good one. She just had to implement it.

Good. On to Caio, said Larry, and Sarah felt her gut wrench. *Your first objective is to give him back his wallet.*

"What can I say about what I saw in his wallet? Should I say something about that?" Sarah asked.

Wait and see how he reacts. I have a feeling that Caio will find a way to solve this problem for you all by himself. This time it was Val talking, and she had a smile in her voice.

"Right," Sarah said, sighing to herself. "First things first." She went upstairs. After getting dressed and putting on a bit of makeup, she took her phone from out of the charger and looked up the number of Matt Greenley.

The phone went immediately to an answering service, as she expected.

"Hi Matt. My name is Sarah Baker. I got your number from Laura at the courthouse. I was wondering if there was a time that I could call you outside of normal working hours." She paused for a moment before adding, "It's a sensitive issue."

She then rattled off her cell phone number and hung up. Her heart was beating fast.

And it was only 7:30 a.m. What was the rest of her day going to be like?

#

Sarah was at the office by 7:45 and ready for Michael when he showed up at 8:15.

"Michael, can I speak with you for a moment?" she asked when he came in.

"Sure, Sarah, what can I do for you?" he said, stopping and leaning over the counter above her desk.

"May I speak to you in private?" she asked. Michael's eyes widened a bit, but he nodded and motioned to his office.

Michael hung up his coat and then sat down behind his desk. Sarah noted that his desk had a closed front. This made her think of the story of Alex and his dad, causing bile to rise in her throat. She fought it back and sat down in front of him.

"I'm concerned that we may have a problem with the Davies deposition set for July ninth," she said.

Michael raised his eyebrows, leaned forward, put his hands on the table and laced his fingers.

"Why so?" he asked.

"Well, the other side wants to depose the children, right?" she said.

Michael nodded.

"I'm concerned about what they will say," she said.

Michael leaned back with a smile like the cat who ate the canary.

"Thank you for your concern, and I understand it. But we have had some very serious conversations with Alex, and I think he understands the repercussions of telling lies in depositions," he said.

"It's not Alex I'm worried about," she said. "It's the younger ones."

Michael sat forward again, eyes now intently focused on her.

"What makes you say that?" he said.

"The youngest son said some very strange things to me the other day when I was watching them," she said. Michael's eyes began scanning her face.

Careful. Careful. Careful. Continue carefully.

"Tell me," he said. Sarah then recounted the incident where Chris had told her that all Alex could think about was sex. Michael's eyes never left her face.

"The last thing he said was that Anne Marie was the one who said that all Alex could do was think about sex," she said. She didn't mention that Chris had also quoted Anne Marie as saying that Alex *needed* lots of sex. She didn't want to overplay her hand. She saw Michael's knuckles go white, but his face was flat and emotionless. He was watching her. It felt like she was being monitored by a lie detector.

You might need to be able to pass a lie detector test one day.

"Listen, we all know that this is the way kids tease each other. But I was worried that if the other side hears something like that, they will have a field day with it. So I thought we might want to assess the younger kids a bit before the deposition."

I'm doing this for the firm. I'm doing this for the firm, she thought over and over like a mantra. She hoped this is what he would read in her face.

At first Michael said nothing. His eyes scanned her face. Then his face relaxed and he nodded.

"Thank you, Sarah. I didn't know about that. And you're right, the other side would jump on that. I will definitely talk to the boys before the deposition."

"Okay. I just wanted you to know. I hope I am not overstepping my boundaries," she said, looking down a bit.

"Sarah, this is exactly the sort of thing that we value from you. You have extraordinary insight and research skills. Never apologize for those. I would have been upset if you hadn't brought this to my attention."

"Thanks Michael," she said, forcing a smile. She hoped it looked radiant rather than psychotic.

Do this carefully. This has to be said just perfectly.

As she got up and started walking toward the door, she could hear Michael opening his briefcase. With her hand on the door, she turned.

191

"Um, Michael. I just had a thought, as you said you value my insight," she said.

Michael looked up at her.

"Well, I'm a lot less threatening than you are. If you ask the boys questions in a formal sort of setting, then they may not be as forthcoming with you as they would with me. They don't really know my role here in the firm. They see me as just some sort of receptionist. So do you think it would be a good idea if I ran them through some deposition questions first, to get their responses in a less intimidating environment? Because you know how good Phillip Seider is at being soft and cajoling with witnesses."

Michael looked at her and smiled.

"Sarah, you're absolutely right. I think that's a brilliant idea. Write up some deposition questions. Probe on this issue. And make sure that you speak with each of the boys individually. I want to know what they will say when the others aren't around to correct them or silence them."

"Should I talk to Alex as well?" she asked.

"Yes. That would be very useful. Get a read on whether you think he will start spouting nonsense at the deposition. He shouldn't, but he has been in more contact with his mother recently, and god knows what sort of things she has been feeding him."

Sarah nodded. "How priority is this?" she asked.

"Get it done by early next week," he said. "And thanks again, Sarah."

Sarah walked out, closed the door behind her and let out a small sigh of relief. She made it through Step One. Step Two would depend on what she could get the boys to say. And she had to accomplish this while keeping anyone from getting suspicious.

#

At 5:30, Michael left the building. By six, Sarah had her walking shoes on and was heading out the door. As she was walking, she heard her phone ring, but didn't recognize the number so she let it go to voicemail.

She was feeling ridiculously nervous about seeing Caio. In truth, she wasn't even sure she would see him. He hadn't told her when he would be on the basketball court. He hadn't said much of anything really. Oh wait, he said he would see her next Saturday, and Karl had just told her he wanted to have a date night with her on Saturday.

Shit.

Just at that moment, she started down the road with the basketball court. Caio was there with Mouse and Ash. It was only the three of them today. When

192

Caio saw her, he immediately tossed the ball to Ash and walked toward the fence. The other two boys exchanged looks and smiles, then said something to Caio that Sarah couldn't hear. Caio just shrugged. Sarah stopped by the fence.

"Hi," he said with a smile as he approached. But his jaw was set, and his eyes searched hers. She suddenly realized with shock that he looked insecure. This made her want to kiss him.

"Hi," she said. "Umm. I needed to tell you a couple of things."

"I can still come by Saturday, right?" he asked suddenly.

"Well, that's the thing. Karl called," she said. Caio's brow furrowed. He looked pained. "I didn't want to but he kind of bullied me into going out with him on Saturday."

"Oh. Okay," Caio said.

"No. No. Wait. Any other day is fine. Really. It's just … well … it was just crappy timing," she said. Caio's brow relaxed but his eyes were still intent on her face.

"Also, umm, you left your wallet," she said.

"Yeah, I know," he said.

"I brought it back," she started, reaching into her purse.

The other boys were starting to walk over toward them.

"I can come by and pick it up tomorrow night, if that's okay with you."

Tomorrow. Her heart bloomed.

"That's perfect," she said.

"Okay. See you then," he said, turning back toward the boys. But he turned again, caught her eye and blinked hard. She did the same. He had done this before. She didn't know what it meant but it felt intimate.

It's cat language, Val said softly. *If you'd ever had cats then you'd know what he just said to you.*

Sarah's heart felt hot in her chest.

Tomorrow, she only had to wait until tomorrow. But what could she say? *I went through your wallet and discovered that you have military IDs that would put you at an age to get social security?*

She had just made it into her house when her phone rang again. She picked up this time.

"Is this Sarah Baker?"

"Yes, it is," she replied.

"Good. Very good. This is Matt Greenley. I got your message, and I think you are right. It is very important for us to speak."

His words didn't exactly surprise her, but his open manner and delivery did.

"I don't have time to talk right now, but is there a night this week that I can call you?" he asked.

Not tomorrow.

"Any time after Wednesday is fine," Sarah replied.

"Excellent. Thursday evening then. Shall we say I call you on this number at seven?" Matt said.

"That would be perfect," Sarah said.

"Good," Matt said. "And Sarah, it wouldn't be a good idea to tell anyone that you have spoken to me. But you already know that, right?"

Sarah felt unreality wash over her again, but her voice spoke for her.

"Yes. I know that."

"Good," he said. "I will talk to you Thursday night then."

Then he hung up. Sarah stood for a moment in her kitchen, realizing that she had now stepped on to another path that there was probably no backing away from.

Chapter Thirty-One

Resurrecting the Dress

Tuesday June 24

Tuesday felt like the longest day of Sarah's life at work. It was getting harder and harder to be there. The only way that she found to get through it was by concentrating on menial, detail-oriented tasks. Today, she chose to collate everyone's billable hours. This was a long and tedious task, but it kept her mind engaged. It wasn't until about four o'clock that she got a call from Andrew Davies, telling her that the earliest time he could bring the boys in was on Monday June 30. This meant that she was stuck in this place, and therefore stuck with Karl, until at least that date. This was not good news.

She managed to get out of the office by 6:45. Caio had told her that he would be by during the "evening" but hadn't given a specific time. So, on her walk home from work, she looked for him on the basketball court, but no one was there. Instead, she found him sitting on her front steps when she arrived home. She should have found this concerning. It was reckless and open, but she found she couldn't make herself care. She was just ridiculously happy to see him. Even the question of his licenses didn't seem so important.

"Hi," she said.

"Hi," he said a bit sheepishly. "I hope you aren't mad that I am here a bit early, but—"

"No. I am really happy you're early," she said.

"I didn't have time to get groceries, 'cause I sort of just came straight over," he said as they went inside. "And I know I promised to make you something good today. But I was kind of planning for next Saturday, so I didn't have time to get what I needed."

"I'm sorry about that," she said, dropping her bag and turning to face him.

"I didn't want to have to do it."

"I know," he said, nodding slightly. "Listen, do you want to eat now? If you do, then I am sure I can find something here. But if you're not hungry yet …"

"I'm not that hungry," she said. She didn't have to say anything else. He pulled her into his arms and kissed her. The window was open, and he must have noticed this because he took her hand and led her upstairs to her bedroom. Once inside, he pulled her on to the bed, but he didn't kiss her. He just held her in his arms.

"I've missed you," he said.

"Me too," she said. "I was starting to worry that—"

"That maybe it was a one-night stand. That I wouldn't be interested anymore. Or that maybe I had come to my senses and realized this could never work. Or that I would realize that I could have so many other people so why would I choose you?"

"Yes," she whispered. 'How did you know?"

"Because I was worried about exactly the same things," he said. "With a few others mixed in."

She looked at him. He looked so young but once again, his expressions didn't match his age. His expression was one of desperation and longing.

"Umm. I saw your wallet," she said softly.

"Did you look in it?" he asked.

"Did you want me to?" she asked.

"Yeah. I did."

"Well, then yes I did. But I have to tell you that it really confused me."

"That's not surprising," he said running his fingers through the strands of hair that hung around her face.

"Can you explain?" she asked.

"Not right now. I'll explain later. I promise. But I knew you would be feeling guilty and self-conscious and all that other stuff … because—"

"Oh, let's not forget the paranoid fear that you might be doing this to try to blackmail me," Sarah muttered.

Caio's mouth dropped open.

"What?! Where did that idea come from? Wait, it's the people in your head, right?" he said, sighing. The openness of his statement and his acknowledgment of this shocked her.

"Well, it's absurd," he continued. "What could I blackmail you for?"

"Well, I … just … well, that's the thing," Sarah said, her mind still stuck on his statement about the voices. "It turns out that I might actually have money. But I just don't have a way to get it."

"What do you mean?"

"Well, Karl asked me to sign a paper, and I secretly took a picture of it. It was a trust. In my name. It was left to me by my late husband."

"And you think Karl is the trustee?" Caio asked.

Once again, he knows legal terms.

"Yes. I think he's the trustee and I think he has been lying to me."

"What are you going to do?"

"I called an attorney that was recommended by Laura at the courthouse. A guy named Matt Greenley."

Caio nodded. "He's good."

"How do you know?"

Caio shrugged. "What did he say?"

"He said he would call me on Thursday, and we would talk about it."

"You haven't told anyone else, have you?"

"No. No one."

"You shouldn't," he said.

"That's what Matt said."

"Well, to put your mind at rest, I don't need money," he said calmly but his eyes looked hurt.

"I didn't really think that. It's just …"

"I know," he said. "You've put up with a lot of shit that you shouldn't have had to put up with, for a really long time."

She wasn't quite sure what he meant, but she loved him for saying it.

She loved him. There, she said it, at least in her own head.

She kissed him.

"You were worried that I wouldn't want you?"

"Yeah. Of course. I have lots of reason to worry about that," he said.

"No, you don't," she said.

He kissed her then, hard. She felt that crazy melting thing that she felt every time he kissed her. She felt like her body narrowed down to only certain points: the center of her forehead, her chest, and her belly, along with all the places where his body touched hers.

He rolled her over on to her back and positioned himself on top of her. She felt the heat of his body. She had never been with someone whose body temperature was this hot. Maybe it was cooking her brain and that's why she felt like she was going crazy whenever she touched him.

He pulled her blouse and bra off and removed his shirt, then leaned back down to continue to kiss her. She kissed him like she wanted to drink him, and he kissed back the same way. She wanted to push herself into him. They kissed until her desire to be as close to him as possible was making her moan. At that moment he pulled back and began to kiss her neck, and then down to her breasts.

When he began to kiss her belly, she realized with shock what he was planning to do.

"No," she said. "Wait, no."

"Sssssshhhhh," he said, as he continued kissing down her body.

"Listen, I haven't. I've never. No one—" she started.

"Sssshhhh. It's okay. Just relax," he whispered.

She lay back and closed her eyes. For a moment she was wildly self-conscious, but then sensation took over.

His lips were on her hips, her thighs, and then the inside of her thighs. And then to a place unexplored by any other lover.

Sarah gasped. The feeling of it was overwhelming. His tongue and his lips finding the tiny places on her body that only she knew existed. She began to moan and covered her mouth with her hand. A chemical wave was taking her and wrenching sounds from her body. She feared she would cry out, that she wouldn't be able to help herself.

She did … and then he was on top of her and inside her. Her thighs began to shake uncontrollably as the pressure built again. She wrapped her legs around him as she felt herself peak again. Everything went red and she threw her head backward. At that moment she felt him shudder and moan.

#

Afterward he gently lowered himself on top of her and rolled them both on their sides. He kissed her face, her lips, her eyes, and the tip of her nose. She stared at his nose, realizing that she had become obsessed with the little bump there.

They lay like this for a while, just kissing softly. Her leg was wrapped around his waist. He was still hard inside her.

"You don't mind this?" she asked after a time.

"Mind what?" he asked.

"Being inside me after sex," she said softly.

"Oh, I stay hard for a long time," he smiled. "If you want to keep going, I can do that too."

She laughed, and when her muscles contracted, he stayed where he was, proving his statement correct.

"That's not really what I meant. I just wondered if it bothered you to have to stay close to me after sex."

"What? What do you mean, 'have to stay close' to you? I want to stay close to you. Why wouldn't I?"

"Oh, well," she suddenly didn't want to explain this. She didn't want to bring thoughts of Karl and her dead husband into this conversation.

"You can tell me," he said, as if reading her mind.

"Well, some people told me that men feel the need to pull away after sex. That it was an evolutionary response. They said that men feel disgusting after sex and … and guilty or something."

"What the fuck?" he responded with wide eyes. "What sort of asshole would say something like that? It's nasty, and incredibly stupid."

"I guess it is pretty mean."

"Yeah, it's mean. It's also really fucking stupid. From a very selfish perspective, if you stay inside the woman then you have a much better chance of continuing to have sex with her. So, if you want to talk about an evolutionary perspective, that's the winning strategy. Unless, of course, you are the kind of guy who can't do that, or who takes a long time to get hard again. If that's the case, then maybe that's why they would say something like that. Fear of inadequacy."

Sarah kissed him hard. He kissed back, his tongue lingering in her mouth. She could feel him smiling.

"Just for, you know, future reference. I have no desire whatsoever to run away from you after sex. But we do need to be a bit careful," he said, pulling back from her and looking at the window.

It was getting dark now, and it had still been light outside when they entered the bedroom. They had been alone together in a bedroom for two hours at least. This was dangerous.

Sarah sighed. "Yes. I guess we should probably go pretend to be studying or something."

"Oh, on that. I had an idea. I thought that I could start teaching you Portuguese," he said.

"You speak Portuguese?" she asked.

"I'm Brazilian. It's my mother tongue," he said with a laugh. "And you've told people that you want to travel. So it might make sense that you would want to learn another language."

"How do you know that I want to travel?"

"Come on. I have been stalking you for over a year. I know a lot about you," he said, then frowned.

"Sorry, that might have been too intense. Did it scare you?" he asked. And Sarah laughed out loud.

"No, it absolutely did not scare me. It actually makes me happy."

"Good" he said with a smile. "This summer, I will give you lessons in Portuguese."

"Are you actually planning to do that?"

"Well, let's put it this way, they say languages are best learned on the pillow," he said with a smile.

"Then I am happy to learn," she said with a laugh. Her stomach chose that moment to growl.

"Right, food," he said, as he pulled out and away from her. He got up quickly and went to the bathroom. The light went on and she heard the sound of running water. She pulled her legs up to her chest and pondered whether she should try to get dressed while he was in the bathroom or wait until he had left the room. She realized that being self-conscious was stupid, as he had surely seen all parts of her naked, but she still felt that way. She wasn't particularly thin, and she wasn't without bumps and bulges. Still, that didn't seem to bother him.

However, before she could finish the debate with herself, he came out of the bathroom with something in his hands. He came back to the bed, kissed her and put her robe and a towel down next to her. She stared at it, perplexed. He had gotten her a robe. Was she supposed to wear it? No one had ever done this before.

"Ummm," she said, staring at the robe. He was pulling on his jeans and looked up at her as he balanced on one foot. He looked strangely like a lion.

"What?" he said as he stood up, then he slapped his head.

"Of course. That was really stupid," he said, picking up the robe and taking it back to her closet.

"Jesus, what would someone think if they walked by the window and saw you there with me, in just a robe? Well, if someone walks by and notices, I doubt we will be able to look particularly innocent, but we can at least make an effort," he muttered to himself as he pulled something else from her wardrobe. He then brought it over and laid it down on the bed.

"I'm starving and I know you are too. Mind if I start dinner? You have something in the fridge, right?" he asked. She nodded, staring at the thing on her bed.

It was the yellow dress she had worn and shoved to the back of her closet after he had been strange with her.

Now, sitting on her bed, he had given the dress a new life.

Chapter Thirty-Two

Stepping Into the Ring

Wednesday June 25

Sarah was awakened by movement in the bed. It was still dark outside. She had fallen asleep in Caio's arms after dinner. She reached out for him, but he wasn't there. She sat up to see him putting his shirt back on. He came over and sat down next to her on the bed.

"Where are you going?" she muttered groggily.

"I shouldn't be here when people wake up," he said, leaning forward and kissing her. "We are taking some chances here, you and I."

She threw her arms around his neck.

"I don't want you to go," she said.

"I don't want to go, but I don't want to get you in trouble either. Now that we know that—well, now that we are this," he said, pulling back from her for a moment and putting his hand to his chest, "I don't want to take ridiculous chances. We don't have to, anymore."

He leaned forward and kissed her lightly. "Listen, I want to take a trip to the city with you. I want to be with you away from this place, where we can be what we are. Are you okay with that?"

"I would love that," she whispered. "But we didn't really talk about anything last night. I felt like there was so much to talk about, so much we should have talked about, but I just wanted—"

"Yeah," he said. "You just wanted to enjoy being together. I felt exactly the same way. I just wanted to be with you and not worry about anything else for a while. I still want that."

"But we kind of do need to talk about stuff," Sarah said. "There's a lot I'm confused about. What I saw in your wallet."

"I know. And I promise I'll tell you, but now isn't the moment. I'll tell you everything when we go to the city. That will give me enough time to try to explain. I don't want to be in this place when we talk about it," Caio said, kissing the tip of her nose.

She smiled. "Did I tell you that I'm obsessed with your nose?"

"My nose? That's what you're obsessed with?" he laughed. "Okay, I'll take what I can get, but I thought other parts of me might be more interesting."

"Nope, your nose," she said.

"Well, then no rhinoplasty for me," he said. "But I gotta go. Come see me this week. Just to say hi for a minute. I'll be there on Thursday and Friday."

"When can you come over again?" she asked.

"How about Monday?"

"Not Sunday?"

"No, I can't on Sunday, unfortunately," he said. Sarah felt her gut twist.

"Why? Do you have a date with some girl or something?" she asked, and then hated herself.

He looked at her and raised an eyebrow.

"You mean with someone my age?" he asked. "No. In fact, if I have to try to have a postcoital conversation with another teenage girl, I will fucking shoot myself in the head."

Sarah waited for the laugh, but it didn't come. He was deadly serious.

"Besides, you are the one here who has an 'official' other, not me," he said, and a note of bitterness crept into his voice.

"Not for much longer," she said, and wrapped her arms around him again. He pulled her to him tightly for a minute before pulling back and standing up.

"I'll see you later," he said, and then he said a word that she didn't recognize, but he said it very tenderly. Before he left the bedroom, he turned to blink hard at her.

She now knew what this meant.

I love you too, she thought, as tears formed in her eyes.

Sarah lay back down and tried to go back to sleep, but her heart ached. She couldn't imagine ever having to see Karl again. She couldn't imagine being able to hide her feelings for Caio much longer. She couldn't exactly pinpoint when she fell in love with him, but she had. It might have been the first time he spoke to her, and she got a glimpse of who he was. It might have happened that early.

When Sarah was finally able to drift back into sleep, she had the dream about the boy in the hole again. This time, she knew it was Caio. She recognized him and he recognized her. In the dream, he told her to go back because he didn't want her to see him like this, but she refused to leave. She looked for a way to

202

get him out of the hole, but she could find nothing. She then went to the edge and was going to jump down, but he told her that she would just hurt herself by doing that. She lay down in the mud next to the hole, never taking her eyes off him, even with tears pouring down her face.

She woke up crying again.

Thursday June 26

In some ways, the blowup that occurred in the office on Thursday helped to keep Sarah's mind occupied with trivial things. Apparently, one of Jason's more important clients was being investigated for insider trading. This sort of case was not a specialty for their firm, but it was a client that the partners were more than happy to try to keep in-house. This meant that there were even more phone calls and meetings and emails than usual. By Thursday evening, Sarah was feeling bone-tired, so when Michael still hadn't come from his office by six, she decided to leave. She wanted to see Caio, and it wasn't like she would be in this job for much longer, if things went her way.

On the way home, she walked by the basketball court, and Caio was there playing with Dex, Ash, and Mickey. Dex was the first one to see her.

"Hey Ms. Baker," he called and waved. She waved back and came to stand next to the fence. Dex was turning to walk toward her but turned around to look at Caio.

"Hey Caio, look who's—" he began but stopped mid-sentence. Caio had turned and was smiling at her and dribbling the ball as he walked slowly toward her. Dex stared at Caio, then back at her, then at Caio as he walked.

"Okay, then. Guess the rest of us will just go play basketball, way over on the other side of the court," said Dex really loud.

Sarah felt like she was suddenly in a spotlight, but Caio was laughing a bit.

"Umm. What was that about?" she asked him as he came up.

"Well, I thought that I wouldn't be able to hide this very well, so I told them that I was going to teach you Portuguese because you wanted to learn another language. They asked if you were going to pay me, and I said that it was really just an excuse to spend time with you."

"You told them that?" she whispered.

"Yeah. But that doesn't implicate you, just me. It goes to the whole 'Caio's got a crush on Sarah' thing that they already believe. But if you keep looking at me like that, then it won't take them that long to figure things out," he said with a smile.

"Do you care?" she asked.

"For you, yes. It's fine for them to know that I'm crazy about you. The other way around could bring you trouble. But hopefully this is all just a temporary situation."

"What do you mean 'temporary'?" Sarah asked, feeling a sudden fear kick in.

"Don't worry. I'm not going anywhere. I just need to come up with a better plan. People won't believe the whole language thing for long. That's just buying time."

"Caio, stop flirting with Ms. Baker," Mouse called coming onto the court.

"See what I mean," Caio said, reaching out to the fence and touching her hand briefly. "See you Monday. I'll bring food this time."

Then he walked back toward his friends.

Sarah backed away and started walking home. As usual, it was physically hard for her to walk away from him. She had just made it in her door when her phone rang.

"Sarah? It's Matt Greenley."

Given her week, she had forgotten that he would call.

"Hi Matt. Thank you for calling," Sarah said, sitting down at her table. "I wanted to talk to you because I think I am a beneficiary of a trust that my late husband set up for me. I think my boyfriend is the trustee, but he has never told me about it."

"Hmmm. What makes you think that you are a beneficiary?" Matt asked.

"Well, he always asks me to sign documents. He has always said that these relate to the mortgage on my house and getting the best interest rate. He always just hands me the document open to the signature page, and I sign."

"You don't ever read the documents?" Matt asked.

"No."

"Why not?"

Sarah paused. "Just after Paul's death, I was too freaked out about everything and overwhelmed."

She thought for a moment about those days. The truth was that it wasn't really Paul's death that had freaked her out. It was more because the voices in her head had become so loud and demeaning that it had been impossible to think.

"And after that?" Matt asked.

"After that, I was afraid of Karl," Sarah said, realizing the truth of it as it came out of her mouth.

"You are talking about Karl Renfield, correct?"

"Yes, how did you know?"

"I did a little research on you before I called. I do that with all my potential clients. So back to why you think you have a trust."

"The other day, I wore camera glasses and created a diversion so I could take a photo of the front page. It was blurry but it was a trust notification."

"Could you forward that to me?" Matt asked.

"Of course."

"As you must know, I specialize in trusts and estates. Sadly, there's no registration requirement here for trusts. However, if you believe that Karl is the trustee, then Patterson and Van Allen will be aware of this trust. Also, do you have a copy of Paul's will?"

"No," Sarah said. "Karl handled all that at Paul's death."

"I see. Here's how I see it. I know a bit about your late husband. I also know a bit about your current boyfriend. I suspect you are correct about the trust. If you retain me, then I can start the process of asking them for information. If Karl has not notified you or if he has attempted to hide things from you, these are grounds for terminating him as the trustee. I am pretty sure that we can do that, but they will fight it."

"I know that," Sarah said. "But I don't have a lot of money to pay you in order to retain you."

"Let's worry about the money part of it later," Matt said. "My hunch is that your trust may be sizable enough for that not to be an issue. And if there has been impropriety on the part of the trustee, Karl should have to pay legal fees, but let's not put the cart before the horse. My first concern is really for your safety."

"My safety?" Sarah parroted back. She wasn't surprised by this. She was surprised that Matt knew it was an issue.

"Yes. Karl is a nasty bastard. If he suspects that you will be trying to take power away from him, he will do one of two things. He will either try to find a way to tie himself more closely to you in a legal fashion. Or he could try to hurt you. The path he takes might be related to what the will says about who benefits if something were to happen to you. Of course, the slayer rule would prohibit him from inheriting from you if it was proved that he killed you, but it would need to be proved that he was the one who killed you."

"Do you really think it's that dire?" Sarah said with a little laugh, trying for levity. It fell flat.

"Yes, Sarah, I think it is. My suggestion, for the moment, is that I will try to do a little secret digging. When you are ready to have me contact Patterson and Van Allen, let me know. At that point, you need to be prepared to get away while everything blows up. Does that sound okay to you?"

"Yes," Sarah said.

Matt was silent for a moment.

"I'm not pushing you, but do you have line of sight as to when you might be calling?" he asked. "I want to make sure that I can give this the time it will need."

"Within a month, no longer," Sarah said. When she said this, her soul felt lighter.

"Good. I like that. Call me when you are ready to fight back," Matt said, and hung up.

Yes, I think it's way past time to fight back.

This was no one's voice but her own.

Chapter Thirty-Three

Karl Unmasked

Saturday June 28

Sarah spent Saturday morning trying to ignore her impending sense of doom about her date night with Karl, and with a bladder cramping like crazy. By her fourth or fifth trip to the bathroom in less than two hours, she felt like she was peeing razor blades.

"Oh great. A bladder infection," she muttered to herself.

Honey, that's perfect. That's an excuse not to have sex with Karl, said Val.

The sense of doom receded just a little bit. Maybe that was an excuse, but would he believe it, or would he be suspicious? *What do I need to make it credible?*

Jesus. It says so much that you are even having to consider this. You probably actually do have a bladder infection. What decent man would want to have sex with a woman if he knew it was going to hurt her? snapped Val.

Indeed, piped up Larry.

"Yes, I know," Sarah said out loud. "Karl is a shit. We all agree on that. We all agree that I have to leave him. I just couldn't make it happen this week. I still want to help Alex and Melissa. I need to do that. And I need to talk to Caio about—I don't know, about what we can do."

You can't actually be thinking about a future with a teenage boy, snapped her mother.

Do you actually believe he's a teenage boy, Isabelle? Larry said coldly.

What else could he be? her mother responded.

I'm not exactly sure what he is, but I would bet my reputation that he's no teenager. There's too much evidence against it, said Larry.

Sarah thought of seeing Caio's licenses and her head began to reel again. They hadn't talked about that. He had left them there for her to see, that was clear. She really should have talked to him about it, but it was such a joy just to be with him when they were together that she didn't want to think about anything but the moment.

Focus. Focus. Focus.

She had a date night "activity" that she needed to tank.

"I can go to an urgent care center," Sarah said. "If it's the same as every other time I've had a bladder infection, they won't find any bacteria immediately."

What do they do? asked Larry.

"They give me a prescription for antibiotics to use if it doesn't get better with lots of water," Sarah replied. "Wait—a prescription. If I get that filled, then it's proof."

But honey, it may not be enough. You know that, right? You might have to sleep with him, Val said gently.

"I can't let him inside me again. I just can't," Sarah said aloud.

She was surprised by the vehemence in her own voice. She had spent so many years submitting herself to Karl without question. Maybe that was because sex with Paul had been lukewarm and infrequent, so she had no real room for comparison. What had been happening with Caio changed the way she thought about this. Sex didn't have to be something you just got through. It was ancient and sacred. If she had never really realized this before, she did now, and she wasn't sure if she could violate the sanctity of this just to avoid suspicion from Karl.

Then you need to be prepared to leave quickly if you have to, said Larry.

Sarah nodded.

But it might not come to that, said Val. *Go to the doctor's. Get what you can. Then do the best you can. We will be here to help you and support you. But you need to get dressed, get your ass out the door, and get to the doctor.*

Sarah knew good advice when she heard it, and she was out the door in less than ten minutes.

She spent a productive two hours at ModernMD that afternoon. It was productive in the sense that she had been right, and the doctor had written her a prescription for the antibiotic Macrodantin. She spent the rest of the afternoon cleaning her house with pine cleaner to remove traces that Caio had been there. Karl may not really care about her, but he had an eagle eye, and if he saw or smelled anything out of order—well, that would be bad. She had just finished changing her clothes and double-checking her bedroom when she heard a knock on the door. She looked at the clock. It was 7:30, time for her date. But Karl never knocked.

Sarah suddenly felt a blind panic hit her. Suppose it was Caio. Wait, he knew she had a date tonight with Karl. He would know not to come, right?

She dashed downstairs but stopped herself when she saw the shadow behind the curtain on her door. It was Karl.

Taking a deep breath, Sarah grabbed the prescription bottle from the table and opened the door.

He knocked. That's an improvement.

"Hi Karl," she said.

"Hi Sarah," he said, and his eyes immediately went to the bottle. "Are you okay?"

"Yeah," she said, stepping back from the door to let him in. "I just have a wicked bladder infection. I went to the doctor today and he prescribed antibiotics. It should be better in a couple of days."

Karl narrowed his eyes.

"That's bad timing. What did they prescribe?" he asked, reaching for the bottle. Sarah had been right to get the prescription. He was suspicious. She had to play this just right.

Karl read the prescription and actually opened the bottle. Then he shrugged. "This stuff isn't very powerful. You should go back if it doesn't get better quickly, but that ruins our date night a bit."

He said this last bit with a smile and a wink that made Sarah feel like she wanted to vomit.

"Are we going out to eat? I didn't cook because I thought we were going out," she said.

"Yes. I made a reservation at the Italian place we went to the other day."

Sarah winced in spite of herself.

"Look, Sarah. I don't want us to associate that place with anything bad. I did all those things because I was really stressed about the situation with Meghan, but that's over now. If we go back there now, then we can change how you feel about it."

Why do you care about that place? Oh yeah, one of your friends owns it. Right.

"Okay," Sarah said, demurring. If they were out of the house, sex became less of an issue.

When they got to the restaurant, Sarah saw Mouse across the room. He smiled at her as she entered.

"I see your friend is here," Karl said as they sat down, and their waitress came over and gave them their menus.

Sarah suddenly had a flash of intuition.

"He's not my friend, but he did introduce me to a kid who wanted me to

209

tutor him. It's a kid he plays basketball with," she said, keeping her eyes on the menu.

"You're tutoring someone?" Karl said. His voice had gone soft and silky.

Dangerous ground, but it was better for her to control how Karl got this information, in case he heard it from someone else.

Sarah looked up.

"Yes. That boy, Mouse, asked me if I would help his friend. He's a kid from a foster home and he was failing his class in civics. So I said I would help. I feel really sorry for him."

"Sarah, you have to realize that most people are where they are in life because, on some level, they want to be there," Karl said.

Even kids, Karl? Even babies? Are you really this much of a shit?

At that moment the waitress returned. Karl ordered himself a steak and a chicken salad for Sarah. Some habits he couldn't seem to break even when he was on "good" behavior.

"I don't suppose he was able to pay you for your help?" Karl asked, when the waitress left.

"He brought groceries. He works at a grocery store, and he was able to get groceries for a discount," she said. It was a believable lie.

"Wait a minute, is he that Brazilian kid who lives with the Fernandez family?" he asked.

"I'm not really sure. I don't know that much about him," she lied.

"Well, if it's him, then I suspect he stole the groceries," Karl said with a sniff.

Sarah toyed with the idea of stabbing him in the hand with his steak knife. Hadn't she had this very same thought the last time she was here?

The waitress came back with their food, and they ate in silence, with Karl scanning the room. When they were finished, Sarah picked up her bag.

"Let's have some dessert," Karl said suddenly.

"Really? You don't usually want dessert," Sarah said.

Warning. Warning. Warning.

"Actually, I already ordered it," Karl said. A few minutes later, the waitress appeared with two pieces of cheesecake, two glasses, and a bottle of champagne. It wasn't cheap champagne. It was Dom Pérignon.

Sarah got a horrible sinking feeling in her stomach.

He is trying to find a way to tie himself more closely to you in a legal fashion.

Control your face. Control your face. Control your face.

After the waitress poured the champagne, Karl held up his hand before Sarah could drink.

"Before we toast, I want to ask you something. I told you that I was sorry about what happened recently but before all that, remember I told you that I had a present for you? Well, this is it."

He took out a small black velvet box. He opened it and inside was a diamond ring.

God no. God no. God no.

Smile Sarah. Smile NOW! Larry yelled inside her head. Sarah looked up at Karl, unfocused her eyes and smiled.

"I see that you're surprised. I guess it's a bit sudden for you. But I want you to know that I was thinking about this before all the trouble. I have been thinking about it for a long time. All I am asking is that you wear it for a while and think about it. We're pretty much married already, it would just be making it official."

And making him a beneficiary. Don't forget that.

Sarah nodded as Karl took the ring out of the box, took her hand, and slipped the ring on her finger. The size of the diamond was obscene and gaudy to Sarah's eyes. People sitting around them clapped, all smiles and congratulations. These were strangers. She saw Mouse looking at her from across the room. The look on his face did not look congratulatory. It looked worried.

Karl looked at her. She needed to say something. *Think of something to say.*

For once fate interceded in her favor. Karl's phone rang.

"Goddamn it," he snarled as he picked it up. Then his eyes widened.

"I'm so sorry Sarah, but I need to take this," he said, as he stood up and walked outside.

With his eyes on Karl's figure standing just outside of the front door, Mouse walked over to her.

"Are you marrying Karl?" he asked. Sarah caught his eye and gave her head a tiny shake but said nothing.

"Right. I understand," Mouse said, quickly backing away.

Karl walked back into the restaurant just as Mouse had gone back into the kitchen.

"I'm so sorry Sarah, but there's a blowup at work. I could get one of the junior attorneys to do it, but it's a sensitive topic. And I know you aren't feeling well. Would it bother you if we cut the night a bit short? That way you can get some rest, and you can think about my offer," he said this with a superior sort of smile, indicating the ring.

Simper. You need to simper.

Sarah smiled and looked down. Karl then held her chair for her and walked her out to the car.

At her door, he gave her a full kiss. He never did this, and it felt like someone was pressing cold meat into her mouth. It was everything she could do not to gag. His phone beeped in the middle of the kiss, and he sighed.

"I have to go," he said, giving her a little smirk and a wink. After his car had pulled out of the driveway, Sarah ran inside, pulled the ring from her finger and threw it on the counter like it was a snake.

At least you were able to leave early. It would have been difficult if you had had to stay there looking at him for too long after his proposal, said Larry.

Well, I guess he got a better offer. Probably meeting up with Meghan somewhere, said Val. *Maybe at that club, what was it—the Stigmata Club?*

Sarah remembered Laura's warning: *Your boyfriend will be none too happy about this, and he has friends that are even worse. If you doubt this, you need to get a look at who goes in and out of the Stigmata Club.* She suddenly felt an intense pressure in the center of her forehead.

I need to go look at that place. Laura said it was on Orchard Street.

Without allowing herself to think much more about it, Sarah picked up her purse, pulled out her keys and walked out the door.

#

Sarah was familiar enough with the location of Orchard Street, but she never remembered seeing any clubs there. The street mainly consisted of shops, restaurants, and coffeehouses, with a few residential properties thrown in here and there. The businesses all seemed to be closed for the night. Sarah drove slowly down the street looking for signs of activity but initially saw nothing.

After blocks of nothing out of the ordinary, she finally got a break. On one side of the road, in front of a closed lighting store, Sarah saw a young woman wearing a leather skirt, leather bustier, and impossibly high Bettie Page shoes. Sarah pulled over and parked in front of one of the closed coffee shops. The girl toddled down the street, stopping in front of a closed knitwear store and adjusting her bustier. Then she tottered a few more feet to a set of stairs where a tall, burly man was standing in front of a door the color of dried blood. The girl said something to the man. He nodded, opened the door, and let her enter.

Sarah was just about to get out of her car for a better look when a woman walked by her on the passenger's side. She was blonde, petite, and skipping in excitement. She was wearing a leather skirt that stuck out like a tutu, a tied-up business shirt, and thigh-high boots. To Sarah's horror, she realized it was Meghan. Sarah immediately let herself slink down in her seat. Meghan walked fifty feet or so ahead, and then stepped into the empty road from between two parked cars. She turned and struck a hip-out pose in the middle of the road, beckoning to someone. Sure enough, not three seconds passed before she saw Karl walk past her car. Sarah waited for him to turn and mark her car. But, for the second time in one night, luck was on her side. Karl had eyes only for Meghan.

Sarah was crouched down as far as she could be and still see. As she watched, Karl and Meghan crossed the road and approached the blood-red door. When the bouncer saw them, he nodded. They were about to enter, when all three turned to greet another person. It was Angela, wearing a leather catsuit and a dog collar with chain still attached. At that point, Sarah lay flat down across the front seats. Karl might have been the most observant of the three in one-on-one situations, but Angela was the one with the keenest eyes in general life. After a few minutes, Sarah sat up slowly. Karl, Meghan, and Angela were gone. Only the bouncer remained.

Heart pounding and breathing hard, Sarah started the engine, but as she checked her rear-view mirror, she saw a large group of people approaching her car. They looked like people dressed for Mardi Gras or Carnival. They were loud, and they were wearing either bright colors or next to nothing. As Sarah watched, they crossed behind her car. It wasn't until they got halfway across the street that she recognized two or three women who worked as paralegals for her firm. They all ran up the stairs. Some hugged and kissed the bouncer before passing through the door.

Sarah eased her car out of the parking space and into the road. She drove slowly, as she didn't want to be noticed and the last thing she needed was to accidentally hit someone at this moment. She didn't want to draw the attention of any of these people—not until she had planned an escape.

Chapter Thirty-Four

Fleeing the Gray

Sunday June 29

You know it wasn't a good idea to go to that club last night without thinking it through, Larry said.

"You wouldn't have wanted me to go and you would have tried to stop me," Sarah replied.

That's true, but we might have been able to help you if we'd known that you were committed to doing it, Larry said.

"Sorry," muttered Sarah.

She was making a small omelet for herself even though she felt sort of nauseated. She had woken up with her bladder cramping even worse than before. She also had a raging headache. She might have thought she was hungover if she had had anything to drink the night before, but she hadn't. This thought triggered memories of last night's events. Karl asking her to marry him. Mouse looking at her with pity. Meghan dressed like a deranged leather ballerina.

"Burn my eyes. Burn my eyes," she muttered.

She immediately sat down at her table as the world seemed to be spinning around her. After a few moments, she felt the sudden urge to pee again and when she went to the bathroom it felt like she was passing knives.

Well, if you had taken the antibiotics, you would be feeling better now. But no, you know better, snarked her mother.

Sarah sighed. She hated antibiotics because taking them turned her into a giant yeast. Still, she should take them. She went back to the kitchen and saw the bottle of antibiotics sitting on her counter. After struggling for a few moments with the childproof top she managed to get the bottle open and shake a pill into her palm. It was bright yellow with black writing on it. It looked like a yellowjacket. Maybe that was why she couldn't bring herself to put it in her mouth. It looked and felt like a little piece of poison in her palm. She put it back in the bottle and closed the top before going to her refrigerator and pulling out a liter of water. She drank about half of it at one go. That should flush things out. Antibiotics weren't always needed.

Sarah looked around her house, thinking about her week and how the events that were unfolding meant she probably wouldn't be living here much longer. The truth was that even if she didn't manage to get any information from the deposition this week, she would still have to leave Karl, which meant leaving her work. She had just enough money saved up to give her six months to find a new job, assuming she needed one. She had a gut feeling that Phillip Seider might be able to help her with references or even hire her.

You know, Sarah. It would be good to pack a suitcase, said Larry. *This situation means that when you leave you might need to leave quickly. So you should get all your important documents and a backup of your hard drive and keep them, along with your laptop, with you at all times.*

You should also go ahead and throw away anything you wouldn't want Karl to find if he got access to this place while you weren't here, said Val.

Sarah nodded. She grabbed a banana and ate it as she sat down at her computer to back up her drive. She did this on one external hard drive. She also backed up some of her more pertinent files on a couple of flash drives.

After she finished this, she found a suitcase and went from room to room. In each room, she scanned for three things: things she would need, things with sentimental value, and things she didn't want Karl to get his hands on. She found quite a few things in categories one and three. What was surprising was how few things fell into category two. Even after living in this house for six years, Sarah had little to no attachment to it.

At around noon, she went to the market to pick up something for lunch. She had hoped that she would see Caio, but no one was on the basketball court. She felt a knife to her heart. She missed him terribly, even if it had only been a couple of days. Her feelings for him were something she could never have imagined feeling. He was more of a man than any man she had known, including her own father. And then there was the puzzle of his age. All the facts were pointing to his being older than he looked—much older than he looked. His knowledge, his language, his behavior, not to mention his IDs. The disconnect between perceived reality and factual reality was affecting her on more levels than she could explain. She had always thought that her small, routine, gray world was simply all there was. But if Caio had really fought in the Second World War, then there was a magic in the world that she hadn't been allowed to believe

215

in. If she hadn't already loved him, she would have loved him for giving her this gift.

While at the store, she walked past an aisle with tomato juice. She normally never had any interest at all in tomato juice, but today it looked good to her. Maybe her body was craving acid stuff to counter the bladder infection. She picked up a couple of small cans along with some mackerel and rice for lunch.

As she walked home, she pulled out one of the cans of tomato juice. She drank it, and it tasted better than she remembered. As she pulled out another one, she noticed that now some of the boys were playing on the basketball court. Sure enough, it was the usual crowd. She spotted Caio among them at about the same time that he spotted her. Without saying anything to the boys around him, he left the game and walked over the fence where Sarah stood.

"Hi," he said.

"Hi." She put her hand up on the fence. It was all she could do in public, but she longed to reach out and touch him, to feel his warm skin under her hand.

Sarah's bladder chose that moment to spasm, and she winced.

"Are you okay?" he asked, moving closer to the fence.

"Yeah. I'm fine. I just think I have a bladder infection," she said. Caio's eyes snapped open.

"Why do you think that?" he asked, putting his fingers through the chain links next to hers.

"Oh, just I am having cramping and having to pee all the time. And I have been getting waves of fatigue all day. I already got some antibiotics from the doctor. Sorry, that's probably too much information," she said with a little laugh. Caio ignored her attempt at nonchalance.

"Did you take them, the antibiotics?" he asked, getting even closer to the fence and looking at her with an unhidden intensity. The other boys weren't openly staring at them. They weren't making fun of them either. They were obviously giving them their privacy.

"No, I didn't take them," she said. "I really just got them so I would have an excuse—well, to not be with Karl."

"Did it work?"

Sarah smiled back and nodded. "Yeah, it did, so that problem was solved but another one came up. He asked me to marry him."

Caio's brow furrowed.

"Yeah. Mouse told me. What did you say?" he asked. Sarah was shocked to realize that he was actually insecure.

"I didn't say anything. He didn't expect an answer in that moment, but of course the answer is no. I'm probably going to have to leave him by the end of this week."

"What?! That's quick," Caio said, putting his hand to his head.

"Is that—" she started but he interrupted.

"No, it's okay. It's really good, but I need to plan faster than I was expecting."

She nodded. At that moment, Dex walked toward them.

"Hey Sarah," Dex said, using her first name for the first time. "I don't want to interrupt, but there's a lady across the street who's staring at you from her window. I mean, not that there's anything to stare at, but I don't know her, and I know how some people like to gossip."

Sarah looked at him and he met her gaze steadily. Then he smiled and grabbed Caio by the T-shirt.

"Okay boy, back away from the woman," Dex said.

Caio laughed, blinked at her and said, "See you Monday," before turning toward the other boys.

Sarah's heart felt so full it could burst. She loved this person. And, even better, he seemed to love her back. The rest of the day, even as she continued packing for her possible flight, this thought came back to her again and again.

And the memory of his voice was the last thing in her head before she went to sleep.

Chapter Thirty-Five

Out of the Mouths of Babes

Monday June 30

In the morning she had to interview the Davies boys, and she was exhausted. It took two cups of coffee before she felt able to function. Sarah had no idea what was causing the fatigue, but it was the worst possible timing. She needed to be sharp and functional today. If she could make it through this and get something usable then she could leave this place with no regrets. She wasn't sure how much longer she could continue working here, knowing what she knew. Plus, she kept imagining everyone she saw in leather outfits. The one bright light of the day was that Caio was going to come over in the evening, and that was a solar flare.

After a tense morning where Sarah kept watching the clock, the Davies clan appeared at 10:30 on the dot. Andrew Davies was an asshole, but he was a punctual asshole. Today, he was wearing a gray suit that looked more expensive than anything Sarah had ever owned. Anne Marie was wearing a brown silk shirtdress that looked the same caliber of expensive. All three boys were present and dressed in casual sporty gear.

Andrew led the boys into the reception area and turned to face them.

"So Anne Marie and I have some things to talk about with Michael, but Sarah here would like to ask you lot a few questions." Andrew looked pointedly at Alex.

"You are to completely cooperate with Sarah, boys. Do you hear me?" asked Anne Marie, taking the chin of each boy in her hand. Chris nodded. Andrew shrugged. Alex maintained a stoic frozen look as if he was refusing to even breathe around her.

At that moment, Michael came out and led the adults into his office.

The three boys assumed their normal positions in the reception area.

"Okay boys," Sarah said. "I would like to take each of you into the confer-
ence room one at a time and ask you a few questions. It's not really a big deal.
It's not official. It's just for us to get you comfortable with the process. Okay?"
All three nodded.

"Alex, can you come first?" she asked. Alex nodded and followed her.

What followed was the most tense and uncomfortable fifteen minutes she
had spent in the office in a long time. She asked Alex about the details of his
daily routine, and his responses were curt at best. At worst, they were surly.
When she got to the last of the questions, about the end of the typical day, Alex
stood up.

"Are we done now?" he snapped. Sarah nodded. She caught his eye for a
minute, and his expression was one of resignation and something else … what?
Pain?

Sarah's interview with Andrew was not much better. She had been pinning
her hopes on the fact that Alex might talk to her in a private setting but no such
luck. Andrew had never been very forthcoming so her time with him provided
little more information than the cereals they ate for breakfast and how unfair it
was to have so much homework.

By the time it was Chris's turn, she was beginning to panic. What if she got
nothing from this, and her grand plan fizzled, then what would she do? Just
walk away?

Sarah plastered on a smile and went to get Chris from the reception area.
She led him into the conference room and closed the door behind them.

"Hi Chris," she said, sitting down on the couch in the conference room. She
patted the spot next to her and he happily came and sat down. He was still
young enough to enjoy adult company without having to put on the jaded "I
am just tolerating you" air of tweens and teens.

"Did your parents explain what we would be doing?" she asked him.

"Yeah. They said that you would be asking me questions. That's all," he said.

"Yes, that's right. But I'll also be writing down what you say," she said, showing him her notepad. She did not mention that she was also recording him on
her phone. She thought it best not to bring that up. Still, the corners of Chris's
mouth took a distinctive downturn.

"Why?" he asked.

"Because I want to remember how you answered the questions. You see,
your mother's lawyer will have lots of questions for you, and someone will be
writing down what you say when he does. We want to make sure that you are
comfortable with all that," she said.

"Do you want me to say something? Do you want me to lie?" he asked.

"Absolutely not! It's a crime to lie in an official court meeting like this. So you shouldn't lie. No one will ever get angry at you for telling the truth," she lied. "Besides, you know how honest Captain America is."

Chris rolled his eyes, but smiled. "Yeah, he is."

"Just be honest. Most of the questions I'm going to ask you are probably going to seem kind of boring to you, but we can always take a break if you need it. Okay?"

"Okay."

"We are just going to talk about what you do on a normal school day. When you get up, what is the first thing you do?"

"I go pee," Chris said solemnly. Sarah smiled.

"Excellent, then what?" she asked.

"On a school day? I go downstairs for breakfast."

"And do you make your own breakfast?"

"No. Anne Marie makes it for us."

"And then what do you do?"

"We go upstairs to get dressed," he said.

The rest of the questioning continued in the same vein. His answers weren't any more interesting or enlightening than those of his brothers. Sarah was still smarting over the fact that she could get nothing at all from Alex.

She was almost through walking Chris through the details of his day. He was openly yawning now. She understood. The line of questioning was boring even to her, but she had to find a detail somewhere without asking questions that, if repeated, would alert Michael to her intentions.

"So, after dinner and TV, what do you do?"

"We go take a shower," Chris said, starting to draw on a pad of paper that Sarah had put down for him.

"Who goes first?" she said, then tried to engage him by saying, "When I was growing up, I would get in so much trouble if I took a shower before my parents at night."

"Oh, we don't have that problem," Chris said, perking up. "We all shower together."

Control your face. Control your face. Control your face.

"Really?" she said, smiling. "All of you?"

"Yep, all of us," Chris said.

"That must be a big shower to fit all of you in at one time. There are five of you," Sarah said, forcing herself to laugh.

"Oh, we go in turns. I go with Andrew and then Alex goes in with Dad and Anne Marie," he said.

Sarah forced herself to keep smiling. She looked over to make sure that the recorder was still running.

"So, you shower with Andrew. Do you guys ever fight or bicker in the shower?"

"No. We just try to get it over fast. Neither of us likes showering."

"What do you do when you are done?"

"We go into the bedroom and put our pajamas on."

"All of you? Your dad and stepmom as well?"

"No. When we go get dressed, they are usually still getting a shower with Alex," he said. Sarah nodded and smiled. This could be it. This was certainly an impropriety.

"What happens when they are done showering?" she asked.

"Then we all put on our PJs and go to bed."

"Do you all have separate rooms?"

"Well, yeah," Chris said, "but we don't sleep in our rooms."

"What do you mean?"

"We all sleep in Dad and Anne Marie's room. The bed is gigantic and much more comfortable," he said.

"All five of you sleep in your dad's bed?" she asked. She found herself speaking more softly, and Chris gave her an odd look. She sat up quickly and coughed.

"Yeah. But it's because their bed is so much better."

"Do you like sleeping in their bed?"

"Yeah, of course. They have a nicer bed. Andrew doesn't always like it, so sometimes he goes back to his room in the middle of the night."

"And Alex?"

"Alex has to stay in Dad's bed," Chris said, then smiled and leaned forward. "Anne Marie said if he's left in his bedroom on his own, he does S-E-X things, and that's not okay."

Sarah forced herself to laugh. So Alex is being forced to shower and sleep with his father and stepmother. No court in the world would think that was okay. They could possibly argue the whole "family bed" psychological argument but the showering was harder to explain. If only she could get this from Alex.

"That's really nice of your parents. I mean, it means they don't get much time to themselves," she said.

"Oh, it's okay. They have lots of time after we go to sleep. I sleep hard and it's hard to wake me up. They could talk, watch movies, do almost anything and I wouldn't wake up."

Almost anything.

"Okay Chris. That's really good. I think we pretty much talked about every-thing that goes on during your day, right?"

"Yeah, we did. For most school days."

"Is there anything you guys do regularly but maybe not every day?" Sarah asked.

"Well, sometimes we barbecue. And sometimes Dad, Anne Marie, and Alex get to go to the club."

Sarah dropped her pencil. As she was leaning over to pick it up, she took some deep breaths. Neither of the other two boys had said anything about this.

Out of the mouths of babes.

"What sort of club is that?"

"I don't know, it's some sort of dance club or something, but Andrew and I are too young to go. We get a sitter on those nights."

"How often is that?" she asked.

"Once a week. Maybe once every two weeks," he said.

"Okay," she said, as chirpily as she could. "We are all done. I know that must have been really boring for you. It was really boring, wasn't it?"

"No, it was okay," smiled Chris.

"Oh, you are just being too nice now. But it's okay, I have to ask people boring questions all the time. I don't mind if you say they are boring."

Brainwash. Brainwash. Brainwash.

"Yeah. They were a little boring," he smiled, and Sarah laughed.

"Do you want me to get you a Coke to drink?" Chris nodded.

"Okay. You can go on back to your brothers and I will get that for you."

Chris trotted out and Sarah sat back on the sofa and let out a long shaky breath. What she had just heard was horrible, but it was something she could use. It wasn't under oath, but if she could get this information to Phillip Seider, he could probably get it under oath. She just had to lie effectively to the parents, and she needed to do that quickly and get the whole group out of the office before they talked about this too much. There was a chance that Chris would tell his father what he said, but she thought it was a slim one.

She got up and found drinks for the boys. As she walked into the reception area with the drinks, Alex's eyes were trained on her.

"Here you go," she said, handing glasses to each of the boys. When she got to Alex, he looked directly into her eyes. She just smiled and pretended not to notice.

"Let me go see if your parents are done," she said, walking toward Michael's office, where she tapped on the door and stepped inside. Michael was sitting behind his desk and Andrew and Anne Marie were in chairs in front of it.

222

"Ah, Sarah," Michael said. "We were just wondering how your questions with the boys might have gone." As she looked between Michael, Andrew, and Anne Marie, she realized that they wouldn't believe it if she said nothing. She would have to make something up to throw them off scent.

"Well. Mostly it was fine. There was just one little thing," she said. All eyes were on her. They hadn't even offered for her to sit down. "Chris did say that Anne Marie was concerned about Alex's over-interest in 'S-E-X' as he put it. And that this was a topic of conversation in the house."

Anne Marie sat up straighter in her chair and folded her hands primly in her lap.

"I *am* worried about Alex and his obsession with sex," she said.

"Honey, he's a sixteen-year-old boy, it's not an obsession, it's normal," said Andrew, putting his hand on top of hers.

This was a nice little performance. Sarah should play her part.

"Well, I don't think any of that is odd. I'm just concerned that Phillip Seider will use it to say you are having inappropriate conversations with Alex."

"I'm his mother, who else will teach him about sex?" Anne Marie said crisply.

"Strictly speaking, you are his stepmother. And Sarah has a point," said Michael. "The court may look at this with concern if Phillip starts probing, so let's make sure Chris knows the conversations that Alex and Anne Marie are having are to educate him."

"Anything else?" Michael asked, scanning her face.

"No. I couldn't get Alex to say much at all, and Andrew was only interested in going back to his comics," she said. The shoulders of everyone in the room seemed to drop by a good half inch.

"That's great. Thank you for that, Sarah. Oh, look, it's lunch. Why don't you go on and take your lunch and we will finish up here," Michael said. Sarah nodded and stepped out of his office. She was just picking up her purse when Michael stuck his head out and motioned for her to come over.

"Did you happen to record what was said today?" he said. Sarah shook her head.

"I just took notes. But I will type those up for you and get it to you by this afternoon," she said.

Michael nodded and closed the door without another word. Sarah quickly collected her things, changed shoes, and walked out the door. She needed to go home and back up what was recorded on to something more secure. She didn't trust putting it on her laptop, even if it was only for long enough to upload to the cloud. She knew that they had all sorts of tracking devices on the work

223

computers, so who knew what shadow copies of things were being made. To be honest, she didn't even trust uploading from her phone to the cloud, because she wasn't good enough at IT to know if that was secure. But there were also other things she had to do. She had a lot of loose ends to tie up, and if she didn't concentrate and keep things organized, she would screw up, and a screwup at this point could be dangerous for her.

As Sarah stepped out of the office building and into the parking lot, she pulled her phone out of her purse and dialed Phillip Seider's cell number.

He did not pick up and it went to voicemail.

"Hi Phillip, this is Sarah Baker. I need to talk to you about an upcoming court case. Could you please call me on my cell phone as soon as possible?" she said, then left her number, slowly and twice. Then she hung up.

She hoped Phillip would understand the message she had left for him. She realized now that her time of being in the shadows was limited.

Chapter Thirty-Six

When a Door Closes

Monday June 30

When Sarah got home, she immediately synched her phone to her home computer and the cloud. Then she double-checked that the copies had been made. Afterward, she started to make herself a sandwich, but was hit by another wave of fatigue.

I'll just go lie down on the couch for a moment, she thought. She had no idea when she fell asleep, but she was awakened by her phone pinging. She sat up quickly and grabbed it.

Sarah, where are you? was the message from Michael. It was 3:30 p.m.

What the fuck? What was wrong with her?

Maybe you just don't want to go back to that hellhole. You have what you need. You don't have any reason to go back, said Val.

"But if I don't then everything starts," she replied. "I need to find somewhere to go before that happens."

Call in sick, Larry said.

Sarah sat up and felt a rush of nausea. She ran to her upstairs bathroom. She made it just in time because when she leaned over, she immediately vomited up the sandwich she had eaten for lunch. She would have no problem making sickness believable. She had barely wiped her mouth when her phone rang. It was Michael.

"Hi Michael," she said, her throat sounding like it had been massaged by a wood chipper.

"I see. I take it from your voice that you are sick," he said. He was trying to be nice, but he was annoyed.

"Yes. I'm sorry. I think I may have the flu. I've been vomiting all afternoon," she said.

"Oh, okay. Then just take care of yourself and we can talk tomorrow. You didn't happen to leave the notes you took on your conversations with the Davies children?" he said. His tone said that he was worried about something.

"No, I have them with me. But I'm sure that I can at least type those up this afternoon for you and send them in," she said.

"Are you sure?" Michael asked but his tone was infinitely less cold.

"That should be fine. It will have to be from my home computer though, is that okay or will the security people have a fit?" Sarah asked, and Michael laughed a little.

"If you are willing to type while you are vomiting, I think we can overlook a little email security slip-up."

"Thanks," Sarah said, and then coughed into the phone for good measure. "Listen, Michael, if you really need me to come in—"

"Oh. God. Stay home. I don't want to get sick. I can just send what files you might need from here. You can log in remotely for your emails. Angela can take the calls. Let me know when you feel better," he said, and hung up.

Sarah smiled a bit. Sometimes Michael's germ phobia was a blessing. She looked up at the clock: 3:45.

Moments after she hung up, her phone rang again. This time it was Karl.

"Hi Sarah, are you okay? Michael said that you called in sick," he said. Good news traveled fast.

"Yes. I think I have the flu," she said, coughing for good effect, although it wasn't much needed. She did actually feel sick.

"Well, I was planning on dropping by tonight."

It's Monday. Caio is coming tonight.

"But if you are feeling sick, maybe it's best for you to sleep," he finished. She took a breath.

Careful. Careful. Careful.

"Thanks Karl," she said, trying to put as much warmth in her voice as possible. "I am sleepy. And I'd like to look good the next time I see you. You know, we have some plans to make." She felt sick saying this, but it was the safest thing to say.

"Of course," said Karl. The words were bland, but the tone was downright smug. "I understand. These things are very important to women. Well, go to sleep and call me when you feel better."

"Thanks Karl," she simpered again, and he hung up without a goodbye. She put the phone down. That whole conversation made her feel sicker.

She went upstairs to the bathroom and looked at herself in the mirror. She was very pale and had dark circles under her eyes. When she was a little girl, she'd had hay fever and often looked like this. She almost looked like she was having an allergic reaction to something. She hadn't had a shower that morning, so she got a quick shower, dried her hair and put on makeup. She then went downstairs to the kitchen and pulled out her computer and the notepad she'd used for the pre-deposition questions for the Davies boys. She needed to use these to validate what she had told Michael and nothing else. That meant she had to write fiction. But not just fiction, fictional dialogue that could be believable to the people who said it, if questioned.

She had just finished this and sent her little novella to Michael when she heard a knock on the door, and she saw Caio's frame outlined in her doorway. She got up and had opened the door before the head rush hit her and she stumbled.

He was in the door in seconds, his arm around her.

"Hey, are you okay?" he asked.

I am now.

God, don't be so sappy.

"Yeah. I just got a head rush," she said. He closed the door behind him. He had his book bag with him, and he dropped it on the floor. He put his hand under her chin and looked at her face.

"Are you sick?" he asked.

"I don't know. I've just been really tired today. I actually came home for lunch and fell asleep on my couch," she said.

He was scanning her face.

"And then later I threw up. So I might be getting the flu."

He pulled her to the side where they were out of line of sight of the window and kissed her for long enough to make her dizzy again, and then led her to her table, where he pulled out a chair for her.

"You should sit down," he said, kissing her again quickly and gently, very gently.

Sarah laughed. For no reason. It was just the joy of being with him.

"You know if you keep kissing me, you might get sick too," she said.

"I never get sick. Ever. And even if I did, that's a small price to pay," he said, this time leaning down to give her a proper kiss. Then he stood up and grabbed his book bag.

"Um. Are we studying something tonight?" she asked.

Caio laughed.

"No. Unless you want to, but that's not what this is about. That was never what this was about."

"Then why the backpack?" she asked.

"Oh. Well, we need to look like we are studying, right? It wouldn't look good if I just showed up here with flowers and food."

He dropped his backpack on her kitchen counter and pulled out some cans of black beans, ham hocks, bacon, cilantro, and onions.

"What's that for?"

"I wanted to make you feijoada. I think you'll like it. I have to use canned beans," he said, looking at the cans as if they were something excretory. "There was no way I could justify soaking beans overnight at home." He shrugged.

"What can I do?" she asked.

"You want to help? I don't mind cooking for you."

"No, I would like to help."

He quickly shot a glance outside. There was no one there. He then kissed her on the nose.

"You can chop up the garlic and cilantro," he said.

"Oh, wait. Before you do that, you should do this," he said and pulled a box out of the grocery bag.

It contained a bottle with UTI test strips. He handed it to her along with a cup from her cupboard. She raised her eyebrows.

"You said you thought you had a bladder infection. So I thought, before you go taking antibiotics, you should at least test again," he said, looking down for a second.

"I think I am actually okay now," she said.

"Well, it's better to be sure. Because I don't want to hurt you, you know. And that could be what's making you sick. Go on," he said, handing her the tube and cup. "And make sure you leave the strip in the cup for at least five minutes. These things are notorious for taking a long time to register a real result, despite what the directions say."

Sarah smiled to herself as she went up the stairs. She was shocked by this, but not unhappy. If someone else had done this, it might have felt like they were treating her like a child. But this didn't feel like that. It felt like they were a couple.

Once in the bathroom, Sarah peed in the cup and put the test strip in it. She didn't feel the burning anymore, but she did sort of constantly feel like she needed to pee. She put the cup on the sink and went back downstairs.

"Did you do it?" he asked. She nodded. "And you left it, right? It needs at least five minutes."

Sarah nodded. Caio suddenly got very quiet. Sarah stood next to him and began cutting up cilantro. She noticed that he was twisting his foot on the ground as he cut and mixed things. He put the beans, meat, vinegar, and bay leaves into a pot with a little water. He then put the heat on high.

"Can you watch this for a second?" he asked. "If it starts to boil, then just turn it down to simmer and put the lid on the pot," he said as he started up the stairs.

"What are you doing?" she asked, suddenly insecure about him seeing a cup of her urine sitting on the sink.

"I need to use the toilet," he said.

"There's a cup—well, there's my cup on the sink," she called up to him, feeling very stupid after she said this.

"Got it," he called back. She turned her attention back to the pot with the meat. They say a watched pot never boils but this one did. She stirred it and put the lid back on. She realized that Caio had been gone for a while. She turned to call to him and found him standing in the door of the kitchen staring at her. The look on his face was so strange that she couldn't even begin to decipher it. He was smiling but his eyes looked wet, almost as if he had been crying.

"Are you okay?" she asked. He nodded and crossed to her. With the window wide open, he pulled her into his arms and kissed her long and hard. She knew this wasn't a good idea, but she couldn't make herself pull away. Finally, he did, just to stare at her face.

"Caio," she said. "We're in front of the window."

He nodded and pulled her back into the living room, where he sat on the couch, pulled her into his lap and began to kiss her again. His cheeks did feel wet against her face.

"Are you okay?" she asked again, pulling back to look at him.

"Yeah. I'm more than okay," he said.

"Did something happen?" she asked.

"Will you go with me into the city this weekend?" Caio asked.

"Can you do that? Wouldn't your foster family have a fit?" she asked.

"If you can go, I can go," he said.

"I would love to go," she said, and he pulled her tight for a minute and then let go quickly.

"Okay. Is there anywhere in particular you want to stay or anything you want to do?" he asked, pushing a strand of her hair behind her ear.

"You know, for as long as I have lived here, I've only gone to the city a few times," she said.

"You aren't from here?" he asked.

229

"No, I was born in Newport, Rhode Island. Then I moved here and went to Brooklyn Law School," she replied. She felt the momentary twinge she always felt when she thought about how she had failed at being a lawyer.

"None of that matters," Caio said, and then his eyes widened. "Sorry. That was rude."

He knew what you were thinking. Did he just …

"Did you just read my mind?" she asked, and Caio laughed a little.

"No. I can't read minds. But I can read faces well. Your face said that you were feeling bad about your past. And you don't have to—" he was about to say something and stopped himself.

"Are you sure that there isn't anywhere in particular that you want to go?" he asked.

"No, I think I'll be happy just to be with you," she said, shocking herself yet again with her candor.

"Then I'll plan it. All you have to do is meet me at the Hudson Hotel near the park. Meet me in the lobby at 10:30. That's all you need to do." After he said this, he kissed her, and they got lost in it yet again.

"Oh shit, the food," she said suddenly, and he laughed.

"It can simmer for hours, no problem."

Seeing his open, kind, caring face, she was struck again by the fact that she had never known a man like this. Would she have left Karl earlier if she had guessed this person existed?

Karl. You need to tell him about what's going on before your brain completely turns to mush, said Val.

"I need to tell you about what happened with Karl," she said, and Caio sat back. His eyes hardened a bit.

"Are you afraid he might show up here tonight?" he asked.

"Well, it's unlikely but if he did—well, he's not nice."

Caio cocked his head and smiled the strangest smile.

"You don't have to worry about that anymore. I won't let him hurt you," he said. Sarah looked at him. He wasn't a big person. And he was significantly lighter than Karl.

"Karl is kind of big. I'm afraid he might hurt *you*," Sarah said.

"He'd be dead before he got a chance to hurt either of us," Caio said flatly, and his gaze suddenly lost all its warmth. For just a moment, it seemed like something else was moving behind those normally warm eyes. But then he shrugged.

"Don't worry, we won't let it come to that. If we hear him, I can find a way out without being seen," he said.

"Listen, that's not the only thing. I need to tell you a few more things about Karl and what has happened this week," she said. And he nodded.

"Well, you know I told you that he asked me to marry him, right?"

Caio nodded again, his face tight.

"He didn't ask for an answer. He said he would give me time to think about it. This all happened just after we had finished dinner at that Italian place where Mouse works. Well, just after that, he got a text and said that he had to go work, and he took me home. When I started thinking about it, I was sure that he was going to see Meghan. Then I remembered Laura telling me about this club called the Stigmata Club, and that I should see it if I wanted to know about the depravity here," she said.

"I know the place," Caio said. "My foster parents cater their events from time to time. That place is a nasty piece of work. I always called it the Death Club."

"What do you mean? Have you been inside it?" she asked.

"It's a BDSM club but that's not the problem. The problem is—well, there's a lot that goes on there that is unsafe and unhealthy. And no, I've never been inside it. That sort of place would be very dangerous for someone like me."

She started to ask him what that meant, but he cut her off.

"Why do you bring this place up?" he asked.

"Well, I sort of went there," Sarah said.

"You went in?" Caio asked sitting up straight and taking her hand.

"No, no. I just sat outside in the car," she said, and Caio visibly relaxed. "But I saw Karl and Meghan go in, along with a few other people from our law firm."

"Did they see you?" Caio said, anxiety returning to his face.

"No."

"Are you sure?"

"Yes. I'm sure," she replied. He looked skeptical.

"Why did you go?" he asked.

"I just thought it might help somehow."

Caio took her face in his hands.

"Listen, Sarah, you shouldn't have been there. That was dangerous for you. You need to be careful."

"There's actually more than that," she said. Then she told him about the Davies case. She told him about the abuse she read about and going to see Melissa Taylor. And then she told him about the things Chris had said to her at the pre-deposition. As he listened, she could feel his hands clench around her fingers.

"What are you going to do?" he asked.

"I'm going to talk to Phillip Seider and send him these recordings. I can't do much with them, but he probably can. But I can't bear the thought that Alex Davies is stuck with them. Oh, and I'll talk to Melissa Taylor," she said.

"You should leave work."

"I suppose, I mean I have enough money saved to live on for a while," she said.

"Don't worry about money. We'll deal with that. And you should call Matt Greenley and get started on your trust. You're getting into dangerous territory with these people."

She was about to argue with him when she realized that he was right. Things were becoming dangerous. She had taken a photo of her trust. It was on her computer. If Karl saw that, she was in trouble. She had spoken with Matt Greenley about said trust. If Karl found out about that, she was in trouble. If Michael or Karl started suspecting that she was colluding with Melissa and Phillip Seider, she would be in big trouble. If any of them got a hint of her relationship with Caio, she was royally screwed.

"Promise me that you won't go back to work. For the moment, you can call in sick. You were sick today, so they will believe it," Caio said. "We can figure out exactly what to do this weekend. Promise?"

He put his arm gently around her waist.

"I promise," she said.

"Promise one more thing. I am going to program my number into your phone. If Karl shows up and you are in any way scared, you call me. Don't wait until something bad happens. In fact, if he shows up unannounced, call me. Or text me. Promise?"

She looked at him. He was so serious.

"Yes, I promise," she said.

"Good. Now we need to get some food into you," he said, lifting her off his lap and getting up. "And you should go check if you have a bladder infection."

Sarah nodded and went up the stairs. The stick in the cup showed negative for all signs of UTI. When she came back down, Caio had laid food out on the table.

He pulled out a chair for her as she came in and she laughed. His brow furrowed for a moment.

"Was that a weird thing to do?" he asked.

"No, it was a nice thing to do," she said sitting down. "It's just not something that I am used to. It's a bit traditional for, well—" she was about to say for a teenage boy but that was starting to sound ridiculous even to her ears.

"I guess I am kind of traditional," he shrugged, sitting down. "I like sports because they always kind of remain the same. It's hard to keep up with all the constant changes in everything else in the world. The clothes, the hair, the slang."

The licenses in Caio's wallet sprang to her mind. The dates on them. And what she had found on his military record. She suddenly felt the world around her shift again.

"How many sports do you play?" she asked, to focus herself.

"Lots. All the North American ones like baseball and basketball. But I also play football, I mean soccer, and cricket. I tried swimming, and I'm good at it but I don't like it. It makes me feel—well, I guess I'm a bit claustrophobic."

From being dropped into a hole and sucked into the mud.

They stopped talking for a moment and just looked at each other. Once again, Caio had an expression on his face that she couldn't decipher, but she knew it was happy.

"Isn't the food good?" he asked. She realized that she had been picking at her beans.

"No, it's really good. I just feel a bit sick is all."

"Then let's go upstairs where you can rest," he said. Sarah smiled.

"Okay. I'm not sure we will rest, but that's okay," she said.

"No, tonight you'll rest. We need to take care of you," he said softly.

He took her by the hand and led her upstairs. Once in bed, he held her and kissed her for a long time. When things became heated, he brought her pleasure with his hands. She returned the favor. Then fatigue hit her again, and she fell asleep in his arms with the smell of him all around her.

Chapter Thirty-Seven

Stolen Kisses

Tuesday July 1

Sarah woke up suddenly, and had to run to the bathroom. She barely managed to get the lid of the toilet up before vomiting into the water. What came up was mostly bile, but it didn't make its exit gently. Even when there was nothing left, she heaved for a good five minutes. Afterward, when she looked at herself in the mirror, she saw that her face was bright red. She was pretty damn sure that she had a fever.

After brushing her teeth, she stumbled back into the bedroom, where she stopped short. Caio was still there. He was lying in her bed, sheets wound between his legs and one arm thrown over her pillow. Seeing him, she stopped breathing for a moment. She had never woken up to find him still in her bed.

Oh god. I could get used to this sight.

Yes, you should be allowed to, whispered Val. *And before any of the other assholes pipe up, I want to say that I never felt what you are feeling right now. I never had a moment like this one in my whole life. You need to cherish this and protect it, no matter what the hell anyone else says.*

"People won't say good things, Val," she whispered.

No, they won't, Val replied. *But fuck them. Being a ghost now, I can tell you that this thing with you and Caio is something you are just stepping back into. It's nothing new. It just got messed up.*

"Are you talking about past lives?" Sarah asked.

Past lives, cross-dimensions, there are lots of different connection points, Val replied.

Valerie, you are on the verge of over-speaking, said Larry suddenly.

"But I want to know—" Sarah began.

And we would love to tell you, but that one is against rules, Larry replied.

234

All this time, Sarah had not taken her eyes off Caio. Suddenly, he sat up, eyes wide, breathing hard. For a moment his eyes were unseeing, then they fell on her. He immediately got up and went to her.

"Are you okay?" he asked, putting his hand to her forehead. Then he nodded to himself.

"You have a fever, but it's not very high. It should be fine," he said, putting his arm around her waist.

"I think I have the flu," she muttered. She was getting drowsy again.

"Ummhmmm," Caio said, leading her back to the bed and getting in with her.

"Aren't you worried about getting sick?" she muttered.

"Nope" he said, kissing her neck.

It felt deliciously good to feel him next to her. For once, he didn't feel hot to her. In fact, his body felt wonderfully cool. She had never felt this comfortable lying with another person. She would never have imagined even wanting Karl to stay the night.

Karl.

Sarah sat up quickly.

"Caio, you need to go," she said suddenly.

"Why?" he asked, sitting up as well.

"I'm afraid that Karl might show up," she said. "I put him off last night by saying I was sick but—"

"But you think he might check up on you?"

"Yes," she said.

"The macho part of me wants to say that I don't care, and that I'll protect you," Caio said, reaching out to brush her hair back from her face. "But I know that isn't smart. I also know that you won't be able to relax. So, yeah, I should go."

He got up as he said this. Sarah had noticed that he wasn't a person to linger once a decision was made.

"But you are to call me instantly if you get any sicker. Call if you start vomiting more, or if your heart does anything weird, or if you start bleeding—"

"Bleeding?"

"Just call me if anything changes," he said.

"Okay. But won't your foster parents think it's weird that you are getting a call from me?"

"If they notice, which isn't likely, I'll find a way to explain it, but it's not really my top concern right now. So, you'll call?" he asked. She nodded.

"I'll text you later to remind you about New York. Remember, 10:30 a.m. at

235

the Hudson Hotel. You won't stand me up, right?" he asked with a smile.

Sarah laughed, but it hurt her stomach. Caio came and kissed her gently, then not so gently, before backing out of the room, blinking at her and then turning to head down the stairs. She could hear his feet on the stairs and then the sound of water running in the kitchen. This was followed by the sound of the front door closing.

She hated that sound because it meant she wouldn't see him for days. She sat up for a moment, realizing that she had not heard from Phillip Seider. She went downstairs and got her phone. Sure enough, she had a few missed calls from his number. She dialed it back and got voicemail. It was still before opening hours. Sarah went into her living room and sat down on the couch, then thought better of it. Instead, she got her phone and called the number of the bookstore where Melissa Taylor worked. It was only 8 a.m., so it was unlikely anyone would answer this early, but Sarah felt a tug to do this. Someone picked up on the fourth ring.

"Hello, oh I mean Reddux Books," said a warm female voice that Sarah knew.

"Melissa?" she asked.

"Is this Sarah?"

"Yes. Do you have a secure email that I can send a voice recording to?" she asked.

"Yes," Melissa answered. She then rattled off an email address and Sarah jotted it down.

"What is this about?" she asked.

"I took your boys through questions and Chris made some statements about Alex showering with Anne Marie and Andrew."

She heard Melissa's intake of breath. Then a soft sob. "My baby." Sarah's eyes started to well up.

"Melissa, I'm going to send this to you. And you need to get it to Phillip, okay?"

There was no answer, only the soft sound of sobbing on the other end.

"Melissa, we're going to fix this. I promise. We will make this right." There were tears rolling down her face when she said this, but she also felt a power beginning to surge through her.

"Thank you, Sarah," whispered Melissa. "But I don't know if there's any legal way to win this. I have tried so hard and for so long."

"Try a little longer," Sarah said, her own voice breaking. With that she hung up the phone. She then sent the voice recording to Melissa and Phillip. She got up and walked around her kitchen for a few moments. She felt weak but she was angry. Finally, she went to sit on her couch in the living room.

I will make this right. I will make all of this right. Even if I have to go to that horrible club myself and videotape it.

Wait. This is exactly what she needed to do. This was probably the only real smoking gun. Get something on video and take it to the DA. The DA would be required by law to do something about it.

How will you do this, when you can barely stand up? said the voice of her mother.

For this day, at least, Sarah's mother was right. Even with all the adrenaline running through her, Sarah was asleep on her couch in less than ten minutes.

Thursday July 3

Sarah spent the rest of Tuesday and all of Wednesday in a fever-induced haze. She got a few concerned texts from Caio, and she responded that she was still okay, even if she didn't really feel it. She got a significantly less warm voicemail from Karl, asking if she was better yet. And the coldest from Michael, who was just barely containing his annoyance that she was away from work.

But when she got up on Thursday morning, her fever was gone and by the afternoon, she was completely herself again. Caio texted her that morning checking in on her. She wished he had called but understood that this would be too dangerous. He wouldn't know who was around. Once he heard that she was better, he was clearly relieved. He also reminded her again of the address of the Hudson Hotel. Sarah smiled at this.

On Thursday evening, as she was standing in her bathroom staring at herself in the mirror, something inside her clicked. She was standing here, when she had a way, or at least a change, to help Alex Davies. She began applying heavy makeup. After this, she went to her closet, searching for something leather. She could find very little, but she did find clothes from which she could make a passable schoolteacher outfit. She also found a wig and an old riding crop that she had from a masquerade party in law school.

That could do …

It wasn't until she was standing at her door that she realized she was serious about going to this club. The voices in her head were trying to talk, but she was drowning them out with songs that she kept circling in her mind. She knew they wouldn't want her to do this. She knew that, just as she knew she had to try. Alex was being abused and his mother was powerless. If she could do something—anything—who was she to deny her responsibility to try?

She got in her car and began making her way toward Orchard Street. When she arrived, there were already cars parked along the street.

Surprisingly busy for a Thursday night, right?

She was about to get out of her car, when her vision dimmed. She found herself inside her own head. Valerie was sitting on the cream couch, with Larry sitting at a desk next to it.

Sarah, suppose there's some sort of membership requirement or card or something. This isn't smart, said Larry.

Stop, Val said to Larry. *I understand why she has to do this. But Sarah, you need to let us help with this. We can keep you safer.*

"How?" Sarah asked.

We're ghosts, Val said. *We can help you be less visible. But you need to keep a part of you connected to us here. If you do, then you will be less physical and physical creatures won't notice you as much—you will seem more like scenery.*

You can't— began Sarah's mother but Valerie whirled on her.

You shut the fuck up! she hissed.

Sarah, take my hand, Val said. Then she reached out to Larry, who came and took Sarah's other hand.

Remember this feeling, keep our hands on you in your mind. And if we tell you to run, then you run.

Sarah nodded.

Open your eyes now, and keep holding on to my hand, Val said.

Sarah opened her eyes. She felt a surge of energy as she got out of the car. It was as if Val's confidence and Larry's perception were flowing through her. Just at that moment, a large group of people, much like the Mardi Gras crowd of the other day, walked toward the club. Sarah looked at one of the men and began to tap her riding crop in her hand. The man laughed, came toward her and put his arm around her.

And just like that, she was swept through the front door with them. No one seemed surprised by her presence.

The inside of the corridor of the club wasn't what she had envisioned. She had expected something dark, and wet with condensation. Instead, she was propelled into a hallway that was painted dark gray but lit in shades of pink, lavender, and green. The walls were decorated with balloons, glitter, and mirrors in such a way as to give the impression of a kids' party or a 1970s disco. It wasn't until she was at the end of the hallway that she realized that the balloons were inflated condoms and that the small pieces of mirror were painted with pictures people being spanked, whipped, and chained. At the end of the hall was a large leather-padded door. One of the larger men pushed his weight against it to get it to open.

When the door opened, the first thing to hit her was the wall of sound. Loud, cheesy, synth-pop music was being blasted over speakers that felt like they must be the size of small family sedans, or at least that was what her ears told her. The next assault to her senses were the flashing lights and strobes that made it hard to see what was happening in the dimly lit room. As she turned to close the door behind her, the smell hit her: alcohol, vomit, piss, shit, and sex. It was a noxious mixture that made bile rise in her throat. She was already battling nausea, and this certainly didn't help. She took a few quick, deep breaths through her mouth, trying to stabilize herself.

As her newfound friends scattered, Sarah saw that she was in a large room decorated in much the same way as the hall, with the addition of whips and chains displayed on the walls. But the decor was not what was shocking. It was the apparel of the people. If Sarah had felt very self-consciously weird-looking in her wig and school teacher outfit, she was underdressed here—or over-dressed, as it were. All around her were people in leather underwear, leather masks, and chokers. Some were being led around on leashes. Some were wear-ing ball gags in their mouths. There were men dressed only in diapers, a few with pacifiers in their mouths. Some people were just naked. Standing out even in a crowd this eccentric were the people dressed as horses. They were adorned with saddles, bridles, and reins that had to have been specially made, probably by Anne Marie's company. All of this in a room that was as large and packed with people as any popular nightclub in the city.

Sarah made her way toward the bar to get a drink. She needed to put some-thing in her stomach to ground herself. She also needed a way to observe the crowd without looking too obvious or like she wanted to engage someone in—well, in whatever they were here to do. She let her "hair" fall into her face in the hopes of obscuring her features even more than her makeup. She also kept the feeling of Val's hand in hers strong in her mind.

She quickly scanned the people standing at the bar, and the bartender. She saw no one she knew. She walked up to the bar and was greeted by a man wear-ing a red leather cupid outfit.

"Hi beautiful. What can I get you?" he asked, but with little intonation and no eye contact. Good.

"Just a Diet Coke," she said, and he was away before she even finished speaking. As much as she would have liked to drink, this was neither the time nor the place. She turned her back to the bar and glanced around the room. It was hard to identify anyone or even really see faces in the undulating mass. But

239

when she looked up, she saw that there were naked men and women in cages above their heads. Occasionally, someone would take a long stick and poke at one of them.

"If you are interested in one of them, you just tell the bartender," said a man to her right. His face looked like he could have been an attorney in any of the firms in the city. But he was wearing a ripped shirt and what skin was showing through had angry-looking red welts. "First timer?"

Sarah felt herself freeze but once again, the voice that came out of her was something she had not expected. It was her own, but calm and confident.

"Yes. I'm a newbie," she said, smiling at the man.

"Dom or Sub?" he asked.

"Dom," she said quickly. "Or Dom wannabe."

The man smiled broadly. "Ooooh. Can I be your first? I love new Doms."

Sarah felt herself smile and even wink at him. "Well, I would but I think I would prefer a woman the first time."

The man made a clown-face frown.

"Isn't it always the way," he said. "But if you want a great first-time experience, you should find Marie."

Marie. Could that be ... ?

"Where would she be, then?"

The man looked up at the cages above their heads. "Well, normally, she would be up there, but someone must have called for her."

The man stood on tiptoe, heaved himself up on the bar and stood. Almost immediately, a bartender arrived and pushed him off. He landed elegantly right in front of her.

"She's at the corner table back there, with her master and some of his closer friends," the man said.

"Thanks," Sarah said and moved forward.

"Come find me later," the man called. "I can do number two—do number two, get it?"

His laugh was drowned out by the music as Sarah made her way across the floor. She knew she had to be careful, but she felt strangely confident. That might have been because most of the people she passed didn't bother to look at her. Or because Val was partially in charge.

She knew that there was something here she had to find. She felt for her glasses. They felt normal on her face. The camera element was well hidden in them. The glasses themselves were black hornrims, which perfectly matched her school mistress attire.

At a booth on the far side of the room, she recognized Karl's dull hair and body language. Rather than approach the table head on, she moved to one side of the room and moved along the wall, glancing between bodies to watch what was happening.

Karl was sitting at the table with Michael, Andrew Davies, Angela, and Meghan. Sandwiched between Michael, Karl, and Andrew were two boys, probably no more than fifteen. They were either naked or shirtless, Sarah couldn't tell. Andrew was leaning with his arms stretched out on the booth behind him, eyes closed. Then suddenly, Sarah saw him jerk and a few seconds later, a woman rolled out from under the table, with enough force that it was clear she had been kicked. The woman was dressed in a pink glitter transparent bodysuit that left nothing to the imagination. It was cinched with a leather belt that looked as if it could cut her in half. As she stood up, Sarah recognized the bronze-streaked hair and voluminous butt of Anne Marie Davies. The men at the table were all smiling or laughing. Anne Marie stood, wiped at her mouth and then moved over to one of the boys sitting at one end of the booth. The boy shook his head but Andrew Davies, who was sitting on the opposite side of the booth, gave him a stern look. He then got up, walked up behind Anne Marie, pushed her to her knees and shoved her head into the boy's crotch.

Sarah pressed the button on her glasses and felt the buzz of photos being taken.

While this was going on, a man wearing a hospital gown and wheeling an IV stand came up to the side of the table where Michael was sitting next to the other young boy. Michael rolled up his sleeve and the man inserted a needle into his vein. The young boy started trying to pull away, but Karl, who was sitting on the other side of him, held him in place. The boy turned his head away as a needle was injected into his arm as well. As Sarah watched in horror, blood began to move up the tube from the young boy, and into some sort of machine hanging from the IV stand. Very quickly the blood then appeared in a tube at the other side of the device and descended toward Michael's arm. Sarah felt rooted to where she stood. It was hard to align what she was seeing with the reality of life as she knew it.

Just then someone touched her on the shoulder, and she jumped. She turned to find herself face-to-face with Alex Davies. He leaned forward and put his lips to her ear.

"You should get out of here," he whispered. He was wearing nothing but some sort of golden pouch holding his penis.

"You saw me? You recognized me?" she whispered back.

"Grab me, kiss me, and pull me into the alcove just there," he said, indicating a small closet near the exit door. Even a month ago, Sarah would have been unable to do this but now she did. She grabbed Alex by the neck, kissed him hard and pulled him back into the alcove.

"I can't talk long. They are waiting for me," Alex said once they were hidden in the shadows. "You're dim, but if someone focuses long enough, you are completely recognizable. Also, your outfit looks like a newbie, so people will focus on you and if Dad or Anne Marie or Karl or Michael can manage to see you, they will immediately recognize you. You don't want that to happen."

Sarah was shocked by his allusion to what her ghosts were doing for her, but she didn't have time to discuss it.

"What are you doing here?" she whispered.

"Everything they ask me to do," he said with a sigh.

"But why? Why don't you tell the police?"

"Are you that naive? Half the powerful people in this community are members of this club, and that's really just the start of it."

"Can't you just run away? I could help you," Sarah said, looking at the deep blue circles under this boy's eyes and understanding them for the first time.

Alex's laugh was more like a cough.

"You don't know who these people are. My Dad doesn't even really know who these people are. I know more about them because he has lent me out to some of them over time, and a few of them have let things slip."

"Your mother said something about your dad being a part of the Illuminati—" Sarah began.

"Sssssh," Alex said, even though they were already whispering, and the music was pounding loudly around them. "That was the sort of shit that landed my mother in the institution. My Dad isn't Illuminati. He's just a pervert, but some of these other people—well, I think they are something the Illuminati could only aspire to be, if even a tiny bit of what I have learned is true. I'm afraid that I am going to learn a bit more than I want to before they finally get tired of me and arrange for my disappearance."

"What? Then you need to get away. You can come with me. I can take you to the city and we can find a lawyer. I can—"

"Listen, that's nice of you, but you would disappear by morning if you tried to help me. And they would punish me by hurting my mother and my brothers."

"Can't you—" she began but Alex cut her off.

"Look, there's no way out for me. I just drew a bad card when I was born the son of a pervert. I drew a worse one when I was thrown in with these people. But there is a way out for you. You need to get out of this city and away from all these people. If you stay in their circles, they'll either kill you or suck the life out of you until you pray for death. For now, I don't think you are important enough for them to notice much if you leave. So get out of this place, go home, pack, and leave town. That way you will be gone just in case someone did clock you while you were here."

He gave her a sad little smile, quickly kissed her cheek and then slid out of the alcove. Sarah suddenly began to shake all over. She closed her eyes and counted, trying to catch her breath. The other person inside her, the one that was so confident, had disappeared, and now she was overwhelmed and terrified.

Where are you guys when I need you? she muttered inside her head.

We are still here, said Val. *You've done so well. But we're losing energy so you need to get out of here now, honey.*

Sarah nodded to no one and moved quickly from out of the alcove back into the main room and toward the exit. She did not look in the direction of the booth where Andrew and Anne Marie were holding court.

Please don't let them see me. Please don't let them see me.

She made it to the door of the exit without being noticed. Unlike when she entered, the hallway was now full of people. Sarah squared her shoulders and pushed through the crowds with a bravado she did not feel.

Someone grabbed her arm and she jerked.

"Leaving so soon?" It took her a mere moment to recognize the man she had seen at the bar. "Did you find our lovely Marie?"

"Found. Saw. Realized she was too much for a beginner like me," she heard herself say.

"I told you that you should have picked me. You still can, you know. Sometimes you need to just shit or get off someone's face."

Sarah started to laugh until she noticed the man's eyes, then she almost choked.

What the fuck?

"Don't worry. I'll be back. But for tonight I have straighter plans, if you know what I mean."

"Oh. A boyfriend who's not cool. Okay. But do keep me in mind when and if you come back," he said, then he drew close to her ear and whispered. "I love the smell of you."

Sarah pulled back, wagged her finger at him, then turned and walked out the door. She was back in her car two minutes later, shaking and crying. She managed to get her car started and drive home even though she didn't remember anything of the drive. Once she was back in her house, she locked the door behind her and put a chair against the doorknob for good measure. She pulled off the wig, false eyelashes, and contacts and threw them into the sink.

She then went upstairs and pulled out the suitcase she had packed. She opened it and added in all the important documents and mementos she had collected. She and Caio were only planning to be gone for a few days, but she packed for longer. She had the nagging intuition that she might not return here again.

Then she lay down, fully dressed, on her bed.

That guy in the club had no pupils. His eyes were blue with absolutely no pupils. And it wasn't contacts, she would know that. What sort of fucked up drugs were they on at that club?

She closed her eyes in the darkness and waited for sleep to come, but it didn't come until the sun was almost rising.

Chapter Thirty-Eight

The Smoking Whip

Friday July 4

Sarah got out of bed at eight o'clock. She had only had a few hours of restless sleep laced with nightmares. What she had seen happening to those boys the night before had repulsed and frightened her so badly that she hadn't even thought to check whether she had been able to get recognizable pictures. Once this thought entered her head, she got up and was about to go downstairs to her computer when she realized she was still wearing the clothes from the night before. She felt as if she were covered in slime or sperm or something worse. She yanked her outfit off and threw it in the corner. Throwing on jeans and a white shirt, she ran downstairs. She took the card from the camera glasses and uploaded it into her computer. When the files opened, she discovered that she had not only taken pictures, but she had inadvertently left the video camera running at some point. There, caught in video, she saw Andrew Davies as he had been slouched against the back of the booth, and Anne Marie coming out from under the booth. She fast forwarded through, and sure enough, she had caught the forced oral sex and the blood transfer. But what she hadn't realized was that she had also captured the conversation with Alex Davies. There wasn't much to see in this segment, but the words were what was damning. As she listened, Sarah felt a chill go up her spine.

"I have to take this to the DA in person."

No. You do not need to get involved in this, Sarah. Send it to Phillip Seider and he can take it to the DA, said Paul, with obvious panic.

Sarah thought for a second. His advice would have seemed sound to her months ago, but now sound advice didn't seem to matter as much. If she put this in the hands of Phillip Seider, she didn't know exactly what he would do with it. She thought he was ethical. She had been told he was ethical, but she had no proof. For that matter, she had no proof that the DA would be ethical.

Don't stick your neck out here Sarah. You need to protect yourself, said Paul.

"Protect myself or protect you?" Sarah snapped back. "Besides, I've been trying to protect myself for my whole life, and what good has it done? I have been paralyzed by doubt and self-loathing, dating an asshole who hates me, and working for Satan's law firm. I'm done trying to protect myself. For once, I am going to protect someone else."

Sarah, Paul may be right on this one. You don't know who these people are. Maybe— began Larry, but Sarah cut him off.

"The DA will take it more seriously if it comes from the person who was there. So I will send it to Phillip, but I will take it the DA myself. Then I will send it to the media."

Sarah, that's a declaration of war with your firm, Val said softly.

"Oh, they can all go fuck themselves. These are monsters, Val, monsters! For once, just this once, I can really help someone. I have a chance to make someone else's life okay. How many people ever get a chance to do that?"

Everyone went silent in her head.

She picked up the phone and called the office of Dave Gregory, the district attorney. The outgoing message said that the offices would be closed for July 4. Of course, it was the fourth of July. She hung up without leaving a message. What would she be able to say over the phone?

Damn it.

Sarah called back.

"Hi Dave. This is Sarah Baker. I work with one of the law firms in Brooklyn. It is urgent that you call me right away."

Sarah then left her number and her home email. The problem was that she had no idea when Dave would pick up the message and she needed to get this done before she met with Caio in New York. She knew that everything was going to change after that trip. She didn't know how she knew it, but she did. Sarah went back to the computer and did a public record and property search on Dave Gregory. Within a few minutes, she had his home address.

Are you planning to go to his house and intrude on his family on the fourth of July? said the voice of her mother.

Shut up, said Sarah and Val in unison.

In truth, this was what she might *have* to do. But she would wait a while to see if anyone called her back.

246

Next, she took out Matt Greenley's number. She glanced at the clock. It was 10 a.m., but that hardly mattered, as it was the fourth of July. He wouldn't be there. Still, she dialed his number. To her shock, someone picked up.

"Is this Sarah?" he asked before she even spoke. He had programmed her number into his phone.

"Yes, Matt?" she asked.

"Yes. I am glad to hear from you."

"I'm ready to start the process. Do you have time to talk about it?" she asked.

"I do, but I would like to talk about this in person. I don't trust the phone for this kind of thing. Can you stop by my offices this morning?"

"I can come now, if that works."

"That's perfect," he said.

Sarah hung up and immediately went to her car. On the drive over to Matt's, she got a text from Caio checking on her. She wanted to call him back but realized that she didn't know where he was or who he was with. She responded that she was feeling better, which was true. He reminded her for the fifth or sixth time the address of the Hudson. He ended the text with xxx. Not an emoji, but xxx.

She smiled to herself.

She pulled into Matt Greenley's Brooklyn office space. It was in a tall glass building. She pressed the button next to his name and was immediately buzzed up.

When she got out of the elevator, Matt was standing at the door of his office. He beckoned her in. The blinds were open, and the room was bright and sunny. The furniture was different from the usual lawyer fare. It was not of the typical masculine mahogany style. Instead, the wood was lighter and homier. He motioned for Sarah to sit on the couch, while he sat in a chair next to the couch.

"You spoke to Laura?" he asked.

"Yes," she replied, not quite knowing where he was going with this.

"She must have told you that our little community here is far from being clean. Not that most legal communities are, but ours is unique."

"In what way?" Sarah asked, but the vision of the boy being forced to hook up to an IV was stuck in her head.

"Let's just say for starters that there's a lot of underworld money here," he replied. Sarah was surprised by his candor. "Then there are the people who pull the strings of those in the underworld, and the even scarier ones who control those who pull the strings."

"This sounds like conspiracy theories," Sarah said, but quickly added, "not that I am discounting that."

"Conspiracy? That makes it sound like these things are secret when they aren't. Power is corruptive, that's not secret, it's axiomatic. There's evil in the world. That's also inarguable. What may be more secret is how that evil finds its way into power, and the way the corruption manifests itself."

"As an attorney, I'm surprised that you believe in concepts like good and evil," said Sarah.

"As an attorney, how could I not? I see both all the time. As attorneys, we see people at moments when they are in transition. Transition brings out extremes. I've seen normal people raise themselves up to the noblest ideals. I've seen monsters transform themselves into angels. I've also seen good men succumb to their meanest instincts."

A picture of Melissa Taylor came into her head unbidden.

"I think there are rivers of these sorts of energies running across our world, and what makes us unique as humans is that we can channel them, the good and the bad," Matt continued. "Sometimes the most difficult thing is knowing if you are doing good or evil, because we don't have the ability to see the long-term consequences of our behaviors."

"Then what can anyone do, if we are holding ourselves to the long-term implications that we can't see or control?" she asked.

"We have to find things we believe in and hold on to them. The people in this community believe they are doing good. Our little community has low crime, high employment, great schools, and lots of opportunity for people willing to work hard. All that doesn't come free. It takes money. This money comes from taxes, investments, and donations. We have low local taxes, by US standards. That means that we are getting money through investments and donations. Do you see where I am going with this?" he said, stopping to look at her.

Sarah thought about Andrew Davies. She had been shocked by the number of businesses that had him as an investor or patron.

Matt nodded.

"You see, we have our shadows and secrets as well. People don't look gift horses in the mouth, do they? And you, my dear, are another gift horse. Your trust is substantial."

"How substantial is substantial?" she asked.

"Tens of millions."

Sarah felt a wave of unreality hit her.

"What?"

"Yes, Paul was a wealthy man from a wealthy family. They had investments in all sorts of things, and some of those investments might shock or upset you. That might be why your husband didn't want you to know about them. I suspect that Karl may have invested the money in places that you would be even more upset about. For this reason, once I put in the request to take over as trustee, citing his negligence in informing you, and the mismanagement of your funds, all hell will break loose."

"I will lose my job, right?" she said. Matt laughed.

"Your job is the least of your worries. In fact, you shouldn't go back to work, just in case someone has seen you here. If I were you, I would plan to move. I will file this at the end of next week but there's a serious grapevine in this town, and they will surely find out before that. That means you will need to leave town early next week."

Sarah nodded.

"I'm serious as a heart attack, Sarah. This is a big deal. I'm risking myself by taking it."

"So why are you taking it?"

"Honestly, because I hate those fuckers at your law firm—and if it's possible I hate Karl Renfield more. A lot of us know how he has treated you for years, and personally it's made me sick. So I'll enjoy sticking it to him. If anyone can do that, it's me."

"Well, it's good to have a confident lawyer."

"Sarah, it's more than my abilities as a lawyer. We were talking of good and evil, but maybe I phrased it wrong. Out there in the world, there are agents of chaos and agents of creation. They exist in opposition, and both sides are very powerful. I have connections to some powerful people in the camp opposing those we will be fighting. Simply knowing and being known by some of these people protects me. Because of that, I am betting that Karl and his ilk won't have the balls to come after me, because that would be baiting very powerful people on the other side, but I can't protect you. So you need to disappear. You can call me, and I will let you know what I need but don't tell me where you are. Do you understand this?"

Sarah nodded.

"Do you still want me to start the ball rolling?"

"Yes. And I'm going to the city this weekend," she said. "I'll move out of my house this week."

"Good. I will try to get access to funds as quickly as possible. Do you have enough to live on without a job for a while?"

"Yes, for six months. I'll let you know where I end up," she said.

"No, don't. Just keep in touch with me by phone or I will call you on your mobile. I think it's better if you keep a very low profile for the time being. Can you do that?"

"Yes," Sarah said. Matt stood up and shook her hand.

"I'll contact you as soon as I hear something," Matt said.

"Thanks Matt," she said, as she walked out the door.

Keep a low profile.

Well, she doubted that the next activity on her list for the day would qualify as keeping a low profile.

Party crashing rarely did.

#

It was nearly eight o'clock and approaching twilight when Sarah drove into the Manhattan Beach neighborhood where DA Dave Gregory lived. Tracking his address down had been easy enough, but now, as she parked in front of his A-frame gingerbread house, she felt a knot in her stomach. The street he lived on was lined with cars. She had no doubt that there would be multiple July 4 parties going on, but she couldn't let that bother her. Alex Davies had likely put himself in danger with some very freaky people by warning her on Thursday night. She was a grown woman, and all she had to do was crash a party.

Sarah got out of her car and walked up to the Gregory house. There was a low gate at the front walk, but it was open. Sarah could see people milling around behind the house.

Yep, a Fourth of July party. Probably with relatives. Probably with relatives Dave hasn't seen in fifteen years. But yeah, she was going to gatecrash.

Unlike the front gate, the door to the Gregory home was not open. It was made of a dark, heavy wood and was engraved by someone who didn't like curved lines. In the middle of it was an oversized brass knocker that pretty much screamed "touch me and I will kill you."

God that's pretentious, muttered Val.

Sarah grabbed the knocker and knocked. A woman in an actual maid's outfit answered the door. For a moment, memories of last night's club adventure came into her head and Sarah wondered if the woman's outfit was going to turn out to be backless.

"Is Dave Gregory here?" she asked. "You can tell him that it's Sarah Baker from Culp, Moore and Rosen."

The woman nodded and turned to walk back into the house. She didn't offer for Sarah to come inside. At least her dress had a back.

"Sarah," Dave boomed as he saw her. He was large, Hispanic, and exuded charisma. He also looked vaguely irritated. He reached out his hand to shake hers as he joined her on the porch. Yep, she was not going to be allowed inside.

"I'm sorry to intrude, Mr. Gregory. But I need to talk to you. It's important."

"Of course. It must be for you to have come to my house on a holiday," he said, smiling only with his mouth. "I'm sure you must have things you would rather be doing, so maybe you can come to my office Monday morning. Whatever it is can wait for seventy-two hours."

He started to turn his back, but she grabbed his arm.

"No," Sarah said firmly. "It won't wait seventy-two hours. It won't wait until tomorrow. By tomorrow I won't have a job, so it needs to be now."

"Okay, Sarah," Dave said, "maybe I can fit you in tomorrow."

"It's about incest," Sarah said. She enunciated the word loud and clear. "If that doesn't get your attention, it's also about sex slavery, forced bondage, and torture. All by members of YOUR bar and my law firm. So, if you don't want to talk to me now, that's okay. I'm pretty sure I can get some interest from the *New York Times* today. Do you want to see the photos?"

She held up her phone and flipped through several photos she had extracted from the video. He visibly paled. He then stepped back into his house briefly, holding open the door with one hand.

"Honey. I need to talk to Sarah for a moment. She's from one of the law firms," he called into the house. Sarah heard a woman's voice reply but couldn't make out the words. Then Dave stepped back out onto the porch with her.

"These are very serious charges Sarah, and against partners of your own firm," Sarah opened her phone to the photo she got of Karl, Andrew Davies, and his son. She handed it to Dave. His eyes widened. Without asking, he flipped through the other photos.

"Does that look like consensual sex to you?" Sarah snapped.

"Who has seen these?"

"Me and a few close friends. I have also backed them up in several places," she said with a moment of unease. The last statement at least was true.

"The boys in the picture?"

"I don't know them. But I saw Andrew Davies's son there, dressed like they were."

"His son?"

"Yes, his son. I spoke with him, and he was not there by choice."

"How old is the son?"

"Sixteen."

"And the adults?"

"Andrew's wife. Michael Angel. Angela Sharp, a paralegal at our firm, and my boyfriend, Karl Rensfield. Well, my now ex-boyfriend."

"Tell me everything you know about the situation."

251

Sarah told him about her conversation with the Davies boys, and her subsequent visit to the club. Dave took notes on his phone. After she finished, he looked up at her with blank, unreadable eyes.

"What was the name and address of the club?"

"It's called the Stigmata Club. But it's not like there's a name on the door. It's on Orchard Street."

"Yeah. I know it," Dave muttered. "How did you hear about it?"

"I can't tell you."

Dave nodded.

"Excuse me for a moment, Sarah. I have a few calls to make, but don't leave just yet," he said as he stepped off the porch and into the yard.

Sarah felt a sudden panic. Suppose Dave was one of them? His expression had been cold enough.

But as she watched him pace back and forth across his front lawn, she realized that his expression hadn't really been cold. It had been repressed anger. His body language told her this.

After a few more minutes, Dave put his phone in his pocket and returned to the porch.

"Sarah, would you be willing to testify to what you have told me?" he asked.

No, you do not need to get involved with this. You have done enough, said Paul.

"Yes, but I may not be around much longer. I think it would be better for me to get out of town for a while," she said.

"That's fair. But you will still be reachable by phone, right?"

"Yes," Sarah said.

"Okay. Leave this with me. I'll handle it," Dave said. "Just don't mention anything to anyone else for the moment."

Sarah nodded. Dave reached out and shook her hand again as he looked directly into her eyes.

He's letting you read him.

"I'm on this, Sarah. Don't worry," he said.

She nodded and then turned to walk back to her car. Of everything she had done, this was the most decisive. She would have to leave now.

The only question left was whether she would be leaving alone.

Chapter Thirty-Nine

Bagels and the Blitz

Saturday July 5

Sarah got out of the subway at the Columbus Circle station, stopping for a minute to look at the giant, silver globe sculpture there. She knew she must look like a tourist, because she was. For as close as she lived to Manhattan, she had never come here. She had always been cloistered in her little section of reality and recently she had been made painfully aware of how limited her experience had been. The world was so big, but she had seen so little of it. Now she was moving into a world that held ghosts, monsters, and love. What else could she expect to find?

She walked past the magazine and hotdog vendors and headed toward Fifty-Eighth Street. Caio had told her to meet him at the Hudson Hotel. When she got to the address, she was momentarily confused. At the spot on the map where the hotel should be, there was just a large white building with small cypress trees in front of it. The building had a weird green strip across it made by green windows and lights. As she stared, a doorman at the front waved at her.

She walked across the street toward him.

"Looking for something, honey?" he asked. His tone was gruff, but his face was not. He was smiling.

"Yes. I am looking for the Hudson Hotel," she replied.

"This is it. Just that way," he said pointing to the door behind him.

Sarah walked through the door and into a room bathed by more green lights. The only thing in the room was an escalator. The whole thing felt very *Alice in Wonderland*. A part of her was waiting for a sign to appear over the escalator that read "Step on Me."

The escalator took her to a large room that was recognizable as a hotel lobby, sort of. Above her was a glass ceiling covered with lush ivy and the walls were thick with the stuff. The rest of the building seemed to be made of steel and wood. At least she could see a reception desk where people with luggage were checking in.

To top this off, everywhere she looked there were unnaturally beautiful people. The entire lobby seemed to be filled with male models and women with legs that took up two-thirds of their bodies. Was there some convention of supermodels and actors? Standing in her simple sundress and flats she felt frumpy and out of place. She wondered if she should just go back downstairs and wait with the doorman until Caio arrived. At least the doorman looked like a normal human being.

At that moment she spotted him. He was sitting on a large rucksack in one corner of the lobby. When he saw her, his face lit up. If the other people in the room were beautiful, then he was a song. Even in a shabby green jacket and sneakers, he radiated an energy that caused people to look at him as he crossed the room toward her.

She started to say something, but he pulled her to him and kissed her, in front of all the beautiful people. Suddenly none of them mattered. She felt herself go limp and fought very hard not to simply fall apart.

"Did you get out okay?" he asked when he pulled back from her. "You are a bit late. I was starting to get worried."

He's worried about me.

She felt lightheaded and giddy.

"Yeah. I just had an appointment this morning. And, well, I think I sort of quit my job last night," she said.

His eyebrows went up. "What happened? Something with Karl?"

"Yes and no." She sighed. "A lot's happened in twenty-four hours. I hardly know where to start."

"Okay. Let's give our stuff to the hotel. Then you can tell me about it over brunch. Wait here," he said, reaching for her bag.

She handed it to him, and he walked quickly over to a woman at the reception desk. At first, she gave him a noticeably skeptical look but after he pulled out his wallet and said a few things, her expression changed dramatically. She took the bags from him with a huge ingratiating smile and actually bowed.

Caio walked back to her with a slight smile on his face. "Let's go get a bagel or something. She said that the room would be ready in an hour."

"But check-in isn't until three, right?" she asked.

"Yep. Our room will be ready in an hour," he said, taking her hand. She felt a tug in her gut again.

Our room.

They found a bagel shop about a block away, but only after more searching than she had expected. Caio was quite picky about where they stopped. When she suggested that they just stop at a Starbucks, he shook his head vigorously.

"I don't want to feed you something crappy," was his response.

They ended up at a place called Pick a Bagel. It was a generic-looking establishment, but it smelled of fresh bread and coffee Caio nodded.

He quickly found a table in the back corner of the place with two chairs sitting catty-corner to each other.

"I've been here before. It's okay. The ordering is complicated though. I can order if you can hold the table. What do you want?" he asked her, as he brushed a strand of hair behind her ear.

"Cream cheese?" she asked, shrugging, and he laughed.

"You want me to order for you?" he asked, and she nodded. He then leaned forward to kiss her on the mouth before turning to get in the line. Sarah noticed a few teenage girls staring at her and she looked away quickly.

She kept her eyes downward, but she could feel the gaze of people on her. She wondered if she was being paranoid or if people really were staring. And if they were staring, was it because he looked so young or she looked so old, or some variation on the above.

Well, what did you expect, Sarah? asked Paul.

They think it looks ridiculous. And it is *ridiculous,* said her mother. But rather than inwardly cringe, Sarah found herself turning viciously on the voice.

Shut the fuck up, she snarled back. *I'm happy. Maybe I'm being ridiculous. Maybe it won't last. But I won't live like I've been living anymore. I just left Karl behind. I just left my job behind. I will probably leave my home behind. So what makes you think I won't leave you behind as well?* She could feel the sting of her mother's shock.

"Hey, you okay?" Caio said, as he returned balancing four bagels on a tray with two coffees.

"Yes, I'm fine. I'm just arguing with voices inside my head again," she said, then started that she had said that aloud.

"Which voices?" he asked, sitting down.

She searched his face for judgment, but she saw none in his dark brown eyes. What she saw was intense curiosity.

"Oh, the ones I told you about. The ones that made my parents get me assessed for dissociative identity disorder."

"Do you still hear voices?" he asked. He was trying to suppress a smile.

"Yes," she said slowly, "do you think I am crazy or something?"

"No, not at all," he said. "I'm just—well, I'm happy to know that we share some things in common."

Before she could ask, he continued. "Do you know the voices you hear in your head now?"

"Yeah, my father and mother and ex-husband. And mostly they just say nasty things," she said, waving her hand dismissively.

"Well, maybe you should tell them to leave you alone."

"I doubt it would do any good because it's just me talking to myself. Probably."

"Probably? Sounds like you aren't sure. Besides your ex, father, and mother, is there anyone else?"

"Yes. My best friend from law school and one of my professors. But they only started speaking recently."

"Did both or either of them die recently?"

"Yes," Sarah said, shocked at the question, and then blurted out, "they told me that they had died recently, so I looked it up. And they had. They also told me other things about them that I wouldn't have known. And ... and ... well, those things turned out to be true."

Sarah felt a sudden jolt of panic. She had just broken every rule that she had lived by for years. She was stepping out of the dark and letting someone see her, really see her, for the first time since her childhood. This was more than sex. It was more than love. It was a level of intimacy she had never even considered. She looked hard at Caio to see if he was going to make fun of her or call her crazy or pull away. But he just nodded.

"Well, maybe they are exactly what they seem to be, the voices of your dead mother, father, ex-husband, best friend, and professor," he said softly, reaching out and touching her hand.

"You mean I am hearing ghosts?"

Caio nodded with a small grin.

"Do you believe in ghosts?" she asked.

"No. Saying you *believe* in ghosts gives the connotation that there's some question about it. I know ghosts exist."

"How?"

"Well, for one, I've interacted with a lot of them over the years."

Wow. How to deconstruct that statement. He's seen ghosts. He's "interacted" with ghosts. And then there was that statement again—over the years.

"You keep saying stuff like that," she blurted. "Like 'over the years' and 'a long time ago.' But you are only—"

"Sixteen? Is that what you were going to say? You don't really believe that anymore, do you?" he asked. There were people all around them, but the world had narrowed down to just the two of them sitting at this small table.

Sarah shook her head but her mind was racing. She was thinking of what little she had been able to unearth about him but how that small amount was world-shattering.

Caio smiled at her and ran his hand over her cheek.

"I left my wallet for you. I wanted you to research me. I'm not sure how much you found because I try to keep myself offline and off record. But there are some things you can't avoid. So, what did you find, Sarah?"

"I found your army record from World War Two," she whispered. "It had a picture, and it was you. It said you were in the army. Is that true?"

Caio nodded.

"But it said that you died in 1945."

"It was a good time to change again," Caio said softly. "I was injured so it was easy to fake my own death."

"The records said that you were eighteen when you died."

"Yeah, when I enlisted they didn't check too hard because I was South American," he said.

"No, I mean couldn't you have pretended to be younger so that you didn't have to go to war?"

"Yeah, but I wanted to go to war," he said.

"Why?"

Caio looked at her intently.

"Because there are some things in life worth fighting for. Some are even worth dying for."

"But how …? How could you? How … just …" she began but he leaned across the table and put his lips on hers. She felt that head rush that she always felt when he kissed her. His tongue was so warm. Everything narrowed further to just the smell and taste of him.

When he sat back down, she was having trouble remembering her name, let alone what she had been talking about.

"We can talk about this in the room. I promise we will. But let's not waste these right now," he said, indicating the bagels. "I got you a classic cream cheese, and a strawberry," he smiled. The world opened again, and her tunnel vision faded. She could see and hear people around her. There was an older couple nearby. The woman was smiling at her.

"What, no salmon?" she said. "I thought that was the real classic."

For a moment, Caio noticeably winced but then he picked up his bagel and took a bite. She marveled again at the way he ate. It wasn't that he had bad manners. He didn't open his mouth when he chewed. He didn't spill things. He didn't eat with his fingers when it was inappropriate. Still, there was something sensual about how he interacted with food. The expression on his face when he pulled a piece of his bagel off in his fingers and put it in his mouth wasn't the same bored, distracted look of everyone else eating around them. If she thought about it, he looked like he was actually tasting his food and not simply consuming it. This small thing brought everything home and made her wonder more about his past and where he came from.

As they ate, they spoke of everything and nothing at all. He told absurd stories about everyone who came in until she was laughing so hard that she almost choked on her food. And he thought nothing of reaching out and touching her at odd little moments. Sarah had never felt this happy. She would have been content to stay here forever, listening to his stories and watching him smile.

She had no idea how long they had been there when he leaned over and said quietly in her ear, "Our room is ready. Do you want to go?"

It was an innocent question, but her body didn't take it that way. She nodded and he got up, pulled out her chair, took her hand, and led her out of the restaurant.

Chapter Forty

The Boy in the Hole Grows Up

Saturday July 5

"I wanted to get back to what you said about the people at your work," Caio said as they walked back toward the hotel. "What happened?"

"Well, I kind of went to the Stigmata Club."

"What?" Caio said, stopping to face her. "You went? By yourself?"

"Yes. And after going there, I realized that it was pretty stupid. But I went in disguise, and I don't think anyone saw me. But I saw—well, I saw Andrew Davies there with Karl and Michael, and his own son. The one I told you about."

Caio put his hand to his face and sighed.

"What did you do?"

"I got pictures of it, and I took it to the district attorney last night."

"You did what? Wait, what did he say?"

Sarah told him what she had told Dave and his responses. Caio listened intently, biting the side of his lip.

"How did you end the conversation?"

"He told me that he would handle it."

"Do you think he actually will?" Caio asked.

"Yes, I do. But it doesn't make much difference for me. Eventually the firm will find out and they will know that it came from me. But it doesn't matter. I can't work in a place—well, a place that … with people who …" she couldn't finish. For the first time since going to the club, her eyes welled up.

"I saw Alex, his son, there. He talked to me and warned me to get out. He said that I had no idea what sort of people these were. He said that even his dad didn't know what sort of people they were. I asked him if they were Illuminati or something," Sarah said, laughing a little in a way that bordered on hysterical.

Caio took her hand.

"What did he say? The boy?"

"He said they were much worse than the Illuminati, or something like that. But he was so hopeless. He said he was doing this just to keep his brothers safe for a while. When I was looking at him, I was—" she stopped for a second, looking into Caio's dark, vivid eyes, so different from the blue, dead eyes of Alex Davies. "Caio, he looked like someone who was just waiting to … waiting to die. I had to do something."

Suddenly she started to cry. Caio took her in his arms. Burying her face in his shoulder, she began to shake. She had not cried throughout all her discussions yesterday, but now it was coming out.

He kissed her head and held her, there in the middle of the street.

"And you said that you weren't brave. That is about the bravest thing I have ever heard," Caio muttered into her hair. "Kinda stupid to go and do by yourself, but very brave."

She held him tight and let herself cry. His body was so warm against hers.

"Listen, let's go on to our room and we can talk about all this in a proper way. And I'm gonna need to make some calls," he said, pulling back from her and taking her chin in his hand.

"About what?" she said.

"About keeping you safe after taking on exactly the wrong people," he said with a sigh. She started to say something, but he kissed her again and took her hand.

"What happened after that? Did you speak with Matt Greenley," he asked, as they crossed the street toward the hotel.

"Yes," Sarah said, wiping her eyes. "He's going to file next week to dismiss Karl as a trustee."

"Did you tell him about these other things?"

"No. I just—I couldn't talk about it."

"That's fair," Caio said. "I'll call him later."

"How do you know so many professional people?"

"We'll talk about that in the room, but I've had to be pretty good with money. So even if you can't get access to your money very quickly, you don't have to worry. I have plenty." Once again, Sarah was taken aback.

As they walked by the doorman, his eyes widened a bit but then he smiled. They entered the hotel and stepped onto the strange green escalator. Rather than standing above or below her, Caio stepped in next to her, and put his arm around her.

"How did you end up in a foster home?"

Caio sighed.

"I ended up with a foster family because of what I look like, and because a police officer caught me sleeping outside one night. When I came here, I hadn't gotten all my paperwork sorted. What he saw was a homeless kid with no paperwork. I had to think fast, and even with that, I ended up in a foster home. Most of the time I can avoid it, but every now and then I get caught by the system."

Sarah felt unreality wash over her again. His walk and mannerisms perfectly matched his physical age. But even with the few glimpses of his life that she had had, she realized he had a wealth of experiences that she probably couldn't even guess at. They walked through the leaf and wood lobby, hand in hand. The people that they passed stared, but most of them also smiled. When they got into the elevator, there were already three or four supermodel-looking girls there, possibly having come from a lower floor.

Or hell. They could have come from hell, given the way they all stared at Caio.

Sarah felt wildly self-conscious for a moment, but Caio never even looked at them. As he pushed the button for the twenty-fifth floor, he leaned in and whispered in her ear.

"Sorry if this place is pretentious," he said. "I think I kinda wanted to show off a bit. If you don't like it here, we can go somewhere else."

"It's fine. Anywhere is fine," she said, and it was true. She was happy to be anywhere with him.

At the door of their room, as Caio was pulling out the key card to get in, Sarah felt a moment of edginess. There was no reason for this. She had no fear of what would happen physically. In fact, she wanted to be alone with him more than anything else right now. The edginess was that she knew that she would learn something that would require a change in her life. And she had already had more changes in her life in the past month than she could ever have imagined possible.

The room they stepped into was small, with dark wood paneling and a bed made in white linen. Sarah only took it in for a second because the moment the door closed behind them, Caio pulled her into his arms. He kissed her long and hard. It was only a few feet to the bed, but they didn't manage to make it. Instead, they ended up lying on the floor kissing. She had no idea how long they did this, because she felt like she was out of her head. What she felt with him was something she had never felt before. It was like her body was screaming some message to her, spelled out in sensation and chemicals that she couldn't completely translate.

In her head, she suddenly heard voices, not from her ghosts but from someone else, from some*where* else.

Excuse me, don't I know you? She didn't remember the words, but she knew the voice. It was her own, but it wasn't.

"You know, I've been searching such a long time for you," Caio said, suddenly stopping and looking at her with moist eyes.

"For me? Specifically?" she asked.

You can't move him, she heard herself say. *He's healing here.* She suddenly saw a vision of Caio lying unconscious on a hospital bed.

"Yes, for you. The only person who makes the risk worth it," said Caio.

"What risk?" she asked, running her hand through his thick hair.

"The risk of trying to have a normal life. The risk I take if I stop running. I never thought I would do that. But with you, things have changed."

I don't want to lose you again. I couldn't bear to lose you again.

Pull yourself together, she told herself.

"I must look awful," she said, trying to ground herself a bit. "I bet my makeup is smeared all over my face and the wrinkles under my eyes look even more lovely than usual."

"You have no idea how much I adore your wrinkles. They are completely charming," he said, reaching out and touching her. "I just want you to get a few more around the sides of your eyes, because those would tell me that you've been laughing more. I want to help you get those."

Sarah felt tears form in her eyes. She didn't even know why. She felt so much that she couldn't explain, and images kept inserting themselves in her head unbidden. Images of men and women with Caio's eyes. Always with her but always being pulled away.

"You need to tell me what's happening here, because I'm scared I might be going crazy," she whispered.

He stood up and held out his hands to pull her up. He then sat down on the bed and pulled her to sit next to him. He was quiet for a long time. Sarah just waited.

"I haven't told you that much because knowing too much would put you in danger. But I think you've already put yourself in danger, so that's not really an obstacle anymore. And I've wanted to tell you, so you would understand me and how I feel about you."

Sarah said nothing.

"So you've already guessed that I'm much older than I look," he said, looking down.

At first Sarah said nothing, waiting to see if he would continue.

"How old are you?" she finally asked.

"I'm afraid that you wouldn't believe me if I told you," he said softly. Then he looked up and his eyes were wet.

"But what I've learned in all this time is that time itself doesn't matter. People say it's what's inside that counts, but the people who say that use it as a throwaway line. The thing is, it's true. The surface stuff degrades over time. But what's inside doesn't. What's real doesn't."

She put her arms around him, and he pulled her to him. She kissed his face and his wet eyes. He took her face in his hands and just stared at her.

How do I tie us together? she thought. *How do I keep us together this time? How do I keep from forgetting? I don't want to lose you again.*

He then kissed her, eyes open and face wet. What they did then was something she had never felt before. It was sex, but it felt different. It was slow and intense and Caio did not take his eyes off her face for one moment. He moved inside her slowly and incredibly gently. When she climaxed, it was slow, long and gentle rather than sharp and explosive.

Afterward, she lay in his arms, with her legs twisted between his.

"I was born in northern Brazil in 1889," he said softly. Sarah's heart skipped a beat.

"They had a lot of slave trade back then," he continued. "I was stolen from my village and taken to work harvesting latex. Well, I was stolen or sold. I'm not sure. But either way, I wasn't one of the best-behaved slaves. Eventually—" he stopped for a moment, and Sarah tried not to move, or even breathe, for fear he would stop talking.

"Well, eventually I pissed someone off bad enough that he beat me until I was nearly dead and then—well, he threw me—"

"In a hole," Sarah whispered, the image from her dream coming back to her in all its vivid intensity. "You were stuck in a hole, and it was muddy."

"Yeah," Caio said, with much less shock in his voice than she might have expected.

"I saw you in my dreams, ever since I was small," Sarah whispered.

"Hmmmm. That was how it happened, then. I saw your face while I was in that hole, it was the only relief I got. I guess your dream allowed you to be with me in that moment. Maybe that's it. That would seem right."

Sarah had questions but kept her mouth shut. She was afraid he would stop talking. She listened to the sound of his heart beating. Finally, he sighed and took a deep breath in.

"I lay in that hole for what felt like years. My life before being sold hadn't been great but I fought to survive … I guess because I was afraid of death," he

263

continued. "In the end though, I was praying for death. I was being eaten alive by insects and worms. That was when a guy from a local tribe found me. And they brought me back to their village to heal me. But after a couple of years, they kicked me out."

"Why?"

"Because I wasn't aging. Something happened to me down in that hole. Something got inside me that prevents me from aging. So I can't. I don't age. I don't even get sick. I can be a carrier for a disease for a time, but my body always eventually kills it. Over the years, I've come to realize the hard way how dangerous it was for people to know this about me. This thing that I have, that I do—well, it can be used. So, I have stayed hidden from the people who would want to do so. Most of the time, I'm successful. I usually stay out of social systems as well, but sometimes I get caught. This time, I got caught because someone else was incompetent and I was stupid. Usually, I get fake IDs that place my current age at eighteen. If it's under eighteen, there are lots of things I can't do. If it's too much over eighteen, people might think it's fake. Even with that, I can never rent cars. Anyway, this time my suppliers screwed up and made the age fifteen. It was a twenty-four-hour turnaround for a new one, so I decided to sleep in the park and I got caught. I was expecting it to be the same as it has always been, but this time it was completely different. This time I was happy to have been caught."

"Why?"

"Because I saw you. I saw your face. I remembered you. I can't even tell you what that felt like, to see you and know you. So I sort of just stayed around for a year, hoping to get a chance to talk to you."

Sarah felt heat in her chest. She sighed and put her head against him.

"But how can you not age? How is that possible?"

"I don't know. I think maybe it had something to do with some virus or bacteria that I got infected with from being in that hole. I was riddled with parasites when they found me, but they all died with the herbs they gave me. So, I don't know, but something changed me."

"That seems impossible," she whispered.

"You don't believe me," he said, leaning back just a bit. "If you want, I can prove it."

Sarah was silent a moment.

"No, you don't have to. I believe you. That's just it. I think I have known there was something really different about you from the very beginning. That you were special. Or maybe just that you were special for me."

He took her hand and held it against his chest.

She could feel her eyes welling with tears.

"What is it?" he asked.

"What are we going to do?" she whispered.

"What do you mean?"

"I mean, what do you want to do?" she said, suddenly a bit insecure.

"I want to be with you. That's all," he said, with that quality that was at once both mature and guileless.

"But how can we do that?"

Caio suddenly smiled.

"You know, *that* I can make work. I never thought I would have the chance to even try for this. So, I'll make it work. But you will have to trust me on some things."

She nodded. "Like?"

"Listen, let's not talk about it just now. I just told you a story I have never told anyone. Ever. In over 100 years, and I am feeling a little emotionally blown out. I just want to say one more thing. Despite what I just said, telling you this may have put you in more danger. That's why I need you to trust me. If I tell you that you need to do something, I need you to trust me on it. And most important, if I tell you not to come near me for a while, then you have to listen to me. It won't mean that I don't want to be with you. It will be for your protection."

She felt a vague sense of unease, and something must have registered on her face, because Caio took both her hands in his.

"Are you going to leave me?" she asked. She was expecting a quick and definitive no. But that was not what she got. Caio just sighed.

"Sometimes I may have to disappear for a while. If that ever happens, DON'T come looking for me. I will always come and find you, but I don't ever want to lead any of these people to you. If they are following me, then they can find you. I won't let that happen. Your first and only concern is to keep yourself safe."

Sarah nodded. She felt the presence of dread crawling up her chest and into her throat.

"Listen, don't think I am treating you like a little girl. Jesus, who am I to think about anyone else like that. But there are things going on here that you won't understand and shouldn't understand. So just promise me that if I tell you to do something, you won't question it. Okay?"

"Okay," she whispered. "But you are scaring me a bit."

"Good," he said. "It's good to be scared sometimes."

Catching her expression, he touched her cheek.

265

"Don't take that wrong. It's just that life exists in opposition. What you saw at that club, the people involved with that, they are just a shadow of that world. It gets so much worse. They get so much worse. There's a depth and breadth to the depravity of what humans can do to each other that you have never known, and I hope to god that you never will."

"I didn't exactly grow up in a nurturing environment and I have spent my life working in law. And then there's Karl. I think I know a bit about depravity," Sarah said.

"That's exactly what I am saying. You think you know it, but you don't. Alex told you that his dad had no idea about the people he was involved with, and he was right. I *do* know something about them. How deep their illnesses go and how easily they manage to justify acts so horrible that you wouldn't see them in the worst sort of horror film. So, yeah, there's a lot to fear in this world. And these people search for people like me because I can be weaponized in fairly devastating ways."

"What do you mean?"

"I mean I could be infected with an incredibly dangerous and infectious disease and then let loose into the general population. But it's not just me, someone who can talk to ghosts can be weaponized as well. So, if they knew about you, you would be a target."

Caio's face looked old, hard, and set for a moment. And this, more than his words, frightened her. Then, just as suddenly, his face relaxed.

"But listen, for all their depravity and horror, people are just as capable of unbelievably noble and selfless acts. We just need to acknowledge the whole spectrum of the world, what it is and what it can be. Some believe in taking sides; I don't."

"What do you believe?" she asked, and Caio paused for a moment.

"I believe in the balance. But I also believe that I have no ability to know how to protect that balance. I can only do that in my own life. Meeting you, knowing you, has shown me that I have been horribly out of balance. I thought I was—"

He stopped and looked at her. Emotions were running across his face so fast she couldn't catch them all.

"Alone," he finally said.

"Me too," she said, tears running down her face.

"Not anymore," he took her back into his arms.

And for a long time, they didn't speak. They didn't need to. But as the light faded outside, the light from the front of their building began to bathe their room in a green that was the color of both plants and poison.

Chapter Forty-One

Love Comes Home to Roost

Sunday July 6

That night Sarah slept better than she had in her entire life. She woke on her stomach with Caio's arm draped over her back. She turned to look at him and he mumbled in his sleep and rolled over to face her. In sleep, the furrows between his brows were nonexistent. His light brown skin looked beautiful against the white of the pillow. His lashes were impossibly long and thick. She reached out and touched the little bump on his nose. This was what she had dreamed about that first night when he surprised her by kissing her. Her hopes had been so limited then. She could have never imagined that one day she would be waking up next to this man.

Yes, man. He looked like a boy, but he wasn't. She didn't even question that anymore, just as she didn't question the story he told her, or the presence of ghosts in her head. These things were a part of the world that she now occupied, a world that was hidden just behind the veneer of the "regular" world she had known. She had been unaware of its existence until just a few months ago but now this was her place, her world, and she needed to learn how to live in it. She suspected that she would no longer be allowed the luxury of insecurity or indifference.

As she watched Caio sleep, she forced herself not to wake him. She wanted to ask him how he had managed to survive in those first years, after he had been cast out into an unforgiving world. How had he dealt with spending over 100 years without any real adult relationships? And how had he made the money that he seemed to have? What jobs had he done—if he had worked—and what were his favorite movies, who was the first person he had kissed? She wanted to know everything about him.

And then Caio opened his eyes, smiled, and kissed her, and all her questions vanished.

They ate a room service breakfast so that they wouldn't have to leave the room. They laughed and talked about little things. Caio's fascination with the progression of movie technology, her hatred of yellow drinks, their shared love of old bookshops. They spoke of all these things as they ate, showered, dressed, and made plans for their day. Normally, Caio was a serious planner because, as he said, "In my situation, you always have to have a plan, a backup plan and a backup plan for your backup plan, just in case your backup plan fails."

"But today, I don't want to talk about anything serious. I don't want to make plans. I don't want to worry about anything. I just want to walk around the city with you and talk. That's it," he said.

And that's what they did.

They left the hotel and walked along the streets holding hands. They took a zigzag route that took them past Rockefeller Center, the Empire State Building, and Gramercy Park. They ate pretzels and laughed. Around lunchtime, they had just finished walking around Chinatown, and they were both hungry, so they decided to eat in Little Italy. They had been walking for hours, but Sarah didn't feel it. In truth, she also wasn't looking at much of anything besides Caio.

Caio scanned the restaurants and dismissed a lot of them as being expensive tourist traps with bad food. Sarah smiled to herself when he did this. She loved food but he took it to another level. Finally, they found a little place that didn't look like much from the outside, but inside felt warm and authentic. The place had red-leather booths with plastic red-checked tablecloths. Every inch of the wall was covered with pictures of celebrities that had eaten there. And, for some odd reason, the owners had felt the need to string multicolored Christmas lights up, down, and around all these pictures. At the back of the restaurant was a group of five or six older men. They were dressed in suits, or slacks with polo shirts, and they were surprisingly quiet for a group that size.

The waiter brought a menu with surprising speed but he was of the eye-rolling, dismissive school of food service. He barely acknowledged them, he just took their orders and sighed a lot. Sarah ordered a classic lasagna and Caio did the same. When the food arrived, it was delicious. They were about halfway through their meal when the dismissive waiter decided to acknowledge their presence by returning unbidden.

"The men at the back would like to pay for you and your son's lunch, but they would appreciate it if you would leave as soon as possible," he said.

His eyes were trained on Sarah, and he was displaying a manner that was feigning politeness but barely covering something else. It was either condescension or vague threat. Sarah looked at the men at the back. Suddenly they seemed a lot more sinister than they had a few minutes before. She looked at Caio and started to pick up her purse. Given the neighborhood, she thought it was wise to leave when someone asked you to do so. But Caio put his hand on hers and shook his head. His eyes had completely lost their normal sparkle and looked flat black.

"She's not my mother, she's my fiancée," Caio responded calmly. "And we will be more than happy to leave when we've finished our food."

Sarah had just enough time to clock the expression of shock on the waiter's face, and to see him turn and walk swiftly toward the men at the back of the restaurant, when Caio's words sunk in. "My fiancée." But before *that* could really sink in, the largest and roundest of the men stood up and lumbered toward them.

"Are you enjoying your food?" he asked.

"Oh, it's lovely, thank you so much," Sarah babbled, praying that Caio wouldn't start something. Caio was probably 140 pounds, tops. The man looming over them was probably twice that.

"My waiter says that you didn't want to accept our generous offer to pay for your meal," he said, leaning on to the table, both hands flat on the tablecloth. The table creaked.

"No, we didn't say that. I just said that we would like to finish our meal. That's only polite," replied Caio calmly.

"Listen young man, you should let your mother—" he began, but Caio had laid his hand on the man's hand.

"As I also told your waiter, she's not my mother, she's my fiancée. Your staff seems to have a difficult time accurately relaying messages."

What the fuck is he doing? Is he starting a fight with a Mafioso?

The man leaned forward and looked at Caio very closely. Caio looked back with no fear or even agitation.

Finally, the man smiled.

"You look familiar to me," he said.

"Lots of people say that. I must have a generic face," Caio responded. The man smiled coldly.

"Well, we are having conversations back there that you might not want to hear." He was about to say more, when Caio interrupted him.

"I am looking at *this woman*," Caio said, nodding at Sarah. "And I am listening to *her*. Do you think I give a shit about what a group of overweight, middle-aged men are talking about in the back of a restaurant?"

269

The man looked startled for the briefest of seconds, and then he laughed out loud.

"So, a wolf in sheep's clothing. Yes, I believe I've heard of you, even if we haven't met," he said. "Very well. Finish your meal. And I am guessing you want to pay for it as well?"

Caio nodded.

The man scanned Caio's face again before nodding and walking away. On his way back to the table, he pulled the waiter aside and whispered something to him. Sarah saw the man scurry away.

"What are you doing? They're going to kill us," she whispered to Caio.

"No, they aren't," he replied.

"Why did you do that?"

"Because they had already clocked us. So I wanted to make sure that they knew I could protect you," he said.

"What? Honey, those guys are huge. And they probably have guns. And—"

At that moment the waiter returned with two menus.

"The owner said that you might like to see the dessert menu," he said, with a tone that was infinitely more respectful.

They ordered pie and ice cream, but Sarah tasted none of it. She was in a whirl.

He just played a game of whose dick is bigger with a potential Mafioso and he won. Who is he? Val asked in her head.

The man I love, was her reply.

Well, that's good because he just asked you to marry him, said Larry. Sarah could feel the smile in his voice.

No, he didn't, he just—

Called you his fiancée, twice, Val replied.

Sarah's heart was burning in her chest and her face felt completely flushed.

#

When they finished, Caio paid the bill with cash before taking her hand and leading her onto the street.

"You said—" Sarah began.

"I know. I'm sorry to put you in the middle of that testosterone battle, but if that guy is who I think he is, then he's someone you don't want to back down from. He was checking both of us out when we came in the door, too much for my comfort. Then he kept looking at us through the meal. He seemed particularly interested in you. I didn't want him to have us followed or to think that I couldn't defend you."

"How did you know him?" she asked.

"If it's who I think he is, a lot of people know of him. He's a figure in darker circles."

"And he seemed to know you."

"He's never seen me, but he may know of me," Caio said, but then he stopped and pulled her toward a shop window, where he took her face in his hands and kissed her.

"But I wanted to ask if you minded what I said back there?"

"It was a bit scary; I mean he was a big guy. I would prefer you didn't pick fights with people who could hurt you."

Caio smiled.

"No, not that, the bit about you being my fiancée," he replied. Suddenly she felt ridiculously shy.

"Did you mind it?"

"No, I didn't mind it," she said softly. He kissed her again. This time longer. Someone said something to them as they pushed by, but it meant nothing to Sarah.

"Okay. Let's take a taxi to the park. If we stay here much longer, it's going to be really uncomfortable for me to walk," Caio said, taking her by the hand and flagging a taxi.

She had never been to Central Park, but it seemed larger and cleaner than she had envisioned. The sky was bright blue above them and as they walked, hand in hand, she could feel the sun hot against her exposed skin.

At some point around 2:00, Sarah saw a familiar building in the distance.

"Oh, that's the building from *Ghostbusters*," she said, pointing and adding, "oh, but you wouldn't remember that—" then caught herself.

Caio raised an eyebrow at her.

"If you want to play that game, then I can start showing you the speakeasies where I used to work," he said with a smile.

"You worked at speakeasies. That was in the 1920s."

"Yeah. I used to work at a place called Chumley's. I almost got caught in raids there a couple of times, but I always managed to get out through the Bedford Street door. To be honest, I think there was an agreement between the police and the owners, because they always raided through the Pamela Court entrance, and we always went out through Bedford," he said with a laugh.

Sarah felt a bit overwhelmed again and shook her head. Caio laced his fingers through hers.

"You've seen so much. It's hard to take in. It makes me feel really, I don't know—"

271

"Young?" he asked and she laughed.

"Yes. Young. And I guess you have traveled a lot as well? You've already mentioned Brazil, the UK, and of course here. Where else have you gone?"

"I've been on every continent except Antarctica," he said with a shrug. "What about you?"

"I've been to DC," she replied. "I went by train once. Actually, I have only ever traveled by train or car. I've never been on a plane. That's crazy, right? To be my age and never to have been on a plane."

They had just happened upon Bethesda Fountain, with pigeons adorning the Angel Statue in the center. A couple vacated a bench just as they walked by, so they grabbed it. The day was hot by now, and it was nice to feel the breeze that brought a cooling mist from the water.

"Where would you go, if you could go anywhere?" asked Caio.

"Oh, probably Hawaii," she replied. "But I guess everyone says that."

"Why Hawaii?"

"I guess it seems wild and natural. Or that's how I think of it," she replied.

"Well, some parts of it are still wild and natural, but nowadays a lot of areas are very built up," he said.

"You were there too?"

"Yeah. Of course. It's like you said, everyone wants to see it. I'm just like everyone else," he said, leaning forward and picking up a small stick from the ground, which he then began to twirl through his fingers. "I lived there for a while. I lived in Kona, on the Big Island."

"Did you like it?"

"I loved it. I had a little house on the beach. It wasn't fancy but it was near the ocean and there were sliding glass doors everywhere. I loved how open it was. And it was safe. All the locals there know you, and once they accept you, they look after you."

"Why did you leave?" she asked.

"To be honest, I just got a bit lonely. I've been looking for you for a long time," he said.

"Did you never have a wife or a family?" she asked, and he shrugged.

"No. I would have loved a family, but no one has ever gotten pregnant with me. I even went through a phase where I was ridiculously reckless. But no, never." As he said this, he was sitting with his legs spread, elbows on his knees, looking at the ground.

"Well, I guess we're a set then. I've always wanted children, but now I'm probably too old to have them," she said with a little laugh. She felt a pang in her heart. How wonderful would it be to have a child? How miraculous to have a child with this man.

He looked at her with an odd little smile on his face.

Finally, he said, "Well, then we can adopt."

Sarah felt her heart stop. She had never expected this response. She had never expected this sort of chance in her life.

"You would want to do that?" she whispered.

"Of course," he replied, sitting up and taking her hand. "I would love to have a child with you."

Sarah felt dizzy.

"But would they let us do that?"

Caio shrugged.

"You can solve most problems in life if you can throw enough money at it. I know that sounds jaded, but I'm not. I'm just practical. So yes, I'd be happy to do that with you."

Sarah felt such heat coming from her heart and from between her legs that she could barely breathe.

"Let's go back to the room," she said.

He stood up, pulled her to her feet and kissed her until she couldn't breathe, in front of the pigeons, the angels, and all the world.

#

They kissed in their taxi back to the hotel. Sarah didn't remember the ride, getting into the hotel, the elevator, or even the room. All she could see or focus on was him, the physicality of him. The way he smelled, the way he tasted, and the way he moved. And they spent the rest of the afternoon in their room exploring only that.

Sarah's phone rang at about 5:30 p.m. Caio picked it up, and saw the number.

"It's Matt Greenley," he said, handing the phone to her.

"Hi Matt," she said.

"Hi Sarah. I just wanted to let you know that I have done a bit of probing and there's sufficient evidence of self-dealing, neglect, and hostility toward the beneficiary. In light of that, I am going to file tomorrow morning. You need to stay away from here after that."

"I know," she said.

"No, Sarah. This is a big deal," Matt said. "It's a lot of fucking money to a lot of dangerous people. They won't take this lying down."

Sarah suddenly got a vision of the fat man at the Italian restaurant.

"Also, Karl has already called asking me to call him back. That tells me he knows I'm going to file. So you need to stay away until I tell you. Staying in the city is a good idea. Call me if you need help or cash," he said, and then abruptly hung up.

"What was that about?" Caio asked her. She explained. He sat up in the bed, naked and cross-legged, elbows resting on his knees and chin on his hands.

"I understand that you need to do this," he said softly. "But it's like you are waving a red flag in front of a bull. First you set their club up to be raided and now you're taking their funds. That's not going to go down well with that particular group of people."

Sarah felt dizzy again but shook her head violently. She had run out of time to act like a scared rabbit.

"Are you okay?" he asked.

"Yes, it's just so much has happened so fast. So, honestly, I am more worried about Karl, at least right now. Matt said that Karl had called him. So he knows and I'm afraid he'll come after us."

"Karl won't be a problem much longer," Caio said, his voice suddenly calm and cold.

Sarah started to speak but he continued.

"It's the other ones I worry about. The older ones. I'm worried if they are part of that hive, they might start getting interested in you. Particularly if—"

"They know about the money?" she asked.

"Despite what I said, they aren't really going to give a shit about the money, at least not the major players. It's the ghosts in your head that would interest those guys. That would interest them a lot. See, you and I have that in common," he said, leaning forward and kissing her.

"You haven't told anyone about that, besides me, have you?"

"I was seen by doctors for it when I was young," she said.

"Oh shit. That's right. But if no one clocked you recently you should be okay. Still, don't tell anyone, right? You never know who's who," he paused for a second.

Suddenly Sarah remembered the little yellow sticky note on Melissa's old deposition.

"Well there is one thing. I found a sticky note that said the client in the Davies case asked for me to do the research on this case—by name," Sarah said. Caio stiffened.

"Tell me," he said. So she told him about the deposition and the note.

"And you didn't know this Andrew Davies person before?" he asked.

"No."

"Did this case require that you use your intuition more than usual?" he asked.

274

After thinking a moment, Sarah nodded.

"Has anyone at the office ever taken a sample of your blood?"

"Well, we have on-site health screening as part of our benefits, so yes. About once a year."

Caio's eyes widened for a moment, then he sighed.

"Right then," he said, nodding and getting out of bed. He threw on his jeans and a simple green T-shirt. Sarah felt her heart spasm.

"What are you doing?" she asked.

"I'm gonna need to go out for a while," he said. "I need to take care of some things. Then, I gotta go back and get some things from my foster parents' house. I need to do that while they are asleep. I also need to see a few people."

"About what?"

"About keeping us safe," he said.

Sarah's face must have registered the panic that suddenly flared in the pit of her stomach.

"Hey, it will be fine," Caio said, coming back to kiss her gently on the lips. "I'll be back by morning. Even if something happens, if somehow something gets screwed up, I'll leave a package for you. Remember I told you that I slept under the bleachers sometimes? Well, if anything ever happens, go there. I will either meet you there or leave something for you there."

Sarah was suddenly overwhelmed by the fact that not even two months ago she thought she could be content with just watching this person. How quickly everything changed.

"Do you think something will get screwed up?" she asked. "Are you going to do something dangerous?"

"No, no. I just like to be prepared," he said but he cut his eyes away from her. "Sometimes things happen, and people miss each other's path. But if that happens, I will leave instructions for you. Just meet me where I tell you."

"Caio—" Sarah began, but he leaned forward and kissed her nose.

"But nothing's going to happen," he said quickly. "I booked the room for a week, so you are going to hang around in the room, spend ridiculous amounts of money on room service and watch questionable movies. I'll be back before you know it."

"But you will come back here, right?" she asked.

"Yes, I'll be back by tomorrow morning. By tomorrow afternoon at the latest. If anything goes wrong, I will call or text you."

"You're sure?"

"Yes, and we have a backup plan just in case," he said, kissing her quickly and then turning to walk out the door.

275

He would just be gone for a night; still, Sarah found herself saying a little prayer to whatever god was in charge of this new world she was in.

"Keep him safe."

Chapter Forty-Two

Karl's Revenge

Monday July 7

Caio had not returned to the hotel by morning. When he hadn't returned by early afternoon, Sarah was in a blind panic. She texted and even tried to call, but the phone just rang, no voicemail.

Maybe he just left you, maybe he realized that your relationship won't work, said her mother but for the first time she was able to dismiss it. She had bigger problems. By the time the sun was setting, Sarah was pacing around the hotel room like a caged lion. Visions of Karl in her head. Suppose Karl had found Caio? But how would he know about Caio? How could he …

Suddenly, panic hit her. She grabbed her bag and began rummaging through it. Her computer was there, but she couldn't find the flash drives or the external hard drive.

Shit. Did I forget those? I couldn't have, could I? All my research about Caio is on those drives. They also have the copies of the audio recording of Chris Davies as well as copies of the damning footage from the club.

Shit. Shit. Shit.

Sarah had to get that out of her house. Even if Karl hadn't found it by now, he might find it later and use it to hurt people she cared about. She grabbed her bag, and ran out of the hotel. The doorman stopped her at the door.

"Can I call you a taxi?" he asked. She was about to say she didn't have the money, but when she opened her wallet she saw a wad of bills there. Caio must have done that when she wasn't aware.

You should stay out of public places.

"Yes. But I need a taxi to Brooklyn," she said. The doorman smiled and nodded, and she was in a hired car within minutes.

When the car pulled into Sarah's driveway, it was fully dark. Sarah paid him quickly and then quietly let herself into her house. She went to her computer to get the external hard drive, but it wasn't there. For a moment, panic gripped her. Her heart was beating in her throat. It was then that she noticed that the drive had gotten pushed under some work papers, along with the flash drive. She quickly grabbed both and shoved them into her purse. Then she turned on her computer and went through the steps to wipe the internal drive.

As the computer was going through this function, Sarah ran upstairs and found the other drive that she had used to record information from the deposition of Chris Davies. She also grabbed the camera glasses and the TF card. It was then that she heard a knock on the door and her blood froze.

Sarah moved downstairs slowly and quietly, sticking to the walls until she could see if the figure behind the smoked glass of her door was Karl. While she didn't recognize the outline she saw there, that didn't mean that whoever was there wasn't an enemy.

There was another knock, and then a male voice that she recognized called "Sarah."

She took a deep breath, plastered a serene expression on her face, and opened the door.

Standing there was Jerry, the police officer, in his uniform, with his hat in his hands.

"Hi Jerry. What can I do for you?" she asked with a smile.

What the fuck is going on. What the fuck is going on.

Sarah, be careful here. Be very careful. This could be a set-up, whispered Val.

"Hi Sarah. Do you mind if I come in?" he asked, looking down. He didn't look dangerous, he looked mortified. In other circumstances she might have found this amusing, if the emotion hadn't looked so devastatingly horrible on his face.

"Of course," she said, stepping back. "Is there something wrong?"

He stepped into her house but stood just inside the door, as if venturing inside would put him in the belly of some beast.

"I hate to even have to tell you this. But, well, there has been a complaint," he said, still looking down.

"About me?" she asked.

"Yes."

"Listen. If it's about my garden encroaching a bit on the neighbor's side—"

"No Sarah. It's not about that."

"Then what is it?" she asked.

"Maybe you should sit down."

"You are scaring me, Jerry," she said as she sat down at her table.

"Look, I know this is bullshit, Sarah, but I have to ask you."

"What?"

Jerry squared his shoulders and sat across the table from her.

"Karl has sent a letter to the department accusing you of having sex with a minor."

"What?" She hoped that sounded convincing enough. It should have been convincing. She hadn't seen it coming. "Karl did WHAT?"

"I know. I know."

"Why would he do that?" she asked.

"Well, that's what I wanted to ask you. Is there some reason for him to be mad at you or to discredit you?"

She sighed. It was time to twist facts as hard as she could.

"He asked me to marry him, and I didn't actually say yes. In fact, I was going to say no and he probably knew that," she said.

Jerry's shoulders visibly relaxed.

"I see. Well, then I understand. But this is low, even for Karl."

"What do you mean, 'even for Karl'?"

"Listen Sarah. I—well—*we* know a bit more about Karl than you do. And most of the people on the force have wondered why on earth a woman like you would be with a guy like him. He's not a very good person."

Sarah nodded.

"I've sort of figured that out in recent months. That's probably something else I should tell you. I contacted the district attorney because one of Michael's clients has been taking his minor son to a BDSM sex club."

"Jesus Christ, Sarah," Jerry gasped. "Should you be telling me this?"

"No, I shouldn't. But I quit my job because I know that Karl and Michael know about it. They've seen the boy at the club because they are both members. I don't want to say more about that club," she whispered, shuddering for real.

Jerry reached out and put his hand on hers. "You don't have to. I know the club. And I know who some of the members are. Although I didn't know about Karl and Michael. And god knows, I didn't know they brought kids there."

"That's why I could never have accepted Karl's proposal," Sarah lied. "I found out Karl goes there. But to accuse me of being with a minor. That's—" she couldn't finish because she suddenly thought of Caio and couldn't say anything bad about him.

"I know. It's disgusting. I wouldn't even be here questioning you if he hadn't sent a letter to the boy's foster parents as well. So now we have to investigate. Do you know the Fernandez family? It's their foster son, Caio Silva."

Sarah sighed and put her forehead in her hands.

"I tutored him in geography and civics. He said he was having trouble and I was helping him. That's all."

"Sarah, did he ever sleep over here?" Jerry asked.

"Yes. A couple of times. Apparently, his foster parents lock him out of the house if he's home later than eight. He would have had to sleep outside. What was I supposed to do? I can't let a kid sleep outside. That's awful."

"So, um. When he was here, where did he sleep?" Jerry asked, looking down.

"On. The. Couch," she said, punctuating each word. "Where do you think he slept, Jerry?"

"Would you be willing to swear to that?"

"I would be willing to take a lie detector, if you want," she said, back straight, staring directly into Jerry's eyes.

I want you to be able to say that I slept on the couch, even if one day you have to take a lie detector test on it.

Jerry looked down.

"I'm sorry, Sarah. Really, I'm so sorry. I know you were just looking out for the kid. You're sweet that way. But that wasn't super smart of you. People talk."

"Well, they should talk about the fact that his foster family locks him out of the house."

"They don't do that. According to them, they worry all night every time he stays out."

"You spoke to them already?"

"Yes."

"Well, then why don't you just ask Caio? He should be able to clear this right up."

"I would, but he seems to have gone missing for the past forty-eight hours."

"What?" Sarah gasped. "You don't think something happened to him. Oh god. You don't think Karl did something stupid?"

She pulled her emotions back in. Her concern was real. But she couldn't let Jerry see how deeply concerned she was. Apparently, she did well enough because Jerry just shrugged.

"You have any idea of where he might be?"

"No. I know he hangs out with those kids who play basketball at the neighborhood court, but I don't know all their names. I know Mouse. He works at the Italian restaurant on Fulton Street. And Dex."

"Okay. Well. I'm sorry to have had to trouble you with this. If I were you, I would stay away from Karl. If he comes round here, call us immediately. If he's willing to lie about this sort of thing, then who knows what he will do."

"Am I safe here, or do you think I should go stay in a hotel?" she asked.

"A hotel might be a good idea, if you can afford it. Or go stay with friends. Karl is bad news at the best of times, and these aren't the best of times."

She nodded as she got up to walk him to the door.

"You know, Sarah, did it occur to you that that kid might have had a crush on you?"

"No. I'm way too old for people to be getting crushes on me," she said. It sounded believable because until three months ago she believed it.

"I think you might be surprised at the number of people in this neighborhood who have more than a little crush on you," Jerry said with a shy smile, then turned and walked down the steps.

Jerry has a crush on me? How did I miss that for so long?

You weren't looking. This was her own voice.

#

After Jerry had gone, Sarah waited fifteen minutes before she let herself out of the house. She wore a dark dress and a gray cardigan to blend in with the night. She moved quickly down the street.

Remember I told you that I sleep under the bleachers sometimes? Well, if anything ever happens, go there. I will either meet you there or leave something for you.

She said more prayers to whatever god led her to this person. She prayed for his safety. He wasn't very big, and he certainly wasn't going to win any physical fights with someone as large and thuggish as Karl. But that didn't diminish him in her estimation in any way. No one had ever made her feel more feminine and desirable than he had. That made him more of a man to her than any man she had ever met. So if Karl was going to try to go after Caio, he was going to have to go through her.

A chill ran through her, and a deep anger. She realized with shock that she would be willing to kill Karl if that was what was needed to keep Caio safe.

She walked quickly down the street, then she ducked through the chain-link fence and worked her way down the bleachers. Sure enough, underneath the bleachers, right near the place that she had planned to hide and watch him, there was a large brown envelope taped to the wood. She grabbed it and pulled it down, tearing the tape and one corner in the process. She opened it quickly.

There were four things inside. She pulled each thing out one at a time. There were two envelopes. One was small but heavy and bulging a bit. The other was a letter envelope. There was also something that was roughly the size and shape of a checkbook or vouchers, but it was too dark to read the small writing. The last was a package. It looked like it could be a jewelry box for a bracelet. It was blue and wrapped with a gold bow.

She looked around quickly but saw no one. She stepped out and walked around to the seats of the bleachers. Still she saw no one close to her. In the distance, there were some boys hanging around a trash can that someone had lit on fire. She smiled when she recognized Mouse's hair in the group, but she didn't see Caio.

She sat down on the bleachers quickly and looked around again. She opened the envelope and took out the first thing that her hand came to. When she pulled it out in better light, she realized exactly what it was, and her heart began to beat harder.

It was a letter with her name on it. It was his handwriting, for sure.

She opened it nervously, but as gently as she could. He had written this; he had sealed it shut with his tongue. She didn't want to be disrespectful with it. The letter was written on real stationery. It was beautiful and thick.

She quickly scanned it. It began with "Dear Sarah" and ended with "I love you, Caio." The words he had never actually said out loud but had never needed to.

"What's this?" she heard, as someone ripped the letter from her hand. She gasped as she saw Karl in front of her, holding the letter. She stood up quickly but had the presence of mind to drop the rest of the envelope behind her under the bleachers.

"Give it back Karl, it's not for you."

"No, I think I'll keep it. I'm sure there will be something in here that will be of interest to a judge."

"No one is going to believe your stupid little lies about me," she snarled.

"Oh, maybe no one will press criminal charges, but your behavior goes a long way to proving that you can't be trusted with money."

"Oh, you know I found out, right?" she snapped, eyeing the letter. She was desperate to get it out of his hands. She looked and saw the boys in the distance. If she called out to them, she wasn't sure if they would come before Karl got away with the letter. She was pretty sure that Dex and Mouse were both there. Mouse, who had been so angry when he saw her eye that day. Suddenly, she had an idea.

She lunged herself forward and grabbed for the letter. Karl held it away from her and pushed her to the ground.

She stood back up and made another lunge for it. She was making her gestures as big as she could. Karl grabbed her arm and twisted her wrist hard.

282

She screamed. It hurt, to be sure, but the scream was dramatic.

"What the fuck is wrong with you, you cunt? I barely touched you," Karl snarled at her as he let go of her arm and pushed her away. He held the letter up and out of her reach.

As he did that, his shirt sleeve pulled up and she saw a huge gaping wound on his forearm. It was festering and black. It looked like necrosis. As she stared, she noticed that he also had a similar black spot on his neck that seemed to be rotting and forming a hole. Swallowing her fear and disgust, she grabbed for the letter again. This time he slapped her across the face and her head was rocked from one side to the other.

"What the fuck is your problem, asshole?" she heard a deep voice say. It was Dex, who had come up from behind Karl and was towering over him.

"This is none of your business, son," Karl responded, taking on his most lawyerly tone.

Mouse ran up behind him.

"Ms. Baker. Are you okay?" he asked.

"Mouse, he has my letter," she said, her eyes pleading. Quick as a flash, Mouse grabbed it from Karl.

"Give that back, you little shit," Karl yelled. Mouse smiled and started dancing backward. But when he opened the letter himself, his eyes got wide and serious.

"I said give that back, son, before you get in any more trouble."

Mouse caught Sarah's eye.

Please, don't let him get it. Please Mouse. Please. She pleaded in her head.

She had no idea what the letter said, but whatever it said, it would be bad in Karl's hands.

Mouse nodded and then turned and ran toward the other side of the basketball court. Toward the garbage can with the fire.

Both Karl and Sarah realized what he was going to do at the same moment. Karl raced after him as Sarah turned around and grabbed the package from behind her. As she ran across the street toward her house, she saw Mouse throw the letter into the fire.

Her heart skipped a beat as she knew Caio's words were burning away, never to be seen by her eyes. But she had bigger problems.

She ran to her driveway and into her house. Once inside, she grabbed her purse and the bag that she had taken to NYC. She then ran back outside to her car. She could hear Mouse's voice. Then she heard Dex.

"You're going nowhere, you asshole." Then sounds of a scuffle.

"Shit," she heard Dex yell.

"Ms. Baker, watch out!" yelled Mouse.

Sarah didn't see Karl yet, but she knew he was coming. She threw open the door to the car and threw her bag in the back seat. She started her car and threw it into gear. She pulled out without looking and floored the car. She glanced in her rearview mirror and saw Karl behind her, chasing her car. She didn't slow down at the intersection, she just ran straight through. She heard the screeching of brakes.

She called 911 and told the dispatcher that Karl Renfield had attacked her, and she was running from him. She asked for Jerry but then hung up. She knew the message would go through and they would search for Karl.

It would also give her an excuse to run like the rabbit that she used to be ... like the rabbit she no longer was.

Chapter Forty-Three

The Hope of a Dream

Monday July 7

As Sarah turned her car on to the highway, she switched on the radio. She was shaking all over and beginning to cry. She tried Caio's number again, but it just rang and rang. He had not picked up his text either. He had worried that something would go wrong, and apparently it had.

Sometimes I may have to disappear for a while. If that ever happens, DON'T come looking for me. I will always come and find you, but I don't ever want to lead any of these people to you. If they are following me, then they can find you. I won't let that happen. Your first and only concern is to keep yourself safe.

She had no idea exactly where she should go but headed toward the airport. There was a plethora of hotels near the airport, security was good, and she could be just another anonymous traveler. And the glimpse she'd had of what was in the packet had looked like a travel voucher of some kind. She wished she could look at the packet Caio left her, but she had thrown the envelope in the back seat, and she couldn't reach it.

Sarah drove at exactly the speed limit and kept a close eye on her rearview mirror just in case someone seemed to be following her, but she saw nothing. She knew that Karl would come after her if he could find her, but she had a head start, there were hundreds of hotels around, and he would have a hard time searching all of them before tomorrow morning. Also, she knew that it was likely he would be picked up for questioning, given the message she had left and the fact that she had alerted Jerry. That meant that she probably had twelve hours to find a better hiding place than a hotel.

Her face was still stinging from where Karl slapped her, but that wasn't the physical thing that was actually worrying her. What was worrying her were the marks on Karl's arm and neck. Something was eating away at his skin. On his arm, she was fairly sure she had seen bone.

I don't think you need to worry about Karl for much longer, muttered Val.

Caio had said the same thing yesterday.

What you need to worry about is that you touched him, continued Val. *And you need to get a shower ASAP.*

Sarah remembered that Val had been a pre-med student before deciding to jump to law.

"Do you know what that was?" she asked Val.

It looks like necrotizing fasciitis, Val whispered in her head, almost as if saying the name of a demon.

"What is that?"

It's also called flesh-eating bacteria. It's normally from a staph bacterium. But it's also mostly on the arms and legs.

"He had it on his arm, and on his neck too."

Yeah. And given the progression of it, he will need amputation of his arm—but they can't amputate his head.

"So he's going to die?"

Yes, I'm pretty certain he will be dead soon. At the very least, he will be confined to a hospital for a long time, Val replied. *You just need to get somewhere to get your face cleaned. If you have cuts, you need to disinfect them.*

At that moment, Sarah saw a Doubletree Inn on her right. She quickly swerved into the parking lot.

Don't park in the front. Even if Karl isn't after you, both Caio and Matt told you that other people will be, said Larry. *Park your car in the back, and take off the license plate.*

"Do you think that is necessary?"

Yes! said every voice in her head.

Sarah pulled to the back of the hotel, took her suitcase out of the car and then pulled a screwdriver from the toolkit she kept in her trunk. She quickly removed the license plates from her car, locked them in the trunk, locked her car, and then rolled her bag to the front of the hotel. As she entered, she noticed that there was a large flat-screen TV just behind the reception desk.

"Welcome to Doubletree," said the dark-skinned brunette at the reception desk blandly, not bothering to look up at her. "Do you have a reservation?"

"No, I'm afraid I don't. Do you have anything available?" she asked. The woman looked up at her with open irritation, until she saw the state of Sarah's face. Then her expression softened.

"Let me see what I can do for you," she said, checking her computer. "I have someone who hasn't checked in yet, you can have that room."

"What if they come in later?" Sarah asked.

"Well, they should have gotten here earlier then, I guess," said the woman with a little smile. "It isn't a guaranteed booking."

She then asked for Sarah's information and wandered off to a back room. Sarah turned her eyes to the TV. Suddenly an image of the Stigmata Club appeared on the screen, and it was in flames.

"Excuse me, I need your help—quick!" she yelled into the back room. The receptionist returned at a fast clip.

"I know someone in that club," she lied as the receptionist grabbed the remote and turned up the sound.

"The firefighters are still at the scene of a blaze on Orchard Street," said a male reporter. "The fire broke out about an hour ago and seems to have started in a club known locally as the Stigmata Club. The firefighters have contained the blaze to one apartment block, so it's not spreading. However, they are still rescuing victims from the club. So far, thirty people have been taken to hospital, with at least ten in critical condition."

Suddenly, behind the man, Sarah thought she caught a glimpse of a familiar shape. There was a person roughly the size and body structure of Caio. The person was sandwiched between two much larger men. She leaned across the reception desk as far as she could.

"Most of the victims who have been sent to the hospital have been severely burned, but a few had different injuries," the reporter said, turning to a woman with glasses who looked extremely uncomfortable. "I have Jennifer Forrester from the health department here with us. What can you tell us about this?"

"Well, a few of the victims seem to have also contracted a resistant bacterium that is causing skin lesions," Ms. Forrester replied.

"Is this somehow related to the fire?"

"At this point we aren't sure, but the bacteria are very rare and the only cases we have seen in this country were also present at the scene of the fire."

"Is this a problem for the public?" asked the reporter.

Skin lesions. That's what you guys call it.

"At this time, we don't see it as any sort of menace to public health as it seems very contained," she said. She was looking at everything around her but the camera.

The camera panned to a woman being carried away on a stretcher. Her face was bandaged but her arms were visible and horribly disfigured by wounds, like the wounds that had been on Karl's arm and neck. Although her face was not visible, Sarah recognized the bronze-streaked hair of Anne Marie Davies.

You need to get a shower now, said Val.

287

"Jesus, that's just what we need, right? Some new crazy-ass bacteria," muttered the receptionist, as she gave her the keys to her room. Sarah nodded, eyes not leaving the screen.

Seriously Sarah, you need to shower! Val repeated.

Then, just before they cut back to the studio, Sarah saw another quick flash of the boy she first saw. Sure enough, he was being escorted by the arm by a larger man. It might have been Caio, but the image disappeared too fast to be sure. Sarah leaned even further across the reception desk, but the live coverage was over and a plastic-looking male anchor and his equally plastic-looking female co-anchor were on screen.

GO GET A SHOWER NOW! Val shrieked in her head, and Sarah jumped. The receptionist gave her an odd look, but Sarah shrugged, took her bag, and headed to her room.

Once inside her innocuous room, with its routine brown-and-white decor, Sarah pulled her clothes off and went to the shower. She had looked up resistant bacteria on her phone on the way up, and was sufficiently panicked to listen to Val. She showered in water as hot as she could stand and scrubbed every inch of her skin. She was pink and a bit sore when she got out of the shower and put on a robe. It was only then that she sat down on the bed and pulled out the package that Caio had left for her.

The plain brown paper packet contained only three objects, now that the letter was gone. The first was a packet containing keys, a few thousand dollars in cash, and a credit card. The second was an envelope with a ticket confirmation for a business class ticket to the Big Island of Hawaii, as well as a car rental voucher and a piece of paper with a name and address in Kona. The ticket was for tomorrow morning from Newark Airport. Sarah stared at these things. She held the keys in her hand and put it to her heart. Caio had touched these things.

"Where are you?" she whispered.

She then took out the last thing, which was a jewelry box. It was a long, blue velvet box with a yellow ribbon. She slowly untied the bow, suddenly a bit afraid. When she opened it and saw what was inside, her heart stopped. She stared at it for a long time. Finally, she closed it gently, and put her face in her hands. She began to cry, and then laugh, and then cry again.

After a good half hour of crying and laughing, she wiped her face, stood up and got her phone out of her purse. She plugged it into the wall, to make sure that she wouldn't run out of battery and spent thirty minutes on it, researching. When she had made her decision, she entered a name into her contacts and then dialed the number.

"Kona Care Center, Dr. Lan's office, can I help you?" a perky woman's voice said.

"Yes. I would like to get an appointment with the doctor. When is your soonest appointment?"

"Are you a new patient?" the woman asked.

"Yes," Sarah replied. She didn't want to give too many details over the phone, given what she now knew.

"Well, we have a cancellation for this Friday at 10 a.m., would that work?" Sarah did some mental calculations.

"Yes, that would be fine."

"What is your name?"

"Sarah Silva," she replied, looking at the name on the credit card that Caio had left for her.

"Very good. We'll see you this Friday, Sarah."

Sarah hung up the phone and hugged herself. She lay down on the bed and began to cry again. In fact, she cried herself to sleep, but this time it was not only tears of sadness.

Tuesday July 8

Sarah's flight the next morning was at 6 a.m. and she was up by 4 a.m., not that she had been able to sleep much. The airport was almost empty when she got there at 4:45. Almost empty except for one person—a person that she knew.

Melissa Taylor was standing in front of the departures board as Sarah headed toward the security line. When Melissa saw her, she smiled, a warm and radiant smile, before coming up to her and pulling her into her arms.

"You did a brave thing. You did such a brave thing," she whispered, and Sarah heard the tears in her voice before she pulled back and they were confirmed in her eyes. "I don't know how to thank you."

"Do you know what happened?" Sarah asked. "I just saw a quick news clip."

"The DA raided the club on Sunday night. As you know, there was a sudden fire last night. It was probably set on purpose to destroy evidence."

"And Andrew?"

"Is still alive, sadly. But the stepmonster died. And the tape that you sent the DA and to Phillip prompted an emergency change of custody. So my boys are back with me," Melissa said.

"Why are you here then? Are you taking them on vacation?" Sarah asked, knowing the truth already.

289

"If anyone asks you, then yes, I am taking them on vacation," Melissa said, her warm eyes suddenly turning frosty. "I let them take my baby away from me once. My own insecurity caused my child irreparable harm. If I stay here, they will find a way to take him back. These people, these monsters, are powerful and real. I know that now. You helped me prove that, at least to myself. So we'll be leaving on an extended vacation."

"Then you will be on the run now? That's a hard life."

"They're my children. If I was willing to be committed for them, then a few years on the road isn't too much to ask," Melissa said calmly. She then turned to look at her three boys, all looking at books at the airport convenience store.

"You love them a lot," Sarah whispered.

"I am their mother. I would die for them," she said, kissed Sarah again, then turned and walked away. The words sat hard on Sarah's heart. Melissa's love for her children was palpable. And those were children by a man who was a monster, a man she didn't love. What if they had been with a man she loved? What would such a bond look like? Feel like?

Sarah shook her head and wiped the tears from her face as she got in the line for airport security.

Later, as the plane took off, Sarah took out the small jewelry box. Inside it, wrapped with another ribbon, was a pregnancy test stick.

Maybe for the first time in her life, something read unquestionably positive.

* * *

Acknowledgement

As always, my heartfelt gratitude goes out to everyone who helped in the creation of this book. So big thanks to Tessa, Addie, Myra, Hassy, Leo, Valerie, Charlotte and Ian, for all their insights, help and support.

Most of all, thanks to my family:

Sebastien, my son and lovingly merciless dev editor, Lucas, my dreamer, who knows what I really meant to say, and Julien, my husband, best friend, and partner for all life's adventures.

For Those Who Enjoyed this Book

Amelie, Lazlo, Hudson, Kara and Dante will return in "The Ghosting Academy".

***

As most people know, reviews make or break authors, so if this book made you feel anything, do please share it, and connect with me at the following:

Webpage: *Lsdelorme.com*
Tiktok: *@lexyshawdelorme*
Insta: *ls_delorme*
Twitter: *@lexyshawdelorme*
Facebook Page: *Lexy Shaw Delorme*

About the Author

Lexy Delorme was born in San Diego, California. After graduating from the University of North Carolina School of Law, various internships and years working in risk, tax, family, and international law, she now classifies herself as a recovering attorney.

With a father who served in the US Military, Lexy had a wandering lifestyle from her earliest days and in her time has been a pop musician, a science geek and a writer for magazines like Bonjour Paris and Playtimes. She was also the author of an app entitled, "The Unofficial Guide To Disneyland Paris". Throughout all of her different careers, her love of fiction has been a mainstay.

Within this eclectic life, she was also one of the first employees at 23andMe, a genomics and biotechnology company based in Mountain View, California and that experience influenced the genetic aspects of her Limerent Series, of which Caio is the first book.

For as long as she can remember she's had characters in her head. As a child, these were the friends she wished to have. As a young woman, the lovers she wanted to find or the people she wanted to become. Writing fiction novels allows her the chance to give these characters a background, a story and a voice.

Having lived in in 3 continents, 9 US states, and 21 cities around the world, including London and Hong Kong, Lexy now lives in Paris with her French husband and two very cool sons. She is currently working on the next books in the Limerent Series.